SABINE BARING

A Story of the Chalk Cliffs

PRAXIS BOOKS

Praxis Books
"Sheridan", Broomers Hill Lane, Pulborough, West Sussex.
RH20 2DU.

First published by Methuen 1900.
This edition Praxis Books, 1994.

This reissue is in a limited edition of 500 copies.

ISBN 0-9518729-6-6

Printed by Intype, Wimbledon, London.

British Library Cataloguing-in-Production Data.
A catalogue record for this book is available from the
British Library.

Almost a century old, *Winefred* is a romantic adventure story which has lost none of its excitement and humour for today's readers. Set in Seaton and Axmouth, on the cliffs of South Devon, the tale of Jane Marley and her daughter has an uncanny relevance even now. Homelessness, poverty, social divisions all present acute difficulties for the central characters. What's more, the forces of nature, in the shape of the cliffs themselves, also take an active role in the story. Baring–Gould's novels were bestsellers in their day, and are currently enjoying a revival of popularity for a new generation of readers.

CONTENTS

Chapter   Page
1. Homeless   1
2. On the Verge   8
3. A Common Chord   14
4. The Undercliff   21
5. Don't   26
6. Over the Punch–Bowl   30
7. A Late Visitor   38
8. On the Pebble–Beach   46
9. Seen Through   53
10. A Rift   60
11. A Proposal   66
12. By Night   71
13. Out of the Snare   77
14. Buried Alive   84
15. Cast Forth   88
16. Job's Secret   94
17. J.H.   101
18. Declaration of War   106
19. Exit Job   113
20. A First Step   119
21. Further Forward   126
22. House and Home   131
23. A Passage of Arms   138
24. Reversed Positions   145
25. The Study of a Face   151
26. A Thorn Bough   157
27. Mother and Daughter   163
28. Most Heartily   168
29. The Shadow of a Change   174
30. A New World   179
31. A Chariot Drive   186
32. At the Milliner's   192
33. In the Square   199
34. Mischief–Making   205
35. The Young Man From Beer   210

36. To Bath   217
37. Confidences   225
38. A Letter from Bath   230
39. The Bath Assembly   237
40. Wanted – Choughs   245
41. The White Cliff   251
42. A Revelation   257
43. A Refusal   261
44. The Gate of Thorns   266
45. Holwood or Marley?   272
46. Over a Tea–Table   280
47. The Curtain Drawn   285
48. The Beginning of the End   291
49. Rent Asunder   296
50. Joined Together   301

Note: Anyone in possession of an original copy of this novel will notice changes in paragraph layout in this edition. This was primarily a stylistic decision, since the 1900 edition frequently employs single–line paragraphs which look strange today. It must also be confessed that the significant saving in paper by running these lines on was a consideration. Apologies to any purists who take exception to this liberty.

Chapter One

Homeless

One grey uncertain afternoon in November, when the vapour–laden skies were without a rent, and the trailing clouds, without a fringe, were passing imperceptibly into drizzle, that thickened with coming night, when the land was colourless, and the earth oozed beneath the tread, and the sullen sea was as lead – on such a day, at such a time of day, a woman wandered through Seaton, then a disregarded hamlet by the mouth of the Axe, picking up a precarious existence by being visited in the summer by bathers.

The woman drew her daughter about with her. Both were wet and bedraggled. The wind from the east soughed about the caves, whistled in the naked trees, and hissed through the coarse sea–grass and withered thrift; whilst from afar came the mutter of a peevish sea. The woman was tall, had fine features of a powerful cast, with eyes in which slumbered volcanic fire. Her cheeks were flushed, her rich, dark hair, caught by the wind and sopped by the mist, was dishevelled under her battered hat. She was not above thirty–six years old.

The girl she held and drew along was about eighteen. She partook of her mother's fineness of profile and darkness of eye. If there were in her features some promise or threat of the resolution that characterised her mother's countenance, it was tempered by a lurking humour that would not suffer them to set to hardness.

This woman, holding her daughter with a grip of iron, stood in the doorway of a farm, talking with, or rather at, the farmer.

"Why not? Have I not hands, arms? Can I not work? Will she not work? Prove us. I ask you why you cannot take us in?"

"My good woman, we require no one."

"But you do. You have needed me. When your wife was ill, and your hussy of a maid had run away – did you not send for me? Did I hesitate to go to you? I left then my huckstering that I might be useful in your house. That was the hour of your need. Now it is mine. Did I not at that time do my work well? Perhaps over well. Your wife said I had scrub–bed the surface off the table and rubbed into holes the clothes I washed. Anyhow I did naught by halves. And your drones, they guzzle and sleep, and when you are in straits – there is sickness, disaster – then they run away. Take me and Winefred."

"My dear Mrs Marley, it is of no avail your persisting to thrust yourself on us. You can't stable more horses than you have stalls. I have no vacancy."

"Your missus has turned away Louie Herne."

"And has engaged one in her place."

"Then give us leave to sleep in your barn, and I'll work in the fields for you, hoeing, weeding, gathering up stones – ay, better than can a man."

"No, thank you. I do not care to have my barn burnt down. You have too much fire in you to be safe among straw."

The woman quivered with disappointment and rage. Erect, with rigid arms and stiff neck, she flared out: "Ay! I could tear down your stacks or fire them. I am 'Dear Jane Marley' when *you* need me. 'Out, you vagabond,' when *I* am in need."

"If you dared do what you threaten," said the farmer, suddenly becoming harsh in tone and manner, "into prison you should go, and then, indeed, your Winefred would be a vagabond, and all through you."

The woman shut her mouth, but sparks scintillated in her eyes. "Mother, let us go elsewhere," said the girl and endeavoured to draw her mother away.

"Not yet," answered the woman impatiently. "Do you not know, Moses Nethersole, that I and my Winefred are homeless? My cottage has gone to pieces, and the whole cliff is crumbling away. The wall is down already, and the lime–ash floor is buckled up and splitting. No one now may go nigh the place. It needs but the hopping of a wagtail to send the whole bag of tricks into the sea. And you – you have the heart to deny us shelter and bread and work whereby to earn both."

"Bread you shall have and a cup of milk."

2

"I will have neither as an alms. I ask no charity. I desire to work for my meat and for my housing. Have I not done so like an honest woman hitherto? Would you make a beggar of me? Give me work, I ask. I seek nothing more."

"Mother, come away," pleaded the girl.

"I will," said the woman curtly, and turned round with an abrupt action. Then suddenly she stooped, stripped off her shoes and, running forward as the farmer backed, she beat the soles against the doorposts.

"There," she said, "there is Scripture for you. I cannot shake off the dust o' my feet as testimony against you, but I can the mud and the oozing of the water from the sodden leather. May that cling there till the Day of Judgment, and bring the blight to your wheat, the rot to your sheep, to your cattle, the worm and canker to your store, and fester into your blood. It is the curse of the widow and the fatherless that will lie on you."

The farmer slammed his door in her face, and retreated to the kitchen. He was a phlegmatic and amiable man, but the fury of the woman, and her denunciation of woes had shaken him; his ruddy face was mottled, and his hand shook as he let himself down into the settle.

"By my soul, she's a vixen!" he gasped.

"Moses," said his wife, "you've done right. If I hadn't been minding ironing of your shirt−front for Sunday, I'd have gone out and given that same vixen a bit of my mind."

"I wish you had, Mary – I'm no match for the likes o' she."

"If I had heard the smallest mite o' wavering in your voice, I would have done so for certain," said Mrs Nethersole; "and so you call her 'dear Jane' do you? Things come out unexpected at times, and 'Mistress Marley' is she? You know as well as I do that she is no honest woman, howsomever she may brag of her honesty. She is just a wild lostrel as has got no belongings, save that girl as never ought to have come into this world of wickedness."

"Mary, perhaps it's all along of it being a world of wickedness that she did come. Jane Marley's case is a sad one. She has been driven out of her cottage."

"Turned out?"

3

"The cliff has given way. You know where it stood."

"Not I – it is on the other side of the water."

"It was on the edge of the cliff, and the rock has been breaking away for some time – that is how she had it cheap. Now it is part down, and they say there be a great crack right along the ground – and the whole cliff will go over, and be munched by the waves."

"That's no concern of ours, Moses; she does not belong to the parish."

"True, but she has worked for us when we were short and in difficulties."

"And was paid for it – and we wiped our hands of her."

"Mary, you are over hard."

"And you are like butter on dog–days. I know you men. Dear Jane, indeed!"

Mrs Marley, with labouring bosom, heaving after the storm, drew her daughter with her into the village street, to the village inn, the Red Lion, kept by Mrs Warne.

She walked in, with a manner almost defiant, and encountered the landlady issuing from the cosy parlour behind the bar, in which a good fire burnt, and where sat a couple of commercial travellers.

"I have come," said Jane Marley, "and have brought my Winefred. Our house is going to pieces under our feet, over our heads, and we are homeless. I desire that you take my child and me. I do not ask it as a favour. Look at my arms. I can work, and will be an ostler for you, and she shall serve in the inn."

"I really do not require you," said Mrs Warne. "I am sorry for your misfortunes, but I cannot help. You do not belong to this parish."

"And are love and mercy never to travel beyond parish bounds?" asked the woman, with her vehemence again breaking out. "Is the tide of charity to flow on one side of the hedge and not the other? Is the dew of heaven to moisten the wool on the fleece of the parish sheep only?"

"Jane, be reasonable. Our duties are limited by the parish boundaries, but not our charity."

"Then extend some charity to Winefred and me, not alms, mind you, only consideration."

"Charity must be governed by circumstances," said Mrs Warne.

"Oh yes," retorted Jane scornfully. "It is like a canal, so much of it let out through the sluices as the dock–keeper thinks well."

"If you will be patient," said the hostess, a woman rubicund, plump and good–humoured, at the moment impatient to be back with the commercials, especially with one who had an engaging eye and tongue. "If you will be patient, I will tell you how I can oblige you. I do not mind taking on Winefred."

"But Tom Man, your ostler, is dead."

"Well, but I must have a man in the stables, not a woman."

"No," said Mrs Marley, "I will not leave the child unprotected in a public house. See me, I have neither father nor mother – no relation of any sort. What my story is, that concerns none but myself; but, such as it is, it has made me alone, with only my child to love. All the love you have to your mother and sisters and brothers and cousins, that with me is gathered into one great love for the one child I have. Where she is, there am I. She is a handsome girl, blooming as a rose. No, I will not let her be seen in a tavern, unless I be near also to watch over her against your leering bagman."

Mrs Warne bridled up. "Bagman, indeed! Tut, woman, surely you may trust me?"

"I can trust none. You are not her mother. You must take us both."

"I cannot receive you both. I have made you a fair offer. If you will not accept, go over the river to your own parish."

Then Mrs Warne retreated into the bar, shut the door, drew down the window and went to the fire and the commercials. Jane Marley left the Red Lion. The cloud darkened on her brow. She said no word to her daughter, but directed her way up the street to a small shop, in which already a light was burning.

In the greensand beds about Seaton, or rather on the beach, washed from them, are found chalcedonies, green and yellow, red jasper, and moss agates, also brown petrified wood that takes a high polish. There was a little dealer in these at Seaton, an old man who polished and set them, and sold them as memorials to visitors coming there for sea–bathing and air. To this man, Thomas Gasset by name, the distressed woman betook herself.

He was sitting at his work–table, with a huge pair of spectacles in horn rims over his nose, engaged in mounting a chalcedony as a seal.

He looked up. "Got some stones for me, Mrs Marley?" he asked. "I hope good ones this time. Those Winefred brought last were worthless."

"No, Mr Gasset, they were not," said the girl. "I know a stone as well as you."

"Thomas Gasset," said the mother, "I come to you with a proposal. Will you take Winefred and me into your service? That is to say, let us both lodge with you. She shall collect the precious pebbles, and as she says she knows one that is good from another that is worthless, she can help polish; turn the grindstone, if you will; and I will go about the country selling them, instead of tapes and papers of pins – or with them."

"My dear good creature," gasped the jeweller – as this dealer in such stones as jasper and agate elected to be called – more correctly a lapidary – "the business would not maintain all three. The season here is short, and I sell in that only."

He looked out of the corners of his eyes at his wife, who was darning where she could profit by his lamp. She pursed up her lips and drew her brows together.

"The business is a starving, not a living," said Mrs Marley, "because it is not pushed. I have just been in at the Red Lion – there are commercials, them travelling for some haberdash or hosiery firm – they work up the trade. It pays to employ them. You make me your traveller. I will go about with your wares to Dorchester, to Weymouth, to Exeter – wherever there be gentlefolk with loose money to spend in such things. It will pay you over and over again. If this sort of working a business can keep those commercials in the lap of luxury in Mrs Warne's bar, drinking spirits and dining off roast goose, it will keep me who never take anything stronger than milk, and am content with a crust and dripping. Let me travel for you and look to this as my home, where Winefred is."

"No," said Mrs Gasset, snapping the answer from her husband's mouth; "no, indeed, we take none under our roof who cannot produce her marriage lines."

"Then I will lodge elsewhere if you will take my child, Mr Gasset. You may trust her. Your goods will be safe with me. I will render account for every stone. You will have as security what is more to me than silver or gold – my Winefred."

The man again peered out of the corners of his eyes at his wife, and again she answered for him.

"No," she said. "I don't doubt your honesty. You have been honest always save once. But there are reasons why it cannot be. That is final." And she snapped her mouth, and at the same moment broke her darning–needle.

Jane Marley left the shop. When her back was turned, Mrs Gasset flew at her husband. "You'd have given way – I saw it by the way you twitched the end of your nose."

"My dear Sarah! It was such an opportunity. The woman is right – my business – "

"Oh! much you thought of your business. It was her great brown eyes – not your agates."

"My dear Sarah! surely at my age –"

"The older a man is, the more of a fool he becomes."

"Well, well, my honey–bee, I didn't."

"No, you didn't, because I was by," retorted the honey–bee, and put forth her sting. "If I had been underground, you'd have taken her in. I know you; yah!" And in the little parlour behind the bar, the comfortable Mrs Warne settled herself before the fire, and drew up her gown so as not to scorch it, and looked smilingly at the more attractive bagman of the two, and said, "Ah! Mr Thomson, if you only knew from what I have saved you."

"From what, my dearest Mrs Warne?"

"From fascinations you could not have resisted. There has been here a peculiarly handsome woman wanting a situation – as ostler. If she had come, there would have been no drawing you from the stables."

"Madame – elsewhere perhaps – but assuredly not here."

The women were all against Jane Marley because she was still good–looking.

7

Chapter Two

On the Verge

Jane Marley wrapped her shawl about her; her head was bowed, her lips set, her grip on her daughter unrelaxed.

She turned from the village, and walked along the shingly way to the water's edge. The Axe flows into the sea through a trough washed out of the blood–red sandstone that comes to the surface between the hills of chalk; but the fresh water does not mingle with the brine unopposed. A pebble ridge has been thrown up by the sea at the mouth, that the waves labour incessantly to complete, so as to debar the Axe from discharging its waters into it. Sometimes high tide and storm combine to all but accomplish the task, and the river is strangled within a narrow throat; but this is for a time only. Once more the effluent tide assists the river to force an opening which the inflowing tide had threatened to seal. One of the consequences of this struggle ever renewed is that the mouth has shifted. At one time the red Axe discharged to the west, but when a storm blocked that opening it turned and emptied itself to the east.

On the farther side, that to the rising sun, the chalk with dusky sandstone underneath rears itself into a bold headland, Haven Ball, that stands precipitously against the sea, as a white cold shoulder exposed to it. Up a hollow of this hill, a combe as it is called, a mean track ascends to the downs which overhang the sea, and extend, partly in open tracts, in part enclosed, as far as Lyme Regis.

There is no highway. The old Roman coast road lies farther to the north, but there is a track, now open, now between blasted hedges, al–ways bad, and exposed to the gale from the sea and the drift of the rain.

But to reach this, the Axe estuary must be crossed. This is nowadays a matter of one penny, as there is a toll–bridge thrown from one bank to the other. But at the time of my story transit was by a ferry-boat, and the boat could ply only when there was a sufficiency of water.

Jane Marley seated herself on a bench by the landing-stage, and drew her daughter down beside her. The wind was from the south-east and spat cold rain in their faces. She passed her shawl round Winefred, regardless of herself.

Presently up came the ferryman. "Good e'en Mistress Marley. Do you want to cross again?"

"Yes – when possible."

"In ten minutes. Will you come under shelter into my cabin?"

The woman shook her head impatiently.

"You will get wet."

"I am wet already."

"And cold."

"We shall be colder presently."

"Poor comfort I call that," said the boatman. "But you was always a headstrong, difficult woman, hard to please. Where be you going to, now?"

"Where I shall be better off than I am here."

Presently Jane raised her face, streaming with rain, and said, "There are springs hereabouts that turn the moss into stone, and the blades of grass are hardened to needles. I reckon that the spray of these springs has watered the hearts of the people; they are all stone, and the stone is flint. I shall go elsewhere."

"It is a long way to Lyme – if you be bound thither. And over the cliffs it is exposed as well, and not safe with the falling darkness. I do not say this on your account. You, Jane, are not one who cares for length of way and badness of weather. But I speak for poor Winefred's sake."

"I am her mother, and I am the person to consider her, not you, Olver Dench."

"No offence meant. But my cat had kittens, and when all were drowned but one, she carried that remaining one about in her mouth everywhere, and never let it go till she had nipped the life out of the kitten; and, I swear, you remind me of that cat."

Then ensued a silence that lasted some minutes. The ferryman

9

reopened the conversation. "I suppose you knew it was coming."

"Knew what?" asked she.

"That the cottage would go to pieces."

"Yes. I got it cheap because of the risk."

"And now, I make bold to ask, what have you done with your furniture?"

"There is not much. What I have is there. I have no house into which to move it. In the parish I am refused –in Seaton they cast me back on the parish, and the parish casts me off altogether."

"You do not belong to it by birth."

"No. I belong nowhere. I have no home."

"But are you not afraid your bits of furniture will be stolen?"

"What if they be? If there be no shelter for Winefred and me, what care I for housing a poor bedstead and a rotten chair? The great grey sea has torn away the rock on which I stood. The wall has fallen, and my house is thrown open to all. Whither shall I go? Where shall I shelter my child? We have no place."

The man shrugged his shoulders. He was a red–faced man with white hair; and in the failing light of winter the red looked dull purple and the white a soiled grey.

"Come now!" said the woman, starting up, "my affairs are none of yours. They touch you in no way. The tide flows."

She did not notice a peculiar expression that came up into his face and creamed it as she said the words, but Winefred, who was looking wistfully at him, was struck by it.

Without another word, he went to the ferryboat, unfastened the chain, and held out his hand to assist Jane in. She thrust his hand aside with a gesture of impatience and stepped in with firm foot, then turned and helped her daughter.

Nothing was said as the man rowed across. The woman was immersed in thought of the most gloomy complexion; the daughter was too wretched to speak. The tears that flowed from her eyes were mingled with the rain that beat on her face. The rower looked from one to the other with a sinister expression. After the boat had grounded, when Mrs Marley left it, he said, "You'll not go away – right away, I mean – without letting me know where you may be; because it might chance – there's no telling – there is hope yet."

He did not complete his sentence.

"There is no hope," said the woman coldly, "no more than there is sun above these clouds and this dribbling rain. The sun has gone down. After nineteen years hope dies." Then she left him, and extending her arm, again grasped the wrist of her daughter.

"Mother," said Winefred, "Mr Dench hates us."

"It matters nothing to us whether he hate or love. Why should be hate us?"

"That I cannot say, but hate us he does."

"All the world hates us, for all the world has money, comforts, shelter, and," she muttered in her bosom, "there are some who have a husband to care for them, and a father to watch over them. We have neither, and the sight of us, as we are, in our need, our nakedness, our desolation, is an offence, like garbage, to be swept aside and cast on the dunghill. Seaton says, Away, across the water! you do not belong to us. And Axmouth says, Away! you were not born here, and we are not responsible for you. Let us warm our feet at a sea-coal fire, and drink mulled ale, and turn into our downy beds – go you wanderers in night and cold and wet – die, but do not trouble us."

Up the steep path that led through the crease in the hillside pushed the weary mother, drawing along her yet more weary child. Yet in the passion of her heart at the contrast her imagination drew she pressed forward fast till arrested by shortness of breath.

Thus in silence they continued to mount. It was a climb of four hundred feet. The woman looked neither to right nor to left. Wet, trailing brambles caught at her garments with their claws. As she passed under a stunted thorn it shuddered and sent down a shower. The flints in the way lay in beds of water; the grass was slippery with rain. Dank and rotting sting-nettles, oozy, but poisonous in their decay, struck at their knees as they mounted.

"O mother," sobbed the girl, when the summit was attained, and the cruel east wind slashed in their faces, splashing them with ice-cold rain, "O mother, I can go no farther."

"How – where can we stay? Answer me that."

"Why should we go on if we go nowheres?"

"No – we go nowhere, for we have nowhere to go to for shelter and food."

"Let us go home."

"The sea has taken it from us."

"Let us shelter somewhere."

"We must find first someone who will take us in."

"There is the Poor House."

"Not for us – we do not belong to the place. And, further, it is full."

"Let us creep into some hayloft."

"They will turn us out."

"Into the church."

"That at Axmouth is locked; that at Rousdon the roof has fallen in."

"Mother, we must go somewhere."

"So we shall – to the only shelter open."

"Is it far?"

"No." She still hurried the girl along, now at a faster pace, for they walked on fairly level down. The day had completely closed in; all, however, was not inky darkness. On looking behind, seen through a blur of mist, could be caught some glimmer of lights from Seaton. There was, perhaps, a moon above the clouds, but the light sufficed only to show that there was not absolute obscurity above.

It was to Winefred as though life was being left behind, and they were plunging into boundless and black despair. A wheeling gull screamed in her ear.

Suddenly her mother halted. The wind lashed her hair, and flapped her sodden gown. She gripped Winefred now with both hands and turning her back to the blast and splashing rain, said "Child! You shall know all now, now that there is no place whatever left for us. Your father has deserted you, he has abandoned me. He did this nineteen years ago. Not a word, not a shilling has he sent me. I know neither where he is, nor what he has been doing. He may be rich, he may be poor. He may be in blustering health, he may be sick or dead. Neither by letter nor by messenger have I been told – and I care not. I love him no more. I hate the man who has suffered us to come to this. Child, if a father can be stone to his own child, if a hus– if a man who has loved a woman can forget her who loved him with her whole fresh young heart – then is it a marvel that other men on whom we have no claim, to whom bound by no ties, are stone also? Child – you and I are alone. We are everything to each other. I have none but you; you have none but me. If I go, you are lost. If you go – I am no more. We are tied up in one another, to live and die together. Come on." Again she turned and faced the tearing, rain–laden wind.

"Mother, I cannot take another step," sobbed the girl.

"We have not far to go."

"Mother, I hear the sea; you have lost the way."

"I know my course."

"There is no path here."

"I know it; paths lead to men and their homes – to firesides and warm beds."

"We are on the cliff."

"I came to the cliff."

"We are drawing to the edge!"

"I know it; we are at the very brow."

"But what if we fall over?"

Then with a hoarse voice Jane Marley said, as she held her child with a firmer grasp, "Why, then, we shall not feel the wind and the cold and the rain and our weariness, we shall say goodbye to a stony world. Where is no other refuge for us outcasts. Locked in each other's arms, mother and child must die."

For a moment Winefred was petrified with horror. For a moment she was unresisting as the powerful woman gathered her up and strode with her to the verge, the water oozing about her from the soaked garments under the pressure.

But it was for a moment only. In that moment it was to Winefred as though she heard the sea in louder tone, multiplied five–fold, laugh and smack its lips, conscious that living beings with human souls were to be given it to tumble and mumble, to pound on the pebbles and hack on the reefs. It was as though she saw through the darkness the cruel ocean throw up spray–draped arms to catch and clutch her as she fell.

But the moment of pause and paralysis was over. With a shriek and a knotting together of all her powers, and a concentration of all

13

her faculties, she writhed in her mother's arms and fought her. She smote in her face, she tore at her hair, she turned and curled, and gathered herself into one muscular ball, she straightened herself, and threw herself backward in hopes of over–balancing her mother. "I will not!" she shrieked. "Let go! I will not." Instead of freezing rain trickling down her brow, the sweat broke out in scalding drops. Her blood surged and roared in her veins and hammered in her ears. Fire danced before her eyes – then there came a falling. O God! – a falling –

And then a stillness.

"What is this?" And a light smote into her face.

Chapter Three

A Common Chord

Almost before she had recovered her senses, Winefred found herself in a cottage, warm, where a good fire burnt, throwing out waves of yellow light as well as grateful heat, and she was being undressed by her mother and put to bed. She was stupefied, exhausted by her struggle for life.

The thoughts in her head were as straws, leaves, feathers in a swirl of water. She knew not whether what she experienced was a phase of dream or a piece of reality. But when food was forced upon her, and a mug of hot elderberry wine put to her lips, she drew a long breath, rubbed her eyes that were brimming with tears, rain and sweat, looked about her and asked, "Mother, where am I?"

"With me," answered Jane Marley.

"Where are we both?"

"Captain Job Rattenbury has taken us in," said the woman. "Enough for you to know at present. Go to sleep and dream away the past."

14

"O mother, did you really intend to throw me over the cliff?"

"Winefred, I would have cast myself over with you in my arms. But that is gonebyes. Forget and sleep."

But none can undergo great excitement of brain, tension of nerve, pass through peril of life, and sleep sweetly after it. The brain continues to start, the nerve to quiver, the horror to come back, perhaps in receding waves, yet with imperceptible decline of force. If the girl fell into a doze it was to again spring up and cry out, under the supposition that she was falling, or to battle with hands and feet, as though wrestling once more to preserve life.

The room in which she had been put to bed was on the ground floor. There was a doorway from it communicating with the front kitchen.

After one of these recurring spasms of fear, rousing her to full wakefulness, at the girl's desire, Mrs Marley left the door partly open between the apartments, so that the firelight might play in at the opening and flicker about the room, and she could hear the murmur of the voices of the speakers, and occasionally catch sight of them as they moved about.

But Winefred was too weary to listen to what they said, and she gradually slipped off into slumber again, once more to rouse with a start, but less terrifying than before, and then again to glide into unconsciousness.

Meanwhile her mother was in the adjoining chamber, and was conversing with the man who was the rescuer of herself and of her child. This man was broad–shouldered, strongly built, with thick tangled grey hair.

He wore, what at the time was unusual, a dense bush of the same grizzled hair covering the lower portion of his face. He had bright, keen eyes under penthouse brows, and a bold, beaklike nose. About his throat was bound a scarlet kerchief. He wore a blue shirt under an unbuttoned, long–flapped, white waistcoat with sleeves. His coat he had laid aside.

The room, as already intimated, constituted at once kitchen and parlour, such as in Yorkshire is termed the "ha'aze," but for which elsewhere a designation is wanting. In it the meals were cooked and also eaten, but the preparations previous to cooking, and the

15

washing–up of dirty plates after, were carried on in the back premises. Against the wall, in a recess by the fireside, was an ancient press, quaintly carved, of oak, with brass scutcheons and hinges, but as though the latter were not deemed of sufficient strength, additional hinges in iron had been added.

On the mantelshelf were skillet, candlesticks, snuffer–tray, a copper mortar, all polished and reflecting the dancing light of the fire. Also a black case that contained gunpowder, there kept to ensure it being dry., Above hung great holster pistols, a pair of cutlasses and a long Spanish gun. Suspended against the wall was a framed piece of needlework, representing a cutter in full rig, the wind bellying her white sails, and the sea through which she passed in indigo blue, of uniform colour and hue. Underneath, in rude characters, also formed by the needle, was "The Paycock in her Pride", and indeed, in one corner, in the heavens, was a repre- sentation of the Bird of Juno, displayed, as the heralds would describe it, that is to say, with tail spread. The whole, though rudely, was effectively executed. There were sundry curiosities distributed about the room – bits of coral, large shells, turning their pink insides towards the fire, a stuffed and mangy eagle, and, under glass, seahorses and flying fish. The man, whose name was Job Ratten- bury, belonged to a notorious family, and was himself somewhat noted in the neighbourhood. He had been, like his father, so it was reported, a mighty smuggler in his youth; he had, however, been impressed and taken into the navy, but had left it, disappeared for some years, and when he came again into the neighbourhood, it was to the cottage he now occupied, which he bought; he then married and settled into a life on land. His wife died, and he was left a widower with one son, Jack; but he lived mostly by himself, and took care to have the lad properly educated. The lad was now lodged at Beer, and was studying with the curate. Captain Rattenbury, as he was called, kept no servant. He cleaned his own house, so that it was beautifully neat and sweet, he cooked his own victuals, knitted and darned his own stockings. He was indeed deft with his fingers and a needle, as "The Paycock in her Pride" testified.

Though living in solitude and quiet, yet Rattenbury was an object of mistrust to the preventive men, who had a station near by. Much was whispered and fabled, but little authentic known relative to his life and pursuits. It was suspected that he acted as a channel of communication between those who imported contraband goods, and those publicans, farmers and gentlemen, over a considerable area of Dorset and Devon, who desired to purchase wines and spirits without paying to the revenue the dues exacted. But nothing positive was known on this head.

"I'll tell you what, Jane," said Rattenbury, "you have put the maid dry and warm betwixt the blankets, but you are wringing wet yourself and your teeth chattering. Strip off your bedraggled clothes yourself. Don't you suppose that I have no female tackle here. my missus has been dead these sixteen years, but I have not had an auction over her clothing; don't you suppose that. I'll just light the candle and unlock the press, and you shall have a change."

He took a key from his pocket and opened the wardrobe. He had kindled a tallow candle at the logs that burned on the hearth, and he held this at the open door. Mrs Marley saw an assemblage of garments suspended within, none belonging to a man, and of all sorts and materials.

"Will you have a stuff or a silken gown?" he asked, and looked at her. He fumbled dubiously among the garments.

"But see – suit yourself – there be of all kinds there. They belonged to my wife. She is gone aloft where they dress in gossamer and swansdown. I keep these for Jack's wife, when he is pleased to marry. But the moth plays the deuce with them. Go either where the maiden sleeps or under the stair, where is a berth. Pass me out your steaming rags, and I'll hang them up to dry. By the Lord, you will be crippled with rheumatics if you do not shift at once. There is your child crying out again! I'll take my fiddle. Give a look in on her, and put on dry things. I'll play her a tune."

"That will rouse her."

"No, it will soothe her. I'll give her no hornpipes, but something soft and slumbrous."

Then he began to hum, "Once I loved a maiden fair". He stood in the midst of the floor, balancing his arms, and dangling his hands to the rhythm of the air. "That will send her to the Land of Dreams. I would play a lullaby, but I know none."

Thereupon he went to a nail to which was suspended a green baize bag, and from the bag he drew a violin. He seated himself at the fire and began to play:

> Once I loved a maiden fair,
> But she did deceive me;
> She with Venus might compare,
> If you will believe me.
> She was young,
> And among
> All the maids the sweetest,
> Now I say,
> Ah! Welladay,
> Brightest hopes are fleetest!

As he played the air he hummed the words. For one so rough, so big, so burly, the execution was marvellously tender and graceful.

He was right. With such a hand on the bow, such melody as this, the trouble of the girl's mind was allayed, as when oil is poured over chafed water. He continued playing, always softly, dreaming himself over this exquisite musical theme, wandering away into changes, as his mind reverted to the one soft sweet episode of his rude career – the courtship of the woman who had become his wife. And as he played the May sun came out and the oak was bursting; he saw meadows in which the purple orchis grew and the delicate "milk maids" fluttered, watercourses over which the marsh–marigolds hung their golden chalices, heard the doves coo and the cuckoo call, and looked into the blue heavens of his Mary's eyes – and the man's face changed, and his eyes filled – "Now, I say – Ah! welladay, Brightest hopes are fleetest!"

Mrs Marley came out of the inner chamber. She was vastly changed in appearance. She has washed her face and smoothed her hair, and in a good stuff gown wore a stately appearance. She was certainly a handsome woman still, though tanned by exposure and lined by care. Job winced when he saw a stranger in a dress that had once been worn by his wife, the thought of whom was still playing over him like a breath of violets.

He laid aside his violin. "That has not kept the girl awake, I warrant."

"No, she has fallen asleep, and there is a smile on her lips."

"I thought so. Sit down, Jane. I will have my pipe and grog, and you shall sip the latter if I cannot win you to have a pull at the first. It will be the most sovereign medicine after the chill. Sit down and tell me all."

"There is nothing to tell."

"There is everything to tell. If I had not chanced to arrive at the right moment, you would have thrown your child into the sea."

"I would have cast myself over the cliffs with her in my arms."

"Why so?"

"Because no one would take us in. I knocked at every door, I told my case in every ear, I appealed to every heart. It was all to no avail; so I knew there was no place for us in the world. We were to be squeezed out of it. Look outside your door and see. Listen to the wind and rain against your window. What sort of a night is this? Not fit for a dog to be out in – yet into it homeless and hungry the widow and the fatherless are thrust. Answer me, which were best? To end our miseries with one gasp, or to lie in the wet and whistle of the wind, shiver and die of a November night behind some dripping hedge in a ditch half full of water? There was but a choice of deaths. It was not a picking between life and death. Which would be worst – the short pang or the prolonged wretchedness? Which would you choose if it were to be your lot – the lot of you and Jack?"

"Jack and I are men. Men do not lie down in ditches to die, or chuck themselves over cliffs. If what they desire and need be not given them they take it by main force."

He poured himself out a stiff glass of grog, then recollecting the woman, gave her some, much diluted, sufficient to drive out the cold and induce sleep.

"Why did you not go to Mrs Jose at Bindon? Everybody who is in distress seeks her."

"Mrs Jose is away at Honiton with her sister nursing her. She is sick."

"Whither do you propose to go tomorrow?"

"I have nowhere before me."

"You do not belong to this parish?"

"No, I was not born here. I have not lived here long enough. But, captain, do not misunderstand me. I ask alms of none; all I require is work to be given me so that I may earn my livelihood, and I will not be separated from my child. See you," her voice softened, and the lines in her face relaxed, as her eyes melted and her lips quivered, "I am a lonely woman. I have neither father nor mother nor sister nor kin. No, nor have I husband neither. He whom I had has abandoned me; maybe, by this time, has taken up with another woman, and dresses and feeds and comforts her." Again her voice and features became hard. She looked before her into the fire. But then again a wave of softer feeling swept over her.

"For eighteen years," she said, with her eyes on the fire, and speaking rather to herself than to the man, "for eighteen years Winefred has lain at my heart. I fed her from my bosom. When she cried, all the fibres of my being trembled. From me she has the very blood that flows in her veins, and her soul is a part of mine, and her first breath she drew out of my lungs. I have done everything for her. I love nothing, care for nothing, hope for nothing, apart from her. I have nothing but my child – no, not a clot of earth, not a brick out of a wall, not a guinea of gold; I have nothing my own but her."

She began to cry, not noisily, but with great tears stealing down her cheeks. Then she was silent. All at once she burst forth, "O God in heaven, Who has put such love into a mother's heart, Thou alone canst understand me. What if aught should befall me, and she were left alone? She is a handsome girl. I was handsome once, and having no father, no mother to care for me, I came into such sorrow as never was. I cannot endure to think that she – my Winefred, my all – should be kicked about from place to place, friendless, or taken up by such as would only blight her whole life. I had rather that she died." She sprang up and her eye flashed. "Rather than this I would do it again. I *will* do it again, and not let the evil soil and rot my pretty flower."

"Be still, good woman," said Job, and he spoke with a gulp in his throat. He took up his violin, and played the same as before. Presently he laid the instrument on his knees.

"I understand you. You speak as I feel about my Jack. I am a rough old sea-dog, and I have been – I won't say what. But all I have saved is for my Jack. I shall make a gentleman of him. All my thoughts are on my Jack." He touched his breast with the end of his bow. "When you talk like that, Jane, you touch a chord here as begins to chime. You and your kid shall remain here. I am getting old, and require a woman to mind the house. As to the pay – we will talk of that tomorrow." She caught his hand and kissed it.

"Nay," he said, "don't thank me. It is the fellow–feeling as does it. I am a father with one child, and you a mother also with one – that is it, woman, that is it."

Chapter Four

The Undercliff

The rain and easterly wind ceased towards dawn. When morning broke a haze hung over sea and land that slowly lifted but never wholly vanished, and left the landscape bathed in the wan sunshine of November, the smile of a dying year.

Jane Marley was afoot early, and went to work immediately. She did what was necessary undirected, lighted the fire, made the kettle boil, and had cleared away the untidy remains of the past day's occupation of the room. When Job Rattenbury came down from his room above and found every preparation made for breakfast, then an expression of satisfaction came over his rugged face. "Right and fitting," said he. "For myself I do not care, but I must think of Jack. He does not like to see his dad make the fire and clean the boots. He wants to do it himself, and we have had a tussle over it. Jack is obstinate. Says Jack, 'Father, I will not have it. You're not my fag. I'll clean my own boots or wear 'em dirty all day.' I say 'There is the difference between us. I was never brought up to be a gentleman, but it is my intent and ambition that you shall be.' And now, Jane Marley, go on as you have begun, and we shall not get across. I'm a rough customer when things go against the grain. You are not one to stand pulling your apron and asking, 'Please, what next?' but buckle to work at once. I want Jack to be comfortable when he comes home, and I must provide that there be none of the little awkwardnesses there have been when he refuses to let his old dad make his bed, sew on his waistcoat buttons, and wash the dishes. Stay here you may, you and the kid, so long as you both conduct yourselves."

But the pact was not concluded till a proviso had been added. "Let this be an understanding between us. You make no advances, and do not aim at becoming aught other than my housekeeper. Because I let you put on *her* gown last night, that is no reason why I should let you step into her shoes. Keep your place, and I am satisfied. Otherwise – there is the door." Thus the compact was concluded.

As there was nothing that the girl could do, her mother bade her amuse herself. Winefred was therefore able to spend the beautiful day in rambles.

The river Axe sweeps to the sea through a trough that has been scooped out of the superior beds of chalk and cherty sandstone, and out to the red sands below. But the chalk stands up to the right and left in noble cliffs, of which Haven Ball forms the eastern jamb, and White Cliff that to the west. From Haven Ball the coast forms one continuous white precipice to Lyme Regis, above a sea in summer of peacock blue.

But, as every tyro in geology knows, the chalk is built up over the green sand, below which are impervious beds of clay. The rain soaking down through the faults in the chalk reaches the argillaceous stratum, and, unable to descend farther, forms innumerable land springs such as come forth at the base of most chalk hills. But where the chalk cliffs rise out of the sea, the water converts the gravelly stratum into a quicksand, and that is liable to be carried into the sea, and this causes subsidences, much as would occur if you lay on a water–bed that had in it a rent out of which would rush that which swelled the mattress.

There had been no sinkages of any importance along this coast within the memory of man. Nevertheless, an observant eye would have noticed that Captain Rattenbury's cottage stood on the undercliff and was on a lower level than the down, but was nevertheless cut off from the sea by a sheer face of precipice. This undercliff formed an irregular terrace that overhung the sea. It was reached by an easy descent from the down above, and lay sufficiently below it to be sheltered from the north winds. His garden was consequently a warm spot even in mid–winter; whenever the sun shone, primroses starred the ground there even at the end of January, and crane's–bill was never out of flower. The entire undercliff raised three hundred feet above the sea, had a ruffled and chopped surface, was broken into ridges and depressed into basins, and was densely overgrown with thorns, brambles of gigantic growth, ivy and thickets of elder. About Rattenbury's cottage was a patch that had been cleared, which served as kitchen garden, and a good but small orchard.

Rattenbury occupied himself that languid November day in pruning his apple–trees. The cottage was of chalk and flint cobbles, with a brick chimney, and was thatched. It leaned against a face of rock, in a manner that would have ensured damp had not that rock been chalk.

The entire undercliff, except for the clearing about the cottage, was a jungle, not to be threaded with impunity by any one wearing serge or broadcloth, for the thornbushes were armed with spines of prodigious strength, and the briars threw about their tentacles set with claws to arrest and tear the intruder. The girl wandered about, diving under the arches of the brambles, peering into the thickets of elders, everywhere disturbing countless birds.

After she had rambled to her heart's content, she returned to the cottage, and saw the captain at his apple–trees, knife in hand. He made a signal to her to approach. "Look here, maid," said he; "you can bear a letter, I suppose?"

"Where to?"

"To Beer."

"Across the water?"

"Naturally. How else get there?"

"I can go there, certainly. It will not occupy many hours – perhaps two."

"Do you know the Nutalls? – David Nutall?"

"There are several of the name. I do not know David."

"His house lies near where old Starr lived. You know that."

"Yes – well."

"Then take the letter. Mind this. No going from door to door, showing the letter, and asking where lives David Nutall. The letter is to be given into no other hand, and that not outside his house."

Rattenbury considered a while. Then he said, "It is a private matter, and no notice must be attracted. Get your mother's box with papers of pins and needles, reels and tapes, and go about Beer, with that, selling. And when you are at David Nutall;s, slip the letter into his hand."

"I will do it."

"And I wish you likewise to find my boy, Jack; he may be at the curate's, he is studying there – that he may be a gentleman. But I want for a bit, tell him, to take him off his studies – it is a tickle concern, tell him, and he is to go to David Nutall's and take instructions from him. Only, mind you, this. Mum as a mouse. My boy, if he is not at the curate's, will be at his lodgings. No one will think anything of your carrying a message from me to Jack – if they come to know you are staying here, But, to make sure, I will give you a pair of socks I have knitted for him. Do not be a fool – mum as a mouse. I will give you a couple of pence for the ferry."

"Shall I go and speak to mother first?"

"No, I will make it right with her. Go at once."

Winefred started on her errand. She crossed the down, descended the furrow through which the track led to the landing–stage of the ferry on the Axmouth side of the estuary. Then she called and waved her hand to attract the attention of the boatman.

Olver Dench did not hurry himself to cross and take over a single passenger, and this one whose capability of paying the toll was doubtful. He sauntered down from his cottage, looked along the road to Seaton, up towards Axmouth, saw no one, slowly launched his boat, and came over leisurely and in bad humour. He took the girl on board, but had got half across before he remarked, "I reckon you and your mother crept into a rabbit hole for the night."

"Captain Rattenbury has taken us in."

"Captain Job!" Dench paused in his rowing. "For how long?"

"Mother is going to be his housekeeper. We stay there altogether." Olver turned blood purple. He said no more, but put the girl on shore. She stepped lustily along. She had taken her mother's box of trifles for sale, which had been left the previous evening at a house in Seaton; she crossed the shoulder of the hill that separates the Axe Valley from the ravine of Beer, a shoulder that rises to the magnificent sea–cliff that is a prominent feature in all views of Seaton.

Then she descended the lane into Beer, a village of one street, shut in between steep hills, running down to a small rock–girt cove. It was a village of fishermen, but every fisherman was suspected of being a smuggler. Those in the place who did not get their living by the sea were quarrymen of the famous Beer stone.

In the main and only street was a house of some pretension and antiquity, that had belonged to the Starr family, hereabouts Winefred began hawking her wares, and as she did so she asked the names of the inmates of the several cottages. After going into three or four and vending some of her goods, she entered that of David Nutall. She saw there an old man, wearing a fisherman's jersey and hat, seated by the fireside smoking, whilst a woman was ironing by the window. Two younger men lounged by the fire talking. Winefred was roughly repulsed by the woman when she opened her box, but the old man put in a word: "Nay, Bessie! Buy a trifle of the maid just to encourage her."

"Are you David Nutall?" asked the girl.

"If I'm not mistaken," he answered.

Winefred drew the letter from her bosom, and put it into his hand. "What?" he asked quickly. "From the cap'n?" The young men at once brightened.

"Yes, from the captain." The young men drew round the elder, their father. It was too dark at the hearth for them to read the letter, and the old man rose and went to the window. He studied the letter with knitted brows, but could not make much out of it. He called the lads to him.

"Ah, father," said one, "I can make out what is printed, but not fist-writing."

"Come here," said David, signing to the girl with the letter. "Can you read what is in writing? Written words, not printed."

"I can."

"Make this out, will you. We are all friends here. There – that line; I can get hold of the sense of the rest of it – or nigh, about."

Winefred read: "At eleven o'clock on Thursday night, Heathfield Cross."

"That will do," said David Nutall, snatching the letter from her. "Tell the cap'n we shall be there. No more. We shall be there. That is the answer. Take this." The old man offered her two shillings.

"No," said she, "mother never takes alms. She earns."

"Well, and you have earned this – as carrying a letter." She held back.

"Mind, child," said the old man, "you hold your tongue about this bit of paper. A word might lose us all."

Chapter Five

Don't

Winefred went down the street in the direction of the curate's house. She encountered the reverend gentleman. He was somewhat shabby in dress, his boots were worn, and his neckcloth far from fresh starched. He had a depressed, crushed look. The girl went up to him confidently, and asked for Jack Rattenbury.

"My child," answered the parson, "he is not at my house, nor at his lodgings."

"I have a pair of socks for him knitted by his father."

"I can give them to him."

"Thank you, a message goes with them. Where is he, sir?"

"I believe on the White Cliff."

"What, wool–gathering? Is he doing that when supposed to be at his studies?"

"You have a pert tongue. He likes to watch the birds."

"Thank you, sir. I will look for him there. It is all on my way back." Winefred, instead of taking the short lane, now made the circuit of the down, ascending by the last house of the long street above the tiny bay, where were a flagstaff and benches, on which latter in almost all weathers fishermen and boys sat and yarned, disputed and smoked.

She asked them about Jack, and learned that he was on the down. "I have socks for him from his father," she explained.

Her way led under and around fragmentary masses of chalk crag belted with flints; and where the flints had fallen out, leaving the surface pockmarked, gulls and guillemots flew about chattering and screaming, and now and again a nimble tern, the swallow of the sea, glanced by.

White Cliff was, in fact, a paradise of birds. The tooth of the storm had gnawed into its friable surface, and bitten out chunks, and scooped caves so as to afford for the birds dry and abundant, and, above all, secure lodging-places where to breed. The brow over-hung, rendering their nesting shelves inaccessible from above, and from below a scramble up the lower sandstone beds was absolutely impracticable owing to their friability.

The white face of the cliff was incessantly changing, though by slow degrees; masses fell off, fresh indentations were formed, and at the base lay a mass of broken rock about which the waves churned; under which and over which, by tunnels and by furrows, the water rushed and returned of a milky tinge. Upon the headland, looking seaward, was the youth of whom the girl was in quest. He paid no attention to her as she approached, indeed did not appear to observe her till she named him, when he turned and confronted her. "What! Winnie, the peddler woman's child?"

Somewhat nettled, the girl stiffened her neck. "It is more honourable to peddle than to lounge," she said. "The peddler does something, and if she were away would be missed, but the loafer is no good to anyone, and is bad company to himself."

"You are sharp of tongue," said the lad, laughing. "I am an unstrung bow just now. If you had been kept with your nose to a Latin grammar, you would wish to lift it to sniff the sea breeze."

"Well," she said, and laughed also, "I have been idling all the morning, and my work now is no more than to bring you a pair of socks from your father, and with it a message."

"Thank him from me for the socks."

"Oh! and no thanks for the message?"

"I have not heard it."

"Well – he says you are to shut up the Latin grammar for a bit, and sit under David Nutall and take instructions from him."

An expression of dissatisfaction came over the boy's face. "And," continued Winefred, looking straight in his eye, "Thursday night at eleven, at Heathfield Cross."

"I thought as much," muttered Jack.

"Well, am I to have thanks for the message?"

"I don't know," be returned, brooding.

"Jack," said Winefred, "put your foot down and say – I won't."

"What do you mean?" he asked, looking at her in surprise.

"I know – or can guess – what it is about. I have not been up and down peddling here and hawking there, and not heard a thing or two. My ears are pointed, and I catch a good deal. Your father is just thrusting you on the same road as he has walked. It is my belief that if the little one of the flat fish said, I will swim straight, he would come out without crooked eyes, and not become a flounder, but be a mackerel. If once you begin to go in and out at the back door, you'll never take to that in the front of the house."

"You do not understand – my father is not a man to be disobeyed."

"I'd peddle before I did it," said Winefred with vehemence. "A peddling woman is honest, and carried her wares slung in front of her, and a – you know what – bears his behind his back. A peddling woman goes about by day along the high road, and is not caught slinking in bye–lanes of a night. You are a fine fellow with your Latin grammar, and learning to be a gentleman, to turn up your nose at my mother because she hawks laces, and then sneak away to cheat the government over spirits. I don't know whether it be a matter of right and wrong, all I know is it don't look honest, and I hate crooked ways."

"I do not see what right you have to dictate to me."

"I am advising only. Why, I will tell you." She turned her

peddler's box round under her arm. "Last night mother and I were going over the down, and it was dark. Mother had her notions as to the way, and she was all wrong. She was making direct for the edge of the cliff; my eyes are younger, and I saw it, and I would go this way when she persisted in going that. Mother is an obstinate woman, and she would go her course; and because I stuck to it she was wrong, she caught me up and was going to carry me along her way. If we have gone three steps farther, we should have bounced into kingdom come, and our bodies would be washing now against the pebble ridge. As good luck would have it, up came your father with a lantern, and he saved us. I would return the favour. You are being drawn along the wrong path by him, and so I turn on you the lantern of common-sense and say, Go right instead of going wrong. This is my advice; take or leave it as you will."

Then Winefred shifted her package again and trudged away. When she reached the cottage on the undercliff, she found that Job Rattenbury was out.

Her mother sat by the fire on a stool engaged in needlework, at the same time that she watched a pot that was boiling. Winefred laid the case of wares aside, and stood drawing in the scent of cooking through her nose.

"Good!" said she, "uncommon – the smell of onions is all over the place; I believe there is going to be beefsteak pudding."

"You are right," said Jane.

"Thanks be to me for it," said Winefred.

Her mother looked up. "You have been out amusing yourself; I cut up the meat and onions and made the pastry."

"But you would not have done it, nor have been here to enjoy beefsteak pudding if I had not kicked and squealed last night. Listen to me, mother."

Winefred got on the table and seated herself there, with her feet drawn under her. "Hearken to what I've got to say. But for me, we, both of us, instead of counting the minutes till the beefsteak pudding is ready for us to eat, would be serving as meals for the fishes. Mother, you are too hasty. Because the rain began to trickle down your back, and your nose was blue, you sought to throw yourself and me into the sea. Now learn a lesson. Don't be hasty again. Winefred

29

and beefsteak pudding for ever! Hurrah!"

"Be serious, child."

"I am. It is a deadly serious question whether I shall eat or be eaten. I give you fair warning, mother, that is now a question I will have put to me again. I will not go over the cliffs however much rain trickles down your back."

"You have no love for me."

"I have so great a love for you, mother, that with teeth and claws, and yells and kicks, I will prevent you from ever casting yourself away or me either. I am in a haranguing, lecturing mood today. I have been giving my mind to Jack Rattenbury, and now I give it to you; and I am in downright earnest with both. I don't like crooked ways."

"Forget what is past," said Jane, in a subdued tone.

"Yes, but I shall take care of myself in the future."

Chapter Six

Over the Punch–Bowl

"Well, mate," shouted Olver, the ferryman, entering the house with a swagger, and casting his cap on the table. "I'm come to spend the evenin' with you. Dang it, in November, they are too long, and one sickens of bein' by one's self. Why! What is the meanin' of this? Women, women about? I don't half like it."

"I do not fit my house to your likings," retorted Rattenbury curtly.

"Hang it, no. I don't expect it of you. But, by George, it is not I only who find the evenings dull alone, I see. Who would have thought this of you at your time of life, and with your grey hairs?"

"If you can't keep a civil tongue in your head, you can take up your cap and sheer off."

Olver struck his fist on the table. "I know better than that. No offence meant – then none should be taken, mate. Come, we'll have an evenin', and talk over old times."

"You are welcome to stay if you will keep in order your saucy tongue."

"Old times! Old times on the *Paycock*! Ah, cap'n!"

Rattenbury signed to Dench to take a seat, and called to Jane Marley to serve supper.

In a very short while the ruffle on Job's temper and countenance was allayed. Olver knew his man, knew that he dearly loved to chat over past days, to furbish up remembrance of old scenes of adventure, recall old comrades and fight old battles. And situated where Captain Rattenbury was, on that side of the Axe where the only persons associated with the water were Preventive men, and all others were farmers and labourers on the land, he was thrown on Olver as an associate.

For reasons best known to himself he kept the men in the service of the Revenue at arm's-length, and such as were connected with the soil, and whose talk was of bullocks, were not to his taste.

As a man advances in life he makes imperceptibly a *volte-face*. He turns his back on the future as devoid of interest to him, that he may gaze fondly at the ground whence he started. Youth values what it can acquire only for what it can make out of it; age appreciates what it holds in hand only for what it was and for the efforts expended in modelling it to what it now is. The present is appreciated, not as containing in its womb that which will be, but for the faded traces perceived in it of past loveliness. As the threads that connect man with his early career break, those that remain are clung to with intense tenacity.

Rattenbury did not like Dench, he even regarded him with repugnance; yet, as there were none other in the place who had been in any way linked with his early life, he endured him as one with whom he could converse with pleasure. But it would be a misconception to suppose that Job Rattenbury lived for the past alone, and that he was without an eye for the future. As far as his own future was concerned he was indifferent, but his ambition with regard to

Jack had a forward look.

Days close in rapidly in November. Rattenbury drew the little blind over his window, and excluded the fishy glimmer of the dying day. He did not light a candle. Candles in those times were of tallow, and were a constant annoyance, as they needed periodic snuffing, but he threw more wood upon the fire, and the whole room gleamed with saffron light that scintillated in the burnished copper and brass articles on the mantelshelf and in the Bristol lustre crockery on the dresser, but nowhere more brilliantly than in those living agates, the eyes of Winefred.

Mrs Marley was engaged at the fire, and was turning out that same beefsteak pudding on which at the moment all Winefred's thoughts and desires hung. Olver's eye observed her every movement, but it did so furtively, and he was careful that neither she nor Job should notice to what an extent she engrossed his attention.

When the supper was served, Mrs Marley and Winefred sat and ate along with the two men, and the girl did full justice to the pudding. That done the women rose, cleared away the dishes, leaving only tumblers and the ale–jug to the master and his guest, that they might smoke and drink and converse together without restraint.

So, as ancient cronies, the captain and the ferryman fell into talk upon times past beyond recall save as a memory, and the *Peacock* was often in their mouths. And as they drank they looked into the fire and drew long pulls at their pipes, and the mistrust, the aversion entertained by Rattenbury ebbed away.

There rose a succession of scenes before his fancy, lighted up with a perhaps unreal halo, such as affection casts over the past, associated with pride at the recollection of a daring and a dashing youth.

All at once Winefred traversed the kitchen. Job caught his violin, and signalled to her with the bow. "Child," said he, "see if you can dance." He threw a crimson kerchief on the floor. "Step on that. Trip and twirl in the midst, and do not ruffle the rag. I have seen it done, and by men."

The girl looked at him incredulously, and with perplexity. This was not dancing, she thought – not such as she had conceived dancing to be.

"Olver," said Job, and he tapped the ferryman on the head with his fiddlestick, "show the little maid how it is to be done."

"I can't dance," relied Olver sullenly, "and what is more, I won't be knocked about the head."

"Yes, you will," retorted Rattenbury, and struck again, contemptuously. "You will do and endure anything for a glass of grog and beefsteak pudding. See! Jane shall bring in the bowl and I will brew. The kettle is singing. Dance you shall, or drink only small beer. Stand up." Then he put the fiddle under his chin, and struck up a hornpipe. The clumsy sulky boatman was constrained to go through some of the evolutions of a dance, to the measure played by Captain Rattenbury. But he did it badly, and Job laid his violin on his knees with a gesture of impatience.

"It is like a porpoise rolling," said he. "Come, Jane, fetch the bowl and lemons and sugar. I have promised it. After the brew I will teach the little wench how to perform." He stood up, signed to Mrs Marley, who took a large ironstone china basin from the dresser, wiped it out and set it on the table. Then from a cupboard she brought the condiments, and Job from a window box produced fine old Jamaica rum. Next, fetching from a drawer a punch–ladle of whalebone, with silver bowl into which was let a guinea, he roared out:

> "Fill me a bowl, a mighty bowl,
> Large as my capacious soul.
> Vast as my thirst is, let it have
> Depth enough to be my grave.
> –I mean the grave of all my care,
> For I design to bury it there."

He flourished his ladle as Mrs Marley brought in hot water from the puffing kettle. The fragrance diffused itself through the room, as the ripe dark rum was poured in, the nutmeg grated, and the slices of lemon were thrown in to swim on the aromatic, generous liquor.

Alas for the punch–bowl! It was one of the institutions of the past. It sent a stream of goodwill that diffused itself over those congregated around it! It mellowed the asperities and sweetened the crudities of those who brimmed their glasses from it. What choice stories, what melodious songs, what sportive sallies did it call forth! And the host ladling forth the spicy liquor was brought into intimate and affectionate relationship with his guests. He was like the sun diffusing warmth, light, life to the planets round. That was quite another thing to the butler decanting champagne into a glass. With the punch-bowl something has passed away out of English social life that cannot well be replaced.

"There, Olver," said the captain; "it was worth attempting and failing in dance to have a smack of such a drink of the gods as this?" Job was in good humour. "Now, little maid," said he, "and you, Olver; and you, Jane, fill out for the girl a thimbleful. I give the toast of the evening, Success to the undertaking."

"Success to the undertaking," said Olver.

"I should like to know what the undertaking is before I drink it," said Winefred.

"That is no concern of yours."

"Then," said she, "success to every honest and daylight undertaking." Job and the boatman looked at each other and laughed. "Come," said Rattenbury, throwing himself into his seat, "let us see if you are as nimble with your toes as with your wits. Dance."

The imperiousness of his manner impressed all with the sense that he must be obeyed. "I cannot dance like Master Dench," said Winefred, "I require teaching."

"I trow not," retorted the captain. "If you have music in your soul, dance you can and dance you will. When I touch the strings every nerve in your frame will tremble in reply. Teach you to dance! Who teaches the gulls? Who the yellow butterflies in spring? Who the leaves of the birch? Who the shining-bodied flies of summer? You'll dance without teaching if there be music in you. If you have none, no instruction will make of you aught but a bungler like him –" and had not Olver withdrawn his head it would have been tapped once more.

"Winefred," said Rattenbury, "I know you have music. With a plaintive melody I rocked you to sleep, with a lively one I shall make you skip. Dance!" He drew the bow over the strings and began a lively air. Pleased at his commendation, and eager to oblige, and finding his command consonant with her inclination, she at once tripped onto the red kerchief that still lay on the floor, and moved her feet and clapped

34

her hands, balanced herself now on one toe then on the other, respon-
sive to the music. It was as Rattenbury had said, the melody provoked
movement, and every change in the air produced corresponding action
in the dancer. Now it was allegro, then andante, now grave, and then
a riot of mad and merry flutter.

"Well done!" shouted Rattenbury. "By Moses, the little wench is
heated. Olver, you could not have been brought to that. No teaching
would have done that. Every nerve in the girl leaped, every pulse
bounded when I touched a fiddlestring."

The boatman growled something about being old and stout. "Olver,
if you cannot dance you can sing – or if you have no music in your
organ you can bellow. Join with me, and we will have the Lights up
Channel." Then he broke forth:

> "Farewell and adieu to you, Spanish ladies,
> Farewell and adieu to you, ladies of Spain;
> For we've received orders to sail for Old England,
> But we hope in a short time to see you again.
>
> We'll rant and we'll roar like true British sailors,
> We'll rant and we'll roar across the salt sea,
> Until we strike soundings in the Channel of England,
> From Ushant to Scilly be leagues thirty–three."

"Now mark," said the captain, waving his bow and indicating points
in the room. "The first light we make, it is called the Dodman. That
it after leaving Scilly – there she is, shining out on the lea like a star.
The Ram's Head – that is next – shining yonder. Then Plymouth, next
Start Point, and after that the light of the Isle of Wight. We steer past
Beechy, by Farley, by Dungeness until we arrive at the South Foreland
light. You see, it's like a picture; all of the points come up one after
another like the stars in the belt of Orion. Now we will sing again:

> "Now the signal is made for the grand fleet to anchor,
> In the Downs at the nightfall to lay up the fleet,
> Then stand by your cat–stoppers, see clear the shank–painters,
> Haul up the clue–garnets, stick out tacking and sheet.

Let every man toss off a full flowing bumper,
Let every man toss off a full flowing bowl,
For we'll drink and be jolly and drown melancholy,
So here is a health to each true-hearted soul."

Rattenbury's face glowed with pleasure. He continued for a while playing variations on the theme, as again in memory he came up the Channel, and smelt the breeze, and heard the hiss of the water, and saw the twinkle of the lights succeeding each other. Then he laid down his violin and said, "Ah, Winefred! you tangle up my kerchief into a knot on the floor. Before long you will be able to dance on it and skip off, leaving it smooth as when laid down."

"Then," said the girl, "Mr Dench must not have gambolled on it first. I have done my best to smooth what he ruffled."

"Come now," said the captain, "Jane, let us hear you sing."

Without hesitation she struck up, "Early one morning, just as the sun was rising," and Job accompanied her, chiming on the strings. A pathetic song to a plaintive melody, but the effect on the singer was not pleasing. On the contrary, as she said of the woes of the forsaken maiden her face darkened, its lines grew deep, and her brow contracted. She did not observe the intensity with which Dench watched her.

Remember the vows that you made to your Mary;
Remember the bower where you vowed to be true;
Oh, don't deceive me; oh, never leave me!
How should you use a poor maiden so?"

The captain noticed the gathering cloud, and turning to the ferryman said, "Come, Olver, it is your turn. On my soul I am enjoying myself famously. I only wish Jack were here. Sing, lad, sing." Then the boatman began to roar out a ballad. He had not gone far before Mrs Marley snatched her daughter to her and hurried out of the room. At the same moment down came the end of Job's fiddlestick on his head. "You dog!" said he. "What made you sing such a ditty as that before women and children?"

"What made me?" replied Olver sulkily, as he rubbed his head. "Why just this – that I wanted to be rid of them. How can we relish our evening when we have such as these interloping and spoiling our happiness?"

"Whose house is this? Whose punch is this? Whose pleasure is concerned?" roared the captain. "I shall have in here just whom I will, without asking your leave; and if I suffer an ill-conditioned cur to sit here at any time, it is that I may have the satisfaction of kicking him if he misconducts himself."

"Keep your fiddlestick off my head."

"I shall rap your thick skull whenever you misbehave."

"I will break it if you do."

"You dare not. There." He struck him again. Olver's face became purple, but he did not fulfil his threat.

"It was for your good that I drove them away," said Dench in a low tone. "You do not know what you are about, taking this woman into your house."

"I should think I knew better than you."

"No, captain, you mistake. Have you considered how folk will talk, what they will say about it?"

"Let them talk and say what they will, I care not one doit."

"You do not know the woman as well as I myself do. She will twist you about her little finger."

Job laughed scornfully. "Bah!" said he. "Look at me – at my bulk, there is no twisting of that."

"She will find out everything you desire to keep concealed."

"Suppose there be nothing?"

"What, there is the undertaking for Thursday."

"Pshaw! She knows which way her bread is buttered."

"You, captain, may have a masterful will, and that you have one I do not deny. But she has one ten times as masterful as yours. She will hold you in her closed hands, shutting them about you, if you suffer it, or if you cross her she will strike you in the face."

"She will do neither. I have ruled men in my day, and *such* men."

"But not one of them a match for her. You never before have had to do with such a woman as this. If she thought she could benefit her child, it is my belief she would regard no-one, stick at nothing."

"And that," said Rattenbury, "that is precisely what I admire in her, ay, and respect. It is with her and Winefred as it is with me and Jack."

Chapter Seven

A Late Visitor

When Olver Dench reached his cottage, that stood but little removed from the land–stage of the ferry, on the Seaton side of the water, he was much surprised to find that his fire was made up, and that someone was seated in front of it with hands extended and knees apart warming himself at it.

He stood in his doorway and stared till his eyes were sufficiently accustomed to the light to enable him to distinguish the occupier of his room and chair. He had not locked his door on leaving. At that period few thought of fastening their houses unless leaving them for a long time, and the ferryman's cottage was usually free to anyone to enter and wait for a passage. A neighbour undertook to attend to the ferry when Dench was away. It was not likely that anyone would desire to cross after dark, but it was not impossible that one should.

The individual by the fire was a gentleman in a bottle–green coat with high collar and brass buttons. The coat was short–waisted but long–tailed. His beaver hat, curled at the sides like a leaf attacked by aphis, stood on the table, and a malacca, gold–headed cane lay there also. He wore two waistcoats of differing cut, so as to allow the lower to show. A thick neckcloth enveloped his throat, and was pinned in front.

Hearing the steps of Dench in the doorway he turned and exhibited a gold eyeglass, through which he had been studying the fire. His lavender trousers were strapped under his boots, and were tight–fitting from the knee down. He was a man of middle age, with slight whiskers elaborately curled, and a forehead apparently high, due to the retreat of his hair. He was a good–looking man decidedly, with mild blue eyes, a well–formed nose, and would have been handsome but for a weak mouth and a retreating chin.

38

Just before Olver entered he had been peering down the tube of a latchkey, and then blowing into it to expel such dust as might have accumulated in it from residence in his pocket. Having satisfied himself on this score he laid the key on his knee, affixed the glass in his eye, and looked into the flames. The tread of Dench made him turn.

"Is that you, the Ferryman Dench?" asked the gentleman. Then placing a hand on each side of the chair he turned it about, so that still sitting he might observe him who entered.

"What! surely not Mr Holwood!" exclaimed the boatman. He took off his glazed hat, turned it about in his hands, and added, "Your servant, sir."

Then he cautiously shut the door behind him. "Good Heavens, sir," said he in a tone agitated and full of ill–concealed alarm. "Whatever has brought you here, sir? This is most risky."

"I cannot help myself. I know that it is unsafe. But I have been prodigiously uneasy, and I felt it impossible to obtain rest of mind without seeing and speaking with you. I have a few days of liberty; I have taken advantage of them. Where is she?"

"Oh! she is right enough."

"But whereabouts is she?"

"Oh! not very far off. Housekeeping to a certain person, unmarried of course."

"Which?"

"Oh! Both."

A pause – Mr Holwood felt in his pocket for his latchkey. "A – clergyman, I hope?"

"Bless your soul, a seafaring fellow, a dissolute dog, been a smuggler – mixed up in – but, ahem! – you are in the Government."

"No, not exactly – in the Foreign Office. You – you don't mean to imply –"

"Never stir in dirty ponds or you wake bad smells. What can you expect? What is born in the bone comes out in the flesh."

The gentleman put his latchkey back in his pocket, folded his hands between his knees, and looked down with a troubled face on the floor; his feeble underlip quivered, and his chin went back as though inclined to dive into and conceal itself in the neckcloth.

39

"I am very unhappy about this. I – I feel a sort of responsibility in the matter, But, my dear Dench, what am I to do? Consider how I am placed. I am a gentleman and well connected. My people are tolerably high in life, and I have a Government situation. It may lead – there is no saying to what it might lead. It is a position that necessitates my taking a place in the fashionable world. That single indiscretion in early youth weighs like a millstone attached to my neck. I try to forget, to make light of it. I cannot. The possible consequences are ever before me, and just now anything approaching to a *dénoument* would be fatal."

"Then why the deuce did you come here and risk all?"

"That is just what I – I ask myself – you know how one feels on the edge of a precipice, an irresistible desire to cast one's self down. I really could not help myself. I felt that I must come here and see and hear how matters stand, so as to take my social – my moral bearings – from circumstances. I would do what is right – strictly honourable and right – but I don't want to hurt my prospects. One must always look to one's prospects in the regulation of conduct, – moral conduct, you understand. A thing cannot be right which hurts one – can it?" He put up his eyeglass. "I ask you as a moralist."

"My dear sir," answered the boatman, "you leave all to me. I am your man, devoted body and soul. No one else knows all the ins and outs as I do. Leave me to manage for you."

"You have always paid her the annuity in quarterly instalments, or monthly, if preferred. I sent it you quarterly."

"Regular as the tides."

"You tell me that she has asked to have it increased. I cannot say but there may be some reason in this, nevertheless I want to be assured that there are to be no undue exactions which might become insupportable." He dropped his glass.

"It shall go no further."

"I hope not." Again up went the glass, and he scrutinised the face of the ferryman. "But, you see, I am in her hands. She can squeeze me till all my juice runs out. If it became known that I had married her, and she were *par exemple*, to arrive in town and assert her rights as my wife, what should I do? What would my people say?

What would they think in the office? And especially at present when I have cause to be sanguine. My expectations are so well grounded."

"Expectations, Mr Holwood?"

"I have a rich aunt, a maiden lady, who thinks very highly of me and my abilities. She is proud and pedigreeish – if I may coin the word. She would never forgive me – never – if she knew that I had united myself to an individual, however well-favoured, without ancestry – a fisherman's daughter, and not able to read or write!"

"Sir," said Dench, "with all due respect, be it spoken, but I think you are vastly indiscreet in coming here under these circumstances. it is now eighteen or nineteen years since you have been here, and you ought to have kept away altogether."

"I felt – hem! – that I must be satisfied. I did not rest easy, not knowing to what extent demands might grow. I desired greatly to hear something about her, and to find out if some compromise might be effected. Is it possible to get her to leave England?"

"No, sir. Not now that she has taken up with that smuggling Captain Rattenbury."

"You stick a knife into me. Has she gone utterly to the bad? I would have done anything, anything in reason for her, if she could have maintained herself in respectability. I have sent her money regularly, as an annuity, paid through you. You have paid her punctually?"

"To the day – quarterly."

"It would be simply fatal were she to appear on the *tapis*." The gentleman pulled out his breast-pin, and poked into the tube of the key in quest of a lodgment there, blew into it again, and replaced the pin. His long white fingers shook nervously.

"See here, sir," said Dench, and drew a seat to the fireside, whereupon Mr Holwood put one hand behind him, the other between his knees to the chair, and turned the chair and himself about, so as to face the boatman. "Jane don't believe as she was properly married. Says I to her, my dear, he was under age, a mere boy."

"But it was not so. I was twenty-one."

"Well, well, sir, she supposes you were not, and that suffices. Says I to her, in the eye of the law, that did for you. It was no marriage

41

at all. And then again, says I, where did it take place?"

"In Rousdon Church."

"True you are, sir, but was not the church ruinated? The roof was off, and no service was ever said in it. She knows that, and in the eye of the law, says I, a church don't hold good if the roof be off."

"It is not so."

"Never mind. She has been led to think so. Then, said I, that is not all, the parson had been unfrocked by the bishop. And in the eye of the law –"

"But was he so?"

"My dear sir, I don't know. But she thinks it so; that is all we need concern ourselves about. You see, sir, we have here with that blessed marriage undermined in three ways, and she is convinced it was a take–in and nothing further in the eye of the law."

"If it had only been as you say!" Mr Holwood put two hands to his chair, lifted it and himself together till he had straightened his legs, then set it down again, with himself upon it. "If it had been so, I should have been greatly relieved. But it was a marriage, irregular in law, yet valid –"

"In the eye of the law," put in Olver.

"Exactly so, exactly. That is my trouble. I move in such good society, and my aunt is worth from two to three thousand a year, and if she came to hear of this she would leave it all to another nephew, a cousin, a curate steeped in methodistical notions. If he got an inkling of it – he is a very serious man, and wouldn't dance or go to a theatre to save his soul – he'd go post haste and tell her about me, on principle of course, and spoil all my chances."

"Then, sir, there is nothing to be done but leave the matter wholly in my hands, as it has been heretofore."

Mr Holwood looked into the fire, and his chin retreated behind his stock. Presently he said dreamily, "I should have liked to have seen her – just once more to have seen her, you understand, without being seen."

"Impossible," said Dench, and struck the floor with his foot. "Sheer lunacy."

"But – the little girl. What is she like?"

"Like her mother."

42

"It could not be contrived, I suppose, that I should see her?"

"It cannot be done, sir, with safety. That girl is as keen as a razor."

Mr Holwood fell to further musing, his weak face assumed an expression of profound discouragement. Presently he said, rather to himself than to the ferryman, "Like her mother, and getting on to the same age. O my God, after all these years, to see the same face again. Has she her mother's wonderful eyes."

"Just the same."

"Dear – dear me! and in her ways, her character –"

"Her mother all over, headstrong."

"Yes, she was headstrong and passionate. She frightened me." He put his hand to his brow. "Merciful powers, one early indiscretion has been the ruin of my life, of my prospects. I have been unable to marry, and very desirable matches have presented themselves. One in particular – highly connected, a family of great influence with the Government, and with a handsome fortune. My attentions have been marked and remarked upon, they have possibly been too pointed; but nothing has come of it, because nothing can. I am obliged to hold back. I cannot contract a new alliance, lest this affair here should transpire, and if that Methodistical cousin of mine had but an inkling of a suspicion he would rout about it till he had turned everything hidden to the surface; on principle of course. I suppose had I ventured to brave the chances and to marry again I might have incurred transportation. I am debarred happiness, preferment. I am in danger of losing my aunt's inheritance. I am tortured by these incessant demands, and by not knowing how to impose a limit. Would you mind holding a light? I am confident there is a comfit in this key. I had some loose in my pocket, flavoured with roses, pink in colour, to keep my breath sweet."

Olver lighted a candle, and held it whilst his visitor explored the key with his breast–pin after the comfit. Then the gentleman blew into the tube again. Dench observed him attentively as he was thus engaged, and a slight curl expressive of contempt formed on his lips.

"No," said Mr Holwood, raising himself and the chair together, "there is nothing in the key. It is with me also as though something – a lump, not a comfit, not at all rose–flavoured – were in me, and

I cannot get it out. It was sweet, too, once. Tell me something about Jane. Has she got to look old?"

"Well, sir, she is still a fine woman, a very fine woman. She has lived in a cottage on the cliff, but you know what our chalk cliffs are, how given to crumble. Hers was so near the edge that it was unsafe; she has been forced to leave it. I have not been there, but I believe a wall gave way."

"Poor Jane, poor Jane," said Mr Holwood dolorously. "I am listening, Dench; tell me more. Has she been – on the whole – steady? – I would say – broadly speaking, respectable?"

"Well, yes, sir, so far. She has had the girl properly educated, thanks to your liberality. She has also sent her to church. Jane herself cannot read or write. You may remember, in the register she set a cross for her mark. I can't say I have seen her much at church myself."

"Ah!" said Mr Holwood, "I always go to church; but," he sighed, "the lump is still there, like the comfit in the key, and will not out."

"Where are you staying, sir, if I may make so bold to ask?"

"At the Red Lion."

The ferryman smiled. "With Mrs Warne," said he, "that is the hostess who has had some trouble with Jane."

"You don't mean to hint that she – she was – hem! was in drink?"

"I can't say what it was. I was not there at the time, but I heard talk about it. Mrs Warne had to threaten to send for the constable to remove her."

Mr Holwood sighed. "Bless my soul, how sad!"

"And at Nethersole's farm it was wusser. They had a to–do to prevent her from firing the ricks."

"Under the influence of – of liquor?"

"I did not enquire. I hear she made a bobbery as well at Thomas Gasset's. I am pretty sure, sir, that the best course for you is to leave Seaton as speedily as possible. Mrs Warne does not know your name, I suppose?"

"Oh no! I have given no name."

"Well, sir, leave everything to me. Why should you, a gentleman, and connected with the Government, be troubled about such scurvy matters as these? I will continue to act as go–between, and Jane

Marley shall never know that you have been here, and doing her the honour to inquire about her. She thinks you still abroad, Governor of – what is the place – Australia?"

"Tierra del Fuego. To this we agreed it should be," said the gentleman dejectedly. Then, after a long pause, he said, "Does she now happen to entertain any hopes, any desires, of seeing me again? Does she ever express a wish for renewal of our old relations?"

He had the key against his tongue twisting it about. Verily the only thing about the man that was braced and taut was his lavender trousers, strained by the straps under his soles.

"Mr Holwood, sir," said Dench, "no; frankly, no. Not a wish, not a thought but to fasten her nails in your face, and tear your bottle-green coat off your back, as a wild cat might do. She loves you no more, she just about hates you with all her flambustical temper. Certainly she don't want to see you again, least of all since she's took up with this Captain Rattenbury."

Mr Holwood winced. He wiped his lips with a silk kerchief and then his tall brow.

"If she were to see you, sir, it would be just like the sons of Sceva the Jew, as we read of in Scripture, and the possessed of the devil."

"Merciful Heavens! Such an incident! if it should get into the papers! If that curate cousin of mine were to hear the faintest whisper of it his ears would go up like windsails."

"Then, sir, go back to the Red Lion, and at daybreak take the coach to Axminster, and thence to town. Leave me to manage matters, prudently, secretly, economically. And trust to no one else."

Chapter Eight

On the Pebble–Beach

Mr Holwood was unable to sleep that night. Before leaving the ferryman's house he had resolved to depart for town by the coach on the morrow, and he had given orders to be called early, and to have some breakfast got ready for him.

But as he tossed in bed the past rose up before him in vivid colours, bringing with it wafts of old sentiment and tremors of old emotions. Scenes of happiness and of error revealed themselves to him bathed in light. Faces rose out of the past and looked at him reproachfully. Perhaps an old fibre in his heart that had once quivered with love was again in vibration.

"Poor Jane," he said, and turned in his four–poster bed. "Poor Jane, would that I could but see her, myself unseen, once again."

Then he racked his brain devising impossible schemes for catching a glimpse of her without allowing himself to be recognised. Next he fell to wondering what his child was like, a child he had never seen, never held in his arms, never kissed, and, in a manner strange to him, he was aware of a void within. He became conscious, as he never had been before, of responsibility, of the terrible truth that not only had he marred his own happiness, but that he had brought about the ruin of another, an innocent victim; and in addition that he would have his child's soul to answer for. He turned again in bed. A fire burned in the grate. It made strange figures on the wall. Reflections as eyes winked at him, a shadow like an arm seemed to be warning or reproaching him with an extended finger.

He raised himself in bed to draw the curtain to exclude this shadow, but they would not meet, and still between them he could see the hand stretched forth signing to him. Unable to account for it, he left his bed, went to the hearth, and found that the shadow was caused by the handle of a saucepan left on the hob at his desire to furnish him with warm water in the morning.

Having arranged the pan that its shadow should no longer offend him, he returned between the sheets, fell into an aimless unhappy tangle of hopes and fears, lapsed into sleep, and if, before dawn, he heard the knocking of the maid at the door, took it as a portion of his troubled dream, was not roused, and slept on, not to awake till full two hours after the coach had gone.

There was now no help for it. He must spend another day at Seaton. If he posted to Axmouth, it would not avail him, he would be too late on reaching that place to catch the London mail-coach. He dressed leisurely, resigned to the situation, and as usual was careful and painstaking about his clothing. He sent for the village barber to shave his lip and chin, to curl his whiskers, and adjust his hair so as to disguise incipient baldness.

Then he descended, very spick-and-span, dangling his gold-rimmed glass on his finger, to the coffee-room and rang for breakfast. In the same leisurely fashion he proceeded to eat his egg and chop and to dip his toast. Occasionally he set his glass to his eye, and raked the walls, to take cognisance of the hunting pictures that decorated them. Having finished his meal, he straightened his back, shook his legs, contemplated himself, and above all the roll of his whiskers, in the mirror; took out a notebook, twisted forward the lead in his gold pencil-case, applied it to his tongue, opened his notes, recollected that he had as yet no account to enter, no remark to jot down, and returned the book to his pocket, and drew back the lead of the pencil.

Then he rang for his beaver and overcoat, was fitted into the latter, ordered lunch, was handed his umbrella, and sallied forth. He was shy of going to the ferry, and letting Dench see that he had failed to catch the coach, so he engaged a boatman to row him to Lyme Regis.

"I will walk along the shore," said he.

"You will find it unpleasant walking, sir," said the boatman; "there are no sands, nothing but shingle."

"Ah, well! Not so far as Lyme. You may set me down short of it. I will walk thence. I rather like shingles. Indeed, I prefer them."

47

After he had been on the water for a while, Mr Holwood said, "Put me down at the dip of the cliffs by Rousdon."

"You know the coast, sir?"

"Ah! – hem! – Yes, I have studied a map. When you have set me on shore, row back and await me at the mouth of the Axe opposite the Chesil Ridge. Then carry me across. I do not choose to make use of the ferry."

"Very well, sir."

The row was comparitively short, and Mr Holwood stepped ashore at a pretty piece of wooded undercliff, where it dipped and allowed a path to descend to the beach. "I will pay you on the Chesil Bank, at my return," said Mr Holwood, and the boatman touched his cap and turned.

When the man was at a distance, Mr Holwood, who had watched his departure, looked around him, and took a few steps along the strand. All was much as it had been years agone, save that then the shrubs, the trees, the herbage had been thrilling with life, and now life had ebbed away, leaves were fallen and strewed the ground, and the grass was grey and sapless.

The sky was not so blue, nor the sea so alive with twinkles, nor the gulls so full of jocund play now as then. But the outlines of the cliffs, the features of the shore, were the same; reef and rubble, the line of torn seaweed and pounded shells still marking the receding tide, the savour of the sea, the murmur of the waves, these were the same.

There lay a mass of fallen rock a little way off – chalk with some flints in it, and behind that there was wont of old to be a pool left by the retreating tide, in which delicate pink and green weed–ace floated, and where a few left crabs ran along the bottom. He looked at it with a swelling heart.

He remembered that rock. A portion of it, facing the sea, was low and level, and formed a seat. On that he had sat many years ago, looking seaward, and then – not alone. He removed his beaver. There was a holiness in the spot, sanctified by sweet, loving, pure remembrances, when life was an open door, and pulses beat with hope and the sun was over all.

Mr Holwood wiped his brow, and let himself down on the stone.

"Merciful Olympian powers," said he in a low tone to himself. "It was here – here it all began." He set his hat with curved brim on the pebbles at his feet. He looked for the little pool – but it was gone, filled with rounded stones. He rested his head between his palms, and his long white fingers played a tattoo on his temples.

At that moment the past was intensely vivid. A barbed past can never be cut out of the memory; it leaves behind its fangs, its canker. It may be covered over, and forgotten, but it reasserts itself inevitably, excrutiatingly, and the fester begins to ooze forth and the wound to gape.

It was so now. On this piece of chalk he had put his arm round Jane's waist and spoken his love into her ear. There where now lay pebbles and a ribbon of torn weed, there in a crystal pool he had seen her frightened face reflected – and into it her tears had fallen.

In all this there was naught to sting and stab. But he recalled something further. It was here, on this same shelf of chalk, that he had sworn – when she confided to him that she would be a mother – that he would stand by herself and her child through life, and he had taken the oath with the deliberate intent of breaking it.

This was the story. When Joseph Holwood had passed his final examination at Oxford, he had come to Lyme Regis for a change of scene and air. His family possessed some influence, and it was an assured thing that he should have a situation in one of the Government offices. He enjoyed a small income of his own, not sufficient to maintain him in luxury, but this, added to a salary derived from his appointment, would make his position easy.

Till he received his nomination – he was promised one in the Foreign Office – he resolved to recruit after his studies, amuse himself at Lyme, boat, fish, bathe, and think of nothing.

So he went there, and spent some summer months in idleness, and in that summer weather and relaxation from all care met Jane Marley, a beautiful girl with large rich brown eyes, a ripe complexion, glorious dark hair, and a regal carriage. An atmosphere of romance surrounded her. Her father, who was dead, had been a smuggler. her brother had been quite recently shot in an encounter with a preventive officer, and she had been left alone, without a known relative in the town of Lyme. There were an independence and an intensity of character in Jane that imposed on the young man. She was a girl not to be trifled with, but one to impose respect. Joseph Holwood fell madly in love with this magnificent girl, and on this very stone he now occupied had declared to her his passion, its honourable nature, and had wrung from her consent.

Above, on the heights, was a parish church, St Pancras, Rousdon, a sinecure, as there was no population within the parish bounds and the church had been suffered to fall into decay, and nothing remained of it but crumbling walls and unglazed windows. In this ruined building a disreputable incumbent of the living, who resided in Lyme, and picked up stray guineas for odd duties elsewhere, was induced to marry the couple for a banknote of five guineas, without licence and without banns.

Holwood had enjoined the strictest secrecy on Jane; he had assured her that his relatives would throw him over, do nothing for him to obtain a situation under Government should they get wind of his marriage. Later on he assured her that so soon as he had his foot on the ladder and was independent of his family he would acknowledge his marriage. The only man in the secret had been Olver Dench, a comrade of Jane's father.

For a while Holwood had been intoxicated by his happiness, but reflection returned with sobering effect. He received a summons to return to town. His appointment had been gazetted. He left Lyme with many assurances to Jane that he would shortly be back.

Not till he reached London, and was among his friends and kinsfolk, did he realise how grave had been the step he had taken. He had left Lyme full of generous resolution that became limp directly he arrived in town. Surrounded by old associations, in the cultured drawing–rooms of the capital, he felt the incongruity of his marriage. He dared not bring Jane to London. To do so would be to affront his kindred, to exclude himself from society, and to bar his prospects of advancement. He could not pluck up courage to ack–nowledge what he had done; he postponed doing so till more convenient. The cowardice which interfered with his doing what was right induced boldness in doing that which was wrong. He returned to Lyme more than once, but was no longer happy with his wife, and under the plea that his duties recalled him, made but short stays with her. He dared not even hint his unwillingness to acknowledge her. His restless manner, his decay of cheerfulness, filled her with apprehension.

One day, on this very stone, she had told him of her expectations, thinking thereby to give him pleasure, and to bring from his heart a new wave of tenderness. Then he had sworn to her to stand by her and her child, and he had taken this oath after having already arranged with Dench to forsake her. He had talked over his embarrassment with Olver, and had settled with him to be his paymaster, and give quarterly to Jane such sums as would be forwarded to him.

Jane had sufficient sense to recognise that the social conditions of herself and her husband were very different, and she had plucked up sufficient courage to speak to him about it. "Joseph," said she, "I understand that you are a gentleman and a scholar, and have grand relations. I should be miserable among them. They would laugh at me and my country ways. That would make you angry, and in defending me you would get across with them. Joseph," she continued, and laid her hand on his arm, and looked into his face with tear-brimming eyes, "Joseph, let it be thought that I am not your widow, only come often to me; come to me and to your child. I do not ask for more. I know that I am an honest woman; but it is no odds to me if my good name suffer rather than that you should be put into difficulties. I can bear that, but I cannot bear to lose you."

It was on her saying this that he had protested fidelity whilst falsehood was in his heart, and from that hour he had not set eyes on her. Olver Dench acted throughout as intermediary. In the first place, he induced Jane to remove from Lyme Regis, and out of Dorsetshire into the adjoining county, and to settle in a cottage on the cliff above the sea. That was one thing gained.

Then he told her, what was false, that the marriage was invalid, as Joseph Holwood was under age, as the parson was under suspension, and as the church was no longer employed for divine service. She had believed him, and had submitted, but she was restive and incredulous at the suggestion that she was abandoned.

Olver Dench brought her money when the first payment arrived, and she had taken it without scruple, as she clung to the belief that Joseph was detained by his official duties, and that his absence was not premeditated. But when, slowly but surely, the conviction was formed in her that he had deserted her and would never return, never acknowledge her or his child, then she refused to receive any more money sent from him. No – if Joseph Holwood repudiated her, in her wrath, her resentment, she declared she would accept thenceforth nothing from him.

When the next quarterly payment arrived, Dench brought the money to her; it was rejected with scorn by the proud and suffering woman. Then the temptation to appropriate it to himself had been too strong for the boatman to resist, and thenceforth as it arrived, he had retained it for his own use.

Once, some years later, a qualm of conscience had come over Olver, and he had sought Jane Marley, with a proposal to supply her with money for her child from Mr Holwood. He, so he said, was settled far from England as Deputy Governor in Tierra del Fuego. But again, and finally, she refused. Thereforth he had felt no further scruples.

Joseph Holwood was unaware, as he sat brooding on the chalk shelf, that his conduct towards Jane had done him more serious mischief than if he had acknowledged his union. This might have damaged his prospects, but that had blighted his character.

As a young man he had exhibited some talent and a certain amount of energy. He had taken a good place in the schools. His conduct at the University had been irreproachable. He had right inclinations, an amiable disposition, and no vicious propensities. Under favourable circumstances he would have become a useful public servant. But his treatment of a confiding and innocent woman, his broken promises, had permanently lamed his character. He had lost clearness of moral perception, and his resolution was radically enfeebled. Thenceforth infirmity of purpose had become a feature of his character. He had not been pushed on in his department because he had proved himself to be capable only as a hack.

He had never married, to the surprise of his friends, but had stumbled into not a few sentimentalities with ladies, had tottered almost to the point of proposing, and then had, abruptly and inexplicably, retreated without committing himself. He was sensible of the insecureness of his position, and indulged in a sneaking regret he had proved himself to be capable only as a hack.

He had never married, to the surprise of his friends, but had stumbled into not a few sentimentalities with ladies, had tottered almost to the point of proposing, and then had, abruptly and inexplicably, retreated without committing himself. He was sensible of the insecureness of his position, and indulged in a sneaking regret that his relation to Jane had been no other than a passing intrigue.

As he thus mused and was unhappy, maundering over the past, he observed a girl engaged on the shore picking up and examining pebbles. She kept close to the line of the retreating tide, so as to be able to select amongst the stones whilst they were wet. Some of these she cast aside after a cursory glance; over others she hesitated, holding them to the sun, and then dipping them again in a hissing wavelet that swept to her feet. A few she retained and deposited in a pouch slung at her waist. As she drew nearer, something in her appearance, something in her manner, something in her gesture arrested, then riveted the attention of Mr Holwood, and starting up and advancing towards her he gasped: "Gods of Olympus! Oh! if it should be *her* child and *mine*!"

Chapter Nine

Seen Through

The girl was Winefred.

Engaged in the selection of pebbles, she did not observe the approach of Mr Holwood; and the rush of the inflowing wave, and the under rattle of the retreat, as the water drew the shingle after it, served to drown the footfall.

When he addressed her, she was taken by surprise, and started. He saw before him a tall, handsome girl, flushed with her walk, with dark hair slightly dispersed by the wind from the sea, with hale cheeks, brown, agate–like, honest eyes, fresh flexible lips, and a well–moulded lower jaw and chin. "Why are you picking and choosing among the stones?" he asked.

"Please, sir, I be looking for chalcedony."

"You should say *I am* not *I be*. But let that pass. Chalcedony–"

"And jasper."

"And jasper; what do you know about them? Are you deficient in grammar and a proficient in mineralogy?"

Winefred looked at him with an odd expression of perplexity and humour in her brown eyes and a dimple forming in one cheek. Now he saw that she had the eyes and features of Jane, but there was in her face something more – a reminiscence of a dearly loved and lost sister, who had been his companion in boyhood, his *confidante*, but who had died of decline just as she attained the age of this child.

"Tell me, my girl, what is your name?" There was a catch in his voice as he asked the question.

"Winefred."

"And your surname?"

"Marley. That is what my mother is called."

He paused before speaking again. A warm flow, as from a broken vein, suffused his heart. He would have liked to clasp the child to him and have said, "I am your father, kiss me, put your arms about me and let me cry." But he dared not do so. Presently he spoke again. "Will you sit by me on this rock and tell me about these pebbles? I do not understand. Why do you gather them? What is done with them?"

She at once took the place indicated, without shyness, with no awkwardness. But he did not seat himself, he stood leaning against the larger bulk of the chalky mass so that he might study her face as she spoke. "About these pebbles?"

"Please, sir, they are chalcedony. Sometimes I get moss agates."

"I understand. But I protest, to my uninitiated eyes they look vastly uninteresting."

"If wet and held to the light you can see through them and note markings in them; if I find some of good colour and very clear, with veins and silklike twists, then the gentlefolk buy them."

"Oh! the pebbles."

"No. Not the pebbles as they are, they have to be polished first. When we had our cottage, there was a grinding stone there, and mother turned the handle and I rubbed down the stone, and then with a little powder and some oil I got polish enough to see whether they really was good for anything."

"Whether they *were*. Excuse me, I interrupt."

"Are you a schoolmaster, sir?"

"I – oh dear, no."

"I thought you might be, and were turning the grinding stone on me." There was a twinkle in her eyes. "Well, sir," she continued, "then I take them to Mr Thomas Gasset, at Seaton, and he gives me a shilling for a very beautiful specimen, but generally eightpence or a groat."

"Ah! That is your pocket money?"

"I don't know about pocket money; it generally goes into my mouth."

"In sweets?"

"In bread and butter. Well, sir, Mr Gasset works the stones up into seals or brooches, or paperweights, or just as so many specimens; and these the visitors buy. And if you be going –"

"You are –," corrected Mr Holwood. Winefred made a slight movement with her arm, as though turning a grindstone.

"If you are going to Seaton, sir, you'll find Mr Gasset's shop on the right–hand side of the street, about a hundred paces above the Red Lion."

He nodded. He was without his hat; now he stooped laboriously – for he was tightly strapped, and wore stays – and picked it up. "And so – she turns the handle of the grindstone."

"What – my mother? Yes, sir. But our cottage has fallen down, and now we have not got the grindstone where we are."

"Where is that?"

"With Captain Rattenbury."

"Of the Royal Navy?"

"No, sir. I don't reckon he was a proper captain, nowhere –"

"I beg your pardon – anywhere."

"Never mind the grinding, sir."

"My dear, polish is everything – you see it in the pebbles."

She considered a moment, then smiled: "Yes, sir, polish is a great deal. I suppose we are all of us rolled up by the great sea of time, alike on the beach, but some are smoothed and shaped – and those are the ladies and gentlemen, and some are left in the rough, and those are such as mother and me."

"You are a shrewd observer. Now about this grinding stone?"

"We shall move it to the captain's house. Will you come and see it on the undercliff? Mother is there."

"I – I – no – no!" replied Mr Holwood hastily. "My avocations call me. I cannot today. On some future occasion, perhaps. Pray, how long have you been with this Captain Rattenbury?"

"Two days only."

"Two days only," he repeated with an air of relief. "I was led to understand – that is to say, I understood you to have said – longer. You are there temporarily, I suppose?"

"No, sir, mother is going to be his housekeeper."

"Oh! –" His countenance fell. He righted his hat on his head. "Does your mother ever speak to you about your father who is dead?"

"He is not dead."

"Indeed; he is not dead. You are sure of that?"

"Yes, sir. He is away somewhere at the other end of the world, I am told."

"Then she speaks to you about him?"

"No, sir, never." There ensued a long pause, which became painful.

"But she thinks of him – a lot."

"She thinks of him!"

"Yes, sir, I can see it, when she sits on the cliff and looks away to sea. She has her mind on him then; I know by the way she loses herself; and if I speak to her she does not hear me. She seems to me to be seeking that place beyond the ocean – they call it Terra del Fuego where he is. And at night, by the fire, she puts her cheek in her hand and looks into the coals. I have to shake her to bring her round."

"And you believe she is thinking of him!"

"I know she is, though she never mentions him." Again a pause. The girl's eyes were on him. He could not bear their penetrating light, and he dropped his on the shingle, which he stirred with the ferule of his umbrella.

Presently Mr Holwood said, "Do you consider, candidly, that your mother is happy? Is she of cheerful disposition?"

"Not over–cheerful, I reckon." He winced. "It is only when I am at my Tomfool tricks that I can get her to smile. I never heard her laugh outright. How can she? Just you think, sir, how it would be with you if your wife had run away and gone to Terra del Fuego, and you did not know what games she was up to there."

The gentleman was visibly agitated. He fumbled in his waistcoat pocket for his latchkey, drew it forth and blew into it. "Some sand has got in," he explained. He was uneasy. he desired to hear more, but was afraid to ask. He desired to see more of that honest fresh face, but he was afraid to meet the clear eyes.

"I suppose Captain Rattenbury is a respectable person?"

"What do you mean by respectable? He is not what you call a gentleman. He's rough on all sides."

"I did not mean that – a – a good man?"

"He has been very kind to us, and is teaching me to dance."

"Oh!" Again his face fell.

"That is a bit of polish, I suppose?"

He did not answer. Presently he said, "My child," and his heart bounded as he used the term. "Your name in Winefred, you say. Does your mother have no shorter, more eandearing name for you than that?"

"She calls me Winnie."

"Well, Winnie, my dear, I trust you are a good girl and say your prayers."

"I say my prayers."

"What has your mother taught you to say?"

"I say, Our Father."

"Anything else?"

"Yes, I say God bless dear mother, for ever and ever. Amen."

"And did you never pray God to bless your dear father, who is – in Tierra del Fuego?"

"He may be my father, but he cannot be my *dear* father. I have never seen him to love him, and he does not care for me, as he never writes or asks anything about me. If he has been in England he has never come to see either of us. He has never sent me a kiss."

Suddenly Holwood stooped, caught the girl's head between his hands, and pressed his lips to her brow. "Suppose, my child, that he has sent you this from the far−away world in which he lives. Why should you not pray for your father? He may need your prayers in Tierra del Fuego."

"What is the good of my saying God bless him, when God cannot do it?"

"Why not?"

"He is a bad man; he has left mother and me."

"Perhaps it was unavoidable. Tierra del Fuego is a long way off."

"No, it is not that. If he had not cut mother to the heart that she has never recovered, she would have taught me to use his name. But he went away wilfully to be rid of her and me."

"You think so?"

"I know it."

"And you have not thought much about him, I suppose?"

"I do not know what he is like. I know nothing about him because mother will not speak about him. But I know he is a heartless, wicked man to desert mother and me."

Holwood said nothing to this. His head had fallen. He took off his nodding hat and set it on the stone. he folded his arms and looked pensively, broodingly at the pebbles.

What would be not now have given had the past been different? Had it been possible now to go back and reconsider his conduct? How happy he could have been in a humble dwelling by the seaside with his simple, beautiful, loving wife, and this glorious child to take to his arms as his own flesh and blood, and for whom to scheme and build castles in the air. But over eighteen years ago he had taken a wrong direction, and to retrace his steps was now impossible.

"Please, sir, you have dropped your key."

"Bless my soul," exclaimed he, rousing himself, "it will be choked with sand."

"There is no sand here, only small gravel."

He proceeded to stoop. But this was a slow and painful process, attended with strainings and creakings. Winefred forestalled him. She had picked up the key and presented it to him, lying across her rosy

58

palm, before his person had described a right angle.

"Winnie," said Holwood in a low tone, "will you do me a pleasure? I am a man of principle – in the abstract. I subscribe to schools for the education of children in the elements of morality. It is to me a shocking thought that a young person of your age and sex should not invoke the blessing of heaven upon the author of your being. Would you like to possess a watch – a Geneva watch?"

He drew from his fob a delicate timepiece of gold, with a gold face. "This," he said, "is a watch that I no longer have occasion for, as I possess a gentleman's repeater that belonged to my father, and which I value accordingly. Would you like to have this bauble? It is a lady's watch."

"I am not a lady."

"Only a little grindstone and shammy leather wanted, perhaps. But no more of this. Will you accept this from an entire stranger, unknown to you by name, but a Patron of Virtue. Include, henceforth, the name of your father in your devotions."

The girl flushed with pleasure and surprise. She put forth her hand – then withdrew it again. "I cannot pray for my *dear* father, but I will ask God to bless my *poor* father."

"Poor! – hem – yes, poor – in Tierra del Fuego, the Land of Fire."

He thrust watch and chain into her hand, caught up his beaver, and walked hastily away, that is to say as hastily as it is possible to walk over a beach of sliding rounded cobblestones.

Her poor father! Poor – not in income, comforts, waistcoats, and hats – but poor in all that makes life rich, love surrounding, and within trust and strength, and self-respect.

Had he remained another moment facing his child, had she seen the tears flow over his cheeks, then, as surely as she discerned the chalcedony or the agate in the moistened pebble, so surely would she have seen the weeping man – one not wholly worthless, not one altogether flint.

Chapter Ten

A Rift

Delighted with her watch, Winefred curled herself up behind the mass of rock so as to be sheltered from the cutting east wind, that in comparative comfort she might watch the movement of the hands, hearken to the ticking, open the case and observe the swing of the balance wheel; even try the key timorously whereby the watch was to be wound, and ascertain in which direction to turn it. The wonder, the pleasure, afforded by this watch surpassed previous experience.

A hand danced the seconds on a subsidiary circle upon the dial. Further exploration revealed an interior where all was dainty mechanism, a diamond on which the pivot worked, a hair–spring of incredible delicacy, and minute wheels of surpassing smallness. The study served to fill the girl's mind with astonishment.

At the beginning of this century watches were not in such general use as they are now; they were costly, and possessed by the rich alone. The farmer had to content himself with the clock, the labourer with the sun, and at night with the cockcrow.

Winefred was roused from her dream of delight by voices, and peering round the hunch of chalk that sheltered her, perceived the chief officer of the preventive service and one of the gaugers. They were in close conference and did not observe her. Mr Holwood had disappeared some time ago behind a headland.

"We shall nab the whole lot," said the officer. "They may show fight, probably they will, as they are numerous and desperate, because we have hemmed them in so close of late that they have not been able to free their goods. We have watched Lyme so closely that there has been no chance for them to run a cargo there. It all goes into that d––d hole of Beer, which it is next to impossible to keep in your eye day and night. And with its freestone quarries and burrows into every hillside, there is a veritable underground labyrinth, in which could be stowed liquor enough to supply the toping squires and merchants of the west for a dozen years. There is no tracking them there, they are in at one rathole and out at another, and verily, the Creator seems to have had smugglers in view when this coast was called up. But we shall draw the net on them this time and bag every Jack with the cargoes. I have sent for the military; there will be too many for us unaided to tackle. They purpose bringing kegs and bales to Heathfield Cross on Thursday night, and wagons will be in waiting to load them for Honiton, Lyme and Dorchester. They will cross at the creek over against Hawkesdown, slip through Axmouth, then up the hollow way, and so to the Cross. I have made my arrangements to catch them whilst lading the conveyances, and if they smell us and drop their goods and run, the military will close up the roads in rear, and they will have no way of escape save that of plunging over the cliffs and perishing in the waters like the swine in the country of the Gadarenes. They will not do that; better be nailed and made to serve in His Majesty's navy than break their necks."

"High time we should catch them," said the man. "They have grown saucy."

"They have grown desperate," retorted the officer. "They have been accumulating cargoes, and have been unable to dispose of them. Now they must do it – and so –" He snapped his hands.

"It is no fault of ours," observed the underling, "if they have been able to run in such a lot. It is this coast does it. That of Cornwall is bad, but nothing to this. The chalk and the channel are against us. Smooth seas and fogs and a coast as full of holes as a hedge beside a warren – what can be done?"

"Well," said the officer, "keep your counsel now. Do not trust even your own men. Some of them may have been tampered with – stranger things than that have happened."

"Well, sir, I suppose they have leaky vessels among them."

"To be sure they have. Were it not so, I should not have been forewarned of this."

"You can rely on me, sir."

"I know I can." And the men walked away.

Winefred heard no more, owing to the grinding of the pebbles under their feet, but she had heard sufficient. It was as she had surmised. She had been employed to convey a message connected with a smuggling enterprise, and the secret had been betrayed by one of the confederates.

She was annoyed at having been involved by Rattenbury in a proceeding with which she had no sympathy; she was troubled at the danger that menaced him and his son Jack, who, she was confident, would not act upon the advice she had tendered. But, further, she saw that if the captain were taken, she and her mother would probably lose the home they had just got into.

Winefred had no decided opinions relative to the morality of smuggling. The atmosphere on that coast was charged with it. her grandfather had been engaged in the contraband trade all his days, and her mother's brother had lost his life in an affray with the preventive men. On this account her sympathies were ranged with those who broke the law, and it was manifestly to her interest to exert herself to protect them in the danger that menaced. But she did not relish the trade that was being so largely carried on in the neighbourhood. It was surreptitious, it ranged with housebreaking and arson. And, as her mother held, it brought no luck on those engaged in it. She had been shown a pint mug with which the guineas had been measured out among the sharers in a successful run. They had not troubled to count the gold. Yet not one coin had remained with her grandfather, and he, to whom many of these pints had been allotted had died penniless. It was not from any deep moral principle that Winefred was opposed to smuggling, but partly because she thought no luck attached to it, and therefore it must be wrong, mainly because it was not an open and daylight profession, and she had a natural aversion from everything that was not manifest and straightforward.

Winefred did not leave her hiding–place till she could do so unobserved; till one man had ascended the path to the station, and the other had taken the beach way to Lyme Regis. Then she came from behind the rock.

She resolved not to mount the track that led up the slope, as it passed the cottages of the coastguard and under the circumstances she deemed it advisable to give them a wide berth.

Her only other way of reaching the captain's cottage was circuitous. It lay along the beach, and she would have to double Haven head and ascend the combe by which she and her mother had mounted on that eventful evening when they were first introduced to the reader.

There was no way up the cliffs between these points; they rise as a white precipitous wall three hundred feet. But she knew the strand – every reef, indentation, every buttress of chalk, and every cave. She had paced it a hundred times pebble–hunting.

On this occasion she did not look further for stones; she had cares that weighed on her mind and occupied her thoughts. So she tramped along till she reached a doubly familiar spot. Immediately aloft stood the cottage she had occupied from infancy. A hedge had skirted the edge of the drags as a protection, and she had been prohibited from going beyond that hedge, even from climbing it.

Now, on looking up, she was startled to observe a displacement of the rock and a dislocation in the hedge. The cliff had parted from the down and taken as it were a step seaward, and was slightly lurching. The hedge was discontinuous, and she could see that a rift had formed that shore deep into where their garden had been.

Winefred was so surprised at what she saw that, regardless of risk, she resolved to examine the phenomenon closely. Instead of treading at the very margin of the retreating tide, where the larger shingle ceased and gravel began, she advanced to the foot of the rocks, and now saw that the cleft descended from the summit to the very base. An entire shoulder or mass had separated from the main body, and was parted from it by a chasm clean cut as by a knife. Not only so, but the portion that had detached itself had sunk. Winefred was surprised at what she saw, and being of an inquisitive disposition, and regardless of danger, she ventured close to the mouth of the chasm. It was torn through the chalky superincumbent beds and through the subjacent sandstone, and a portion of turfy down had moved seaward, but had done so without oscillation, for it had not been so shaken as to break into fragments and strew the shore with dislodged masses. On the contrary, it had parted from the mainland with a minimum of violence, and it was in sinking that it had detached itself.

Winefred first peered into the rift, then cautiously entered it, and looked up at the white walls barred with strata of flints, some of which were snapped across by the disruption.

No stones were falling. No further movement was perceptible. With beating heart the girl not only entered the chasm but pursued her course up it. The sky above showed as a white silk ribbon. Abundance of light flowed in from the mouth and from above, but the air was chill and the smell damp and earthy.

The bottom was encumbered with fallen blocks of chalk, white as lumps of sugar, and over these Winefred scrambled fearlessly. A belt of what is locally termed "fox-earth" showed above the floor, and from it distilled water in tears.

She could distinguish a cavern – one of those subterraneous reservoirs which in the calcareous beds had received and held the water that percolated down through the pervious rock till it had itself been drained by the water filtering to a still lower level.

Winefred climbed with hands and feet over a mound of refuse, then down the side, and found that the rift still penetrated farther and lost itself in darkness. It was obvious that the cleavage had been incomplete, the block that had parted from the down had not completely effected its insulation, or there would assuredly have been a streak of light at the farther end.

Winefred was familiar with cliffs, clefts and caves; they presented to her no terrors, were invested with no mystery; but she was scarcely aware of the actual risk she underwent. Such phenomena may be safely investigated after they have definitely settled themselves, but hardly whist in process of formation. Nevertheless she advanced, and now she saw that the chasm had a limit, and that this limit was composed of a slide of rock and flint and earth from above forming a sharp incline, up which it woud be feasibe to scramble and possibly by this means to attain to the surface of the down. This would save Winefred a long circuit; moreover, the adventure offered the zest of novelty, and she was hungry.

Before proceeding, however, she peeped into the cavern. It was apparently extensive, penetrating some way, but dwindling in size as it receded. The floor was level and dry. Then Winefred began to mount the rubble shoot. The fallen chalk and earth had to a large extent dropped powdery, so that her feet sank, but here and there she came on cores of hard stone and then on beds of flint caked together. She passed a discoloured vein cut in section, where water charged with iron had run and had stained the rock.

As she continued toilfully to work her way upwards she observed how complete the dislocation of the beds had been. The stratification of flints was not continuous on both walls. The bed of silicious nodules on one side was repeated on the other at a depth of ten to fifteen feet, showing that the cleavage had been brought about by sinkage. The silence in the cleft was absolute save for an occasional downpatter of dry earth or pebbles, but there was no considerable fall whilst Winefred was there.

The ascent was laborious, nevertheless the girl prosecuted her attempt with resolution, and was finally successful in attaining the turf, but in a condition so soiled that she knew she would be scolded by her mother. When Winefred was at the surface she saw that for some distance beyond where she had come out, the turf was torn, as cloth might be ripped by a sharp tug.

The chasm was in process of extension, and eventually would stretch across the entire headland and detach it altogether. Now she saw why her mother's cottage had given way. It had been planted on that portion of the crag which had subsided. But the subsidence had been uneven, one-sided, so that what remained of the house was on an incline, and a lateral crack from the main rift had reached and thrown down one of the walls. In places the turf looked like a pane of glass that had been struck by a cricket ball. It was starred with radiating fractures.

The girl leaned over and looked down the gulf out of which she had emerged. It seemed of prodigious depth and utterly dark. The lips were not above fifteen feet apart at top, the wall on the land side descended perpendiculary, whereas that on the farther side was slightly inclined.

Only at the extreme end of the chasm where she had mounted was it possible to climb to the top, and it was obvious that the rent was gradually but surely prolonging itself.

Chapter Eleven

A Proposal

Jane Marley was at the kneading trough, with her sleeves tucked up, and her hands in the dough, when a shadow thrown upon her made her look up, and she saw Olver Dench at the window. He nodded to her through the window, came to the door, opened and entered without ceremony. "How do you find yourself this morning, mistress?" asked the ferryman, seating himself. Jane made a gesture indicative of impatience.

"The captain is out," she answered curtly.

"I have not come to see the captain."

"The house is not a show-place like Colyton Castle."

"I have not come to see it."

"Then you have no business here."

"That is an uncivil address to an old friend."

"I do not recognise any friend." This silenced him for a while. He observed her, with her sleeves rolled above her elbows, her fine moulded arms, her handsome, if somewhat stern, face, the full lips, the fine sweep of the jaw, the copious, dark hair with warm glints in it, the ripe complexion, and he thought what a good-looking woman she was.

She continued to knead the dough, in total disregard of his presence, and the sun entering through the latticed window played over her arms, the dimpled rosy elbows, her swelling bosom, over which the breast-piece of her white apron was pinned at the shoulder, and it flamed occasionally on her pouting lips. Then, after a considerable pause, Olver Dench began once more.

"I have come here, Jane, not on the captain's affairs, but on yours."

"Mine, you will favour me not to trouble about."

"When I say yours, I really mean those of your child."

At once she was interested. He saw that. Her arm remained stationary for a moment, the hands plunged in the dough. Then she resumed work with increased energy. She tossed her head and said, "My child is under my care, and her affairs in no way demand your meddling."

"That is just as you will," said Dench with assumed indifference. "But I would bid you bear in mind that you are at present under the roof of one of the most fanciful, humorous, and shortest–tempered of men. He will welcome you today, and if you offend him turn you out of doors tomorrow. He is headstrong, and has brimstone in him, by George! and you have sparks enough in you to make a conflagration probable. Unless you knuckle under to him, he will thrust you and Winefred forth – and you will be once more as you have been – homeless. Did you ever hear tell of the visit made him one day by two gaugers who wanted to overhaul the place? He received them, seated on a keg, with a pistol in his hand. Masters, said he, this little cask is full of gunpowder, come near by another step and I will discharge my pistol into it – and we three will march together. They made for the door. That is your man; wilful, desperate, overbearing. If you cross his will in any particular he will send you to the rightabouts. That will not matter for such as you, but it will be bad for Winefred."

He perceived by her heightened colour, by her quickened breathing, that he had touched Jane where most sensitive.

"Do you know, mistress, why Captain Job has taken you both into his house?"

She made no other answer than a shrug of the shoulder.

"I will tell you: I will lift a corner of the crust and let you see what is the meat in the pie. Was not your father, Topsham Marley, associated with him in most of his ventures? What did he gain by that? Did he leave you comfortably off? I always heard tell that there was money to bury him, but nothing over. Your brother Philip, he was with him also. What profit came to him out of the partnership? When Philip thought that he was pulling the chestnuts out of the fire for Job – he getting the burns and none of the nuts – Philip and he came to words and they parted company, and Philip started on his own account. He was at once betrayed and shot. Take my word for it, certain big men with large dealings will not allow the little men to succeed. The iron pot breaks all the cloam pipkins that float on the same water."

"You do not dare to tell me that the captain caused my brother's death?"

"I do not say that I know he did. All that I pretend to say is that I was not the only man who noticed the curious coincidence. No sooner did Philip start on his own bottom than he was put out of the running. It is a singular thing, if you are interested in such matters, to observe how the wholesale dealers go free, and how the little retailers get nabbed. What profit had Topsham, what had Philip out of their ventures? Did your brother leave anything? I reckon it was the same tale with Philip the son as with Topsham the father – enough to bury him and not a penny over. Now look at Job Rattenbury. He has bought and is fitting out a cutter for his son Jack, and is going to set him up as a gentleman. He does not spare money where Jack is concerned. Cash seems as plentiful with the captain as elderberries on the undercliff. He has made a fortune where others have failed. Some have sown, but all the harvest goes into his barns. If right were done all round, your father ought to have died a rich man, and your brother would have been alive this day, and you and your child not be homeless and destitute."

"As to Philip," said Jane, in a quivering voice, "it is well known he was killed in a scuffle with the preventive men."

"Yes. But how did they know when and where to drop upon him? And why, if they did come on him, did they shoot him instead of running him into prison?"

He was silent now for a while to allow what he had said to sink in and produce the desired effect. He watched the woman's face; the muscles were working, and her cheek glowed. Her eyes he could not see. After a long pause, he proceeded, "It is rough on us men that we should get, not kicks only, but leaden bullets put into us, and he all the ha'pence; but it is a crying iniquity that his son Jack should be bought up to be a gentleman and your Winefred should be left a beggar. Answer me this. Did not your father and brother endure the labours, the buffeting of wind and wave, the risk from the gaugers?

68

What for? That Jack should have a spick–and–span painted cutter with gilt figurehead, and spout Latin grammar. He will rattle the guineas in his pocket, and when Winefred holds out her hand will cast a copper into the dirt and bid her bend and pick it up."

Jane's whole frame trembled.

"So it is – the widow and the orphan are robbed, we underlings must not complain that we are badly served. But it makes me mad to hear how he swells and brags over what he is going to make of his boy Jack. And there are you and your Winnie having to curtsey and say, Thank you sir, when he offers you a crust of bread and pulls a bit of his thatch over your heads of a November night. We should combine to get our rights; combine against wrong and robbery."

"How can we combine?"

"I will tell you. The captain is a rich man. I know it. He admits it. Whence came all his money? From the sweat and blood of men like your father, brother and me. I also worked under him once, but I would not endure the injustice. Glad I was to get out of the concern and take a ferryboat, and thankful I am when I get a score of passengers to put across in the day. look you, Jane; if that ferry were worked the way he does the other business, at the end of the day he would say to me, 'Here, Olver, is one ha'penny, but nineteen pence ha'penny goes into my pocket, and I'm going to lay it out in picture books for my Jack.'"

"How can we combine?" she asked again.

"I'll make you a proposal," said Olver, but he spoke hesitatingly, and seemed reluctant to deliver it till he had further worked on the mother's passions, and blinded her with anger and envy. "I say that what the captain has accumulated ought of rights to be divided into four equal parts. I allow that he has a claim to one–quarter, but I have to another – that I do assert; and then, if you had what properly belongs to you, the two remaining quarters should be yours, as the shares of your father Topsham, and your brother Philip, who was not married, and so his share comes to you – for Winefred." he paused, cleared his throat and set a hand on each knee.

"Now, Jane, I bargain that you and I combine to secure out lawful property, of wehich we have been defrauded. Lord! what thieves go to prison and what rogues run free! It makes my bile run over to think that his nipper Jack should be toasting in the bar whilst we sit on the doorstep in the cold. We must put our heads together. There is naught done without combination."

"How – what is to be done?"

"That is just the secret. Can you guess why the captain houses you and the girl? It is because he knows that he has wronged the widow and the fatherless, and his conscience gives him a pinch now and again. He thinks to hush it by allowing you such scraps as he would cast to a dog, Towler, if he kept one – which he don't. Jane –" Olver spoke slowly, and with his eye fixed on her "–Jane, you are on the spot, and I looks on it as the wonderful ways of providence bringing you here. You keep your eye wakeful, and keep an eye in the back of your head also. You discover where he hides his piles of money. Hidden it is somewhere, sure as I sit here. Now, Jane, I want us not only to put our heads together but to join hands."

"What do you mean?"

"Well, if you find that out for me, and help with the partition, I'll make you my wife, and then you and your kid will have a home of your own."

"Your wife!"

"Ay – I knew what you would say. But where *he's* gone is a long way off, round the other side of the world, and he has married a Spanish woman there, with sugar plantations and slaves, and they have a fine family. He'll never show his face in England. He daren't, I tell you. So we may as well –"

"You!" The woman turned and faced him, in a flame of scorn. Her eyes sparkled, she breathed passionately through her rigid nostrils, her bosom heaved. "You – you dare propose this to me?"

He stood up. "Why not? I speak for your advantage."

"For my advantage – to be with you – head to head, hand to hand – with you!" She quivered with fury, her very hair bristled. "You? If I had you between tongs, I would throw you into the ashpit. Leave this house!" Olver's face turned plum colour.

"Jane! Will you dare try it on without me?"

"Leave this house," she cried, pointing to the door with her hands covered with strings of dough.

"Jane," said he, "I have said and let you know more than I ought. But I warn you to beware lest you take a step in this matter independent of me. Take care how you hunt and beat the thickets without me. I am not a man to be trifled with. If I find that you are going behind my back, I will tread you and your brat into the earth, as though you were snails."

Chapter Twelve

By Night

On her return to Rattenbury's cottage, Winefred was thrown into a dubious condition of mind. She had purposed to confide everything to her mother, to tell her about the present of the watch and what she had overheard. But on coming into her mother's presence she saw that the time was unpropitious.

She knew her mother so intimately that she was aware that the communication must be deferred. Mrs Marley was one of those persons who, when possessed by an idea, and that one of an exciting nature, are incapable of attending to any other, or on whom the communication of another of agitating nature completely unhinges the reasoning faculties and produces an irrational explosion of feeling. Winefred saw at a glance that something must have occurred during her absence which had upset her mother.

She therefore merely inquired where Captain Rattenbury was, and was told curtly that he was out – a fact sufficiently obvious. Job had informed her mother that he would not be home till the morrow, but Jane Marley did not think to give this information to Winefred. Not knowing this, the girl said no more, determined to caution the captain on his return. She went into the back kitchen and to the larder cupboard and provided herself with food, her mother saying nothing nor noticing what she was about, nor did the ticking of her watch attract attention.

Thus the hours of the short November afternoon slipped away, and Mrs Marley seated herself at the side of the fire knitting, with her gown turned up over her knees lest it should scorch and with her arms still bare, glancing in the firelight. Winefred occupied a stool, and fell to studying her mother's countenance and listening for the footfall of the captain of his hand on the latch. She was in no little anxiety. The day was Thursday, and the attempt to disperse the goods to their several destinations would be made that night, and a few hours must determine the fate of the smugglers.

She saw that a storm was raging in the interior of her mother that troubled her wild soul and tossed her feverish blood. But Mrs Marley was clearly indisposed to allow her daughter to know what had aroused it. The expression of the woman's face was now angry, then hard and remorseless, flushes of passion swept across it, and then all colour deserted it. At moments her eyes were as though exploding into fireworks, and at the next were dull and lifeless.

Every word of Dench had been as fulminating powder in her soul. Till the interview with him she had entertained no suspicion against Rattenbury; she had recently regarded him with gratitude for having received her and Winefred into the cottage, and she was an impulsive woman, strong in her feelings, whether in liking or in hating. But now, all at once, his conduct appeared to her in a new light. He was no longer a benefactor, he was an oppressor, who had grievously wronged her father and procured the death of her brother, and was rendering to her a tardy and wholly inadequate compensation.

She did not stay to inquire whether the words of the ferryman were justified, whether the charges he made were founded in fact. It sufficed her to see that there was probability in the assertions, and womanlike she accepted them as unassailable. She had been robbed, her child robbed, and all for the sake of Jack Rattenbury, that he might be cockered up and transformed into a gentleman. A smouldering fire of rage against both father and son consumed her heart – a sense of injury ate into her soul and filled her with gall.

Suddenly she started, turned fiercely on Winefred and said, "Why do you stare at me? Go to bed; it is time. Disturb me no further." She was a woman that would be obeyed, to be turned from her purpose by no reasoning, amenable to no persuasion. Of this

Winefred was so well aware that she did not attempt opposition. She at once rose from her stool and noiselessly crept to the little room that has been arranged for her under the stair. But, although in obedience to her mother Winefred went to bed, she could not sleep.

There could exist no doubt that the captain had been betrayed, and that, unless forewarned, his capture was inevitable. The coastguard and the military would draw together along every road and lane and enclose them as in a battue. When he should come in there would still be time to warn him, unless he arrived very late. Where was he? Who could say? It was unlikely that he should have told her mother. He might have gone to Lyme to see after the carts, or to Beer to make the final arrangements for the transport of the casks from their hiding-places to Heathfield.

She turned the problem over in her brain and sought a solution. Suppose that Rattenbury did not return that night, by what means was he to be communicated with, how was the danger that menaced to be averted? He had saved her life, he had sheltered her, she was bound to do everything in her power to save him. Of that she had not the smallest doubt, and her resolution was formed to do her utmost, even in despite of her mother, should she offer opposition.

After an hour Jane Marley fastened the house door and retired to her room. She would not have run the bolt had she anticipated that Rattenbury would return that night. Her action convinced Winefred that he had told her mother not to expect him back. What could she do?

She listened to the ticking of the clock and awaited the striking of the hours. When ten o'clock sounded, then she was well aware that not another minute must be lost. Noiselessly she crept out of bed and clothed herself; she hearkened whether her mother stirred, but heard no sound. On tiptoe, her shoes in her hand, she stole over the kitchen floor, and with caution she slowly drew the bolt.

The moment the door was open, a rush of cold air fanned the embers on the hearth into a glow; but she hastily passed outside, shut the door behind her and breathed freely. She was, at any rate, safe now from obstruction by her mother. Even if the latter had heard her, pursuit would be in vain; she could easily elude it among the thickets and in the dark. She drew on her shoes. All within was still, she had not been overhead, her mother had not been roused.

Her heart beat furiously, and she was frightened at her undertaking. It was not that she was alarmed at being abroad and at night, but she was well aware of the magnitude of the issues dependent on her action.

If she failed – the goods would be confiscated, the band broken up, and the captain imprisoned for a lengthy period. At his age he might not live till his term expired.

The stars twinkled, a crescent moon shone, there was frost in the air. Winefred had formed her plan, and she knew her way. She had to ascend from the undercliff to the down, and the chalky path lay before her as though phosphorescent. There would have been complete stillness but for the mutter and fret of the sea and the piping of the wind.

The smugglers would certainly have preferred less light and more noise, a howling wind, a blinding fog, and a booming sea. Above every sound Winefred could hear the throbbing of her heart.

She was now upon the down, where the turf was short, strewn with flints bleached by sun and rain. She crossed it, and descended into a deep, lateral combe, through which a trickle ran into the river. Here were trees, but they were bare of leaves. Beyond stood the crest of Hawkesdown with its earthworks thrown up, none knew by whom, but haunted, in the opinion of the people, by a ghostly warrior with a fire–breathing dog. She was now among fields, and in a tangle of lanes, but she knew her direction, and although the ways twisted, she made as straight as was possible for the crest of the opposite hill, and for a while skirted a fir plantation that lay like an ink blot on her left. She was not able wholly to escape the shadows of the pines, for she was forced to enter by a gate, the hedge being too thick and thorny for her to scramble over it. In the gloom she became uneasy, alarmed, thinking that eyes were watching her, and that mysterious beings lurked among the branches, ready to leap upon her. To her excited imagination it was as though there came to her whisperings from among the bushes. She walked faster, turning her head from side to side, and sometimes looking over her shoulder.

At the beginning of the present century "free trade" was in repute among the daring and adventuresome along the coast. Smuggling was a passion, like poaching. Those who were engaged in it rarely abandoned it. It was gambling for enormous stakes – the profits were great, but, on the other hand, so were the risks. If now and then a cargo was run and sold, and the profits measured out in pint mugs, on another occasion an entire cargo was confiscated. Not only was freedom jeopardised, but life as well. Neither "free trader" nor coastguard was nice in the matter of shedding blood.

Smuggling methods were infinitely varied. The game was a contest of wits as well as of pluck, and in that lay much of its charm. The spice of danger attending it attracted the young men instead of deterring them.

In order to obtain information relative to the trade, so as to be able to "nab" those who prosecuted it, the Government had paid spies in the English and the foreign ports. It sought to undermine the integrity of those combined together in the trade, and to encourage treachery. So well aware of this were smugglers that no mercy was shown to the man who was detected in clandestine communication with the preventive service men. He was sometimes dashed over the cliffs, sometimes taken out in a boat and literally beaten to death with a marline–spike before his body was committed to the waves.

There was something to be urged in extenuation of English smuggling. Customs–duties were first imposed in England for the purpose of protecting the coasts against pirates who made descents on unprotected villages and kidnapped men and children to sell them as slaves in Africa, or who waylaid merchant vessels, plundered and then scuttled them. But when all such danger had ceased, and the pirates had been swept from the seas, the duties were not only continued to be levied but were made more onerous. It was felt that there had beenm a violation of compact on the side of the Crown, and bold spirits entertained no conscientious scruples in setting at naught the law of contraband. The officers of the Crown instead of pursuing, capturing and hanging Algerine pirates, proceeded to seize and consign to prison native seamen.

It was in this light that the matter was viewed by the water–dogs about the coast; nor was this confined to them, the opinion was shared by the magistrates, country gentry, anbd parsons. Three classes of men were engaged in the business. First came the "freighter" – the man who entered on it as a commercial speculation. He engaged a vessel, purchased the cargo, and made the requisite arrangement for the landing. Then came the "runner", who conveyed the goods on shore from the vessels; and lastly the "tub–carriers", who transported the kegs on their backs slung across their shoulders.

Captain Job Rattenbury had at one time been a "runner" but he was now a "freighter", and to be that a man must be a capitalist.

Winefred had reached the Roman Road, the Fosse Way that ran from one end of England to the other, and, by the light of the stars, being chalk–paved, it gleamed like a belt of silver. But on it was observable something creeping like a slug in the uncertain light.

The girl watched it as it approached. That which she saw was a train of tub–carriers. With audacity, and with a prospect of success due to this very audacity, the train was advancing along the high roads, contrary to the wonted tactics of the free traders, but in reliance on the guard of the coast watching the shore, and the lanes leading from it.

There were over a score of men in the line, and all had blackened their faces. They were moving a large amount of run goods from the hiding–holes of Beer, for dispersion among the taverns and gentlemen's houses that were expecting consignments.

Winefred watched the black mass worm itself along uphill. She held back at first in the darkness of the hedge. It was her purpose to start forward to arrest Captain Job as soon as he came abreast of her. Several men went by. Two – four – eight, it was not possible for her in the feeble light to distinguish one from another, and the faces were all black.

"Who goes? Halt!"

Instantly the advancing line stopped, and one stepped forward, strode towards Winefred, who had moved and attracted attention, and said, "Who is there?"

"Captain Rattenbury! O Captain – where is he?"

"Who asks?"

"It is I – Winefred. You have been betrayed."

Chapter Thirteen

Out of the Snare

In a moment Winefred was surrounded by men. There was something alarming in their appearance, with blackened faces. One, a tall, vigorous fellow, apparently young, stood forward and questioned her.

"What! Winefred Marley?"

"Yes – I want to speak to Captain Rattenbury. Where is he?"

"He is not here. I am his son."

"Jack! – You! Your father has been betrayed. I overheard the officer from Lyme arranging to take you all. He has sent for the soldiers. He knows that you are to meet the carts at Heathfield Cross."

"When did you hear this?"

"Today – some hours ago – on the beach, below the station. I was behind a rock, and they did not see me."

"Why did you not speak of this before?"

"Your father was not at home, or I would have done so. I waited, expecting every hour to see him come in. Now I have run away whilst mother is asleep."

"You are a brave, good girl," said the young man. He turned to the men. "What is to be done?" he asked.

"We must go back," said one or two.

"You must not go back," exclaimed Winefred. "Indeed you must not; the soldiers are on the road from Musbury."

"Then forward."

"That will not do. The coastguard in force are watching at Heathfield Cross."

The men were silent. After some consideration, in a dead silence, Jack said, "There is but one course open. We must creep along the

77

lanes to Hay and Buckland, and stow our goods wherever we can."

"Do you think that possible? I suspect that they are drawing in from east and west, and have taken the precaution to stop all the earths to the north." Winefred knew by the voice that the man who spoke was David Nutall, to whom she had taken the captain's letter.

"I know they will have done that," she said. "I heard them say as much. They intended drawing a net round you, and leaving you no way of escape save over the cliffs into the sea."

Again an anxious silence ensued. Then one asked: "Jack! how about the undercliff? Has not your father got runs and rat–holes there that would contain us all?"

"No," answered the young man. "He is too wary for that. He knows that the very first place that would be searched would be his cottage."

"There is something in that. Then there is no help for it; we must drop our goods – there in yonder plantation I advise – and get away singly as best we may."

"We shall be caught and detained till the whole of this bit of country has been put through the sieve, and if they find the tubs – we are done for."

"It is a bad job."

"I vote we fight rather than lose our goods."

"There are too many. We should be overpowered."

"I do not relish losing everything without making an effort to break through."

"I can tell you what to do," said the girl, "and also where you may conceal everything."

"Where is that?"

"Today I saw that the cliff has parted under mother's cottage. The rock is torn in half, and I climbed the crack from the beach to the top. Where I went up you can go down. The crack is quite new and is narrow. At the end it is choked with earth and stones. If you have ropes you can lower the kegs and then steal away by the coast and by water to Beer. Then let the soldiers and the rest draw together; they will take neither you nor what you are carrying. They will not know what has become of you. No one knows of this hiding–place but myself – there was none a week ago, only some cracking of the surface that tumbled down our wall."

The men consulted in an undertone. "If the soldiers do come along the roads from all sides they will meet to shake hands, that is all," said Winefred. "I should laugh to see their faces."

"The girl is right," said Jack. "Winefred, lead the way at once." Then again the men formed in line, and she, walking beside the young man, headed the procession.

"But where is the captain?" she asked.

"No occasion to be alarmed about him," answered Jack. "Trust to his cleverness. They can do nothing with him if he has nothing in his carts. He is going, he will say, to fetch hay from Axmouth which he has contracted to deliver at Lyme."

Winefred led the way, partly along lanes, partly over hedges, through gates, under the boughs of the young firs. She was fearless now; her only care was not to stumble on any of the preventive men.

She laughed in her heart to think that she who had lectured Jack against smuggling should herself be involved in one of these illegal ventures. But what she was doing was not for the sake of gain, but in discharge of a debt of gratitude. Jack, however, was ill at ease. He did not relish the business on which he was engaged, and he was drawn into it solely by obligations to his father, who needed his services at the time, which was one of emergency.

As he walked along he considered the magnitude of the risks he ran, imprisonment and its consequences, the closing against him of every honourable profession. Should he escape, then he was firmly resolved never again to engage in such a transaction, – not, however, because of its danger, but because it was repugnant to his tastes rather than not consonant with his principles.

The old man had been associated with the trade all his days, took a pride in it, he could not leave the groove, did not desire to do so, looked on his profession as manly and honourable. He had no wish, no thought, but that Jack should continue in it, but carry it on upon a grander scale, and it was with this in view that he was furnishing him with a fast–sailing cutter. But Jack felt a repugnance against deliberately, at the outset, entering on a career that placed him in antagonism with the laws of his country. Of moral scruple he had not an atom, nor did any moral objection enter into the composition of Winefred's dislike to the trade. His objection was founded on inexpediency; hers on the business being one of "hole and corner", as she termed it.

"No," said Jack, half to himself, "never again."

"What never again?" asked Winefred in a whisper. He did not answer. He was not responsible to her for his thoughts.

"Jack," said she in a low tone, "why did you come out tonight?"

"Why," he answered, "for one reason, because you told me not to do so. A man hates to be ordered about by a woman."

"Even when her advice is good."

"Yes. Because she orders one way, there is something in him that forces him to go contrary."

"I always thought that men were fools," said Winefred. "Now you tell me that they are so, and I believe you with all my heart. Women are men's good angels."

"That you are tonight, Winnie." He looked at her trudging by his side in the uncertain light, and he thought how much he owed to her. It was she, and she alone, who was leading him out of the toils. But for her intervention, in another half-hour he would have been in the hands of the officers of the Crown.

The men did not speak, and Winefred comprehended that it was not for her to break the silence. The train had crossed the brook, and was now mounting the hillside that led to the downs which overhung the sea. The growl of the waves became more audible.

Presently they were on the common, crossing it as a black worm, aiming at one point towards which Winefred led confidently. "We shall need a light," she whispered.

"Not on the cliff. We should attract attention."

"No, in the chasm. I am not a fool; why should you consider me one?"

"When we reach the place –"

"We are almost there now. Walk cautiously. If one were to fall over it would be worse than falling into the hands of the guard. Bid them halt."

Jack elevated both his arms, and the convoy stood still. With precaution, observing every yard of ground in front of her, Winefred advanced. All at once she stopped dead, looked back and said, "Hist!

Here is the crack. Do not come to the edge lest it break away."

Jack Rattenbury stepped up to her, and she showed him the mouth of the rent. He could see a black irregular stain; in the feeble light it did not show as a gulf. It might have been ink run over the turf – but ink in floods. How deep it was he could not conjecture, for it showed no depth, only level backness.

"How far down?" he asked.

"To the very level of the beach," she answered, "except at the end where the tear begins, and there it is choked with earth and stone that has crumbled and tumbled in. You will not be able to carry the kegs down; the slope is as steep as a spire, and is broken in places by bits of rock, and in others soft as dough. You must lower the tubs."

"Rope!" ordered Jack, turning to the man nearest. Then, "Someone will have to descend."

"That will I," said the girl, "but I must have a light."

"It is surely unsafe for you to attempt it."

"Not at all. I have climbed it. I know what it is like. I have led you so far, I will go through with my enterprise. Let me have a lantern."

One was passed to young Rattenbury. Winefred stepped along the fringe of the rent till she reached its extreme limit. "I can descend here in safety," she said, "but it is not easy work, and a heavy man might sink in the rubbish; see, I am over the edge already. When I am lower down I will light the lantern. It is a little difficult at first to descend, but it becomes easier farther down. Do not fear for me. I learned how to do it today – I mean yesterday: it is past midnight now. You shall follow me after you have lowered the casks."

She disappeared into the black chasm. It made the heart of the young man stand still for a moment. He expected to hear a heavy fall. Then a white hand was extended out of it, and he let her take the lantern. "Is there room for me also?" he asked.

"No; it is steep and narrow. Give me a flint and steel."

In another moment he saw a splutter of sparks, then a glow that brightened as the girl breathed on the ignited tinder. Finally came a burst of yellow flame. She had kindled the candle, and this she at once placed in the lantern. Now only could he see the wall of the chasm, and the flintstones glistened in it like eyes. Below all was impenetrable darkness.

"Have no fear," said Winefred cheerfully, and began the descent. Jack watched the light as it danced down. It was seen here, then there, as she circumvented some fallen block that had lodged and wedged itself in the chasm. Then boldly she mounted another, and leaped down from it. Next moment she was struggling through soft chalk like a snowdrift. Then a shoot of stones was sent bounding down the incline, dislodged by her feet. Jack dared not lean over lest he should occasion some of the friable chalk of the edge to give way and fall upon her.

The star diminished in size. Now it was invisible, then only discernible by the faint glow it cast on the walls. Anon it flashed forth once more. It seemed to Jack as though an hour had passed before the light became stationary, and a voice, confused by the echo of the sides, came up to him, "I am at the bottom, – lower the kegs."

"Stand back," shouted Jack in reply, "lest the falling stones crush you!"

"I will go to the mouth," answered Winefred. "But I leave the light where it is. Lower at once."

Winefred guessed rather than heard what he said, and she placed the lantern in the cave she had observed on her ascent. By this means it was sheltered from stones that might be dislodged and fall. But where it was, it cast a halo upon the white wall opposite.

As soon as Jack conceived that Winefred was beyond reach, he bade the men pass a rope through the loops attached to the kegs, one after the other, and let them down into the abyss. When the slackening of the cord assured him that a cask was lodged, then he cast down one end and drew the rope up to this with more than one man at a time to stand on the edge and let down the butts. The operation was consequently somewhat slow, nevertheless it was in time brought to a conclusion, and then he told the men that they must descend at the extremity of the rift, reach the shore, and make the best of their way home. By means of the ferryboat all could cross. On the morrow, at about the same hour, they would return and move the goods and dispose of them as seemed most advisable, after he had consulted with his father.

The men could descend only singly, lest one following another should send down stones on him who preceded him. Then Jack leaped into chasm and vanished.

The men looked at each other. Said one to his mate, "I think I shall slip over the downs."

"Aye," said a second. "I had rather risk the chance of running into the mouths of the sharks than go down yonder."

"And I," said a third, "shall turn into the straw in Bindon barn, and lie there till daylight. I am not disposed to go underground without the assistance of the undertaker."

"We have our orders," said one of the young Nutalls.

"That's right, my boy," spoke old David. "Follow me," and he went over the side.

Jack Rattenbury descended step by step in the darkness. It was a difficult and dangerous downward climb, to be executed only with an extreme caution, but he achieved it. He had not, however, reached the bottom before he was greeted by Winefred, who had taken the lantern and held it so as to assist him.

"Look," she said. "Here at the side is a little cavern. I have already rolled in two of the kegs. When the men are down we will stow the lot in there."

Slowly, and in single file, the men arrived, with a few exceptions. "Make haste and get away," said Winefred. "This has been a longer business than I thought. Leave me the light and I will dowse it at the least alarm. I can get the kegs in, and no one can see them when there."

"You are a brave girl," said Jack. "I thank you, and you shall be well rewarded."

"I want no reward," she answered, "except this, that you say 'I won't' if this sort of thing is proposed again."

"Well – I won't. I swear it. This is the last time."

Chapter Fourteen

Buried Alive

"You cannot stay here alone," said Jack; "I will remain with you."

"You must rejoin your men. Leave me. Your way is to the mouth of the Axe, and mine – I will go along the beach till I reach the path to the station – no, I dare not go that way. Some of the angry and disappointed men might meet and question me – Why out at night? I would confess nothing, but they might suspect something and search along the shore and find this rent. I will climb up by the way I came down, and get home as fast as may be, after I have got the kegs rolled into the cave and concealed."

"I do not like to desert you here at this hour."

"Time with you is precious. With me it is only a matter of concern to relieve my mother's anxiety and alarm should she chance to wake and miss me."

The young man laid his hands on the girl's shoulders. "Winefred, I shall never forget what you have done for me tonight. I cannot find words in which to thank you, but my heart is full."

"Well, go."

"Good night, Winefred. Henceforth we are no mere strangers, but friends."

"Yes, till we quarrel."

"For that there must be an occasion." Then he started.

She listened as his feet displaced the pebbles on the strand. She listened till the roar of the inrolling tide drowned his steps. Then she went back into the chasm. The lantern still threw a sickly light on the white wall opposite.

She had to pick her way among the kegs that encumbered the floor, and lift or roll them up a heap of soil before the mouth of the cave. The barrels were happily small. A tubman carried a pair of them, one slung at his back and the other in front of him. They were heaped up where they had lodged on their descent. The loops of rope attached to each, and inseparable from such run tubs, loops furnished by the dealers in France who consigned the spirits to the smugglers – these greatly facilitated the transfer.

Winefred got several into the cave, where they now encroached on the entrance. The girl entered and busied herself with arranging them along the side.

Then she left the natural improvised cellar, and recommenced rolling and hauling the casks. The cave, as she observed, had been severed in half; a portion of it certainly penetrated through the portion of the cliff that had split away from the main bulk. She looked and saw the crown of the arch just showing above the floor on the farther side of the chasm, at a considerably lower level, thus proving that the separated bulk had sunk in splitting off.

She examined the small opening that showed, that she might see if it were feasible to stow any of the tubs there, and so obviate the labour of rolling or carrying them uphill. She threw in a stone, and it fell, rolling over, indicating that the floor of this portion of the cavern was tilted at a steep incline. Satisfied that it would not do for her to attempt to force any of the tubs in there, she resumed her toil of carrying them to the upper cavern. She worked on diligently, but the work was trying, and she became exhausted and hot. Then she seated herself and wiped her face with her sleeve.

The smell of the spirits pervaded the air and made her giddy. As soon as she had recovered her breath she rose, and, finding the entrance again encumbered, she again went within to roll the casks against the sides. That she might see where to place them she planted the lantern in the middle. She counted the kegs. She had ranged more than half the entire number, but she doubted whether she would have strength to store all. Moreover, she was becoming anxious to go home lest her mother should discover her absence. Not only was this so because of the alarm into which Mrs Marley would be thrown by her disappearance, but also because, should she miss her, she would assuredly rush forth and rouse the neighbourhood to search for her, and this, under the circumstances, might lead to detection of her part in the rescue.

Stirred by this thought, she took up the lantern to resume her task, when – with a rush and a rattle – down came a mass of chalk–rubble and soil from above.

Happily the fall took place without the cave in the chasm, so that none of it touched Winefred. She was, however, frightened. She stood holding the lantern, breathless, expectant of more, waiting till the cataract should cease.

Considerably alarmed though she was, she did not at the moment suppose that her position was endangered. She congratulated herself that she was under cover when the avalanche occurred. Had she been outside the cave she would have been struck down and buried by the fallen masses.

Owing to the feeble light diffused by the candle through the horn sides, she was unable to see far and discover the extent of the fall. It was some minutes before she ventured to approach the entrance. There were stones on the floor that had not been there before, and she was able to distinguish a bank of earth where had been the cave door. Moreover, a strong smell of brandy, far stronger than before, pervaded the air.

Dread came over her, like a cold wave rolling down on and enveloping her – a dread lest the mouth be choked. It was an imperious necessity for her at once to ascertain whether there remained any way of escape.

She threw open the door of the lantern to afford more light, and then she saw that a mass of rubble mounting to the summit encumbered the entrance, and apparently completely choked it. Winefred found that she must climb this; she did so, tearing and rolling down the pieces of chalk and marl and sand before her.

She thrust the lantern before her, to see if any glimmer shot through and reflected itself against the farther wall of the cleft. She looked to see if any indraught caused the flame to waver.

The earth and stone were heaped dense to the very summit, and to what a depth above the mouth of the cave without it was impossible for her to conjecture.

To add to her terror and bewilderment, the fumes of the spirits became stronger and more pungent, stupefying her brain. The stones in falling had stove in some of the barrels, and their contents oozed forth. Winefred's heart stood still for a moment as she realised the full meaning of her situation.

Then she staggered down the heap and retreated to the farthest recess of the cave, set the lantern before her, looked into the light, and for a moment became the prey of despair.

But Winefred was young, energetic and brave. She studied the candle. How long would it last? How long would it be before day broke?

But when daylight came, none would penetrate into this vault where she was interred alive. Yet, possibly there might be some rift, some eyelet-hole through which it might enter and reveal a way of escape. What was the time?

She put her hand to her belt for the watch that had been given her. It was not there. She had not brought it with her. She left the lantern where it was and went again to the entrance, and worked with hands and feet to roll down and tear through the dead mass of rubble. She worked on till she was blinded with sweat and tears, till her head whirled, till her powers were failing, and then she reeled back to the depths of the cave to see the wick of the candle fallen over and burn uncertainly in the melted grease.

She put her hand to it.

It went out.

Then she threw herself forward on her hands, gasping, her pulse leaping, her brain swimming.

"I am buried alive!" she cried. "Oh, mother! what will she think? What will she do?" Her hands gave way, she fell on her face and consciousness deserted her.

Chapter Fifteen

Cast Forth

Jane Marley was roused from her sleep before dawn by the sound of someone entering the house. Then she heard the door being locked and barred, and a heavy tread was on the stair.

She knew at once that Captain Rattenbury had returned, earlier than he had proposed, and she had been prepared to expect, and at ease in her mind she laid her head again on the pillow for sleep. But not an hour had elapsed before she again heard a hand on the door, followed by loud knocking. She paused a while, expecting the master of the house to respond; but as he did not do so, she opened the casement and asked who caused the disturbance.

"We want Job Rattenbury," was the imperious reply.

"He is abed, asleep."

"Open the door."

"I will call him – the house is his, not mine."

"The fox is awake, never doubt."

"Who are you?"

"King's service men. Now will you unbar?"

"I will call the master. You must have patience till I slip into my clothes, and can light a candle." Some words were whispered outside the house, and in obedience to orders a couple of men went about the cottage to guard the back. The moon had not set; it was dark.

Jane was not ready for some time. It took long in those days, before the phosphorus match had been invented, to light a candle. Flint and steel had to be struck till sparks falling ignited tinder. Then a sulphur match had to be applied to the smouldering fire, and when the match blazed then only could the wick be ignited. It was for this reason that usually a rush–light was kept burning in every house. Burglars might break in and plunder it before the master could get light by which to see them.

It was true that ashes still smouldered on the hearth in the kitchen. Jane had heaped them up purposely before going to bed, so as to save her the trouble of striking a light in the morning, with the inseparable risk of skinning her knuckles, but she did not have recourse to the embers: she deemed it advisable to detain the men without as long as possible, so as to allow the master time to secrete anything he desired to conceal before the servants of the Crown were admitted.

But before she was ready to go to the door, his tread was audible on the stair; he descended leisurely, and as she entered the kitchen with a candle, she saw him with towzled head, rubbing his eyes and half–clothed. "Jane," said he, "who are these disturbing me in the night?"

"The gaugers," she replied.

"What do they want with me?" he asked.

"They are outside – ask them. How should I know?"

He undid the bars and turned the key. "So!" said he. "What is your business here at this hour?"

"We must search the house."

"Have you a warrant?"

"No – we do not require one when the scent lies strong. The drag leads this way."

"I do not demand one. Come in. For what are you in search?"

"Oh! you know well enough," said the officer in command, entering. "There has been at least one cargo that has to be dispersed tonight, but the rascals have snuffed us, and have slipped away. We shall catch them yet. But as a preliminary we will look for their tracks here. If they have taken to their heels they cannot have carried off their burdens. They must be deposited somewhere. You confounded old rogue, who are at the bottom of it all, we shall not let you off if we can find a thread of rope by which to hang you."

"It is a little dark for finding such a thread," said Job. "Jane, light all the candles in the kitchen to assist the gentleman. There is a pair of horn spectacles of my grandmother's I can lend the officer."

Suddenly Mrs Marley cried out – "My child! Winefred! Where is she?" She had discovered that her daughter was not in her bed. She had vanished. "Where is Winefred?" cried the mother, forgetting everything in a paroxysm of maternal anxiety. "Captain Rattenbury, where is she?"

"How the deuce should I know?" answered he angrily. "I am not a nurse."

"Where is Winefred?" cried the woman again. She ran distractedly to the door, and called into the darkness, repeating her child's name. She waited, listened; no answer. She came back to the preventive men. At first she thought that, frightened by the noise at the door, the girl was hidden in the house, or had run forth at the back, and she felt the bed. it was cold. It could not have been left recently. Clasping her hands, standing before the men who had entered, she entreated, "Tell me, where is she? What has become of her? Have you taken her? Did you suppose she could have told you anything?"

"My good woman," said the officer in command of the search party, "we know absolutely nothing of your child. We have not seen her. Do not disturb us now. We have our duties to attend to, and cannot look after runaway wenches."

The men dispersed through the house. They sought on every side. They sounded the walls, tapped on the floors, but could detect no signs of a place of concealment. One man took a candle and examined the hearth, he called for a besom and swept it. He tried the light up the chimney, and struck the bricks with a hammer. All in vain.

"What is in that cabinet?" asked the officer, indicating the oak wardrobe clamped with brass and iron.

"You are welcome to look," answered Rattenbury. "It is not locked. Old clothes. Are they contraband?"

One of the men threw open the doors and revealed the ranges of garments; he swept them aside. "Women's gear," said he in a tone of vexation.

"I may husband my wife's old suits without your leave," retorted Captain Rattenbury.

"No liquor anywhere?" asked the officer.

"Yes, a flask of Schiedam for my own consumption," sneered Job. "You will find that under the seat in the window. I will not begrudge you a drop to wash down your mortification."

"You infernal rascal, you are too deep for us. But we shall be even with you yet."

"The loudest–ticking clocks tell the worst time," said the captain; and then added, with a twinkle of the eye, "Do you suppose that if I were what you take me to be I should be so soft as to stow away goods where a parcel of green fools would look for them?"

The officer bit his lip. "Come away, my hearties," he ordered.

"My child! Where is my child?" pleaded the frantic mother, whose attention had not for a moment been distracted from her own loss. She clung to the officer as he was leaving.

"My good creature, I know nothing about her."

"But you have seen her. You have seized her to get some information out of her."

"No such thing. We have not cast eyes on her."

"Then you may see her. Send her back. She may be dead. If you find her –"

"Pshaw! A girl is not to be accounted dead till all other probabilities are exhausted. Look for her yourself. We have other things to attend to."

"Sorry you have been detained so long for nothing," sneered Captain Rattenbury, bowing. Then he shut the door on the baffled visitors, and at once his expression underwent a change. He did not replace the bolt. He stood for a moment observing the restless woman, who paced the room with her hands to her brow; her hair had not been tidied and bound up when she left her bed, and now it floated over her shoulders.

"Captain, where can she be?" she asked, suddenly facing Rattenbury.

"I will tell you, mistress," he answered, and his lips were set hard and his face was menacing. "These sharks may have denied having swallowed her, but *they* know. She ran into their mouths."

"What do you mean?" She stood breathless before him, with her hands down, her arms rigid.

"What do I mean? Why this. The job of tonight finds its explanation in her absence. We have been betrayed. Someone who has known our secret has told it. That is the sense of all this disturbance.

And there was no one else who could or would turn cat-in-the-pan. I sent her with a letter to Beer; and, like a fool, David, to whom I sent it, let her have a peep into it, and learn what was intended for his eye alone. Why is she away? Because she stole out as soon as it was dark to sell me and my mates to those devils at the station. Go there – you will find her there. Olver was right; I was a fool to have pity and house you. Who expects gratitude of a woman, or that she can keep a secret is as one who expects a cat to keep from milk. However – they have not got what they reckoned on. They have not caught me sitting on my eggs, and from what they say, the rest have stolen away. None else knew about the plan save your girl. No one else could have blown upon it."

"It is false. She knew nothing. She has done nothing."

"Where then is she now? Know she did – that David admitted to me. She did not tell you, lest you should spoil her little game. This is how I am repaid for what I have done."

"Repaid!" exclaimed Jane harshly, rendered furious by the charge laid against her child, coming on her at a moment when maddened with anxiety as to her fate. "Repaid, say you," she repeated, and her eyes flamed. "Who is it who has sold and betrayed his mates, over and over again? If he is served with the same sauce he has mixed for others – I rejoice."

"Woman, I do not understand you."

"Yes, you do understand me; but you will not allow that you do. How is it that my father, who worked with and for you, and spent himself in pushing your schemes, died in poverty, whereas you are rich?"

"Rich! I am not rich."

"Oh, yes, you are – though you pretend to poverty."

"You are a spy on me, are you?" demanded Rattenbury, with manifest alarm in his manner, movement, and tone of voice.

"How is it that my father died poor? Answer me that," asked Jane.

"That is easily explained. He did not lay by his money. He had not that bird-lime rubbed into the palms of his hands that makes money cling – no thrift."

"It was not so. You sucked him as an orange and then threw him aside. And my brother Philip –"

"What of him?" asked Job scornfully.

"You had him put out of your way as soon as he became inconvenient, when he had broken with you and set up for himself."

"Who told you this?"

"You see I know all."

"You have imagined all this. It is arrant falsehood. There is not a spice of truth in it. These are the fancies of a madwoman. You shall leave my house."

"Yes, cast me forth now. I hope in my heart that it be true that Winefred has betrayed you. But I do not believe it. You who betrayed my kin, ought in all justice to be betrayed in turn."

"Leave my house," shouted Job. "I was unwise in taking you in to watch me and go behind me in what I take in hand. I swear I believe now that you sent your child to call the sharks together."

"You believe that?"

"I do; you are capable of anything. Olver said as much. By my soul I know it. You would have killed your child had I not stayed you. And now in your crazy rage over fancied wrongs you would finish me. I see it in your tigerish eyes, in your wild and furious manner. You are not to be reasoned with, not to be trusted. Gather up your duds, and be gone."

"But my child!"

"Go after her – go to where the sharks are. They can give you an account of her. I allow you ten minutes to clear out – no more. Good Lord! what a loss is ours tonight, and all through you and your girl. If you were not a womwan, I would strangle you."

Jane cast herself at his knees. "She is not with the coastgaurd. She knws nothing. Help me to find her. I will forgive what you did to Philip and my father."

"Forgive!" he shouted. His face flamed. "*You* forgive! That is news! Begone!" He stopped, caught her under the arms, lifted, carried her bodily, and flung her outside his door. "I have harboured you too long. If either of you were dying on my doorstep, I would not open to take you in."

Chapter Sixteen

Job's Secret

The frantic woman lay in a heap at the door, crouching against it, in such a tumult of brain and heart, of distress at the loss of her child, and rage against the captain, that she was incapable of rising. She remained panting, biting her fingers, beating her head, and sobbing.

But the very violence of her emotions exhausted their force, and presently she rose to her feet and reeled away.

Whither should she go? In what direction look? Already a cold light was beginning to show over the Rousdon heights. A November day was at hand. The bushes deepened into intense blackness in contrast with the paling skies. The fangs of chalk seemed to gleam as teeth exposed against her.

Rattenbury had bidden her seek Winefred at the coastguards' station, but the officer had declared his ignorance of the whereabouts of the girl. The charge of having betrayed him made by Captain Job served as an excuse for ridding himself of guests whom he had come to regard as encumbrances if not as enemies. Jane knew her daughter sufficiently to be aware that the charge was groundless. Winefred was not one to show treachery to the man whose house had sheltered her. But whither was she to turn?

She took some steps towards the preventive station rather because she knew not where else to go than with any expectation of obtaining tidings there. She had not gone far before she came upon a man, one of the service, on the watch. At her demand he replied that he could supply her with no information.

"It is of no use whatever your going to the station," said he; "no one there can help you."

She turned irresolutely and wandered not knowing whither she went, first in one direction, then in another. Her appearance was forlorn; half-clothed, with dishevelled hair, and with face white with despair. She came repeatedly on men upon the watch. To each she put her question, always to receive the same discouraging answer. In her dazed condition she did not consider that it was strange that she should encounter so many men on the alert at so raw an hour. She could think of but one topic – her loss.

Then an idea came glimmering into her clouded brain, that possibly her child might have strayed into Axmouth. And yet why? What cause could have drawn her from her bed and from the house at night? She took a turn in the direction of the village; the lane she followed led from the down by a sharp descent to Bindon, an ancient and picturesque house, once a mansion of the Wyke family, now occupied as a farm.

The light was widening. She opened the gate in the wall and entered the court before the dwelling. The house with its gables and broad mullioned windows, bore a peaceful, smiling appearance. In the grey dawn the yellow illumined windows winked at her in friendly fashion. As the unhappy mother rapped at the door, a stout, motherly body bounced forth with her lap full of wheat for the pigeons. She drew back with an exclamation – then bade Jane enter, drew her into the hall, where a fire was burning and candles were lighted, and at once recognised her. Jane Marley told her what was on her mind.

"Sit down," said the farmer's wife, whose name was Jose, "sit down and have a cup of tea. Mercy on us, you look shivered and scared and starving, and as if you'd been up all night. It is of no use your trying to think when the stomach is empty. I've attempted it scores of times and failed. Do not fret till you have a cause. I have been the mother of nine children."

"I have but one."

"Then I have had nine times your worries. Bless you! children will be children. They with their pranks are always giving us heartaches; but if we was sensible we would not worry. She has been playing a trick on you to see how you would take it."

Mrs Marley shook her head.

"You eat a rasher of bacon," said Mrs Jose. "It is wonderful how different we see things when the stomach is full to what we do when it is empty. Spectacles are nothing to it. All will come right. That is my experience, especially when we are expecting ills. When the evil drops on us it is when we are not on the look-out. What I have found, time out of mind, is that when I have been terrified with fancying disaster was on me, it has been a token that good luck was on its way. There was my Tomasine. I missed her. I made sure she had got smothered in the mud; but it was only she was settling with her young man the day they were to be married, and he was a warm man with several hundreds, and had as fine a breed of sheep as any in the country. My Samuel fell off a waggon, and I thought he had broke his neck; he was laid up a bit – but it prevented him from enlisting; he was mad on soldiering, and he might have been shot. Now he is settled as a gorse jobber and doing finely. Be still now, puss!"

The last words were addressed to a kitten that was rubbing against her skirt, and finding that no attention was paid to her, proceeded to claw into the garment. "Milk in good time," said Mrs Jose; "there are others to be attended to besides kitties. Drat the canaries, what a clamour they keep up! Of a morning all creation is on the alert, and all, every member of it, thinking only of itself and its stomach. Mrs Marley, you sit in the chimney corner, warm yourself. You shall have a dish of tea in a jiffy. I can smell the bacon, it is being fried. I hear that you have been scampering all round the world seeking work, and you did not think of coming to me."

"This house is so large –"

"More the reason I should require help in it. I dare be bound we can find a corner for you. Martha Ann has gone home with a housemaid's knee, and that has made us short of hands. Those canaries must be looked to, or they will crack my ears. Do not trouble about your girl, she will turn up all right."

The kindliness, the cheerfulness, the confidence of that woman soothed and encouraged Jane. She took the seat indicated by the fire, and Mrs Jose unhooked the cage of birds to give fresh water and groundsel to her vociferous pets. She talked the whole time, now to Mrs Marley, then to her servants, to the cat, to the canaries, her herself. Then hearing the tread of one of the farm men, she dashed out of the hall to give him orders, and was back again in five minutes.

"The boys know all about it," she said to Jane. "Ebenezer is going with milk into Axmouth, and he will make inquiries there. They tell me someone has been lying in the barn, but he has left. Timothy got a glimpse of him, and protests he is a Beer man, from over the water. Trust the lads – ours are good as gold – they will make inquiries everywhere. I hope you like my bacon. I do not over-salt it as do some. I keep it in malt-combs. That makes hams and sides rarely sweet. It is a pity that this house looks west. One ray of rising sun is said to be worth a dozen of the rays of the sun when setting. Are you better, Mrs Marley? There is more colour in your cheeks; and let me give you a comb and brush and you shall do up your hair. You look like a wild woman. As to Captain Rattenbury – it is all nonsense. If you like it you may come here, but I suspect he knows when he is well off, and he will not find anywhere a woman more handy, frugal and clean to keep house for him. The old man is failing. He has led a rough life, and that tells in the end."

Jane Marley rose. She put her hair together, smoothed her dress, thanked Mrs Jose, and said she could rest there no longer, she must go forth and seek her daughter. "Take my advice," said the farmer's wife, "always look well at home before searching abroad. Many a lost article for which you have searched the roads lurks in your pocket. Go back to the captain's on the undercliff. Back the child will be to a dead certainty. She will be wanting her breakfast. All living beings want that, and young things – desperately. It is a law of Nature's, so look and follow that."

The advice given by Mrs Jose was reasonable. Jane was not in a condition of mind to understand the reason of it, but the direction given commended itself to her instinctively. As she went up the lane, she felt that her knees gave way and that her breath was short. The excitement through which she had passed told on her prowess, and her strength failed. She made her way over the open upland to the descent leading to the undercliff. On the way she had passed no man. The coastguards, baffled, disappointed, had been withdrawn. Perhaps they also, like all other members of creation, sought their breakfasts. Jane followed the path among the bushes till she reached the house of Rattenbury. In place of going to the front door, which she supposed would be fastened, she went round to the back of the cottage. Whether the captain were within she did not know, nor concern herself to consider. She sought not him, but Winefred. If he were out – well. If within, and he opposed her entry, she would withdraw when satisfied that her child was not there.

She lifted the latch noiselessly and entered the back kitchen. This she traversed, and finding the door ajar into the front apartment, that served as parlour and sitting–room, she thrust it open with a finger, and entered. As she did so, to her surprise, she saw the captain on a stool before the wardrobe, both the valves of which were thrown back; and the rail from which depended the garments from crooks was drawn forward beyond the depth of the cabinet, so as to prevent the closing of the doors.

Further, she perceived that this rail was actually the front of a drawer which must have been contrived to run back when pressed into the depth of the wall, or the rock against which the cottage leaned. Into this drawer Rattenbury was dipping. She stood motionless and speechless in her astonishment, gazing at him. A double set of pegs or crooks was affixed to the rail, the hooks set alternately, so as to allow of a double range of garments being suspended in the wardrobe, hanging clear of each other, and completely concealing the backboard of the closet. These clothes – gowns, cloaks, petticoats, shawls – were now brought forward and hung clear, suspended at a distance of two feet six inches from the back of the wardrobe.

Jane saw the captain extract a little bag from the drawer. He then moved on the stool and slightly turned himself about as he proceeded to thrust the bag into his breeches pocket. At the same time he leaned his shoulder against the rail to thrust the drawer back into its place. As he did this he caught sight of her observing him.

At once his face became livid, then turned purple. With an oath he sprang to the ground, ran to the hearth, snatched down a pistol that hung above the mantelshelf, and, grasping it by the barrel, turned on her and raised his hand to fell her to the ground.

"Watching! Spying! –" He could no more; a splutter of foam, not words. As he leaped at her, she sprang back, raising her hands to protect her head; but at the same moment he went down in a lump on the floor as though the pistol butt had fallen on his head instead of hers.

Jane Marley stood for a moment uncertain what had happened, and what should be done. Had his ankle turned, and would he pluck himself up again, once more to rush at her? Or had he been felled by an apoplectic stroke? After a brief moment of hesitation, seeing that he made no movement to rise, uttered no sound, she stepped forward, bent over him, and endeavoured to remove the pistol from his grip. But the fingers were tight locked and she could not disengage them. She turned his head and saw by the face that he was unconscious.

Then she laboured to unloose his neckcloth and his shirt–collar; she forced him over on his back, and was by this means able to dash water into his face. As he lay thus, his hand gradually relaxed, and the pistol fell from it. Jane immediately secured it, and replaced it on the crooks above the mantelshelf whence he had taken it. Was the man dead or in a fit?

The wardrobe doors were wide open, and the range of old clothes still projecting into and depending in mid–air in the room. Jane had sufficient shrewdness to see that it was advisable to replace all before she summoned assistance. Mounting the stool, she looked into the drawer and found that it contained purses, small canvas bags, wooden and metal boxes, and at once satisfied herself that they were filled with money, gold mostly, some silver.

She caught her breath, then breathed heavily, and her heart beat fast. She did not immediately close the drawer, but remained staring at the wealth that was amassed there before her – the accumulations of a man, saving, unscrupulous, daring, and so cunning as never to be caught – the spoils of a long, adventurous life.

Looking about her she saw the captain to whom all this gold belonged lying on the lime–ash floor, his face grey, his eyes open, but expressionless. They saw nothing, the brain knew nothing of what she was doing. She thrust the drawer back in its place. It slid on runners let into each side. It moved smoothly, noiselessly and when in place was so ingeniously contrived that no one could have guessed at its existence. All the hanging garments retreated with it, and showed as though suspended in the most ordinary way from a

99

rail attached to the back of the closet. So firmly did the drawer fit that when Jane Marley pulled at the pegs she failed to make it oscillate to such a degree as to indicate that it was moveable. She descended from the stool and shut the wardrobe doors over the range of female dresses.

Again she looked at the prostrate man, and now saw that his eyes were on her. There was in them a flicker of intelligence. She thought, but could not be sure, that he knew her and was aware what she was about, but his mouth did not move. He made no attempt to speak. There was no token of resentment in the eyes, and the features were drawn, distorted, but expressionless. When the cabinet was shut, and the secret secure, then Jane endeavoured to lift the captain and remove him to the adjoining bedroom, which she had occupied, and to lay him on the bed. But his weight was too considerable and too dead for her to be able to effect her purpose and after several unsuccessful attempts she abandoned them. It would, she realised, be necessary for her to leave the cottage and summon assistance. She stood over him for a few minutes considering.

Then she noticed that the little bag he had begun to thrust into his pocket had fallen out and was on the floor. She stooped, picked it up, and, assured that it contained coin, unloosed the string that bound it and filled her palm with guineas. Then hastily, with a sense of fear, she poured them back into the bag, and kneeling by the prostrate man thrust it into his breast pocket.

Having done this she drew a long breath, as freed from some weight that had come across her heart; she unbarred the front door and opened it. As she did this a cool breeze puffed in, and the rising sun sent a stream of gold over the floor and the figure that lay motionless upon it. Jane looked back, holding the latch in her hand, musing.

Then she stepped to the side of the prostrate figure and said, "Job! Captain Job! your secret is now mine."

Thereupon she turned to leave the house and run towards Bindon to summon aid.

Chapter Seventeen

J.H.

At the same moment, as Jane was on the threshold and about to shut the door behind her, Winefred appeared, but Winefred so covered with soil, so be–chalked, as to be hardly recognisable. Yet Jane knew her at once.

In the conflict of emotion in her heart the shock was too great. She reeled and caught the doorposts, and stood speechless, her mouth open – staring.

"Mother! have you missed me?" Jane was unable to answer. She gasped for breath. Behind Winefred was a young man. "Mother, have you been frightened?" Then, still speechless, Mrs Marley pointed to the figure on the floor. Instantly, with an exclamation, the young man dashed past her, and knelt by the prostrate captain.

Jane's head was dazed. For a moment the earth spun round, and a blue cloud rose and enveloped her. She would have fallen had not her daughter caught and sustained her. Winefred led her within to a seat, and as Jane entered she shrank from the captain. She put her hands before her eyes and reamined breathing hard, and trembling in every limb. After a while she withdrew her hands, looked at the young man, and asked, "Who is that?"

"It is Jack – Jack Rattenbury," answered Winefred, who still had her arm about her mother, afraid lest she should slip down in a faint.

Jane remained silent and motionless for a minute, then with a sharp turn of the body shook herself together, rallied her senses, and said, "Run, run for a doctor – I had been out searching for you, Winnie, and when I came back I found him thus." Jack stooped over his father, endeavouring to get him to speak, but although old Rattenbury's eyes rested on him, and his mouth moved, he was unable to articulate words.

"He has had a fit," said Mrs Marley, as she stood up, almost herself again. "If you are Jack, help me to carry him to bed. I have tried to lift him, but have failed. I had not the strength; he is a heavy man."

"No, mother," said Winefred. "Jack and I will do that. You are too shaken."

"Yes," said the young man, rising, "that is the proper thing to be done. But lest he suffer from cold, and there is no fireplace in another room, we will have a bed moved in here."

Winefred now removed her arm from encircling her mother, and the three proceeded to make the stricken man as comfortable as possible under the circumstances. Then said Jane again, "Run for a doctor. He must let blood. It is the right thing to be done in such a case. Do you go, Jack, and Winefred and I will attend to your father till your return." Jack once more bent over the captain, took his hand and spoke to him, and again Job Rattenbury laboured ineffec- tually to utter some words. At the same time his eyes turned to the wardrobe.

"I cannot catch his meaning," said Jack. "There is something on his mind, something he is most desirous to communicate. Can you guess at his meaning, Mrs Marley?"

"No," answereed Jane, compressing her lips. "You are wasting precious time, and risking the loss of his life to dally thus. Go for the surgeon at once; he must breathe a vein."

The young man nodded, looked at his father, and left. When he was gone, Jane turned to her daughter. "It is in vain. No doctor can mend him. But I am glad that the young man is away. Now" – she clutched her daughter's hands – "tell me all. Tell me where you have been – why you have been away."

"O mother," said Winefred, "it is a long story. Must you have it at once?"

"I must know all. Why is he – that Jack, with you?"

"But for him I should not be here now!"

"Why so?" Then Winefred related her story. She told that she had overheard the directions given by the officer of the coastguard to his man, how that, knowing that the smugglers were to be trapped, she had done her utmost to caution them and save them from plunging into the snare. "You hear this!" exclaimed Jane in a tone of triumph, springing from her chair, and going before Rattenbury. "You hear this! you – you who dared to say that she had betrayed you. She betray! She has, on the contrary, been the saving of your band. I am glad you lie thus, stricken down, judged by God for what you said."

"Mother," pleaded Winefred, drawing the excited woman back to her seat, "do not speak to him in that fashion. listen to the remainder of my story."

"You do not know what he has done," said Mrs Marley. "He came here last night and because the guards were out, and his plans known, he would have it that you had betrayed him, and he drove me from the house. He lied when he said that you had called the preventive men about him, and now God has beaten him to the ground for saying it." Looking again at the man on the bed, she cast at him, "You – listen to what follows." Winefred continued her story to the fall of the rock, without interruption from her mother, who, however, at times nervously, sympathetically gripped her hands, and throughout with eager eyes looked into the face of her child, trembling and breathless to hear the sequel.

"And then?" she asked, when Winefred paused.

"Well, mother, after Jack Rattenbury left, so he has told me, he walked along the beach, but he felt uneasy at having left me behind and alone, partly on account of the gaugers being about, and angry at having lost their prey, and partly because of the crumbling and fall of the rock, so when he got with the rest of the men opposite the Chesil Bank, he would not cross over with them, but turned back and retraced his steps till he came to the place where the rift had been formed. But by this time it was quite dark, for the moon was down. On reaching the chasm he could see no lantern, nor hear a sound; he was afraid to call out lest he should draw attention from the men who were about on the cliffs, and were drawing together as if they had a scent. Then he went along the beach, but saw nothing, and he did not well know what to do. He could not ascend by the path lest he should run into the arms of the coastguard, so he turned and went back again. He thought he heard voices aloft, but was not sure. He did not like to go home – I mean to Beer – without some knowledge of what had happened to me."

"Go on."

"Then at last the dawn came, and he returned to the cleft, and he saw that there had been a fall of rock, not very great, yet there certainly had been one, for the mouth of the cavern was hidden. He clambered over the rubbish and called."

"And you answered?"

"Mother, it was like this. I had fainted. I do not know how long I lay insensible. I do not know whether it were a real faint or I slept – when I came round, came to know anything – then I saw something like a star, just a little point of light. Mother, if I had not seen that little star, I do not think I should ever have come to my senses again, but have gone dazed, or slept or fainted off again into endless night. But when I saw that pinpoint – it was no more – then my mind and my life came back again to me; and I began to think and to remember, and I knew what had happened. and was able to consider what should be done. I guessed that the star was just one little bit of opening left that had not been covered. I daresay when the rock fell it was covered, but the heap sank and let this tiny hole appear. Through it came the light and the sweet morning air. I scrambled towards it, and then, just then, I heard him call, and I cried in reply. He heard me, and I tore away with my hands at the soil on one side, and he cleared away without as fast as he could. We were like a pair of rabbits. At length an opening was made through which I could wriggle like a worm. Look at my hands –"

Her mother clasped her to her heart. She could not speak. "But," said Jane, after a long pause, "you might have escaped without him."

"Yes, perhaps, but not so soon. Then Jack and I built up the entrance, so that none might find it till such time as he could come by night and flit all the goods away. He came on with me here." Winefred looked towards the bed, "I suppose the excitement of the night has been too much for the captain. And, O mother, it nearly killed me. You did seem frightened and ready to fall when I came upon you at the door. Mother, dear, I do not like the way his eyes watch us. Do let me put up a screen."

"He cannot hurt you now." Then, starting up, "But, Winefred, you have not had anything to eat." She looked at the clock; it had stopped. "I do not know the hour."

"That I can give," said the girl. She went into her bedroom, if so the recess could be called under the stair, and produced the watch that had been left by her beneath her pillow.

Her mother stared at the gold timepiece. "How came you by that?"

"It was given to me, mother."

"Who gave it you?" asked Jane, as she snatched the watch to her and turned it about. There was some enamelling on the back in blue and white.

"A gentleman gave it to me. I should have told you before. Indeed, I intended to tell you yesterday, but you were in an ill-humour, and so I waited and then the chance passed."

"I have seen this watch before. I know it well," said Jane, in a muffled voice. Again a sense of giddiness came upon her. So much had occurred, such a rush of strange events had passed over her, such a storm of various emotions had torn her, that she hardly knew what was happening now, or was likely to happen next.

"There was a gentleman who came to me yesterday on the beach when I was picking up pebbles. He had very curled whiskers, and was sprucely dressed. He wore a fine hat and a green coat. He gave me the watch."

"Did he say anything to you?" asked Jane in the same low, suppressed tone. She held the watch in her hand and turned it about.

"Yes, he spoke of you, mother; he continued asking about you, and what you were doing, and where you had been. He was strange in his manner."

"Did he tell you his name?"

"No; but there are initials on the case, J.H."

"It surely must be he!" said Mrs Marley. "He would at one time have given me the watch – it is the same; but I could not read the hours then; I have learned that since. It is he. Why did he not come to see me? Did he say he would do that?"

"No, mother, he was in a hurry."

"Where was he going?"

"He did not say."

"Tell me – tell me something more. What was he like? I do not mean his hat and his coat."

"He was rather a handsome man, but he had hardly any chin, and that spoiled his face; and he was forever fumbling with something, generally a key; and he blew down it, and turned it about at the end of his tongue. But when he spoke of you I thought he was going to cry."

"It was he," said Jane, and she knitted her hands together about the watch on her lap.

"Who, mother?"

"Child – you met your father."

Chapter Eighteen

Declaration of War

As soon as Winefred had eaten something, had changed her dress, and cleaned her face and hands of the soil that had adhered to them, Mrs Marley despatched her to Bindon to inform Mrs Jose of what had occurred. The farmer's wife was so kind–hearted that Jane knew that she might calculate on receiving prompt assistance from her.

When the girl had departed on her errand, Jane sat brooding with her eyes on the floor. Occasionally she looked at the man extended in the bed, but his eyes were now shut, and he seemed to be asleep; consequently her services were not in immediate requisition, and she was free to think over what had taken place. But her mind was in a turmoil, and she was incapable of arresting the succcessive pictures, fancies that whirled around in her head, to consider one apart from the rest.

To think clearly is not given to all. By some it is acquired through education, but to others education aggravates the confusion. A totally ignorant person with a limited range of ideas is accordingly often a far more valuable member of the community than one whose head is a ragbag stuffed with odds and ends, new and old, unco–ordinated. Nature has not furnished every brain with nests of boxes into which to sort its ideas; but education of a proper sort should be directed to the inculcation of mental tidiness, and not to the accumulation of articles which serve only to make the confusion worse compounded. Herein is the radical defect of out national educational system. We stuff our children's brains with facts more or less valuable, many of no importance whatever – the height of Chimborazo, the number of gallons of water rolled down by the Mississippi, the population of Timbuctoo, but make no attempt to cultivate observation and develop the reasoning powers. A Scots child's mind is made to digest what is put into it, that of an English child only to gorge facts. Therefore in the race of life, he is left behind; he lies his length sleeping off his surfeit, whilst the Scotsman steps into and walks off in his shoes.

Jane was uneducated; a woman of strong feelings and few ideas, who was accustomed to be governed by one thought at a time. Now her contracted mind was in a turmoil with the crowding in of many and diverse thoughts – the reappearance of her husband or betrayer, whichever he was; the wrong done to her by the captain, as shown by Olver Dench; the peril of life in which her child had been placed; the discovery of Rattenbury's hoarded gains; the stroke that had cast him speechless and powerless before her, at the moment of discovery; all these matters mingled and entangled themselves in her mind inextricably. She strove hard to fix her attention on one subject only, but at once another started up to claim consideration.

As she sat thus, the door opened and the ferryman entered. "Hey, Jane! So the captain is down. Just heard the tidings from his son. How came that about? Had a brush with the sharks? They have been about in the night, I hear. Where is he?" Jane pointed, and Olver went to the bedside, called to the sick man, and said, "How came this about, captain? I saw Jack, but he was in such a vast hurry he could tell me no particulars, so I came up to learn them myself, and to see if I could be helpful. Don't be down–hearted. You will pull through. How came you hurt? A knock over the head?"

The stricken man opened his eyes. "Come, give an old mate a word," said Dench.

"He cannot speak," Jane explained. "He has not spoken since he fell. Jack has gone for a surgeon to let blood."

"A stroke is it, and not from a cutlass," said the ferryman. "Who would have expected that, old man? On my soul, I thought you would never have come to an end like this, like a sick cat before the fire. But it is a queer business, too. I reckon they thought to have you fast. By my liver, I am inclined to think it is shammed, so as to throw the enemy off the scent." He looked intently at Rattenbury, and satisfied himself that the man really was ill. Then he turned himself abruptly about, came before Jane, and said in a low tone, "He is tricky as a fox, but there is no deceit here. His game is played. How came this about?"

"I was away at Bindon. When I returned, he lay his length on the floor."

"He will not speak again until he chirps Alleluja in kingdom come," said the ferryman. "Let the surgeon do his best, he cannot pull him round. I am glad Jack is gone. That leaves the house clear for an hour. Jane, I spoke with you the other day about sharing, and you would not hearken. The chance has come again, as though offered by an auctioneer, so that hearken and consent you must, unless you are a bigger fool than I take you to be."

"Winefred has gone for Mrs Jose," sair Jane with a flutter of alarm at her heart.

"Then we have but half an hour at our disposal. In that half hour we must discover where the captain has hidden his money."

"I will be no sharer with you."

"Oh, so! You will have it all to yourself! That will not answer."

"Leave the house; you have no right to be here," said Jane Marley.

"Eh!" mocked Dench. "You give orders as though you were mist-ress; orders you have no power to enforce."

"Jack Rattenbury shall know of this."

"Let him know." He stood mustering the room with his eyes. "I shall improve my mind a bit. Jane, be advised and offer no opposition. I tell you we are in the same boat. We have both been cheated. I want no more than is my due. I am an honest man, and I diddle nobody – but then I don't choose to be diddled myself – and if you have spirit you will be of the same mind. We will leave a third for Jack, and divide the rest between ourselves. I shall search the house if need be, whether you like it or no."

He had spoken in a low tone to Mrs Marley. Now he went to the side of Job Rattenbury, and said aloud, as though addressing one who was deaf: "Mate, we have been old friends for over a score of years. You can trust me. Your time is not long and you know it. You desire to say something, and cannot fashion your mouth to the words. You would tell me your last wishes, and how I am to dispose of your property, and where your cash is stowed. What do you say, governor? You will trust me. That is as it should be. Try your hand, hold out your flapper to show that you comprehend me."

The paralysed man made an effort to extend his arm. "That is brave. You can use your fingers. What say you to writing your wishes? But, understand, mate, you must say first where your money is, and then, in due course, how you would dispose of it. I will bring you a slate; there is one hanging there by the chimney–breast, I will hold it before you, and you shall scribble thereon what you like. I ask for no copyhand. Rely on me. I can keep counsel."

He brought the slate, and, seating himself on the bed, placed the pencil that was attached to the slate in the sick man's hand. Captain Rattenbury had his faculties now, he clearly comprehended what was desired of him, and he made an effort to respond. He held the pencil awkwardly between his fingers and began to write.

"That is fine," said Olver. "I can read that. *I*, capital *I*. Go along, governor." Again the pencil moved. "Yes – right enough. *F*. What comes next? – So, it is an *E*." The sick man paused. The pencil had slipped between the wrong fingers, and required readjusting. Dench placed it again between thumb and forefinger. Jane looked on uneasily.

"Right, old mate, an *A*. What follows *FEA*? – So! an *R*. You fear! Come now, what do you fear? is it Death?" Job Rattenbury turned his eyes in the direction of Mrs Marley. Then with a clumsy, shaking hand he made a scrawl.

"I cannot decipher that. It is like a spider. Try again, old man. Ah! *J*, is it? What next?" Again the pencil scratched. "An *A* now. *I fear Ja–*. Come, finish." But the captain's powers were exhausted, the pencil fell and the hand after it. In vain did Dench replace it, the fingers could no longer clutch nor direct it. Rattenbury made painful attempts, but all failed.

"No good," said Olver at last; "and, drat it! there does not seem to be much daylight in what he has written. Jane, can you make anything out of it?" She vouchsafed no reply, but looked towards the door. "Ah!" said the boatman, "expecting some from Bindon, are you? Then no time is to be lost."

He took the captain's clothes and examined them. "No keys! That tells something. But what have we here? A bag of gold."

"Leave it," said Jane; "thief that you are! Jack knows of this. Take it at your peril."

"I hope to find more than this," said Olver. "I shall look upstairs first."

"Stay" exclaimed the woman, springing to her feet. "You shall not search. The preventive men have been here already and have looked into every corner and probed every wall. They found nothing."

Olver laughed. "They hunted after kegs of brandy, looked for large hiding–places. I know better than to do that. There will be none such here."

"You shall not go," said Jane, and attempted to intercept him.

"Beware how you interfere with me," threatened Dench. "The captain can't speak, and I shall make sure that you do not if you interfere with me in my work. Jane, be reasonable. What I want is my own money. I do not intend to take anything that by right should belong to you and your Winefred. We have both been pillaged by this man! hands off! let me pass!" It was not possible to oppose him. He was the stronger of the two. He mounted a few steps, then descended again.

"A staircase," said he, "is a rare hiding–place. I must try every step." He examined each riser and footplace, but fruitlessly; then Jane heard him ransacking the chamber overhead. This engaged him for some time. He clearly believed that Captain Job had concealed the money in his bedroom, and he left no corner unexplored. Presently, dissatisfied with the result, angry and impatient, he descended, lighted a candle and mounted again to search a recess he had discovered in the roof, formed by a set–off from the chimney. But this also was disappointing. He came down once more, blew out the candle and replaced it in the brass holder on the mantelshelf.

"No," said he contemplatively, "there is nothing aloft. Not a box

110

there, not a drawer is locked, and I have overhauled all the bunks. No keys in his pocket. He is deep." He planted himself in a chair, placed his elbows on his knees and set his chin in his hands. His cunning, wicked eyes roved about the room. "Dang it, Jane," he said, "it is somewhere. He is not the man to bury his money in a bank. Besides, had he done that, there would have been a pass–book. I have not found one anywhere. I have looked into every chest and turned out every drawer, and poked into every nook upstairs. This room is not ceiled or I would have said there was a place between the plancheon and plaster. But that cannot be. Now I'll rummage the inner room."

"That has been mine," said Jane. "And that hole under the stair is where my Winnie has slept."

"It is more likely to be in the kitchen," said Dench. "He would not trust it where a woman made her lair. But if here, it will not be where anyone else would make a hiding–place, as beneath the hearthstone or up the chimney, nor under the floor. It is certain to be in the very last place that would occur to any other man but he."

He went to the clockcase. "This is not going. Is there aught stops the works?"

"The clock has run down," said Jane Marley. She was uneasy, fearing lest he should find the hiding–place, but she did not allow her feelings to transpire. She assumed a sulky mood. He turned to the window and lifted the lid of the seat.

"There is a box here."

"Yes – a box."

"He keeps his grog here; and where his grog is, there his money will not be. Too many itching fingers after the bottle of spirits to make that safe." He tapped a bit of wainscot, but it sounded dead.

"There are shutters," mused he; "what does a man in a cottage want with folding shutters? As well expect to meet with a pierglass. They hide something. Excuse me, Jane, if I darken the room whilst I look." Still his search was without result.

"I am hanged," growled he. "But, ha! there is still the wardrobe left." He crossed the room to the closet beside the fire. Jane's heart rose into her mouth. Dench threw open one of the doors. He hesit-ated a moment about unbolting the other valve; did not do so, but groped in the pockets of the dresses that were there suspended in double range; he was disappointed in those he searched. Then he unhasped the second valve, and closed the first, that he might submit the rest of the clothes to the same search. Had he looked over his shoulder, he would have seen a light spring into Jane's eyes.

"By my liver," said Dench to himself, "I did suppose that I should find his wife's old rags as his bank." He drew some of them aside, and laughed contemptuously. "See – those fellows who have been before me have riddled the backboards with gimlet holes. By Moses!" – he started back and shut the door.

What alarmed him and interrupted him in his search was the passing before the window of Mrs Jose and Winefred. When they entered he was standing beside the bed of Captain Job, with a look of commiseration on his face.

"Drat it," said Olver, "it may be womanly, but I can't help it, only a man does not care for females to witness his condition." He wiped his eyes. "Just come to take a farewell of my old mate. Not long for this vale of tears. But we mustn't repine, must we, Mrs Jose? Scripture –" Mrs Jose did not regard the ferryman. She pushed past him. He was no favourite of the farmer's wife. Moreover, Olver was at a loss how to finish his sentence. He was not primed with texts. Mrs Jose went at once to the side of the sick man.

Dench took occasion to draw back, and nudging Jane Marley, he said in an undertone, "A word outside with you." She hung back. "I must have it," said he behind his hand. "It is of serious importance."

After a little further hesitation she yielded, and accompanied him without. He conducted her a few paces from the cottage to a spot that was not overlooked, and which was beyond earshot. Then, turning upon her in a threatening tone, and with a menacing actions, he said, "Jane, I have been bawked, but it is there. It is certainly there. But he is deep, deep as hell. Find it, and I shall made it worth your while to confide in me. It is the strictly right, square and honest thing I want to do, that the poor devil may have rest for his soul where he is going. You would like to have peace of mind on your deathbed, and it is a Christian duty in us to redress a great wrong he has committed, so that he may have a happy death. He robbed your father, your brother, you and your child, and he has robbed me. All

I seek is to do what is right and take what is properly mine, and give you what properly belongs to you. Make me your friend and not your enemy."

"A friend!" said Jane contemptuously. "Of what value to me would be the friendship of a man who steals from his friend when that friend is unable to lift a finger to protect himself?"

"Steals! steals!" echoed Dench; "you take advantage of me as being a woman. I would reclaim only what is mine own, and that for the benefit of his soul. Beware lest you get hold of anything without taking me into partnership."

"I do not fear you – bully as you are," said Jane; "for I know enough to make you shake before me."

He laughed scornfully. "What do you know?"

"Tell me this, Olver Dench: What happens when a man has betrayed his mates?" The colour deserted his cheeks.

"You have said enought to let me see that it was you who gave information. I have but to speak the word to David Nutall."

"Come, Jane, let us be friends."

"No."

He remained silent for fully a minute. "Enemies then?" he asked at length, in a voice little raised above a whisper.

"Enemies if you will. Friends never."

Chapter Nineteen

Exit Job

When the doctor arrived he gave no hope of permanent improvement. The captain, said he, must be kept quiet; supposing that nothing were allowed to agitate him, he might in part recover his faculties, but this was rather to be desired than to be anticipated.

Mrs Jose carried off Winefred. It was advisable that the girl should not be in the house, and Jack and Mrs Marley undertook to sit up with the patient during the night, taking their watches alternately; Jack to wake the first part.

Between twelve and one the young man roused Mrs Marley and retired to bed. His father was in much the same condition, apparently; he had remained perfectly quiet, and had slept.

Jane left her bed on being summoned. She had not taken off her clothes. She found the fire made up and the kettle on the boil at the side. Jack had been sitting before the grate, and had made some grog, sufficient to moisten his throat, and to help him to spend the hours, but he had taken a moderate amount only.

Jane seated herself near the sick–bed and took her knitting. The captain's eyes were closed, not shut, and she could see the glitter of the eyeballs under the lashes; but whether he slept imperfectly, or whether he was half–awake and was observing her, she could not decide.

There is no occupation like knitting for breeding thought. A man smokes to encourage concentration of his mental faculties; but a woman, when she knits, diffuses her thoughts, they spread like the antennae of a sea–anemone in all directions, and lay hold of every– thing that drifts by in the current of memory, to draw it in, twist, distort, magnify it, take it into the innermost receptacles, and there suffer indigestion from it, often in the acutest form. As Jane worked with nimble fingers her mind was busy, busy mainly over Job's accumulations. Not for an instant did she question the suggestion that they were acquired by defrauding her father and brother, nor did she doubt that her brother's death had been procured by the man now lying powerless in her presence. She had not inquired of others whether what Dench had thrown out was an opinion generally entertained, whether it had any foundation whatever. She accepted the assumption as a self–evident fact, and started from it.

Jane Marley was in no little degree concerned about her own future and that of her child. The captain would not last many days, and she would then have to leave the undercliff, as the house would pass to Jack. It was a freehold, acquired originally by squatting on the land a generation ago.

To be on the trudge again was not a prospect Jane relished. It was true that Mrs Jose had offered to take her and Winefred in – but that was not intended to be for a permanency, only whilst the maid was recovering from white swelling. Moreover, Jane knew so much of herself as to be aware that by temper she was disqualified to live as one of an establishment with other servants. Indeed, the mistress who did not fall out speeedily with Jane must be of a peculiarly fore-bearing temper. Jane was wilful, unyielding and passionate. She knew it. Whither, then, was she to go? What was she to do?

Her husband had been in the neighbourhood, but had not visited her, and had vanished again, after seeing and speaking to his child. She could not build on the hope of obtaining assistance from him, even had not her pride revolted against the thought of soliciting it.

In a day or two she would have to make up her bundle and leave; then Jack Rattenbury would take up his residence there. The house would be his own, with all the money it contained; and he would take his ease, rattle the coin in his pocket, fling it about, and be what his father intended – a gentleman.

It is a hard thing for one who has land and home, an income and kindred, to enter into the feeling of desolation and hopelessness that possesses the heart of one who is absolutely adrift in life, without a single attachment, without a single point in the outlook, on which to fix the eye and to which aim.

Jane Marley's life had been broken at an early period – made purposeless by no fault of her own. If she staggered, it was not that her head was light, but that the ground gave way under her feet. When young, when possessed of the elasticity of youth to carry her forward, and form for herself a future, she had been cruelly wronged. Now she had passed the turn of life, the sap was withdrawing, the forces of her soul were in decline, and her heart became sick at a prospect without an elevation in it – a future that was all cloud.

For herself she felt little concern, her life had been a failure, and to that she submitted. As she knitted and observed the ball of worsted at her feet, she thought that this wool was being used up with a purpose and to a profitable end, whereas the thread of her life had been involved in a hopeless tangle. Winefred was on the verge of womanhood, and promised to be handsome, but this very fact was fraught with danger, and might occasion her ruin, as it had been that of her mother before.

Jane's heart was on fire. She was prepared to do anything, every-thing in her power to assure to her child a healthy and a happy life, but the means of obtaining this were not available. She had harrowed and cross-harrowed her brain, tearing up all her experiences, search-ing after what she could not find. She had lived hitherto a precarious existence, tramping over the country, hawking ribbons, pins, needles, tapes and ballads. On the mean profits she had maintained herself and her child. She had done more. She had been so intent on quali-fying Winefred to take a position superior to her own that she had sent her to school, and had kept her there. Was it not, said she, due to her own defective education that she had been unable to retain her husband's affection?

But she had not been able to save money. She had no little store on which to fall back. She had received offers for Winefred from farmers' wives to take her as a servant; but these she had refused, partly for a selfish reason, because she could not endure to be separated from her daughter, but also because she did not choose that Winefred, the child of a gentleman, should definitely adopt a menial life in a farmhouse till every chance was gone of placing her in a superior situation. The poor mother could find no gate out of her difficulties.

As her fingers worked, tremulous with the fever of her brain, the thought of the meeting of Winefred with her father rose into prom-inence. It had been unsatisfactory, in that he had made no promise to the child, he had done nothing for her, save give her a watch, unsuitable to her position, were her position to be one of poverty. But was not this gift an earnest of a purpose to do something more? It was well that he had seen her, for he must have observed that she was educated, and altogether other from what her mother had been.

If only some opportunity were to arise whereby the girl might be lifted to a higher shelf, so as to show J.H. what she really was, what capabilities were in her, what cause he would have to be proud of her, then Jane would be ready to efface herself, or remain far away in the background and in obscurity. Why should Captain Job be able to convert his cub into a gentleman and she be debarred from raising her child? What had Rattenbury himself been? What had been his wife's birth? Both came of the seafaring class, neither had derived from gentle blood. They had occupied a position to which they had been born. Why then should Jack be promoted? On the other hand Winefred had a real gentleman for her father, and had therefore a half claim to be a lady.

Moreover Jack was to obtain his advantages and advancement by means of money accumulated by the old smuggling adventurer through the despoiling of others, even of her father, and by the sacrifice of her brother. She had a right to some of the store. It did not belong to Captain Job because it was under his roof, and in his cupboard; it belonged to the men who by their blood and sweat had earned it, and she entered into their inheritance, acquired their rights. Olver had spoken the truth; in all common equity the money was hers. Dench had forfeited his rights by the betrayal of his mates. She was shrewd enough to see that Olver could only have known of the expedition, and of the attempt to trap those taking part in it, by having been first privy to it and then by having betrayed it. To herself Jane said that the sum she required was not large, just sufficient to enable her to tide over her present difficulties, to secure a home, to establish herself in a little business – a small shop, perhaps. Thus furnished, her future would be secure, and there would be a prospect open for her child. This – the having a shop – had long been an object of ambition, so as not to be compelled to tramp over the country exposed to every weather, away from her child, carrying her pack.

How much had Captain Job saved during his long career? Surely it could be no robbery if she were to deduct from it the modest sum that she so greatly required, and to which she had a moral right. She stood up, laid her knitting down on the chair, and went to the wardrobe, then halted, and going to the window closed the shutters. Then she stood, with her finger to her lip, listening to make sure that Jack was asleep upstairs. She heard his heavy breathing. he was young – sleep sealing up eyes and ears so soon as his head was laid on the pillow.

She took the candle from the table, and holding it aloft looked at the captain. He lay as he had lain for many hours, motionless, apparently unconscious. Then she replaced the candle and went again

117

towards the wardrobe. Something caught and lightly restrained her feet. She looked down, they were entangled in the worsted of her knitting. She stooped to disentangle them. Next she lightly opened the doors of the wardrobe, and putting her hands to the pegs drew the rack forward.

She could not well look into the drawer without a stool. She therefore sought this; it had been thrust into a corner. She brought it forward and placed it before the range of dangling garments. Then she stepped upon it to examine the contents of the drawer. She had previously seen purses, bags and boxes. She opened one of the latter, and found that it contained banknotes. She untied a bag, it was stuffed with sovereigns. In a purse were a number of old guineas. She lifted the lid of a small japanned case –it contained jewels. The value of the stones she could not guess. She took up a brooch and held it so that it shone in the feeble glimmer of the candle. "Ah!" thought she, "how well this would become my Winefred!" All at once she started, and her heart stood still. She was plucked from behind.

In a moment she turned, and was frozen with fear. The palsied man had rolled himself from the bed to the floor, and with a supreme effort had wormed himself along it till he reached where she stood. With one hand he had stretched forth and laid hold of her dress that he might drag her away from his store.

But the effort had been the last of which he was capable, and when Jane stooped to wrench her garment out of the hand that clutched it, it was already that of a dead man.

Chapter Twenty

A First Step

The funeral of Captain Rattenbury was conducted with that pomp and circumstance so dear to the West Country heart. The entire neighbourhood attended from both sides of the estuary of the Axe. Indeed, the village of Beer was for the afternoon denuded of its inhabitants; for, although only men were invited to the interment, yet the women flocked to it as well, to express their sympathy with the bereaved and their respect for the deceased, with copious gush of tears and flutter of kerchiefs, and to hang about the door of the house of mourning in hopes of being able to squeeze in and taste a little of that spiritous consolation which flows freely at the funeral of an adult, the absence of which from that of a child deprives it of its zest and popularity.

Olver Dench thrust himself forward officiously, acting as though he had been constituted master of the ceremonies and dispenser or steward of the refreshments. Mrs Jose, always forward in kindly help as she was ever prompt in kind intent, was there to assist Mrs Marley. She had boiled the salt beef at the farm, and baked the saffron cakes in the Bindon oven. She had thoughtfully retained Winefred at her house, and had told her mother that it was her purpose to keep her there till something was settled relative to her future disposal.

When the ceremony in the churchyard was at an end, a sense of relief manifested itself among the sable mourners in a hum of conversation interspersed with sallies of cheerfulness and splutter of laughter. A black stream now set in the direction of the cottage, where the bearers might recruit after the muscular exertion of carrying the corpse, and the mourners after the tension of their feeling.

The undercliff habitation could not possibly contain all, and it resembled a hive about which the bees were thick, some entering eagerly, others emerging reluctantly, wiping their lips. Olver retained hold of a flask of spirits, and poured out to everyone, accompanying each libation with a word on the irreparable loss the community had sustained, and on the unapproachable merits of the deceased, accompanied also by confident assurances that he was then smiling down on the mourners from aloft. Then he threw out observations on the good luck enjoyed by Jack at having come in for the fortune accumulated by the thrift of his father, who has been the most unselfish man he knew, toiling that Jack might enjoy, amassing that he might spend.

The ferryman did not fail to impress on all present that he had himself been the most intimate friend of Captain Job, associated with him throughout their lives, that they had lived as brothers, and that he had been constituted orally by the departed the guardian of Jack, and, added Dench, "Please God I will do my duty by the lad, for ever and ever. Amen." Then, as his cheeks grew redder and his face more glossy, he moralised with greater unction. It behoved them all to take lesson, and so to order their lives as to be able to die as happy as had the captain. It would be well were their hearts in the right place, as was his. That was their great secret. All were doomed to fade as the lilies and to wither as the grass. Let them, therefore, lay up treasure for their children to enjoy, and comrades to be left behind to lament them.

Then he diverged into more or less open allusion to Jane Marley. He named no names, and he said nothing, but he felt all the deeper that it was a sad thing for a man when ill and dying to be in the hands of hirelings, who had no interest beyond grabbing what lay strewn about, and whose solicitude was wholly for themselves and not with the patient. But these insinuations were made only when not liable to be overheard by Jane and Mrs Jose. As his face glowed like a November setting sun, and assumed a gloss like young holly leaves, he became noisy, talking louder, excessive in his officiousness, demonstrative in his grief, and effusive in his piety.

"I think," he said very boisterously, "that we'll lift up our voices

120

and sing John Wesley's favourite hymn, 'For he's a jolly good fellow'." Mrs Jose hastily interfered.

"Well, ma'am, we'll take it slow time, like a hymn."

As this did not meet with approval, "Then someone start any hymn as is suitable – I ain't very familiar with psalm–tunes."

The influx of mourners was incessant, for no sooner had one set been refreshed than another battled its way in at the door to be regaled as well, and the first set, which had departed by the back door, made the circuit of the house, and appeared again at the front, fresh for new consolation.

The saffron cake and the cold beef were in request, but not to the same extent as the spirits. As each ate and drank he heaved a sigh, and said, "Ah, well! Us shan't see the likes of he again," or "He died beautiful – 'appy as a hangel," or some similar commonplace. It was part of the etiquette to heave a sigh and utter a moan, and make a pious observation. At length the rapidly declining day put a term to the entertainment, and caused a diminution in the concourse of applicants for cake and liquor. When the last had departed, Dench cast himself into the armchair and said, "Darned if I ain't pretty nigh done up. Now it is my turn to touch a drop."

"There is none left," said Mrs Jose, who had quietly removed the bottle, "and what is more, you must clear out of this. Jane and I are about to wash up, and then we must carry back to Bindon the dishes and glasses that I lent for the occasion."

"Well," said Dench, "it can't be said but that we did it handsome, and I reckon they enjoyed themselves – prodigious. As to clearing out – I don't see it, but I'll help to clear away."

He set to work accordingly to make himself useful. He was, in fact, impatient to be rid of the two women. He replaced the chairs against the walls, brought in wood and made up the fire. He mounted the stairs and drew up the blind in the bedroom above, and as he did so peered into everything. The chamber had been well searched before; he searched it again now.

He did not descend till the women were gone burdened with baskets that contained glass and crockery. When he came down he saw Jack standing at the window, looking forth into the dark night that had set in, with an expression of sadness and in an attitude of dejection.

Olver said cheerily, "We'll have out another bottle and smoke. Care killed the cat. Make this your home. Draw a chair to the fire and close the shutters, there is a good fellow. I'm a bit fagged – I've worked hard today. But blow me if I would not go through it all again for your dear old father. Ah! he was my most familiar friend. We knew each other from boyhood, and he valued me for my poor gifts. Hanged it I know what he saw in me – but there was something that made him cling to me. He trusted me above anyone in the world. I am one of your straight men, you know. When he was bad with the stroke, and you had gone for the doctor, he could not speak, but he made eyes for the slate, and I understood him, and brought it to him, and he wrote on it, 'I fear Jack, that he's thoughtless, and may waste his inheritance. Be a father to him, old friend. Tell him to intrust his money to you and beware of a bank.' There," said the ferryman, taking down the slate, "you see it here. Drat it – only 'I fear Ja–,' the rest was there, upon my soul, I can swear to it; but there have been a deal of people in the house today rubbing against it with their shoulders, and they have rubbed the most of it out."

"What you tell me seems too much to get on to the slate," said Jack, but without exhibiting a lively interest in the communication.

"Oh, not a bit. You see the commencement," said Dench. "What follows has been brushed away. Then you father turned the slate and finished on the other side. Ah! that is gone. I warrant you that Jane Marley has done this. She is deep and she does not like us. A bad lot that. Do not trust her. If she had been able to write, there is no saying what she might have added and passed off as his last will. There has been no will found, I believe."

"None. I do not think my father made one."

"No. He would have informed me if he had. He did nothing of importance without advising with me. But you may take this as the expression of his last wishes, and I can swear to every word. Jane Marley was present, saw him write, and because she spited me has cleaned out the scribble – all but the beginning. What has your father left?"

"I do not know – except debts."

"Debts! but there is plenty of money for wiping them out." Jack shook his head. "I say there must be."

"Then where is it?"

"That is just what I supposed you knew. He did not tell me, though we were so intimate."

"I have no idea as to what he was worth, and where he placed what he had."

"My dear boy, he never spent one–tenth of what he made. He has been a hoarding man ever since I knew him, close and frugal. On himself he spent nothing."

"But he never stinted me; and that is how the money went."

"Fiddlesticks! He ordered you a cutter, that don't cost a trifle."

"But it is not paid for."

"He was not the man to order when he had not the money in hand wherewith to pay."

"There were fifteen pounds in a bag in his pocket," said Jack; "I know of no more. That will meet the cost of the funeral, but not leave much over."

Dench went to the window seat, lifted it, and took out a flask of spirits. "I don't understand. There must be money."

"To be frank with you," said Jack, "I have no faith in money made in the way he has been speculating. It may come in freely, but it runs out again as freely. It is drawing water in a leaky bucket. I have heard Mrs Marley say that her father died as poor as a rat, and he had been in the business since he was a boy of fifteen. It has been the same with my father."

"But you have heard him boast that he intended to make a gentleman of you."

"Yes, precisely because, like a gambler, he reckoned on his next throw being successful."

"He has spent a lot of money on your education."

"Yes, and he has ventured a lot of money in the trade – of late he has not been able to realise. The lookout has been so sharp that he has had no returns. You know how this last affair has ended."

"Nothing has been confiscated."

"No – nothing has been sold."

"I am not satisfied. On the whole he had been a lucky man, and, by the foot of Pharaoh, a man like him is not ruined by a bad job.

123

Let us look round. If we find anything, you know what was his last desire, that you should intrust it to me – make me your banker. You see this slate? He was vastly against you keeping it yourself. He knew how thoughtless and wasteful young men are."

"We will talk of the disposal of the money when we have found it," said Jack. "I will go round with you, and we will search, but I have formed no very great expectations, so shall not be downcast if we find nothing."

Every candle was lighted, and Jack and Olver thoroughly explored the house together. This was now the third time it had been searched; but on this occasion the ferryman was not hurried. He had the whole night before him.

They took down all the garments suspended in the wardrobe, Dench felt every fold, examined the linings, beat them with a stick. They searched above the receptacle, they looked under it. The only thing they did not so was to draw it bodily out of its place, and this they did not attempt because it was fastened into its place by crooks driven into the wall, secured with screws that had become rusted into their place. Jane Marley's bedroom was subjected to a search so thorough that the two men omitted nothing.

It was during this investigation that Jane returned. She watched them as they continued the exploration, and held the candle for them. "We will let the fire out," said Olver. "I will go up the chimney and examine that."

But when this also proved fruitless, "I wonder," said the ferryman, "whether he stuffed that violin of his with banknotes. A hundred-pound note don't take up a terrible space."

Again he encountered disappointment. "We will rip open each pil-low and mattress," said Dench. "I've heard of large fortunes being secreted thus, and that is just where no preventive men would look for kegs." He unpicked a seam, thrust in his hand, and groped through the feathers of pillows and the wool of flock mattresses. Had there been a guinea secreted in either he would have fingered it. But there was nothing of that sort – dust only and that not of gold. Olver was puzzled, angry, disheartened.

"Can it be anywhere outside the house?" he asked. "Jack, tomorrow with the daylight we will give up hours to the search and

124

leave not a stone unturned, not a bush unexamined. I'm darned, but it is somewhere."

With a hard, unmoved face, Jane Marley had watched and attended on the two men. She had been with Mrs Jose to Bindon, helping to carry back the articles lent from the farm for the funeral feast. As she had neared the house Mrs Jose had said to her, "Jane, Winefred has got a valuable watch, worth forty guineas, I should say, and she tells me a strange tale about it – that she has met and talked with her father, who gave it to her."

"Yes, it was so."

"But, Jane, what does he mean by it? Is he going to recognise her?"

"Not immediately. She must be educated. But she is to be brought up to be a lady."

"A lady! And he will supply the money needful?"

"The money I have. I am to have more as I require it. I shall give up peddling."

"I am glad. He has behaved very badly. I am glad he sees the error of his ways, and will make amends to you and to her. It is a step in the right direction."

"A step. Yes." Jane considered. "Yes, it is a step."

"A first step. The rest will follow."

"Yes, others will follow."

"They must." Jane said no more. Nor did Mrs Jose till the door of Bindon was reached. There the farmer's wife had said, "I do not know the rights of the story, and this is not the time for it to be told. But what about the name? Is Winefred still to be Marley?"

"Winefred is to be no more called Marley, but is to bear her father's name, Holwood."

"And you?"

"Oh! I am nothing. I matter naught. I have been known as Marley. I am going back, but Winefred is beginning. That makes the differ-ence" and as Jane walked in the darkness back to the undercliff, she said to herself, "It is done. I cannot draw back now. I have taken the first step. But Winefred shall be a lady."

Chapter Twenty–One

Further Forward

The search outside the house proved as barren of results as had been that within. The undercliff was so broken as to offer many places in which with ingenuity and some labour recesses might be formed in which much could be concealed. But to a hiding–place of this des–cription there must be a track; and the fallen elder–twigs, and scattered leaves, the straggling binds of bramble armed with terrible hooks, the thickets of thorn undisturbed, showed that no runs had been made from the house to any particular spot.

Discouraged, Olver leaned his elbows on a mass of chalk, laid one huge red hand over the other, palm downward, looked across the block at Jack, who was beyond, and said, "I'm darned, if this is not one of the worst jobs I have ever been in. I wish your father had wrote down on the slate where it was he had stowed the money."

"That is, if he had anything to stow."

"He must have had. He did have – else why should he have been in such a fear lest you should squander it?"

"If something had been saved and put away, we must have found it." Dench remained looking steadily at Jack, but his thoughts were elsewhere.

"You don't think," mused he, and he spoke to himself rather than to Jack, "you don't think as how Jane Marley may have scented it, and have secured it, and got it now in that chest of hers. We have looked everywhere else. She is away now at Bindon. Let us prise open the lock and search it from end to end. I warrant it is there. It can be nowhere else that I can think of."

"No," answered Jack emphatically. "To that I will not consent. If she chooses voluntarily to open, that will be another matter, but in her absence, without her knowledge – never."

126

"Why not?"

"Because it is not right, and she a poor woman. I would rather let her have it than commit such an outrage."

"You would, would you?"

"Certainly," with some heat. "Besides, I owe Winefred a debt of gratitude, and I will not repay it by an insult offered to her mother."

"Well! men are made in different fashions and out of various clays. What, then, is to be done?"

"There is but one thing can be done – accept the situation. I must make up my mind to knock about till I can find work that will suit me. I have not expected much. If there had been much, my father would have given me to understand that it was so."

"He has done this. He has told me and you plainly that he was resolved to make a gentleman of you."

"He has given me education, and it is that which makes the gentleman."

"Fine! Education is a rare advantage if you have money to back it up; money without education is a halting horse; but education without money is one foundered in all four legs. What will you be? Not a fisherman. Your education is thrown away for that."

"I intend to sell the house."

"Sell the house!" echoed Dench, and lifted his hands in astonishment.

"I must do so. If I had a little income I might live here in it, and idle. I should not relish that. As I have no income I cannot occupy it. I must look out for a situation, and not being a snail I cannot travel with my house on my back."

"You have the cutter."

"That cutter is of no use to me unless I know how to employ her."

"Oh! there is employment easy found."

"Yes, but not such as I care to undertake. I know what you mean. Besides, my education is so much capital invested. I must see if I cannot make it render interest."

"But the house –"

"It holds me here, and just here no work suitable for me is to be found."

"Darn me!" said Olver, looking musingly at his hands, "I'd not sell

127

the house till I had torn down every stone, and had sifted every peck of dust."

"And found nothing, and thrown away what little value the cottage possessed when standing."

"I do not see," said the ferryman, "that this is a house that will fetch a price. There is no field or paddock attached to it. There are just four walls and nothing further. If you were to take to the sea and carry on your father's business, then the place is well enough. And yet, after this late affair, it is a little blown upon. And then Jane Marley's cottage has gone to pieces. These cliffs are not sure; you cannot say what may happen next. Purchasers might argue that it was an unsafe tenure, not worth much because so insecure in its foundations. It might last a hundred years, or it might go tomorrow. I am shot if I would sell."

"I have thought it well over," said Jack; "no other course is open to me."

"You may let the cottage."

"Who would take it? It is only fit for a labourer in Bindon, and their hands are all provided for in Axminster. Besides, I am in want of money."

"You will sell furniture and all?"

"Yes, everything."

"Then take my advice and dispose of the house first. You are separated by the mouth of the Axe from Seaton, and Seaton folk will not come here to get furniture; but if the house be sold, then the purchaser may bid well for what is in it, that he may have the whole bag of tricks together, and not be put to the extra trouble and cost in new rigging."

"There is something in what you say. The sooner it is done the better. I shall speak to the auctioneer, and have the crier sent about."

"Well, if it must be, I say so as well."

The young man walked away to go to Beer, where he had been in lodgings up to his father's death. He had matters to arrange there. Dench remained in deep thought for some time. He was completely puzzled, and could not resolve what he should do. In the event of the cottage being sold, would it be advisable for him to buy it? But it could be of no use to him, and his ambition pointed to a public–

house. To risk his money on the chance of finding the captain's hoard was altogether too precarious. Three times had the cottage been ransacked, and each time fruitlessly. Yet Olver was not satisfied. Rattenbury had boasted to him over his grog of his intentions with regard to Jack, and Rattenbury was not a man to lie, though he might exaggerate. He had not obscurely intimated that he was possessed of the means whereby he could carry out his intentions.

Dench returned to the cottage, and as he entered he took with him the chopper which had been driven into a bench that stood by the door. It was used for cutting up the fuel. By this time Mrs Marley had returned. "Jane," said he, "don't look sour and turn crabbed. It must be done. Young Jack laid it on me, but I don't like doing his dirty work. He might have come and taken the job in hand himself, but he is a sneak, a miserable sneak, and he has gone to Beer and bound me to do it."

"What is it?"

"He bade me break open your chest. He says that the captain's money has not been found, and that you have laid your hands on it. Says he, make the old cat give up the key, or break the lock off the chest. Turn everything out."

Her face flushed with anger. "You take me for a thief!"

"Not I. I don't think you clever enough. But Jack – it is Jack's demand."

"There is the key." She threw it at his feet. Dench picked it up. She looked at him frowning and with scorn. He went to the chest and searched, once more to be disappointed. He returned to the kitchen, gave her the key and seated himself. He said nothing, but leaned his head in his hand. Think as he might, he could hit on no other place in which to search.

"Jane," said he at length, despairing of finding what he sought, and changing the current of his thoughts, "what are you going to do? Jack has made up his mind to sell the old place and every stick in it."

"Sell the house!" Mrs Marley considered. She put her knuckles to her lips.

"What will you do? Where will you go? I reckon you will have to make up your mind as to that."

"Where I go, and what my plans are – these are no concerns of yours," she answered. "I shall find a home somewhere."

"May not an old acquaintance – a friend you will not allow me to call myself – ask a civil question without meeting with a rude answer! Why, Jane, I have known you since you were a little girl. I knew you when you met with *him*. I know all about that bad business, and I have known you ever since, and have admired how you have kept yourself respectable. I should be a bad sort of a chap, and altogether without heart, were I to let you go and not ask about you."

Jane answered, somewhat mollified, "I shall take a house suitable for Winefred and me in our altered condition."

"Well now," said Dench, "I don't understand that. Altered is for the worse, I suppose."

"I should have said in our bettered condition. Winefred's father has acknowledged her, and will provide that she be brought up as a lady." The colour faded instantly from Dench's face, and his jaw fell. He looked at her with blank, fishy eyes.

"He has acknowledged her! It is not possible. You lie."

"It is true. Look at this. See the gold watch with his initials on it. He gave it to her as a token that he would provide handsomely, liberally for her. We shall take a house in which she can live as a gentleman's daughter ought to live. For myself I care not. I am not, I never have been, a lady. That is why he deserted me. But with her it is different." She raised her head, and there was triumph in her eyes and a flush in her cheeks.

"It is false," gasped Dench. If what Jane said was true, then Mr Holwood was reconciled to his wife. he had recognised his daughter. If so, his own knavery would be discovered. Not only would the quarterly supplies cease, which for eighteen years he had appropriated to himself, but he would be called to task for what he had done, and would have to answer for it in court.

"Have you squared up with him?" he inquired, with his attitude and tone of voice expressive of uneasiness.

Jane was too full of pride to consider him. She answered, "I have not met him. I am in no hurry to do so. There is too much calling out against him in my heart, that is like a kennel of barking dogs, for me to forgive. But Winefred has seen him, has talked with him, and he has promised her that he will deal by her, I will not say generously, but as he ought."

"I do not believe it. He is in Terra del Fuego."

"He is returned. What say you to the watch? I knew it immediately. He had offered it to me once."

"I see no proof in the watch. It may have belonged to the captain, and you –"

She cut him short. "It has his initials on the back."

"J.H. are common initials. John Hall, the cheesemonger, has the same."

"Whether you believe or not matters nothing to me," said Jane, still swelling with pride. "All Seaton, all Axmouth, everyone shall perceive that we are not as we were; that my Winnie has no more occasion to go along the beach picking up chalcedonies, nor I to trudge the lanes, hawking pins and needles; but that Winefred is a lady, a real lady, with money to spend, dressing like a lady, doing nothing – like a lady. When I hear from Jack Rattenbury, I shall know when to leave this cottage, but do not think that I will take orders or advice from you."

Chapter Twenty–Two

House and Home

Jack Rattenbury found that a good many bills descended on him after his father's funeral. He had no means of checking them, as he had not come on any account–book, but he had little doubt that the debts had really been contracted, for they revealed that the captain had been engaged in an extensive business as "freighter"; not for some years taking any part in the active carriage of goods, but providing the cargoes and negotiating the sales. To the French ports he had despatched West Indian groceries procured in England, and from France he had received consignments of brandy. And in both transactions the goods had been run without regard to Customs duties. So long as sugar was at famine prices in France, and large profits could be made on spirits and tea in England, the contraband trade attracted to it the most adventurous on the coasts.

Neither the vessel built for Captain Job nor the stores last ordered had been paid for. Jack had made up his mind not to follow his father's business, which, though it might be very profitable at times, was also liable to great losses. He liked the sea, but saw clearly that if he took to it he would be more or less brought into relations with the men who had acted with, under and for his father, and that it would be difficult for him to keep clear of "free trading". He liked books, and his inclination turned to some occupation on land where what he had acquired would prove serviceable.

The day of the auction came on speedily. It were well, thought Jack, to have the sale at once, that he might be free to go where he would find work, and have money wherewith to meet his father's debts. Happily the day was bright, and although a cold wind blew from the north-east, the sun shone – a November sun, pale and without warmth. Yet at that time of the year, the very sight of the luminary is cheering.

A country auction is a curious sight. It was even more so at the beginning of the century. Auctions, like funerals, are wet or dry, and a dry auction, like a dry funeral, attracts few assistants and provokes little enthusiasm.

A dry auction is colourless, cold, sordid. Emulation among would-be purchasers is languid, and the sums realised are inconsiderable. It is otherwise at a wet auction, so entitled because spirits are freely provided and distributed; at that faces glow, hearts warm, competition waxes keen, the humour of the auctioneer sparkles, and the prices fetched by the articles offered are often altogether disproportionate to their intrinsic value. Messrs Hawkes and Squire were in good repute as capable men who understood how to play upon the tempers of a circle of hesitating purchasers, how to pit one against another, to cover a defect, and enhance the value of an article exposed to sale.

"No," said Mr Hawkes, "that won't do. We must not begin with the 'ouse. We must not bring it in late, with this here drivin' and freezin' wind. We'll do as Mr Rattenbury proposed, and very sensible it was of him. We'll have out the cloam and the glass and the jugs and togs first, and get 'em up to a lively 'eat, and then run the 'ouse afore they get cold again. There's a rick of firewood, and an old set of harness without an 'oss to wear it, that I can see, and some garding tools, a chopper and a block, and the clinkum clankums as we can bring out. Mr Squire, you get the liquor well in, ply 'em freely, ripen 'em up before we put up the 'ouse. The order ain't professional, but in such a wind and such a season, and when the space within is limited – it can't be helped. Folks'll be goin' when they get cold."

"I think we will begin," said Mr Squire. "They have got through a gallon of gin already."

"Right you are," responded Mr Hawkes, and mounted a chair set against the outside of the house near the window, where there was some shelter against the wind. He was a florid man, with very large, white whiskers, and a white hat with a black band round it, all the lower part of his face large and heavy, small dark eyes and dark brows. Before him were benches, and a table crowded with crockery and sundries grouped into lots.

"Now then, gentlemen and ladies, by your leave and if you please. Time is up, and the trump of duty calls. I may say, though it may be unprofessional to say it, that in all my career it has never been my good fortune to have had come into my hands the disposal of so eligible and desirable a collection of articles as those which it is my privilege and pleasure to submit to you today, together with one of the most desirable and convenient residences ever offered on the south coast of England. Ladies and gentlemen, I will just read over the conditions of sale, so that later no dispute and difficulty may arise." Mr Hawkes proceeded to do as he proposed, but in so hurried a manner that nothing he read could be understood.

That formality concluded, he took his hammer in one hand and received a basin from his assistant in the other. "The first lot,

133

gentlemen and ladies, that I submit to you is of the highest desirability. It is a washing basin, the jug has been mislaid – but that is of no real importance. The basin is the thing; and washing is also the thing. The man or woman who does not value a basin is a man or woman who don't wash, and it is washing that differentiates the civilised man from the savage. If anyone here be setting up house, here is an opportunity that may not occur again. I see several young men present hovering on the verge of matrimony, or contemplating it as a possibility in the near future. Cleanliness is next to godliness, and if there be one of them who would desire to enjoy an 'appy 'ome and a beautiful wife, let him buy this basin."

"Thickey basin is cracken," shouted someone from the crowd.

"Cracked, is it? possibly – but still eminently serviceable. Let me tell you, Mrs Bunce – it was you who made the observation – that many a head is also cracken, as you term it, but is nevertheless an eminently serviceable head. With this basin goes a soap–dish and – thank you, Mr Squire – an eligible teapot. A most desirable lot."

He waved the last–named article, holding it by the spout adroitly, concealing in his hand the broken nozzle.

"This teapot, you will observe, has a sound handle, and has its lid attached. Many a teapot is rendered useless by the loss of its lid. This one not only possesses its lid, but also the flower or knob at the top. This pot" – his face became withering in its scornfulness – "this teapot, I hope, Mrs Bunce, you will not pronouce cracken," and he tapped the sides. "Ah! Mrs Bunce, come round, I thought as much – Two shillings. Two shillings offered for the basin, soap–dish and teapot."

The woman called Bunce vainly protested that she had made no offer. She was unheard. "Two shillings for this lot. The price is ridiculous. If Mrs Hawkes were here she would not allow the chance to slide. Ah! I thought as much, Mrs Jose, two and six. With those cheeks like ribstone pippins, and at so high a polish – she is the lady who simple ravens after soap. That you, ma'am, three shillings. Every gentleman and lady must possess a soap–dish. That is right, three and six. Again, Mrs Jose. I admire your judgment. Some know a good thing when they see it, others don't. Another sixpence. Someone bid another sixpence? Going for three and six, going,

134

going, gone for three and six – given away."

And Mrs Jose of Bindon became the possessor of a cracked basin, a soap–dish without a strainer, and a teapot with broken spout.

After this start the auctioneer knew that he would do fairly well.

"Mr Squire, lot number two, if you please. I thank you kindly. A pair of bellows and a nautical almanack. Very good, very. Wind and tide. Who will offer?"

"What year?" shouted a seaman, with reference to the date of the almanack. Mr Hawkes did not answer. He was occasionally deaf.

"Now then," said he hastily, "a pair of bellows, without which no wife can manage, and a nautical almanack indispensible to every sailor or boatman. Such a combination is most appropriate; the husband and the wife each has a share in this lot. One shilling! I misunderstood; surely no one offered so paltry a sum. Come – another sixpence. That is right. One and six. Anyone bid further? Right! Two shillings. Two and six, and dirt cheap. Take it, young man. Your name, I believe, is Temple."

After a pause, "It is fresh out here, ladies and gentlemen. If you will pass round the glasses you will obtain a little warmth applied in the right place. Stoke where the fuel ought to go: under the boiler. Lot number three." He held up a picture.

Then a sailor called out, "Where is the Paycock?"

"The Paycock? What does he mean?" asked the auctioneer of his assistant. A whispered communication ensued.

"Oh! the Peacock, a study in wools, is withdrawn. Filial feelings, which we all respect, et cetera. But what have we here? Daniel in the Lions' Den, with crimson velvet curtains fringed with gold bullion, hanging down in the den, and the prophet depicted, very properly, in adoration. Light streaming from above. In the remote distance aloft – King Ahasuerus, wasn't it? – gazing on the sublime scene with emotion. A scriptural subject – Daniel in the Lions' Den – one shilling. Yes, ma'am, eighteen pence – sir – two shillings. The velvet curtains are alone worth that. Half–a–crown. So good for your children, help to make them realise the sacred narrative. Three shillings. Give pleasure and instruction combined to little Tommy, and make him say, 'Mammy, I have read about Daniel in my Bible' –give – thank you, three and six. Right – four shillings. Going,

135

going, gone."

Thus went on the sale, briskly, each article fetching more than it was actually worth, as is generally the case in small sales to which the Jew dealers do not think it worth their while to go. At a large auction they combine against the public, and control the sale in their own interest, running up an article only when bid for by someone outside the ring. In a small sale the profits go into the pocket of the seller, in a large one into those of the dealers.

When the sale was in full swing, the bidders were warm, and rivalry had been excited, some bidding out of mere wantonness, some out of ostentation, some to prevent others from possessing what they themselves did not want. Then Mr Hawkes put up the little house and scrap of land on which it stood.

Considerable hesitation at once manifested itself, and there was a long pause before an offer was made. The undercliff was a snug spot for a man to live at who had no business and could afford to be idle; it was unsuitable for anyone else. However, the agent for the owner of the Bindon estate offered thirty pounds. It might serve as a labourer's cottage. It would not let for above four pounds, and would require some outlay in repairs. But the main objection against it lay in its situation near the cliff, as it was uncertain how long it would continue habitable. It might last a lifetime or go to pieces like Jane Marley's cottage on the morrow.

Then a retired tradesman of Seaton held up his hand. The agent again offered; a third bid; then an old maid from Lyme. The sale moved but sluggishly. Mr Hawkes looked towards the agent. But he shook his head; he had been instructed not to go above a certain specified sum.

Jane Marley stood by the window. She had thrust her way to the front, and was near the auctioneer; she leaned one elbow on the sill and looked up into his face. He held his hammer aloft, gazing about him, with an encouraging word cast at one, then another, but without response.

"Seventy," said Jane.

He turned sharply about. "Seventy pounds offered for this desirable residence, worth a hundred and seventy – a freehold, mind you. Who says eighty? Come, Going for seventy. You could not build it under two hundred. Now, Mr Frank. The fruits of life are, in your ripe and green old age, to sit under your own vine and fig-tree."

"And possibly have the ground fall away under one," said the tradesman, and shook his head.

"Seventy. Going, going! I am really ashamed. Stay a moment. Madam, we shall expect caution money."

"Here is the entire sum."

"Gone!" said the auctioneer. "And now we will proceed with the rest of the furniture. Step inside. Ladies and gentlemen, oblige me, and step within." Silence among the crowd. Those assembled looked at one another with astonishment.

A woman who a few weeks ago had in vain sought shelter for herself and child, one who had been regarded as the poorest of the poor, suddenly put down seventy pounds and became owner of a house and freehold property.

"Upon my life," whispered one to a neighbour, "hawking must be a paying trade."

Mrs Jose worked her way with her elbows to Jane and shook her hand. "I am rejoiced," she said, with her face bright with smiles. "You have a house of your own now; the rest will follow."

A friend whispered in her ear, "Where did the peddling creature get the money?"

"The little maid's father has come down handsome," answered Mrs Jose in an undertone.

"How can that woman have got hold of such a sum of money?" asked a seaman of Olver Dench.

"Hist you!" answered the ferryman. "By robbing the captain." Though he said it in a whisper, he spoke sufficiently audibly to be overheard by those around, and those who heard repeated it to such as had not. Jane saw eyes fixed on her full of mistrust. But she threw up her head; and as the sale proceeded bought the wardrobe that had not been disturbed, beds, tables, and most of the furniture.

"Mother!"

Jane saw Winefred beside her. "My child! my child! We have been wanderers. Now we have of our own a house and home."

Chapter Twenty-Three

A Passage of Arms

For a while a feverish delight and pride in her new possession filled Jane Marley to the exclusion of every other sensation. For the first time in her life she was mistress of a house of her own. Her former cottage had been rented, and rented cheaply, because of its precarious position.

But if proud, that pride circled about her child, and had nothing to do with herself except so far as that Winefred was her own. It was of the girl she thought when she had the house put in order. She sent for mason, plasterer, carpenter, and paperhanger, and not only put it into repair, but transformed the interior. It was with a bounding heart that she brought Winefred to see the cottage when the tradesmen had left it. She had not suffered her to go to it whilst in their hands. It had been largely refurnished. The windows were curtained, the front kitchen converted into a parlour, and papered and ceiled. The house was clean and bright, and in Mrs Marley's eyes a fit residence for a princess.

"O mother," exclaimed Winefred, "this must have cost a great deal of money. How did you get it?" And when Jane hesitated, then the girl answered herself, "I know: Mrs Jose told me that it came from my father. But, O mother, the people do not believe this. They are wicked and cruel. They say that you stole the money from Captain Rattenbury when he was sick. It is shameful. As if my own dear mother could do such a thing!" And with a sudden impulse of affection, she threw her arms about her mother's neck, and kissed her passionately. "Mother, do not mind what they say! When I hear these spiteful, false words, I give it them back again, and make them jump, I assure you."

The abrupt change in Mrs Marley's condition had, in fact, excited comment. It formed the main topic of discussion in Axmouth, Seaton and Beer. It was disputed over in tavern and in kitchen. The Beer men, who had had extensive dealings with Rattenbury, spread over a good many years, declared that it was preposterous that he should die without leaving money, and money to a considerable extent. He had not spent much at the village shops, but had dealt with wholesale merchants. No concealment had been attempted when freighting at Beer or Seaton for the French coast. The English Government was not called upon to investigate too minutely into the destination of goods shipped for the Continent. But concealment was sought on the return voyage, when the boats were laden with spirits from France, or China teas from the Channel Islands.

The Excise men were of the same opinion as their adversaries at Beer. Captain Rattenbury was undoubtedly a man of substance. he had defied them too long with impunity not to have made a good thing out of his business. If there had been now and then a run of ill luck, and some cargoes had been confiscated, he had recouped himself over and over again by others that had been successfully landed. He had been a slippery man, and a most successful one. That he should die and leave no assets was incredible.

The matter was looked at from every light, discussed by all, whether competent or incompetent to form an opinion, and Mrs Jose was the only person who accepted Jane Marley's explanation of her sudden accession to what was, comparatively speaking, wealth.

Most loud and decided in his verdict was Olver Dench. His red face flamed when the subject was broached, and he spoke with a vehemence and quivering emotion that betokened rage – rage that his friend had been robbed and his friend's son left destitute. The ferryman had ostentatiously offered hospitality to Jack, who had accepted it, just because he would be near the cottage till it was sold, and after that he continued to remain with Dench, because he had nowhere else whither he might go till he found for himself a suitable situation.

And being daily associated with the ferryman he had the opinion drummed into him, till his previous scepticism as to his father's wealth yielded, and he came to accept the view that he had been defrauded of his patrimony. But when and by what means Mrs

Marley had appropriated it remained obscure. Every evening over their grog and pipes the matter was brought up and debated, but always without their arriving any nearer to a solution, till at last Jack became weary of the topic. Not so Dench, who was possessed with it, and could turn his thought to no other.

What perhaps conduced to lead Jack to believe in Jane's having robbed him was not so much Olver's arguments as her own conduct. One day she came to him on the cliff where he was by himself, and said, "Jack, I am sorry for you. You have been left in poor circumstances. But the case is not so bad as you suppose. The captain was good to me. When every other door was shut against my child and me, then he took us in, warmed and fed and lodged us. I was then desperately poor and wholly friendless. Now I am better off and not quite alone. I will do what I can to assist you, and I will gladly give you a hundred pounds."

"A hundred pounds!" echoed Jack, taken aback. Then, after a moment's consideration, he said, with constraint in his manner, "I thank you for the offer, whether in way of gift or loan, but I will not be holden to anyone but myself. I shall fight my own way. I thank you, but decline positively."

He turned and walked away musing on this offer. To Dench he spoke of it. The ferryman blazed at once like powder on which a spark has fallen. "That settles it," he said. "She would not have offered the money unless uneasy in mind. Mark you, if she be so ready to give you a hundred pounds, she keeps back three times as much for herself and that kid of hers. That makes four hundred, and next she will be offering me another hundred to bottle up my thoughts and not let them fizz out at my mouth. Is it reasonable that Winefred's father should put down a solid lump sum? – put so much money into the hands of an ignorant, half–crazed woman, who has heretofore never had a piece of gold wherewith to bless herself? Not likely, is it? Consider what the father would do in such a case as she pretends – that he has repented of his wrong and is making amends. I do not say he has. I do not believe in her story at all. But let us suppose that he did come here, see Jane Marley and Winefred, and promised to do his best for them. He would undertake to furnish them with a little money paid quarterly, but would not give three, or four or five hundred pounds to her to play ducks and drakes with. That is not likely. Moreover, he is not worth so much as that."

"You know Winefred's father?"

"I know something about him. He has been Governor of a place called Terra del Fuego, and I do not suppose his pay has been so good as that he can put his hand in his pocket and say, There are a few hundreds – take, and I will give more when you have thrown these away."

"But he gave the girl a gold watch."

"How do you know that? The woman Marley says so. That watch may form part of the plunder of which you have been robbed."

"Then again," said Olver, "what inducement had the woman to offer you such a sum?"

"Because my father was kind to her and took her in."

"Pshaw! He did that. Because he offered her his situation to be maid–of–all–work, to cook his meals, clean the house, make the fire; in return for which she was to be taken in, together with the girl, and to receive half–a–crown a week, is that it? That is no ground for such a fit of generosity coming upon her. No, no. She has stolen the captain's money, and would salve over her conscience that tortures and stings with one hundred pounds given to you. I see it as clear as daylight."

"It looks bad," said Jack in a tone of discouragement. "But, Olver, not a word about this to anyone else."

"You should have closed with the offer. Half a loaf is better than no bread."

"I could not do it," answered Jack, and so the matter dropped. The feeling that pervaded the neighbourhood made itself very evident to Jane Marley and Winefred. The mother was indifferent, but it provoked the liveliest resentment in the girl. Winefred was fired with indignation that her mother should be thought capable of dishonesty, and she winced and chafed at the gibes cast at her, or at the insinuations she could not openly resent.

The neighbourhood had conspired to hold aloof from them. No one save good Mrs Jose would speak to either, except on matters necessitating exchange of words. When mother or daughter came into Axmouth or Seaton heads were turned aside, or they were stared at insolently and remarks made behind their backs, perfectly audible and never complimentary. Jane held up her head the highest, became harsher in manner and more peremptory – even with her child.

Winefred complained to her of the slights to which she was subjected. "When we were poor," said Mrs Marley with darkened brow, "then we were cast out. Now we are rich, we are hated. As they cannot take our money from us, they slander us. We can rub along very comfortably without them. I would leave the place had I not bought the house. I would not have bought it had I thought it would come to this. You shall have richer dresses than any other girl in Axmouth, and go to church to let them see it."

This was not the way to allay suspicion, and disarm hostility. Winefred felt it, and shrank from the display her mother forced her to make. She was eminently unhappy; she had not been so continuously wretched before. The imputations cast on her mother angered her. There was an ever open sore; she was sensitive, hearkening for a word, observant for a look or gesture that referred disrespectfully to her mother.

Winefred had never made friends. Her mother had sufficed. To her she had clung, to her looked up, in her believed. To hear her mother spoken of as a vulgar thief, a woman taken compassionately into a house, and using her opportunity to rob the man who had shown her mercy – this was intolerable to the high-principled, keenly sensitive child.

Knowing that to speak on the matter to her mother only served to make the latter more irritable, Winefred at last shut up her trouble in her breast; but it haunted her by night, it accompanied and over-shadowed her by day, and this served to embitter her against the little world that surrounded her. The sole person in whom she could confide was Mrs Jose, and on her sympathetic bosom she shed floods of tears, whilst the good woman patted and soothed her.

But although Mrs Jose might comfort her she could not drive back the growing sense of resentment wherewith Winefred encountered everyone else. Not only was the girl wounded by finding her mother charged with dishonesty, but a new self-esteem had been quickened in her, born of the insistence of her mother that she was a gentleman's daughter, and was destined to be a lady, and to occupy

142

a position high above the heads of those who now depreciated her.

A lonely child is liable to become proud, and a wronged child waxes resentful. Hitherto Winefred had been sharp with her tongue, with a good-humoured tartness, but now the cutting words she uttered shot from an angry heart. She must fight her mother's battles, and defend her mother's character with what weapons she possessed.

The cottage that had been owned by Captain Job, and was now the property of Mrs Marley, stood, as has already been said, on a sort of terrace a few feet below the level of the down. This terrace had been formed at some unknown period by a sinkage. It was not extensive; it comprised an abrupt dip and a congeries of isolated humps and prongs of chalk, lost in dense thickets of ivy, thorn, and briar, above all of elder. In spring the depression showed like a sea of white blossom, and in autumn it was purple with the berries.

So sheltered was the spot from every wind, save that wafted from the south over the sea, that flowers grew thereon throughout the winter even, and the sap began to return in the hollow elder-sticks in January.

Jack Rattenbury came there one day, a warm winter's day, impelled by recollections of his childhood, for among these rocks and brakes he had been wont to play. He was in low spirits, as he was out of employ. His future was uncertain. He had been given no definite direction for his energies. Into the smuggling trade he would not enter, and he was half inclined to offer for the British navy; but a common sailor's life at that date was not attractive, and the European war being over, many of the crews of our men-of-war had been discharged. Moreover, he was, by inclination, disposed to take some situation in which his education would be of service to him.

He had picked a bit of elder and was chewing it, as he sauntered into a little dell in the midst of the thicket, where the turf was broad, and which had been to him in the old days a garden of wild strawberries. Hearing a movement, he turned his head, and next moment Winefred burst through the bushes and upon him. She was better dressed than he had been accustomed to see her in the past. She wore a winter bonnet trimmed with turquoise-blue ribbon, and a navy-blue gown. She was a handsome girl, with full dark eyes, arched brows, a straight, well-moulded nose, the face somewhat long, mouth and chin firm, and expressive of resolution, the forehead wide and rounded, and her hair dark. Her cheeks were glowing; they deepened in colour when she saw him. "Why are you hiding here?" she asked. "Have you come to spy on us?"

"I am not hiding. If you are suspicious, I take it you have something you are afraid may be seen."

"I saw you stalking on the down."

"Oh, then you have tracked me!"

"I – come after you!" exclaimed Winefred, contemptuously. "Well, if I have, it is to warn off trespassers."

"I am not trespassing. This was my father's land once, and my playground."

"It is yours no longer."

"You are right, no – I believe this is no-man's-land, and that which my father owned and your mother bought does not include this thicket. If it be hers now, she must have laid out some more of that mysteriously-got money to purchase it from some other proprietor."

"Mysteriously-got money," said Winefred angrily. "Speak openly, or say nothing."

"I have my thoughts."

"Yes," said the girl; "you, bred in dishonesty, a sneaking, night-prowling smuggler, who would have been kicking his heels in prison at this present hour but for me, one such as you thinks that none can have money which has not been crookedly hooked in."

"Have done, Winefred, I owe you something."

"We are quits. You helped me out of the cave, but I could have scratched my way forth without your aid, and I warned you and helped you to slip out of the net spread to take you. You owe me nothing, and I owe you nothing. The account is settled between us. I do not desire to be indebted to a smuggler. You, like all the rest, wonder that your father left nothing when he died. But ill-gotten gold makes itself wings."

"In that case, all my father's gold will come swarming out of your mother's pocket, like ants on an August day when they get their wings and desert their heap."

"You are a coward, to insult a defenceless woman," said Winefred passionately. Her face paled with anger, and she turned sharply and ran away. Jack swung himself after her, caught her by the arm and flung her back into an elder-bush.

"You little fool," he said, "you were dashing right over the brink. You see, whether you will or no, you must owe something to me." It was a fact. He had rescued her from plunging over the precipice concealed only by some bushes. She looked, saw that what he said was the truth, and without thanking him when sullenly away.

But Jack, as he sauntered from the spot, was dissatisfied with himself. "I have been too sharp with her," he said. "If there be a fault it lies with her mother, not with Winnie. I did wrong. With a girl one should not attempt a passage of arms."

Chapter Twenty-Four

Reversed Positions

A fit of depression came over Jack. Happily in youth such fits are not of long duration.

The excitement of the funeral and sale was over, and a sense of solitariness weighed on the lad. He had no relatives. There were conections at Beer, but these were all more or less closely implicated in the contraband trade upon which Beer flourished, though ostensibly it occupied itself with fishing. Jack considered it expedient that he should keep clear of them, and it was for this reason especially that he had accepted Olver Dench's offer to lodge and board him.

But he did not like the ferryman. There were in him a rancour and a low cunning that revolted him, and Jack resolved not to take the man into his confidence, nor ask his opinion on any matter of consequence. He had no occupation and very little money. His idleness was involuntary. He could nowhere find a situation that was suitable. He was young, inexperienced, and with a very limited range of acquaintance. Beer was a hamlet, Seaton and Axmouth small vill- ages. Of towns he knew nothing, with town dwellers he had no connections. His education had disqualified him for any such place as was available near at hand, and far afield he had no one to point the way to a situation. Inexperienced as he was, he was lost. He was impatient to earn his livelihood, but powerless to find a place in which he could earn it.

The sole offer he had made to him was one he could not accept. This was from the chief officer of the Preventive Service. He could not take this lest it should arouse alarm and resentment in the men of Beer, who would suspect him of entering the Service to betray what he already knew of their secrets. His impatience to do something, and his inability to find anything to do, became so distressing that he lost his cheerfulness, became moody and silent. He had been to Lyme, where he had endeavoured to obtain a place in a lawyer's office, but the vacancy was filled. He tried a bank, no clerk was needed. He visited Colyton, he went to Axminster, to Honiton, but found no vacancy anywhere. Business was stagnant, trade depressed; clerks of some standing were receiving their discharge, no young hands were being taken on.

Meantime his small supply of money was ebbing away, in another week his purse would be wholly drained. If he could not find the employment that was suited to him, he must look out for some to which he must suit himself. The condition of inaction became intolerable, and his discouragement acute. Better anything than nothing, he said to himself, and he resolved to take any work that he could get.

When he had formed this resolution, he went to the nearest farmhouse, that of Mr Moses Nethersole, and knocked at the door.

"Come in!"

He entered and said to Mrs Nethersole, who alone was there, "I beg your pardon, I would speak to the master."

"Take a seat, Jack. You may speak out to me. Moses and I are one."

He was a good-looking lad, and whatever their ages, the women

146

looked on him with a favourable eye. "Thank you kindly," said Jack, "but it is something particular between him and me. I will go out and find him and speak without disturbing him."

"Oh, he is busy, as usual, doing nothing. He is in the shippon. When you have seen him, come back and have a glass of cider." Jack left the house, and before long he found the farmer, who was looking at a cow that had inflammation.

"You want me? About what?"

"Just this, Mr Nethersole. I am weary to death of doing nothing. I want work. Will you give me employment? I was not brought up

> To plough and sow, to reap and mow
> And be a farmer's boy

but I will do my best."

"Can you thatch?"

"I have not learned."

"Then you cannot do it. Thatching a rick is not an acquirement that comes by the light of nature. What do you say about hedging? A good hedger is worth a great deal. Dickon Spry – the hedges he built up, though he did some when he was a boy like you – are as good now as they were seventy years agone. Tate Wetherell was set to hedge after Dickon's death, last fall, and they are down already that he set up. You must know the sort of stones to use, and which end to drive in, how to wedge them tight, and how to fill in behind. It is an art."

"I will endeavour to learn."

"Thank you kindly, try on someone else's hedges, if you please. How about ditching?"

"Anyone can dig."

"I beg your pardon. Anyone cannot so as to lay a drain. There are drains and drains. I have know many a hundred pounds thrown away as completely as if chucked into the Axe mud by setting men to drain as did not know the trade. It is a sad misfortune, young man, that all the time and money that were spent on your education in what is of no profit to man or beast, were not employed in setting you to learn from an old farm labourer what is useful. You cannot

147

mow – you would cut your leg off with the scythe. You cannot plough a straight furrow – you would be upset at once. You cannot shear a sheep – you would cut off the flesh and kill the poor beast. You could not milk a cow dry – but would spoil its udder. No scholars for me, thank you. Look at this cow – it has inflammation and will die. There goes twenty to twenty–five pound, all through the ignorance of Richard Piper."

Discouraged and sad at heart, Jack walked away, and forgot to call for his glass of cider at the farm. When Moses Nethersole came in, his wife said to him sharply, "What did Jack Rattenbury want with you?"

The farmer informed her. "And you have not engaged him?"

"Of course not."

"He was a born fool," said the woman. "Had he applied to me and not to you, I'd have took him on, sure as I'm alive. He's a fine, upstanding, good–looking lad. We could well do with such as he."

Crestfallen, Jack made his way into Seaton. He knew that the farmer was right. His hands were not horny for labour, and although he was willing to learn, he might spoil a great deal in the process of learning.

He directed his course to the Red Lion and went into the bar, where Mrs Warne was sitting alone, looking into the fire, and dreaming of commercials. At a sign from the hostess he seated himself near her. "Shall I draw you a half–pint?" she asked.

"Thank you, yes," said he, "but I have not come here for bitter beer. I have bitters enough without adding to them. The fact is, my few shillings are nearly run out."

"Into Dench's purse?"

Jack did not answer this. Turning his hat about nervously, he said, "I want you to find me some occupation, Mrs Warne. You are a dear good creature, as everyone knows."

The landlady looked at him with a friendly eye, and pursed up her lips. She had been knitting a stocking – a large one – possibly for her own leg, possibly as a Christmas present to a traveller high in her good graces. She scratched her nose with the knitting–pin. Presently her face brightened.

"There is a postboy short," she said, "at Cullompton. The young man there, at the Castle Inn, Jack Spratt is his name, has had a fall, and a curious sort of fall too. he was thrown forward from a hoss and fell on his toes, and with the jerk his toes twisted up on end, like the markers for a game of whist. They had to cut the boots off him, and they can't get the toes down again. I never heard the like before. You are accustomed to 'osses, I suppose."

"No, but I can learn."

"And how about your riding?" Mrs Warne poked at him in the cheek with her knitting-pin, and narrowly escaped putting out his eye.

"I daresay I could do that."

"Ah! but there is a style about a postilion. To see him from the windows of a calash rise and fall is a picture. You will have to wear a white beaver hat, and a tight yellow jacket, and lily white don't-mention-'ems. You'll do that?"

Jack remained silent. He had to swallow his pride. Then Mrs Warne's face clouded. "No," she said, "it will not do. They will want at the Castle a boy about Jack Spratt's build to get into his suit, and you are twice too stout; you'd explode the garments like the old cannon as they fired when Queen Caroline was let off. But I have another idea." Again she thrust at him with her knitting-pin. "You are a scholar. At Cullompton there has been a split among the Methodists, and they have set up a new connection. My sister, who is a groceress in a large way, has taken twenty shares in the new chapel. So far there have been no dividends. They have a tidy chapel, well warmed and lighted, but have not secured a satisfactory preacher. They have tried several, but they do not draw. One had a club foot. Another took snuff, and that the stricter people said savoured of the world. A third was husky in his voice and had no delivery. So they decided that none of these preached the unmixed Gospel, and the shareholders are in a pretty stew about their dividends. What do you say now to trying your powers there? I will recommend you to my sister, she carries weight, and will put you in – and draw you must and will."

Then a tender light came into Mrs Warne's eyes. "Lord, Jack! for certain you will draw. You are young, good-looking, and unmarried, and if you are of an amorous disposition –"

149

"I will never do," sighed he, as the vision of the groceress in a large way who carried weight rose before his mind's eye.

"No," said Mrs Warne; "but if you can't be of the fondling description, you can be denunciatory – but that requires beetle brows and pebbly eyes. Well, you know best. I can tell you of something else. You go across the way, up street to Thomas Gasset. He was in here the other night having a pipe and glass, and he was saying how he missed Winefred, and how he might have employed her to push his wares in the season – and now she is a grand lady. There is no saying, he may take you on as a traveller; and oh! to be a commercial!" Mrs Warne held up her hands in ecstacy. "Commercials is 'eavenly!"

So the lad went forth, leaving his half–pint half drunk on the table, to seek the shop of the lapidary. The establishment was small and shabby, but shabbier was the little man with spectacles on his nose and unshaven chin, no collar but a soiled neckcloth, who sat at a table engaged on setting a cut pebble.

For some time he did not look up. He continued upon what he was doing; but he had seen the boots and lower portion of the trousers of Jack as he entered and knew that they did not belong to a purchaser. Consequently he did not hurry nor desist.

"Well?" he asked at length.

"Mr Gasset," said Jack, "I have come to ask you if you require someone to act as your agent with your cut stones, seals and brooches, and get them disposed of for you."

"Jane Marley was here proposing the same thing for herself. But I was to take both in. Two women would have eaten all the profits. You are a growing lad, voracious in appetite. I could not afford it."

"But I would go about."

"Consider the expense and the uncertainty. I am too old to run risks. The profits are very small. No; I must go on in the old way."

He nodded to Jack to leave. As Jack left the shop Mrs Gasset entered. "What has young Rattenbury been here for?" she asked.

Gasset slowly informed her, still working on the pebble.

"And you refused him! You are an old idiot. He would have been the making of us, he is so good–looking."

Chapter Twenty-Five

The Study of a Face

"I suppose you have not been asked to Bindon?" said Olver, as Jack entered the ferryman's cottage.

"No; for what?"

"Only Mrs Jose is going to have a Christmas party for her servants and farm labourers, and she always on these occasions invites the young folk of Axmouth, and has the church musicians. I thought it not likely she would have asked you."

"No, for she knew I could not attend so soon after my father's death."

"Exactly; I thought as much. She is a motherly body, and always thinks and does the right thing. But for that you would have been invited. I only wish I had been. I have tasted her pickled hams; there are none like them. And she does not stint the liquor. What is the matter with you?"

"I have had some knocks-down. These take the curl out of one's spirits, but I shall be all right again tomorrow."

"Excuse me, Jack, if I give you my opinion. I think you are going to work in the wrong way. A man's success in life depends on his seeing where to put his foot, and then and there putting it down. If you want to cross the Axe mud you must step on the stones, otherwise you go up to your waist. Now, Jack, there's a fine field open to you as the son of Captain Job. But you will not enter it. I've seen an ox – just the same; the farmer wanted to drive him into a pasture rich with buttercups, but, bless your soul! he would bounce into a milliner's shop instead."

Jack took up his hat again and went forth. He was weary of Olver Dench and his persistence in urging him to pursue his father's

151

business. Full of discouragement that made his heart sad, he wandered about till the day closed in, and then, for lack of anything else to do, he resolved to go to Bindon, not to take any part in the festivities, but from a distance to observe them. The weather was favourable, the air mild, although the season was mid–winter. Bindon, as already intimated, had a front court closed by a wall. With this wall the house formed a quadrangle. The porch and hall windows faced the entrance, looking into a turfed enclosure, whilst a chapel occupied one wing, and the other was given up to barns. The chapel, never consecrated, had been erected for divine service in 1425, when the mansion was the residence of a squire with retainers; but when Bindon declined to be a farmhouse, the building ceased to be associated with worship and was given over to secular purposes.

As the lonely lad approached, he saw the twinkle of lights, and heard the hum of happy voices. He would not draw near, lest he should be recognised, and this led to an awkward situation. He hung about within hearing of the music and voices. Bindon had never been surrounded by a park, but it has pleasant, sloping grounds, well studded with trees and broken with rock. It was something to Jack to be near his fellows, and to know that if he was sad others were happy.

As the darkness deepened, the risk of being recognised became less, and he drew near. The barn had been cleared, lanterns had been suspended from the rafters, and as these shed but a feeble light, they had been supplemented by hoops stuck with candles, pendent from the tie beams. On a barrel at one end sat a fiddler, the clerk in Axmouth church, and near him a solemn man, the tailor, who worked the bass viol. Another, Hopkins, the shoemaker, warbled on the clarionet.

In the days gone by, at the beginning of the century, every country church had its village orchestra. At that time the detestable harmon–ium and the strident American organ, the phylloxera of sacred music, had not invaded and exterminated village concerted music.

The floor was occupied by dancers. Mrs Jose, her broad, rosy face all smiles, looked on. But the number of those who figured was inconsiderable. The girls were shy, shyer still were the lads; and only

152

a few of the bolder spirits and the most confident in their legs began to dance. But by degrees, under the influence of the music, of the persuasion of the hostess, of the desire to make the most of so rare an opportunity, shyness yielded, and the number of footers on the floor increased. The light, according to our modern notions, was not brilliant, but the twilight of tallow candles and horn lanterns sufficed, where hearts were light and blood was aflame.

The barn had a large door under a penthouse roof for the reception of sheaves to be tossed in from a laden wagon, to be piled at one end and thrashed on the floor in the middle. It was lime–ashed at the extremities, but the floor, on which the flails played, was of oak boards, beaten hard and smooth.

But the barn was provided as well with slits unglazed, through which light and air by day entered the barn when the great doors were shut, and through which now flowed the light and the sounds from within. To one of these Jack drew near. He could look through and observe the fun without himself being noticed. This was the more certain as the loophole he selected was behind the barn door, thrown back to allow those who were hot to issue forth and cool themselves, and to enable the dust tossed up from the floor to be carried out by the draught and dissipated. Lest an excess of chill winter air should enter, only one of the valves was opened. At any moment, if necessary, it might be shut. But the air, if humid, was not frosty, and none complained of cold.

Concealed behind the door, Jack peered into the interior, leaning his elbows on the ledge that projected from the slit. He felt no desire to be within. It would not have been seemly for him to have taken a part in the merrymaking so soon after losing his father, and the tone of his spirits was not in keeping with a festival.

He knew by sight most of the girls present, but none of them interested him particularly, though several had pleasant and even pretty faces. The soft light from above toned down any slight roughnesses or irregularities there might have been in complexion and feature; and where the faces were kindled with pleasure, the eyes sparkled, and the colour mounted, none could be plain, and a taste must be fastidious that does not see beauty in the fresh and well–formed faces of the West.

As to the young men, they were cheery, perhaps a little noisy in their mirth, and only such were clumsy as had laboured at the plough in deep tenacious clay. Jack wondered whether happiness abounded alongside with ignorance, and was more sparse with knowledge; whether education did not spoil a man for the enjoyment of simple pleasures. He would have found no satisfaction had he been within, dancing with the rest. He would have felt himself out of accord with those present. He was separated from these young people mentally, and was no longer capable of sharing in their pleasures as he was debarred from taking part in their pursuits.

But he was not the only person who was solitary, isolated, that evening. Over against him sat Winefred on a bench against the barn wall. A flaming ring of candles threw a comparitively strong light upon her face. No lad had spoken to her, none had invited her to dance; although, as Jack could not fail to discover, she was far handsomer than any other girl present.

Nor did those of her own sex associate with her. They held aloof, and if they noticed her it was in a captious spirit: they whispered and pointed at her gown or her trinkets and tittered. It was unfortunate; it was provocative. Her mother had insisted in dressing Winefred for the occasion in a manner wholly unbecoming the sort of entertainment to which she had been asked. A handsome dress, bracelets, and brooches were resented by the girls present as an attempt to outshine them in their humbler stuffs and cheap ornaments.

To do her justice, Winefred had entreated her mother not to oblige her to appear overdressed, but Jane Marley could not understand her shrinking. She regarded this as an opportunity for the assertion of superiority over the other girls of Axmouth, an opportunity to be seized on and enjoyed. Winefred was keenly alive to the awkwardness of her situation, but was too proud to show how wounded she was by the slights put on her.

She could not, she would not stoop to solicit the friendship of girls who regarded her mother as a thief. It would be solely on condition that they acknowledge her mother's integrity that she would relax towards them. So long as they held her mother in suspicion, so long would she hold aloof from them. Consequently she did nothing to disarm the ill-feeling that existed against her. None ventured to attack her openly, being afraid of her sharp tongue. She was well aware that around her was the flicker of animosity, like summer lightning, of which one cannot say where it will strike.

The girls to whom her mother had sold ribbons, laces, papers of pins and reels of cotton, resented her sudden elevation to a position – as far as money went – far above them. The boys followed suit. They took their tone from their partners. She made no attempt to attract them by graciousness of manner. Those few who had approached her were repulsed.

But although the girls were jealous of her, they were as well in awe of her, and did not dare to carry their hostility too far. They were alive to the fact that she was very good-looking, and that a little display of amiability on her part was alone required to bring the young men about her in a swarm.

Peering through the opening, Jack watched Winefred's face as he had never before been able to observe it. He wondered why she was there, so manifest was it that the entertainment afforded her no pleasure. Others wondered as well as he. A couple was standing outside, leaning against the door, in the shadow of which he was concealed. "Do y'mark her, Joe?" asked the girl.

"Yes, I do, Bessie. She is tart as a green gooseberry, and will curdle Mrs Jose's milk."

"Why has she come, Joe? I can tell you. To outflounce us girls, and to make mock at you lads. She thinks herself in her finery as high as the clouds above us."

"She is vastly pretty," said Joe.

"Oh! if you think so, go and ask her to dance."

Jack did not remove his eyes from her. She certainly was pretty. She was more than pretty – most of the girls present were that – but she was above them in beauty as she transcended them in dress. The brow, broad and intelligent, was lighted by the candles above, and set off by her profuse dark hair. Her eyes were lowered, and the long lashes swept her cheek. The face was long, but formed an oval, and the chin, if pointed, was not too sharp. The delicate, sinuous lips would have made the mouth delicious but for the expression of bitterness that compressed them. There was no brightness, not the suspicion of a smile, in her face, more than in that of a corpse.

Winefred was certainly unhappy. Jack was convinced of that. She sat there, in the midst of gaiety, without partaking of it, suffering internally, yet afraid to let this be seen, lest it should be made an occasion of jest. She kept herself under control. The tension of the muscles showed how great the exertion was.

Was it her fault, asked Jack of himself, that Winefred was left so completely alone; that no one, except at intervals Mrs Jose, spoke to her; that she dared not lift her eyes lest she should encounter looks of animosity? Was it so very certain that her mother had done that wherewith she was charged by the general voice? Was not that charge formulated to express the envy and spite of those who saw the woman who had been under their feet lifted above their heads? And even if Mrs Marley had done him this wrong, was her daughter a partaker in it? Consciously, certainly she was not. Asking these questions, and thus musing, Jack continued to watch the face.

He was sure that the hardness in the countenance, the twitching of the set mouth, and the convulsive knitting of the hands on the lap were due to effort to suppress tears that were welling up in her heart.

A sense of softness come over Jack. This girl, like himself, was alone. And the feeling that she, as he, was friendless, made him wish he could creep in unseen and sit by her side. He would say nothing, he had nothing that he could say, save this, "Winefred – I believe in you." Every now and then her head sank, and the light no longer fell over it, but bathed her glossy dark hair, and then for a moment her chin rested on her heaving bosom.

By an effort she reared herself, looked quickly round at the dancers, fearful lest weakness should have been detected, and with defiance in her glance. All at once, as though consciousness came over her that she was observed, she moved uneasily on the bench and looked straight before her at the slot through which Jack was looking. No dancers at the moment intervened, and she saw him.

Her eyes fell at once. Jack could not be sure whether she had recognised him, but that she had seen that someone was watching her was obvious from her movements. He drew back, and again was the unseen hearer of a conversation relative to Winefred.

"Bill," said a girl, "I have caught you sidling towards that stuck– up minx of a Marley or, as she is pleased to call herself, Holwood.

I know you want to make up to *Miss* Holwood because of her hundreds of pounds, and to be off with Susie Finch."

"It is not so. I swear to you it is not so. You attack me because you are disappointed that Jack Rattenbury is not here."

"It is an untruth, a wicked untruth. What care I for Jack Rattenbury? He is too saucy to speak to such as I – with all his learning he had of the curate."

Then they passed away to patch up their lover's quarrel elsewhere. Jack pressed to the window slit again. And again he looked across the barn at Winefred, and once more their eyes met.

Her lips contracted, her brows knit, she started from the bench, and strode across the floor to the barn door.

He turned, thrust back the valve, and dashed away into the darkness.

Chapter Twenty–Six

A Thorn Bough

Jack trudged down hill. The night was not dark. Mrs Jose had purposely chosen one on which the almanack informed her there would be a moon, so that the young people might not have to return in the dark. She was a considerate woman in all that she undertook. But nearly all those who were assembled in her barn, came from Axmouth, and would go home together. "However," said Mrs Jose, "a moon won't hurt and is advisable."

Aloft great white clouds were drifting like icebergs in a polar sea, but below there was little wind. Occasionally, when one of these clouds came before the moon it partially eclipsed it, but was itself transformed into a luminous haze, with a halo about it.

Bindon grounds had been well timbered. Already, the finest trees had been cut down, and the grounds had been curtailed and cut up for the accommodation of cattle. Beneath the trees the shadows were as ink blots, but otherwise the sward was silver. A sufficient dew had fallen to catch the moonlight and be converted by it into pearl. Jack walked down the road to the gate at the bottom of the descent, where the stream that whispered down the valley hushed for a moment as it dipped under the little bridge before the gate that opened on to the old Roman road which descended as a phosphorescent ribbon to Axmouth from Lyme, a stretch of the Fosse Way that led direct from London to Land's End. But at the gate he halted.

Here, in place of a stately entrance of piers, surmounted with balls, proper to give admission to the domain of a great mansion, was a shabby farmyard gate, for Bindon had been deserted by its gentle owners before the reign of Queen Anne, when park gates of this description came into fashion. On the wooden bar of the gate Jack leaned and considered. He heard men talking as he stood on the road. He could see lights twinkling in the windows of Axmouth.

One long single–sided street constitutes the village of Axmouth. The houses were on the right, on the left the dancing stream, and the distance to the beach was a quarter of a mile. From below the churchyard wall, that was lapped by high tides, a pebble path led to the point at which the ferry crossed. Dench lived on the farther side, but a call would bring him across.

If he walked down that attenuated village street, Jack knew that he would encounter men leaving the tavern, or lounging in conversation in the moonlight, and would run the gauntlet of mothers on their doorsteps awaiting the return of their daughters and curious to ascertain with whom they walked home.

In the clear silver glare he could not expect to escape recognition, and he was certain to be addressed and questioned as to whether he had been at Bindon, whether there were not grand "goings–on" there; and if he said he had not been one of Mrs Jose's guests, then he would be questioned as to where he had been, and why he was returning that way. In the humour in which he was, Jack shrank from the ordeal of undergoing so close a catechism. He was disinclined for conversation. Consequently, instead of pursuing his course, he turned back, resolved to repass Bindon, and take the way above the house that led down the shallow combe running parallel with the

Axmouth Valley, and which would lead him to a point somewhat nearer the mouth of the river, but equally convenient for the ferry. It was true that by this means he was describing the letter C, but this mattered not. Time was to him no object, and his limbs insensible to fatique. Young couples loitered about outside Bindon in sufficient amorous warmth not to regard December cold, and Jack avoided them by keeping well up the hill slope and under the trees, and by this means regained the road above the house. The road, however, at once dwindled to a path. The downs have of late years been enclosed and made to grow turnips instead of heather and gorse. It was not so then, consequently the path to the common was not required for wagons and carts, and was weedy and unconsidered. It was closed against the down by fir-poles run across the gap.

There was a thorn-tree here that threw a shadow over the rails. The leaves had been shed, but so dense was the tangle of interlacing boughs and twigs and spines that the shadow was more bewildering and blurring than if it had been a blot.

Jack came upon the extemporised gate abruptly and unexpectedly. He was not thinking of the barrier. his mind was occupied with other matters. He would have run against the larch-poles, had not someone who leaned against them turned sharply at his tread, confronted him and asked what he was about.

He started back in surprise, but recovered himself instantly, and said, "Who are you blocking the way? This is no toll-gate."

"What are you about, running after me?"

"I – I run after you? Let me know who you are, who supposes such nonsense?" He saw next moment, for she who had spoken stepped forward into the blaze of silver light.

"Do not come near," said she. It was Winefred. "I have plucked a branch of thorn from the tree, and will strike you in the face if you venture."

"There is no need for a thorn branch when you have a needle in your mouth."

"Why have you followed me?"

"I did not know you had left the barn."

"That is false. You have been watching me."

"I have been to the Axmouth gate, but I changed my mind and

came back."

"You have been watching me. I saw you. What right have you to stare me out of countenance?"

"A cat may look at a Queen, and a poor lad like me may look at a clawed cat, I reckon."

"I will not be peered at. At revels, clowns grin through a horse-collar – but to cut grimaces through a slit in a wall is not a Christmas pastime."

"It is not forbidden to look on at a dance."

"I will not be stared at like a bearded woman or a spotted boy at a show. Why have you pursued me?"

"I have not pursued you. I will not say that I was not thinking of you as I came along the lane and stumbled on you, for I was."

"And what, pray, were your thoughts? Here is a penny, to pay for them, though I warrant that it is beyond their worth."

"I was thinking of you. Yes. I saw that you were not enjoying yourself."

"I was enjoying myself bravely."

"No, you were not. You were vastly unhappy. I saw how your mouth worked. You came away, not because I stared you out of countenance, but because you could no longer restrain your tears."

"It is false. I came away because I would not be exposed to any rude Peeping Tom."

"Peeping Tom saw you – naked as Godiva – that is your bruised and wretched soul, that was bare to me. I saw how it suffered."

She stamped, but said nothing. Her bosom was heaving with passion, but she switched to and fro with the thorn branch as a precaution lest he should approach; then she turned and struck at the improvised gate as though she must strike something; after that, feeling that her courage would give way unless she looked the lad full in the face, she reverted to her former position, fronting him.

"I really do not know what concern one has with the other," said Jack. "Stand aside that I may remove the poles; then go through yourself or let me pass."

But she would not do this, or did not hear his demand. There was something brooding in her mind that must out before they separated. "Yes," she said, with suppressed emotion, "we have a good deal to do with each other. You know what folk say of mother and of me; not that I care – no, not this." She bit off a piece of the bark from the thorn twig and spat it forth. "If there had been the smallest foundation in what they say, why did they not set the constables to work and have mother and me arrested and sent to prison?"

"No one has accused *you* of any crime."

"But they do charge mother, and that is the same thing. You do. I remember what you said when we met last, on the undercliff. If the money we have now to spend were indeed yours, I would dash it in your face, shower it over your head, strew the ground with it, not keep one farthing. I would strip off my smart clothes and go forth in my old patched gown once more to peddle tapes and thimbles. You believe my mother is wicked? You believe it? Answer me."

"Nothing, as you say, has been proved."

"Then you have no right to accuse her. You have no right to believe us capable of having done it – of having one penny which is not justly our own."

"I do not know what to think. Of one thing I am quite certain – you are blameless."

"That is as much as saying that my mother is guilty. She could not do it. She could not do it. She would not do it. When did she ever cheat in a matter of a finger's breadth of ribbon. Did not she always sell thirteen for twelve, never eleven, never, never? I know my mother, I have known her since I was a little babe, and I never, never knew her do what was not just and true. She could not be a thief. As for those people around, all but Mrs Jose, let them chatter and slander and backbite if they will. Let them think evil in their hearts, for their hearts are muddy wells that give forth naught but slime. But you – you should be nobler – better – and yet it is you –

O! my mother, my dear innocent mother! my mother who –" Her heart swelled to choke her. She bit her lips, fought with herself. She could not speak, more, she would have betrayed her weakness by falling into a convulsion of sobs.

"May I undo the barrier?" asked Jack, after a long pause. Winefred had withdrawn her face into shadow, lest he should see it.

"As you will," she answered shortly. Then, as he was engaged in

161

removing the fir-poles, and his back was towards her, she broke forth again in rapid speech.

"I know that you are at the bottom of this league formed against us; you and Olver Dench set all in movement, stir up the hive and send them forth with their stings to fall on mother and me. I know what you do – you represent yourself as a lamb and us as wolves. You feeble, bleating lamb! Baa–aah! Look at me, you say, I have no wool. I have been plucked by them."

He raised his hand in deprecation.

"Yes," she said vehemently, "do not deny it. You are greedy after compassion, and so you represent us as rogues, and when everyone points at us and screams out 'Thieves!' you come sneaking up to see the effect, and how we bear it, and burst into laughter if we wince. Mother has no deadlier enemy than the ferryman; you know it, and you go lodge with him, and together you two men contrive schemes against us defenceless women. There is not a child but looks at us with fear, as monsters of wickedness; not a woman who does not think we infect the neighbourhood. And then, when we are stung and torn, you creep up to gloat on our tears. You will not stand forward openly; you peep through holes. It gave you pleasure. You chuckled and rubbed your hands because no girl spoke with me, no lad asked me to dance – because there, in a crowd – I was alone – quite alone." Her bosom tossed like a stormy sea. "But what care I for being alone? I am glad that I am so in the midst of a rabble of mean and spiteful girls and country clowns."

"Winefred–"

"How dare you call me Winefred? I am –"

"Oh! I forgot. Miss Holwood."

Then all at once her anger gave way. In a lower tone she said, "Call me what you will. I do not care. I sold laces and pins and needles – pins at a ha'penny a row. Yes, I am a tramp, a common huckster. Say what you will. I know I am honest, and I know my mother is as clear as sea–water. Say what you will, you and that bully Dench. I am alone, and there is none to protect me. Insult me as you choose. It is fine sport for men. They can worry us and do not fear having their fingers bitten. I cannot defend myself against a brute like Dench and a coward like you combined against me."

"Winefred," said the young man, "I also am alone, utterly alone in the world. In that we are alike. But there the likeness ends. I am poor, you are rich. But in my poverty and solitude I thank God I am not as you are, full of malice."

"Of malice!"

"Of resentment and rage."

"Have I not a cause? When everyone is set against us, when we are worried and baited, can we curl up and take it calmly? The hedgehog can do that because of his prickles. If I were to scream out all would laugh. When I shut my lips you sneer and say I am holding back my tears. Let me through."

Without another word, without a good-night, but dashing a blow at him, a harmless stroke with the thorn bough, she thrust through the gateway he had made and went forth upon the down.

Chapter Twenty-Seven

Mother and Daughter

When Winefred entered the cottage where her mother was, she seated herself on a chair against the wall, and let her hands drop on her knees. Her mother, who was knitting, looked up and said, "Back so soon!"

Winefred did not reply, and the woman continued at her work, but she jerked the worsted, and let slip a needle that fell upon the floor. "Why are you returned so soon?" she asked, after she had stooped, picked up the fallen pin, and recovered the dropped stitches.

"I had enough of it," answered the girl shortly. Jane looked at her, but Winefred turned aside that her mother might not see her face.

"You are not cold, I reckon," said Jane, "so you do not come to the fire. Have you danced?"

"No."

"Have you supped?"

"No."

"Why did you leave without your supper?"

"I have had enough of it," again answered the girl. Mrs Marley rose, went into the kitchen to the larder, and brought in food, which she set on the table, but Winefred made a motion of refusal. "I am not hungry, I cannot eat."

"Something has gone wrong," said her mother. "Tell me what it is."

"There is nothing to tell." Her mother did not press her. She knew the ways of her child, knew that her heart was full, and that she feared to speak lest she should expose herself and distress her mother. She resumed her work and allowed the food to remain on the table. Ever and anon she looked from the stocking she was knitting to the girl seated with her back to the wall.

Jane Marley had not changed her style of dress with her altered circumstances. She wore the same plain stuffs simply put together as heretofore, but her face had undergone a change; it had become harder, more lined, more gloomy.

After a quarter of an hour passed in silence, and the situation had become irksome, Mrs Marley said, "Winnie, this will not do. Something has happened to offend you. Are you angry because you have not had a dance?"

"I do not wish to dance. I would not dance with one of them."

"Why not? Is it because you are above them?"

"It is because I will not touch the hand or speak in friendly way with anyone who says that you are wicked."

"Winnie, you should not be too haughty with them."

"I am not haughty. I care nothing for my smart dress. You know, mother, that I was against putting one on. It is not that."

"This cannot go on. I have had a talk with Mrs Jose; she thinks there must be a change."

"Let there be a change. Let them acknowledge that you are an honest woman."

"There is nothing for it," said Jane hastily, and her hands trembled; "but this – you must go to school."

"To school!"

"Yes, a boarding–school."

"Will you come with me?"

"No, of course not."

"Well, then, you are the most wonderful mother that ever was. Once you would have thrown me over the cliffs–"

"No more of that."

"Because you could not bear to be parted from me."

"Now it is necessary. Mrs Jose thinks so – I feel it."

"I will not go."

"You must go. It will be for your good. You are to be brought up as a lady. I have been turning over in my head, and see that it must be so. You are too good for these clods, and not good enough for gentlefolk. You must be set to learn the manners of those with whom you will associate."

"I do not wish to leave you, mother."

"You will have to do so. It is I, not you, who will suffer. You will be among young people, and share their games and learn their lessons. I shall sit here knitting, thinking, my head turning and my heart aching – alone."

"You must not be alone."

"My child. It is my place to think for you, and to endure what must be for your benefit. The time will arrive when you will be married. You have been made to feel in a fashion what it means to stand alone, and to have no man by you to fight your battles. There is no farm lad you would take, and no gentleman who would take you."

"But, mother, my father had no such thoughts."

"And what came of it? He deserted me because I did not belong to his class. It would be the same with you – and that shall never, never be." Her face became darker, sterner. "I have known what desertion means. I once loved and trusted and tied up all my hopes to one man. And for nineteen years I have eaten out my heart in wrath and resentment because I have been forsaken. I have not slept, I have tossed on my bed, night after night; I have had a fire here, in my bosom, burning me, week after week, month after month, expecting, desiring, and never seeing him return, never hearing of him save that he had gone away, gone out of England, so as to be removed from me, put the wide ocean between us, lest I should go after him; and there, where he is, I doubt not he had found some other woman better suited to him than myself."

"But, mother, he is in England again."

"Yes – in England, but will not return to me. You he may receive, but me – never. And I did him no wrong – never, never, in word or act or deed. Only I was a poor, ignorant and common girl – that was my sole wrong."

Her fingers worked rapidly. "I have no hope, no care for myself. All I think or hope for concerns you. Winefred, I would throw you over the cliffs rather than that should happen to you which was my lot. You must learn to become that which I never was and never could have been, and so you will not only find a husband, but also keep him."

"I do not wish to be married."

"Marry you must. You cannot stand alone. You are a well–grown and a handsome girl, but unless you have education all that does more harm than good. I was – so all said – a very handsome girl, and what came of it? I caught the fancy of a gentleman, and he married me – whether it was right and good marriage I do not know, but I have begun to think it must have been good and holding, or he would not have run away so far to escape from me. After a while he grew cool, and shook me off, shook himself free of me as Samson shook off the cords of flax, as though burnt with fire, wherewith the Philistines had bound him. He never came near me again."

"But, mother, you say that it is he who is finding the money for buying this house and for my education as a lady."

Mrs Marley looked down suddenly, and her colour deepened. She did not answer directly, but after some pause, said, in a hesitating manner, "He has not come near me. He may care for you, because he can make a lady of you, but for me he cares not, he can make nothing now of me. It is too late. If you get a husband who is a gentleman, you must be able to hold him fast. He will not run away from you if you have money and retain the purse, but above all – not if you have education. It was not because I was poor, but because I was untaught that *he* left me. It has been as a worm in my brain. To school you must go, and so escape that misery which would be yours if, like me, you were no scholar."

"O mother! If I must go away, do you come also. You cannot be happy here."

"I cannot leave now. I have bought this house. I hold to what is mine. As to the people and what they say, I heed them not. It frets me only when it hurts you. There is nothing they can say or do that will either lift me up or cast me down. I must bear my woes."

"Are you really unhappy, mother?"

"I am what I am. Do not concern yourself about me. I have my sorrows and my shame. You are free. What they say falls on me, not on you, and I wish that you should be away from their chatter and their fangs. You have a future, I have none. Me they are welcome to tread and knead into the dirt if only you go unspotted. My life has not been so happy that I care what befalls me in what remains of it. I value it only for you. But your life is just opening like a June rose, and I must shelter it from the wind. Understand me, Winnie, whilst you are here, you are the butt of every girl who is inclined to be spiteful. Where all seek to hurt, you cannot escape without bruises. When you are elsewhere you will make new friends, get into another class, and begin a fresh life that I do not understand, but this is what I have set my heart upon, and this is the ambition that fills me."

Winefred stood up, flew to her mother, and they were locked in each other's embrace, sobbing on each other's shoulder. High as heaven, deep as hell, is mother's love, self–effacing, capable of all self–sacrifice; and infinitely tender, clinging is that of the child to the mother, when that child has neither brother nor sister, nor father, on whom love may be dissipated. Jane Marley was the first to re–cover herself. "Dear child," she said, "I lived but for you – and for that very reason I part with you. I send you away."

"I will go," answered Winefred through her tears. Then she departed to her room. Her mother had appointed for her that recently occupied by the captain, but it had been ceiled, renovated, trans–formed, and turned into a bright and pretty bedroom fit for a girl. She extinguished her candle. She did not undress and go to bed. She sat at the casement. The room was warm. It was above the parlour, in which the fire burned all day. There was no necessity for artificial light, as the moon shone brightly. Sitting at the window, she looked out on the chalk rocks, dazzling white in the moon, then disappearing as a cloud passed over the face of the luminary, but again shortly to flash out again. Winefred looked indeed at these white prongs of rock, but she did not notice them. The bitter expression had faded from her lips, her brows were no longer knit; her hands were pressed to the temples, for her pulses throbbed painfully.

She was alone. But not so solitary as others might be, even as Jack Rattenbury. She had her mother to fly to, to rest upon, to hold in her arms, but he – he – poor lad, had none. She regretted that she had spoken to him with harshness.

Chapter Twenty–Eight

Most Heartily

Jack went his way, dissatisfied with himself, with Winefred, with the whole world. Why had the girl spoken to him, looked at him, defied him as she had done?

It was perhaps natural, reasonable, excusable, that she should regard him with an unfriendly eye, in consequence of what was rumoured relative to her mother and his father. If this story were baseless, as possibly it was, then both women must feel acutely having so gross an act of dishonesty laid to their charge, and be predisposed to look upon him as an instigator of the calumnies that had caused them intolerable annoyance.

That Winefred was wretched Jack had read in her face. He pitied her, and yet he was angry with her for the manner in which she treated him. If the women were innocent, he said to himself, they did not act in such a manner as to disarm suspicion. And whether guilty or not they were not a pleasing couple, Jane Marley with her furious temper, Winefred with her pride. The world is a looking-glass. As is the face that you present to it, such is the face that looks back at you. Assuredly Winefred made no attempt by gentleness to win back for herself those who were alienated, not through any fault of her own doubtless, but because of the suspicion that dogged her mother. Had the girl possessed a good heart, would she have spoken to Jack as she had done?

"Bah!" said he aloud, as he kicked before him the flints that strewed the down and glistened in the moonlight, "Bah! What is she to me? I will cast her out of my thoughts."

But it is sometimes easier to form a resolution than to adhere to it. He found himself reverting incessantly to the picture of the frowning girl with clenched hands on her lap, seated in the barn, alone amidst many, or to her in the moonlight menacing him with the thorn branch.

So he walked back to the ferryman's cottage, and, avoiding conversation with Olver, threw himself on his bed. Dench had, indeed, sought to detain him by asking questions as to where he had been, whether he had obtained employment, and what he proposed for the morrow, but the boy answered that he was wearied and indisposed to talk.

"He will be brought to it yet," said the ferryman to himself. "Those Beer fellows, and above all David Nutall, are a bit shy of me and suspect something. But if I have this greenhorn here, and can thrust him in among them, I shall know all their movements, and can sell them in a lump when I have a mind to."

Since the disposal of the house that had belonged to his father, Jack had not been up to it; he had avoided it. But on the morrow, after another day of ineffectual search after employment towards evening he walked over the down at the head of the cliffs and descended to the undercliff where the cottage stood.

It had been renovated, and in part remodelled since its purchase. The wall had been whitewashed and the roof repaired. The fence before the house had been put to rights, and the little garden had been dug up. Brambles that had straggled across the path leading to it, and overswaying boughs, had been pruned back.

Jack looked at the house. It was certainly a pleasanter dwelling now than in his father's time. A house in which a woman is at once assumes a neatness and a charm which one occupied by man only does not and cannot possess. A light sprang up in a window. Someone was within, and he saw the shadow of an arm upon the pane that was raised to draw a curtain. He beat a hasty retreat. He recalled how on the preceding night Winefred had accused him of running after her. He was fearful of being seen near the house by someone either coming out of the door or approaching from the down. It would not be easy for him to account for his presence there. Winefred would be strengthened in her persuasion that he spied on her actions. Then the blood rushed to his temples. She might even conceivably suppose that he had taken a fancy to her, and that it was her charms that drew him to the house. He! – he had taken a fancy to her!

He hurried away, not by the path, lest he should encounter the girl or her mother, but through the bushes, and he stumbled over stones, and caught his foot in briars. He came upon the open space which he had been wont to regard as his garden, and where he had had a brush with Winefred. He stood still there and shook himself, but he could not shake off the thoughts of that girl. The air there was charged with the smell of decayed leaves and mouldering twigs. Every step was upon dead vegetation, and every tread brought out an exhalation of death.

In vain did he force his mind to other matters; it would turn with perverse persistency to Winefred, and he saw her in his fancy pursue him with an angry light in her eyes, and every branch that smote him seemed to him to be struck by her hand.

On the following day Dench absented himself and asked Jack to mind the ferry. When he had put a passenger across he returned, slightly dipping the oars in the water, to fall into a dream and think of her. On that afternmoon he heard a call from the Axmouth side, and on going from the cabin saw that Winefred was waiting to be put across. He flushed crimson, and his heart fluttered. He was angry with himself for feeling excitement. He crossed and held out his hand to assist her on board, but she leaped into the boat unaided.

She took her place, and looked resolutely at the Chesil Bank, not once at him, nor did she open her mouth to speak. Again, on reach–

ing the shore, did he offer his hand, and she dropped into it a penny, but would not touch it.

In an hour she was back again, with some purchases she had made in Seaton. She looked him in the face now, but with a stony eye, and demanded to be put across. Although whilst in the boat she would not look at him, yet he could see by her uneasy movements on the bench that she knew that he was watching her. he saw her bend her brows and purse her lips.

She left the boat hastily, casting the penny into it, and shortly after Jack saw that in her hurry she had neglected to take up one of her parcels. He hurried after her, caught her up, and presented it to her. "I thank you," said she coldly. "Here is for your pains," and offered him twopence. He coloured angrily and withdrew his hand. "Take it," she said. "I refuse to be indebted to you for anything."

"I will not take it."

She threw the coppers on the ground and pursued her way. Jack put his foot on them and ground them into the mud.

Occasionally he encountered her in a lane; when this was so he could see by her manner that if it were possible for her to slip out of his way down a sidepath, she would do it; if it were not, she tossed her head and passed without a word.

One day the fancy took Jack Rattenbury to revisit the rift that had been formed when Mrs Marley's cottage had been ruined. The kegs that had been secreted in the cave had all been removed. What induced Jack to go there, whether it were curiosity to ascertain what alteration had taken place in its aspect, or whether the association of the place with the eventful night when he escaped by it from the preventive men drew him there, he did not himself know.

He crossed the estuary and sauntered along the beach. The tide was ebbing and leaving on the pebbles ribbons of weed and a thread of froth. Turning sharply round an angle of the cliff he came on the mouth of the chasm, and stood, breathless, not knowing whether to retreat or to go forward, for there before him, on a mass of fallen chalk, sat Winefred, her head in her hands, sobbing.

The lad, after a moment's hesitation, took a step towards her. She looked up quickly, flushed, then turned pale, rose and faced him, with defiance in her countenance. "Again – spying!" He was too

171

surprised to speak. The sight of her tears had taken the courage out of him. "Now you have seen me," she said, "you can go again."

"I did not come here to see you. I did not expect to find you here. I came to look once more at the cave."

"It is choked. You know it."

"I did not know it. I have not been here since I helped you to get out."

"That is false. You removed all the smuggled goods."

"I did not. It was done by others. I told them where they were concealed."

"I do not believe you."

"I have my faults, but lying is not one of them."

"But slander is. I know you tell lies of us."

"You are mistaken. Never have I said a word against you."

"But you have against my mother."

"I cannot tell exactly what I may have said concerning her, when a certain matter has been discussed, but I may say, and I do sincerely assure you it is true. I have most generally spoken in her defence rather than against her." Winefred was silent.

"I am sorry to see you in trouble," said Jack. "You have been crying."

"I am angry at being followed and spied on."

"You were in tears before I disturbed you."

"Yes, I had been hearing an amusing story: it made me laugh and cry at once."

"Who speaks untruths now?"

"Am I to ask your leave and to curtsey before I am permitted to shed a tear?"

"Oh no! We have nothing to do with each other."

"Nothing at all. I desire you to keep out of my way, but you are continually running against me or running after me. Why do you do it? Do you suppose that I carry about with me your father's gold."

"Engage the Seaton crier to march before you wherever you go, and ring his bell and call – Clear the way, fall on your faces, or hide. Miss Holwood comes." She burst into tears again.

With an effort she mastered her emotion. "If you will go and bray through the country that you have seen me cry, say the reason why.

I have been crying because I am going away, going among strangers."

"You are?"

"Yes."

"I wish that were my luck."

"To pry after me?"

"No, that I might find work. Why are you going away?"

"To be made into a lady. My father is a gentleman."

"And where is this wonderful change to be made?"

"I will not tell you. Of one thing I am glad. For that I shed no tears. I shall be relieved of your presence."

"I cannot get away from Seaton. I am like one of the pebbles here, rolled up and down, forward, backward – and always on the one ridge. Is your mother leaving also?"

"She is not. This is Mrs Jose's doing. That is to say, she has found a place where I am to be. She has got distinguished relatives who live in the best society. I am to go to them. They are to roll me up and down, forward and backward, till all my roughness is rubbed away."

"Ah! you – but you are a precious stone – chalcedony, a hard one. I – I am rolled, but only to be ground on nothing."

Winefred was slightly softened. She said, "Have you consulted Mrs Jose? She is everyone's friend, and helpful to all in difficulties. But if she offers you the place of button boy to her relatives, I shall refuse to go to them."

"You must dislike me vastly."

"I hate you."

She looked steadily into his troubled face and, and after a pause, added, "And do you not hate me?"

"Well – I suppose I do. Perhaps so. Yes, of course I do."

"As I do, most heartily."

"Yes, most heartily."

Chapter Twenty-Nine

The Shadow of a Change

Everything in this world is comparative, there is nothing absolute. All creation is in scale from the animated germ to the man, through all the ranges of invertebrate and vertebrate life. And man is not a culminating superlative, for mankind is in itself a wondrous ladder made up of degrees. Taken physically, intellectually, socially, he is situated on a stage with stages above and others below him. Indeed every man in his several aspects or component part is but relative. He may be handsomer than another, but not so clever, or handsomer and more clever, but stand on an inferior social rung.

Now when Mrs Marley informed Mrs Jose that nothing would satisfy her short of the introduction of Winefred into high society, Mrs Jose ran her eye up the scale of her kindred and acquaintances, and said with confidence: "My dear Jane, I can put her into the very 'ighest, short of a title. It is that of Tomkin-Jones of Bath' and as Jacob's ladder lost itself in heaven so did that social scale up which Mrs Jose looked land itself in the transcendent blaze of the Tomkin-Jones parlour. "Yes," said Mrs Jose, "it will not do to have the girl here longer; it is curdling her soul, like putting over much cider into milk posset. You are right. We must get her out of this place if she is to be reared as a lady. If you keep poultry on the same ground they get the gapes. We must shift the hutches. We will send Winefred to Bath."

In Mrs Jose's pleasant face little dimples formed. "Yes, Jane," said she, "but I'm thinking Mrs Tomkins-Jones is not in the best circumstances, though she be so high. You cannot expect her to do it for nothing. It is her misfortune to be unable to teach manners for the pleasure of the thing. You see it is just the same as giving lessons on the piano – one has to be taught the fingering – and that fingering in social life they call tact. Only them as knows it can teach it."

"I will pay – and that gladly. What I desire is, that my Winefred should become a real lady."

"Learn the fingering – that is all she requires," said Mrs Jose. "In 'igh society they hold themselves above shoppies. All things don't agree with everyone. There is my cat is ill after eating herrings. You must not let out that you have been a hawker. We know that by nature all are equal. Scripture says so, just as hams be when they come from the pig. But, my! what a difference there be in the curing! It is that which gives style and flavour, and makes a prime Wiltshire or a Yorkshire stand out above your raw green hams. It is into the pickle you must put Winefred, and I'll see to it, and the pickle must get right down into her bone. I don't approve of glazing and flummery, and when you cut in – nothing but saltpetre. If she is to dress and act as a lady, she must think and feel as a lady. When I see an old woman dressed very young, I say it is mutton with mint sauce, served as lamb; we will have Winefred real, and she has a right to be that, for her father was a gentleman. Mrs Tomkins–Jones is my cousin, but I don't presume on that. She was a Stripe, and that was the name of my mother's family."

"And do you think you can persuade them to take my Winefred – if I pay?"

"I will try. They used to keep their carriage. I don't say that they do so now. But it is not forgotten that they did. Keeping your carriage and pair – it sticks to one just as the smell of lavender does to your linen if you have kept them together."

Mrs Jose considered. Presently she said, "But not a breath of a word about the huxtering. You know very well, Jane, I want to be delicate, but I can't help myself, I must explain. There are Mrs Ball, the greengrocer, and Mrs Trant, who has the drapery. Have they ever asked you to take a cup o' tea with them – I mean at the same table? No, they would say it would not be fitting and proper, because you were a travelling hawker. You see what a difference it makes your having a shop counter fixed, and one you carry about with you. Now the Tomkin–Joneses are above Mrs Ball and Mrs Trant as the lark is above the barndoor poultry. So you may conceive that if she knew what you have been –"

Jane Marley's face became stern. She interrupted Mrs Jose with, "Put me aside. If I can get my Winnie into that family I will not stand in the way. I have stood in my own light long enough, and will not spoil my child's future. It is because I am not a lady that I have been as a cloud tossed by the tempest, and never able to find repose. *He* supposed that she could not be much, come of such as me; but when he saw her, then he discovered his error. There is the stuff in her –"

"Yes, and all required is that it shall be properly cut out."

"Tell your friends that her father was a gentleman who has lost his wife."

"But Winefred will speak of you."

"What then? Say that she has been reared from the cradle by a nurse, a common sort of woman, as can't read or write; you can say, if Winefred does not speak as ladies should, or in other little things goes contrary to their ways, put it down to me, say that she learned those manners and speech of her nurse. But, mind you, tell them that she has good blood in her, and that whatsoever is faulty comes of me, her nurse, and of that they are to rid her."

"I don't much like saying that, Jane. I am a woman who always speaks the truth."

"It is the truth. I have been her nurse. I held her to my bosom and soothed her when she cried. No one else ever did that. And her father did lose his wife – that is to say, he ran away and left her. He went abroad, they told me, to the other end of the earth, and put the rolling seas between us. There is no lie about that."

"Well, well, we shall see. I will say as little as possible."

"You must say," said Mrs Marley, with her fingers knitted, embracing her knees, and looking stonily before her, "you must say as how Winnie is accustomed always to call that low thing her mother, because she has not known any other, though that creature is not worthy of her; but you may also say that the nurse loves her" – Jane's eyelids flickered and her voice became less harsh – "loves her, worships the very ground on which she walks. You can't go too far in that, and if you will you can go further and say that it was time the child should be taken out of such degrading associations and be put with gentlefolks, for and because" – Jane threw up her head – "she has gentle blood in her, and because this was her father's wish."

The woman seemed to feel a bitter pleasure in disparaging herself. She went on: "The child is young, and she will be unhappy at the outset, and be longing to be back with her mother, as she styles that person who brought her up. But in time she will grow out of that and make new friends, and will learn new ways, and then – then there will be a great gulf fixed between her and that common woman who was her nurse, a gulf so wide and so profound that there will be no passing from the one to the other. I must make up my mind to that. I see that it will come. But I will endure it for Winefred's sake." Drops stood on Jane Marley's brow, and there was a fire in her eye, but no signs of unbending.

"I will do my best for her," said Mrs Jose. "I will myself take Winefred to Bath – and to say the truth, I should like to see my high relations again, and have an excuse for a visit. Milk always gains a flavour from what it is set nigh. That is why you can't well have meat in a dairy. I shall come back with quite a smack of gentility."

Mrs Jose mused. "We must go to Lyme," she said after a while. "I will take her there with her trunk, thence we shall get to Dorchester, and so on by coach. It can be done."

"When?"

"Next week."

All at once Jane's eyes were as windows against which rain has beaten, and the woman broke down utterly. It was like the collapse of a great oak. The distress, the despair of the mother were so great, so overwhelming, that the kind-hearted farmer's wife could only stand and look on, unable to offer consolation, powerless to stem the rush of passionate sorrow. She allowed her to give way without an attempt to check her, and tarried patiently till the first burst was overpast. Then she said gently, "Now, Jane, try to come round again. Yourself has willed it, and all for the good of the young girl. This life is full of crossroads and branching lanes, and we don't all walk along it two-and-two like the Odd-Fellows going to church on Club Feast. A few years will pass, and you will then be proud of Winefred, proud to look at her, to hear her speak, to see how beautiful and ladylike she has grown –"

"But so far – far from me."

"Jane, every thought in your head, every feeling in your heart will be swallowed up in pride. I will tell you my ideas, Jane. You go on consuming your black and miserable thoughts, and it makes you wretched – just like the kitchen cat as will eat black beetles and grow lanky on it – but think of things bright. Trout grow fat on Mayflies. Consider this. Winefred with her handsome face and nimble tongue is certain to catch the fancy of some great gentleman. How can you say but that this may be a lord? My people – I beg their pardon – the Tomkin-Joneses live in the most fashionable square in Bath, and although they don't keep a carriage and livery servants just now, they see carriages and footmen go by their windows. And anyone who casts an eye on Winefred is sure to fall in love with her. It will be worth going through something for the sake of what may, must be."

Jane was quieter. She said, "When she has a house of her own and is married, I shall ask to be allowed to darn the socks and hem the dusters." She drew a long sigh. "O Mrs Jose, you do not know how I have longed for this! Yet now it is about to be, I feel sick at heart."

Then a maid looking in said, "Missus! I say, missus!"

"Well, Betsy, what do you want?"

"Please Missus, there be young Jack Rattenbury staying about, and sez he wants to see you."

"What does he want?"

"I don't know, but I reckon he do want something of you."

"Bless the boy," said the good-natured woman, "they all do that. Tell Jack to come in."

Chapter Thirty

A New World

After a tedious journey, such as travellers had to undergo at the beginning of the century, whether they journeyed by coach or by private carriage with post horses, Mrs Jose and Winefred arrived in Bath. Mrs Jose sought quarters for herself in a modest tavern, as she could not, dared not thrust herself on her grand relations. Moreover, before formally visiting their house, she had to change her gown, wash off the soil of travel, and give fresh curl to her hair.

When all these preparations were accomplished, she conducted Winefred to the Tomkin–Jones residence, a corner house of a square. The door opened into a narrow street, and the house had but a single window on each storey that looked into the square. Nevertheless it was numbered, and esteemed itself as belonging to the square, and not to the street.

Before Winefred Mrs Jose endeavoured to disguise her nervousness, but the attempt was futile, her excitation was perceptible at every point. A more than ordinary carnation mantled her healthy cheeks, her broad bosom heaved tumultuously, the movements of hand and head were spasmodic, and she showered advice as to comportment on the girl at her side, in the distraction of her mind repeating the same items a score of times.

As the door was approached, "My dear," whispered the farmer's wife, "how do I look? Is my bonnet straight? Just see that my flounce is not curled up behind." On the doorstep Mrs Jose stood in perturbation, unable to decide which was the correct proceeding, to knock or to ring, or to knock and ring, or even to ring and knock. She was relieved of her embarrassment by the door opening without her having summoned the attendant, and by the maid appearing with letters in her hand for the post.

Mrs Jose now announced herself, and informed the domestic that she believed she was expected, and inquired whether Mrs Tomkin-Jones and the young ladies were at home. The servant postponed the commission with the letters, and led the way to the drawing-room on the first floor, up a narrow and steep staircase. Mrs Jose followed, treading lightly as if dancing among eggs, and Winefred mounted after her.

They were shown into the drawing-room, an apartment that had a window into the square, and smelt of carpet cleaned with ox-gall. The paper was drab, with bunches of flowers on it; and the curtains were of a heavy green, and looked as if they had been dyed. They were protected against the sun by a second set of curtains of muslin.

The chairs and sofa were encased in chintz tied about the legs; and the looking-glass frame above the mantelshelf was enveloped in yellow gauze. At each end of the shelf stood a candlestick of brass hung with cut-glass prisms, some chipped, one missing. Next to these, on the inside, were two vases filled with spills of twisted coloured paper; and in the middle was a French ormolu clock, under a glass shade, that did not go, and was surmounted by cast figures representing the Flight into Egypt.

The circular rosewood table that occupied the centre of the room had on it a posy of shell-flowers under a glass bell; and mats of coloured wool and steel beads – these latter somewhat rusted – were dispersed over the table to receive nothing in particular. A few books radiated from the bunch of shell flowers, selected to lie on the table, not on account of their contents, but because of the gilding on their covers. The chairs in the room also radiated from the posy at set intervals. The fire was laid but not lighted. The fire-irons were highly polished, but apparently never used. In a dark nook lurked a meagre little poker of black iron that was employed when the fire was alight and needed stirring. The blinds were drawn when Mrs Jose and Winefred entered, but the maid drew them up partially, not wholly, lest too much light should enter and take some of the dye out of the dismal curtains. The carpet, recently relaid after cleaning, represented sprays of seaweed floating on the surface of the bottle-green deep among sprigs of coral forming rococo octagons.

Mrs Jose seated herself timorously at the edge of a chair, and looked around her with an expression of mingled awe and pride. Presently she pointed at the shell flowers, and said with bated breath, "Wonderful, are they not? That I call a real work of art. Must have cost pounds. Just fancy, all shells, not real flowers. Tell me, dear, do I look very hot?" Satisfied that she was not overheated, Mrs Jose's eyes rambled about the room, then fell on the floor.

"My dear, never before have I seen the carpet without a drugget over it. Wonderful, is it not? It really makes one feel as if one must either dislocate one's ankle or plunge knee–deep in the ocean walking over it. That is high art. Is the bow under my chin pulled out properly? Hush! I hear them coming."

The heightened colour left her cheek. But no – none arrived. It comported with the dignity of the family not to exhibit over-cordiality in the reception of a relative of an inferior social stage.

"My dear!" in a whisper, "when Mrs Tomkin–Jones comes, if she graciously speaks to you, answer with a ma'am just once, or perhaps twice. Not too many ma'ams, or she will think you have been in a shop. You understand?"

The house, opening into the street, but pretending to belong to the square, was perhaps typical of the Tomkin–Jones family. That family affected to belong to a social order above that to which it actually pertained. But in this it was not peculiar. With few exceptions most people aim at appearing, socially or morally, what they are not. And it is well that they should do so, for it is precisely this straining upward after something higher which is the motive principle of civilisation. Through ten thousand ages the negro never felt this, and therefore remained where he was when first planted in Africa.

There are insects that assume the appearance of leaves, or twigs among which they feed, there are birds that adopt the colouring of the soil on which they cower, but with men capable of cultural advance it is just the opposite; and it is precisely this aiming at something above and other than their surroundings that differentiates them from the beasts. There are exceptions. One has heard of a nobleman who studied to look like and talk like, and think like one of his grooms; but this is a sport on the race, such as ought not to be in a civilised world at all. But it is precisely because the trades-man seeks to look like, live like, think like, and behave like the gentleman, that the entire middle class has risen to the same cultural level that was attained by the highest class a generation or two ago. And this mighty and magnificent upheaval in mind and manner will continue to manifest itself so long as those who stand at the apex of civilisation maintain their high qualities of breeding, courtesy, refinement and self-respect.

Presently Mrs Jose caught her breath, flashed a frightened glance at Winefred, rose from her chair, surveyed her face in the mirror, sat down again, and looked eagerly at the door. The handle turned, the door opened, and in rustled Mrs Tomkin-Jones, stiff, stately, cold. Mrs Jose rose and bowed profoundly. Winefred also stood up. The reverence that possessed the farmer's wife had infected the girl. She looked inquisitively and respectfully at the lady.

Mrs Tomkin-Jones was tall, wore a "front" of chestnut with little curls ranged on each side of her brow over the temples, and a lace cap that concealed the junction of the old and real with the new and false. Here again was an instance of that unreality illustrating the upward strain of humanity which aspires to perpetual youth, and resents and disguises the ravages of decay, because it possesses within it the instinct of eternal bloom. Mrs Tomkin-Jones bent her head and extended a hand in reply to Mrs Jose's salutation, with condescension in her manner, but so as to convey an unmistakeable hint that no familiarity would be allowed.

"I hope, Mrs Jose, that you enjoy your health as usual?"

"Thank you kindly, ma'am, middling."

"And Mr Jose also enjoys rude health, as usual?"

"Pretty well for the time of year. But he's always took in his kidneys."

"We will waive details. And this dear child you wish me to receive temporarily under my protection. An engaging face," said Mrs Jones, putting up the gold-framed eye-glasses. "But the arrangement of the hair might be improved, and the complexion is too weather-tanned and," raking her from head to foot "the dress leaves much to be desired. Her name, I think you told me, was –"

"Miss Holwood."

"Any relation to the Holwoods of Lambton? The late Hon. Mrs Holwood was, as you may – as, of course, you do not know – was a daughter of Viscount Finnborough. A family – that of Finnborough – of affluence, but what is better, of antiquity and distinction."

Neither Mrs Jose nor Winefred could answer this question.

"I hope," said Mrs Tomkin–Jones, after a pause, "I hope you have not felt the cold. We do not usually put a light to the fire till the afternoon when we expect visitors. Perhaps you will do me the favour of coming into the dining–room, in which we ordinarily sit – at all events of a morning. The room is more cheerful, and the young ladies are there. I myself feel shivery in this reception room, and am obliged to be careful about my health. My dear doctor laid it on me to avoid sitting in cold rooms, specially at this time of year. You will, I know, oblige me. You will be pleased, Miss Holwood, to make the acquaintance of my daughters, and they are ardent in their desire to make yours."

She rose. "Excuse me if I lead the way. The staircase is objectionably narrow, two can hardly descend together, which is an inconvenience at dinner–parties, but since my bereavement, since the irrevocable loss I have endured, I have not had the spirits to entertain. My daughters, no doubt, would prefer a more distinguished and ampler residence, and perhaps – but this serves temporarily, temporarily, you understand – though I believe the doctor, had he lived, would not have sanctioned it. We have a position, you comprehend, that ought to be kept up. Allow me – this is the door." She threw it open, and a blast of colour smote in the faces of those entering.

The dining–room had a red flock paper on the walls, and dull crimson–red curtains at the window. The Turkey carpet was covered with red drugget. The furniture was of cumbrous mahogany and leather. On the black marble mantelshelf was a black marble clock. The sideboard was heavy and too large for the room. The sole picture on the walls was the portrait, very flat, of the late Dr Tomkin–Jones, in a black suit and white cravat, and pasty face against a background of red curtains.

"My daughters, Sylvana and Jesse," said Mrs Jones; and two young women, who had been crouching over a very small fire in a very elevated grate, rose.

The elder was somewhat like her mother, but had her father's cadaverous complexion and a spiteful expression. The younger,

Jesse, was pleasant-looking and almost pretty.

"My dears," said Mrs Tomkin-Jones, "I need not introduce you to our good friend and remote kinswoman, Mrs Jose, who sends us at Christmas such excellent hams and geese and all kinds of good things. But I beg to introduce Miss Holwood, who belongs to the Lambton family you know, connected with the Finnboroughs, whose carriage and liveries, brown turned up with scarlet, you are so familiar with."

Sylvana rose frigidly and inclined her head, but Jesse darted forward, caught Mrs Jose in her arms and kissed her.

"My dear," said her mother reproachfully.

"My aunt," said the girl, "and an old darling."

"Well, not absolutely, not exactly an aunt," said Mrs Tomkin-Jones. "Please, however, do not forget Miss Holwood."

The farmer's wife's face flushed with pleasure, and a kindly light kindled in her eyes, hitherto awestruck.

"You would like to see your room," said the lady to Winefred. "Jesse will show you. Her name is Jesse not Jose. Jesse, my dear, do not gush; gushing is unladylike."

When the younger daughter had withdrawn with Winefred, Mrs Tomkin-Jones signed graciously to Mrs Jose to take the seat lately occupied by Jesse Jones. She lowered herself slowly, solemnly, into an armchair, and brought her mittened hands together so that the fingertips met. "Of course, it is understood," said the lady, "that I do not generally put myself to so great an inconvenience as to take in a perfect stranger, but you have been so considerate in remembering us with your excellent hams – and the turkey – well, I am disposed to oblige you."

"Besides the payment," threw in Sylvana. "That was a first consideration."

"You are mistaken, my dear," said the mother with vexation. "That was the very last consideration."

"Oh! and for that you stickled so much over the terms?"

"My dear, do not be vulgar." Then to Mrs Jose, "Of course you understand that levers would not have lifted me from my resolution to receive no one."

"You have been advertising, mamma."

"My dear, will you be quiet? I enjoin on you silence. It is low to interrupt. Nothing, my good Jose, would have induced me to open my doors to one who is exceptionable in the matter of birth. I rely on you that in this particular case all is right."

"Her father is a gentleman, and desires to introduce her into good society; her education has been unfortunately neglected," stammered Mrs Jose.

"I quite understand that. Do you know him?"

"No, I have never seen him. He is, or had been, abroad, I have been told. I think he was Governor–General of a place called Terra del Fuego. He came home, I have heard, but is back again in foreign parts."

"Ah! A Colonial appointment. Exactly. And her mother?"

"Mr Holwood lost his wife before his child was born – I mean soon after it was born," answered the good woman with growing confusion of face and uncertainty of manner. "But really you must not ask me too many questions. I do know nothing about the family, but that they want the maid to be properly educated, and they are ready to stump up."

"Stump, Mrs Jose!"

"That is to say pay handsomely."

"There is no thought of payment entertained by me. No sum that could be mentioned would adequately compensate for the attention, the direction, the correction that will be lavished on the young lady. I do not sell my services," said the widow severely; "if it be deemed right that an honorarium should be offered, I resign myself to it. But the large circle of my acquaintance, their distinguished quality, and my wide experience enable me to impart to any young lady placing herself under my protection an air of refinement that is the exclusive privilege of the aristocracy and I venture to say that you would have to go far afield to obtain advantages equal to those offered under this modest roof. Oh! here they return, and apparently good friends."

As the two girls entered the room, Mrs Tomkin–Jones examined Winefred with a critical eye. "Country made or mismade," she said. "*Nous allons changer tout cela*. And now, my good Jose, may I offer you something to eat or to drink? We shall be going out for a drive in ten minutes, and I must haste with my dressing. I am so sorry that I did not think of this before. A biscuit now? A glass of sherry? No – then – excuse me, a cruel fate bears me away, a social necessity – I must dress before my drive. Trust me. I will do my best by the young lady, and when you see her again, you will find her transmuted."

Chapter Thirty–One

A Chariot Drive

"Madam! the chariot is at the door."

"Bless me! not dressed. I ordered it for three o'clock."

"It is now on the stroke," said Jesse.

"Dear, dear, the clock has stopped. Jesse, you forgot to wind it up last week."

"I did not know it was my duty, mother."

"It is always your duty when I forget to do it. I shall be ready instantly. Winefred – I understand that is your Christian name, and a very charming name it is – we will drop formality, and no more call you Miss Holwood – I will show you Bath, or the Bath, as it was wont to be called."

"And the chemist where the celebrated pill was compounded?" asked Jesse.

"My dear" – Mrs Tomkin–Jones rose to her full height – "I hate profanity. Remember that your father wrote out the prescription, if you desire that your days may be long in the land. Now, Winefred, put on your things. Sylvana, are you coming?"

"No, mamma, not if I am to sit with my back to the horses."

"You forget your breeding, child. A visitor, of course, sits beside me."

"I know that, mamma, therefore I decline."

186

"You will come, Jesse?"

"As you wish, mamma, and show to the admiring visitor the City of Bladud, Beau Nash and of Tomkin–Jones."

"My dear, eschew flippancy."

In a quarter of an hour the ladies were ready, and descended to the carriage. This was a somewhat battered conveyance, let by the hour, drawn by a horse that had known better days, as had the chariot and the driver. The steed leaned forward, so that but for the counterpoise of the carriage he would have fallen headlong on his nose. Thinking that the general aspect of the conveyance, driver, and steed, left something to be desired, Mrs Tomkin–Jones said in her grandest manner, "Everything may not be quite as might be desiderated, but I study safety above all else. It is my first consideration, and one is compelled to sacrifice appearances to that!" – she shrugged her shoulders – "I can rely on this chariot. The horse I have known never to fall, though it sometimes coughs. The coachman I knew by long acquaintance – I mean employment – as one who does not drink. One cannot be too cautious. An inebriate driver, even with the most sober horse, may do terrible things. Moreover, Baker is attached to the family by cords of gratitude, as he was attended in a case of considerable internal complication by my dear husband. The horse has good blood in him. Observe the nose and the hanging underlip – it was a characteristic of Charles the Fifth. Will you favour me by stepping in? The cushions and lining have a smell – a mouldy, damp, strange savour – but it is wholesome, and was particularly recommended by the dear doctor in cases of hay fever – from which I suffer."

Winefred had never sat in any other carriage than a carrier's van or a mail–coach, and she was in no mood to note the defects in that she now entered. Her heart swelled with pride. She was made much of, was indulged, treated with some deference. She had passed into a new world in which the atmosphere was new. She was away from the suspicion, the slander of Axmouth. She would not have been a woman and young not to have felt elated at the thought that she was rich, and on account of her riches was respected. Yet withal she was uneasy at her surroundings, so different from any wherewith she had been acquainted, and she was afraid of exposing her ignorance.

Her mother had so often and so earnestly commented to her on lack of social culture as having been the cause of her own undoing, as having blasted her entire life, that Winefred, standing at the threshold of a new career in which this desideratum was to be acquired, felt timorous, lest she should make some great mistake, commit some solecism at the outstart. "Hah!" said Mrs Tomkin-Jones, throwing herself back in the chariot, "there passed by Lady Vire de Vétte. How unfortunate that she was looking in the wrong direction and did not catch my eye and my greeting."

"Mamma," said Jesse, "there is Aunt Jose on the footway, shall we take her up?"

Mrs Tomkin-Jones did not hear her. She was studying the chimney tops of the houses on the opposite side of the street, and so failed to see Mrs Jose. "Baker!" said the lady, "drive to Miss Prance, the milliner." Then half to Jesse, half to Winefred, "It is essential that we get our dear child equipped properly. Then we will go on to the mercer's."

Winefred looked from side to side with undisguised admiration. She saw Mrs Jose, caught her eye, and smiled and signed to her. So also Jesse, who kissed her hand.

"The Abbey," said Mrs Jones. "My dear doctor, of whom I am the relict, lies there. He has a suitable, elegant monument. So also does Captain Shadrach Jones, his father – also with a neat memorial. Perhaps you would like to see them. Baker!"

"No, mamma," said Jesse, "it is the possessed with devils who frequent tombs."

"My dear, don't be irreverent." But she did not insist on dismounting at the Abbey. Presently the widow said, "I presume that the creature chose those dresses for you."

"What creature?"

"The woman, you know."

"What woman? Do you mean Mrs Jose?"

"Mrs Jose! Oh, dear no. She is not a creature or a woman, but a distant relative – very distant – of ours. I mean that individual, person, nurse – whatever she was, who looked after you in your childhood."

"Oh! My mother!"

"Well, yes, that worthy being whom you have been accustomed to so designate. Ancient domestics of that description are estimable, and, up to a certain point, useful; but beyond that point are liable to become insufferable nuisances. It is so difficult to get them to realise what is their proper place. They want the delicacy of intuition which should show them when to fall into the rear because no longer wanted. They are given to presume and become intolerable. It was high time for you to dissociate yourself from an individual of this description. You must excuse my frankness, but association with such a *personale* has already infected your intonation. In a few years it would have been hopeless to have attempted to eradicate it. Happily, at your years, the vocal organs are still flexible and the ear has not been deformed. Yet dialect is not to be got rid of as easily as an unbecoming and unfashionable suit of clothes. We shall have to exert every effort on our part, meeting with response from you, to master this defect. What was the name of that woman?"

Winefred's face became crimson. She moved uneasily on the seat. All her pleasure in the drive and at the novelty of the scenes was gone. Jesse, sitting opposite, misinterpreted her distress and attributed it to the references made by her mother to Winefred's provincial dialect and unfashionable gown. But such reflections in no way wounded the girl. That which troubled her was the slighting reference to her mother. She would have burst forth in vindication of one who was inexpressibly dear to her, but was restrained by recollection of the urgency of her mother, and of Mrs Jose, not to allow herself to be drawn into a revelation of the true connection that existed between them. She was quite aware of the delicacy and difficulty of her situation. She passed under one name, her mother under another, and the circumstances were too obscure for her to be able to explain how this was.

Happily the current of Mrs Tomkin-Jones's thoughts was diverted. She turned to Winefred and said with solemnity, "We are now approaching – look on the right. You will see a chemist's establishment with the Royal arms above the shop window, and the inscription accompanying it, 'By Royal Appointment.' It was there that the celebrated pill –"

189

"I thought as much," said Jesse, interrupting her mother, "the bread pills were certain to be rolled forth."

"*Bread* pills, my dear!" exclaimed Mrs Jones indignantly; "your lamented father was not the man to prescribe bread to Royalty. I do not relish this tone. Had it not been for professional rivalry, your father would have had a baronetcy conferred on him, and I should have been Lady Tomkin-Jones. The pills did it."

"Rather, they did not do it," asserted the irrepressible Jesse.

Mrs Tomkin-Jones drew her lips together as though about to whistle. This was expressive of indignation. She said no more on the matter, but sighed. The lady was wont to sigh when her mental corns were trodden on.

She had stiffened her back in pride as she approached the chemist's shop. It became stiffer with indignation at her daughter's levity and lack of reverence. But the shop passed, she relaxed and sank back into a dignified position, and said, "Ah! by the way, what is her name?"

"Whose name?"

"That of the domestic."

"Do you mean, ma'am, my –"

"For heavens sake, do not address me as ma'am."

"What shall I say – Mrs Tomkin-Jones?"

"That is almost worse; it stamps a person at once. Only servants of lodging-house type address one thus. Neither, if you please."

"I will try to recollect."

"What was the name of the nurse?"

"Marley – Mrs Marley."

"And, I presume, you have fallen into the habit of calling her mother or mamma?"

"I did not fall into it, I grew up with it."

"Most reprehensible, but under the circumstances explicable and excusable. That sort of female is given to presume and push, and requires to be taught its place. I have little doubt she did her utmost to spoil you." Winefred was shaking; anger, resentment swelled her heart.

"That sort of female," said Winefred in a quivering voice, "is one

190

to love and reverence."

Jesse saw that something had gone wrong. She touched her mother with her foot and shook her head. "Well, it is flattering to the self-esteem of individuals of an inferior order to have a child of good blood and name in their charge and to be able to attach it to them. But you ought to have called her Marley, or nurse – no more." The tears filled the girl's eyes, the colour rose and fell in her cheeks as mercury in a barometer before a hurricane.

Jesse, who saw her distress, and was vexed with her mother, said, so as to produce a diversion. "Now, mother, the story of the pills – anything but this Catechism on your Duty to your Inferiors."

"No, my dear, I will not tell the story of the pills, as you so pertly call it. The narrative touches the Crown, and whatever touches the Crown should be treated with respect, even if its association with the name of your august father did not exact that it should be approached with decorum. Oh! there is Frank Wardroper! Here! Baker! stay! I wish to speak with a gentleman." Then signing to a young man irreproachably dressed, she turned to Winefred, and said in a low tone, "Son of Sir Barnaby Wardroper, you know. I will introduce him. An eligible acquaintance."

The chariot was arrested, and to the signalling of the gloved hand and bobbing head, the youth approached with raised hat and graceful bow. After the usual salutations had been interchanged, with remarks on the weather and inquiries that were mutual as to health – "Allow me, my dear Mr Frank, to introduce you to a charming friend from the green lanes of old England, a flower from its most rural nooks. Mr Wardroper, my dear Miss Holwood, Mr Frank Wardroper; she belongs, you know, to that delightful family, the Finnboroughs – allied that is. So unfortunate that the Viscount has left Bath; he and Lady Finnborough would have been so charmed, you know. My dear Mr Frank" – aside into his ear, but audible to Winefred – "an heiress, daughter – sole child of the Governor–General of – I forget – one of out most vast and important of the Colonial possessions – a veritable goldmine." Then she pursed up her lips, winked and nodded, and made symbolic gestures with her hands and parasol, as though unfurling something – the rent–roll of Winefred and pouring forth something, the plunder of the Colony of Tierra del Fuego. "By the way, Mr Wardroper, you are a man of exquisite taste, you know, and, I wonder, I wonder now, whether you could be induced by any poor words of mine to take a seat in our equipage, beside Jesse, and accompany us. In fact, positively we are going to the milliner's and dressmaker's to rehabilitate my dear little country friend here, and you are such a judge, have so fine a perception in colour and cut, such tact as to fit, that I feel we should acquire an incalculable advantage could we secure your opinion."

"Delighted!" said Mr Wardroper. The steps were let down, and the young exquisite, who was such a connoisseur in dress, was admitted to the carriage.

"Between you, me and the post," said Mrs Tomkin–Jones, setting up the stick of her parasol beside her mouth, "my country friend here has been allowed to run wild in the hedges like a rose of June. Her distinguished father is a widower, involved in diplomacy and all that, you know, and quite unable to attend to her education. She has been left too much in the hands of vulgar domestics, and – well, you know the result. *Des lacunes, comprenez vous – soyez l'aimable et n'y prenez attention – cependent elle est charmante.*"

Winefred turned hot and cold. She knew that she was being discussed in a language she did not understand; above all – what she suspected was that some disparaging remark had been made relative to her mother. She was already beginning to feel that her new position would be one of discomfort out of all proportion to its advantages. But suddenly, with a start, she put up her hand and exclaimed – "Oh!"

Chapter Thirty–Two

At the Milliner's

"My dear," said the relict of Tomkin–Jones, MD, "if I may be allowed the impertinent question, why did you say 'oh!'?"

"I – I think I saw someone I know," answered Winefred, colouring.

"None of the Finnborough! Do not say that. We will drive on – or turn the carriage. In which direction? I did not see the liveries. Perhaps on foot."

"Yes."

"The Viscount. No – positively. You must introduce me as an old and valued friend, you know."

"It was not – I am not sure. I may be mistaken, but I think I caught a glimpse of my father."

"Your father! Not possible. Not returned from the Colony? I see – to be advanced. He knows that you are here. He will call and inquire."

"I am not sure he knows that I am with you. It was arranged without him."

"He must have arrived quite recently. Prodigious! My dear Mr Frank, let us procure the last edition of the *Bath Gazette*. We shall find him among the fashionable arrivals."

"The new number will not be issued till the day after tomorrow."

"True – we must remain in suspense. Or shall we inquire at the principal hotels? This will be quite an accession to our circle, and a heightening of our pleasure. All the more reason, if her father be here, that Miss Holwood should appear to the best advantage. I wonder now, whether he designs to take her out with him, to be the belle of the assemblies of what's the place! How good of you, Mr Frank, to assist us with your counsel. I suppose it will hardly do to ask you to our table to take pot-luck with us? Our circle is but one of ladies."

"A garland of imperishable roses," said Mr Wardroper. "I shall be more than happy."

"Nonsense, Mr Wardroper – pot-luck, remember. Upon my honour, I believe there are but scraps in the house, and I expect only rissoles or cottage pie."

"Mamma, you know that you ordered a head and shoulders of salmon, and that Mrs Jose has brought us two beautiful ducks."

"Prodigious! I had forgotten."

"Really," said the young man, "what is on the table will be immaterial to me in such society, where eye and ear are in a thrill of ecstasy." He took off his hat and bowed round.

"Oh, Mr Wardroper, excuse me, what an elegant new ring you are wearing!" said the widow. "How did you come by it? If not asking impudent questions, is it a present or a purchase?"

"If the ring meet with your approval, that is its highest value. It is actually my father's signet ring. His hands have become so crippled with rheumatism, and the joints of the fingers so swollen, that he is no longer able to wear it, so he has transferred it to me. It is an heirloom."

The young man removed a fine engraved cornelian, set in gold, and handed it to Mrs Tomkin-Jones. "Your arms, I presume?" she said, looking at it.

"Certainly – a chevron between three choughs. The crest a Cornish chough. Though, I protest, I have not the smallest idea what the bird is – whether it exist, or is extinct as the dodo, or fabulous as the wyvern."

"But I know it," said Winefred.

"Martlets have, I believe, no feet," said Mrs Jones.

"But these have legs and beaks of sealing-wax scarlet," said Winefred. "Otherwise they are as black as ravens. They are clever birds and build in our cliffs. We had one about a year ago, but a cat got at it. He was tame and loved to be stroked and caressed and talked to. He would run up a ladder like a squirrel. But oh! he was mischievous, once he got at mother's box–"

"Do you mean your poor deceased mother's jewel-case, or only the workbox of your nurse?" asked the widow.

"I mean where were the tapes and pins and buttons," answered Winefred, colouring.

"Really," said the young man, "I protest that you make me desirous to see one of these birds. Conceive my ignorance in not knowing what a chough was, and yet bearing three of them on my shield and one on my helm."

"It would be pure," said Mrs Tomkin-Jones, "to have one, tame, in the square garden. I suppose that it would remain there, were the wing clipped. But there are cats."

"Oh!" exclaimed Winefred, "our bird would have been able to keep away from the cat if it had not been ill, but it had swallowed a brass thimble and was heavy and dropping. If you had it in the house, nothing would content it but to trip upstairs to the very garret."

"Elle est ingenue, n'est pas?" An aside of Mrs Tomkin–Jones to Mr Wardroper. Then, "It would be really too charming to have one of these birds in the garden."

"I can get you a pair," said Winefred. "When I go home I will see to it. You can have only young choughs, but their beaks and legs are orange the first year; it is not till the second that they become scarlet. The wild, full–grown birds cannot be caught. They are becoming scarce. I think that the jackdaws are driving them."

"How gratified Sir Barnaby will be!" observed the relict of Dr Jones to young Wardroper. "How it will amuse him to see in the flesh hopping about in the garden the choughs that are engraved on his plate, and worn on his livery. Ah! here we are."

To a woman there is no happiness more sincere, more honest than that of spending money freely on her personal adornment. Next in degree is that of spending it on the decoration of another. Such as have not money at command to lavish, enjoy a very real and full happiness when the chance comes to them to dip freely into another person's purse regardless of the object for which they dip. Mrs Tomkin–Jones had felt poignantly her inability to sweep into every shop in Bath, and run up bills commensurate with her social importance, and worthy of the memory of the late MD, the Maker of Bath. But now her bosom swelled, and every pulse tingled with pride, because she was able to exhibit before the shop assistants that she was a woman who, if she did not spend much herself, was able to introduce to them such as could do so. The consciousness of importance gave stiffness to her back, amplitude to her bosom, elevation to her chin, and passed in electric rustles through the folds of her gown. The mere looking through an assortment of materials, the matching of ribbons, the balancing of trimmings against the textile fabrics they are to enrich, afford a joy to the female heart such as no man can enter into.

When the preliminaries had been discussed and determined, then ensued the second act of the drama, the ascent to the measuring and fitting room, from which man is as absolutely excluded as of old from the mysteries of the Bona Dea. Mrs Tomkin–Jones described a circle with a sweep of her skirts and said to Jesse, "My dear, I am sure you will remain here with Mr Wardroper, whilst I attend Miss Holwood above!" Then to the young man, "I am truly sorry, but do you mind?"

"To be left with Miss Jesse is like being given custody of the Crown jewels," answered he. When Winefred and Mrs Tomkin-Jones were gone, Jesse turned with a laugh to Frank Wardroper and said: "It is positively bad. We are boring you intolerably."

"Not at all. My soul lives in art."

"You are laughing at us."

"Set your mind at rest. Do you not see that the proper dressing of a lovely girl is a matter of transcendental importance? It is like the setting of a fine melody to rich and appropriate harmonies, it is the clothing of a poetic idea in a cloud of expressive, illustrative words. Be a jewel ever so fine, it exacts proper meaning."

"Is this your own?" asked Jesse bluntly.

"It is from my father – like the ring. I do not pretend to originate, only to embellish."

"I have no great interest in dress."

"You are wrong. Excuse my saying it, but you are. You have, you say, at home salmon and ducks. The whole charm, delight of our prospective meal will consist in their being well dressed, stuffed and garnished. There is style in everything, in language, in painting, in cooking, and in clothing, and no woman is justified in forgetting this."

After the lapse of a quarter of an hour, the feet of Mrs Tomkin-Jones appeared on the stair, followed by the gradual unrolling of the lady, next by that of Winefred, and then that of the shopwoman, as they descended from the measuring department. A placitude, an elevation, an illumination invested the countenance of Mrs Tomkin-Jones, as though she had endowed a hospital, or was about to give her body to be burned in martyrdom for the Faith.

"Will one of the young men call my coachman," said the lady

with dignity. "And, Miss Finch, you will remember my instructions about the *ruche*."

"Home!" ordered Mrs Tomkin–Jones, accepting the offices of the shopman, when he shut the carriage door, as undeserving of recognition, being of everyday occurrence. "Since we live in the same square, Mr Frank, my carriage will take you to your door after having set us down."

One of the party alone was dispirited and indisposed for conversation, and that was she whose money was being spent, and whose person was to be adorned. A fibre of her soul had been jarred. On reaching the door round the corner, the ladies descended. Frank Wardroper had jumped out.

"Baker shall drive you on," said Mrs Tomkin–Jones grandly.

"Not at all – we are but five doors off."

"He really may as well."

"I am already out and on my feet." He took off his hat and bowed.

"*Au revoir*," said Mrs Jones, "*à sept heures.*"

On entering the house, Winefred, who had become somewhat pale, laid her hand on the arm of her hostess and said, "I should wish to say something."

"By all means, my dear, when?"

"Now, but not in the passage."

"The hall," was Mrs Jones's correction. "Is it concerning the tulle for the Assembly Ball? I myself question the ribbons."

"It is not about any dresses," answered Winefred.

"Well, here, come into the dining–room. Sylvana! No, she is not there, and the fire is low. Goodness, how the smell of last meal hangs about! Why did she not open the windows? As to the domestic servants, they think of nothing. Now, my dear, what is it?"

"Shall I come in?" asked Jesse.

"Yes," said Winefred. "I should wish you to hear what I have to say." She shut the door. Mrs Tomkin–Jones drew off a glove, and then threw up her veil.

"Very well, yes, my dear."

"It is one thing only," said the girl. Jesse saw that she was in earnest, that her communication would not concern the dresses. She said to herself, "That girl has a temper, and is going to fly out."

"It is one thing only," repeated Winefred, looking straight at the widow. "What did you say to the gentleman in a foreign language?"

"To Frank Wardroper? In what language? I speak several."

"I cannot tell what tongue it was, but it was not English."

"Oh! I did say something in French, I remember. But of course you know French?"

"I do not. You know that I do not."

"Every lady is familiar –"

"I was not brought up as a lady."

Mrs Tomkin–Jones was confounded, but she recovered herself. "No, my dear child, I know you were left in charge of an ignorant person who neglected –"

"I was sent to a Dame's school, but I did not learn French there. That matters not. You were, I think, alluding in French to my – to my – Mrs Marley. You used some words; that was before we entered the shop. If they concerned me I do not care, but if they reflected on her, I *do* care. I care with my whole heart and soul, and" – the tears were near filling her eyes – "I have heard you call her a person, a creature, a thing, and what you said about her in French I know not, but it was not civil or you would not have spoken it in a strange tongue. What did you say?"

"I really do not recall."

"It does not matter. But, madam, consider this. I will not have Mrs Marley spoken of, in English or in French, in a way that is not respectful. None but I know what she has been to me, nor how that there is no one in the world to fight her battles but myself. No one but I know how good she is, how true, how honest, how loving; those who snap and sneer at her are not worthy to buckle her shoes. A word spoken against her, in ridicule or in disparagement, I *will* not bear, I *cannot* bear. I cannot tell what I might say or do if I heard it again. But of this I am certain, I will throw all the advantages away from me which I might gain by being here rather than hear it again. I would rather leave the house and go back to her once more."

"It does your heart credit," said Mrs Tomkin–Jones, who was really a good and well–meaning woman.

198

Then Jesse burst forth: "Let me kiss you. Now I know that I shall love you. If mamma says a word against her, I will stamp on her corns, and she has soft ones, too!"

Chapter Thirty-Three

In the Square

The day was pleasant, the sun shone, and the spring buds were swelling. In Bath vegetation is in advance of that elsewhere. The crocus was passing and the daffodil was coming on. Clouds, mountainous, snowy, were piled up in the blue sky. The sun was warm, in the garden of the square it was possible to sit out and enjoy it. The hills about Bath, and the houses that encompassed the square, cut off the cold wind.

Mrs Tomkin-Jones, because numbered as belonging to the square, possessed a key that admitted within the rails into the precinct where grew seringa and snowballs, was wintry grass, and where accumulated scraps of paper, the waifs of the street. By means of the key Winefred had admitted herself to the garden, and was seated on a bench enjoying the sun, occupied with thoughts the reverse of sunny.

The girl was not reconciled to her surroundings. She had begun to doubt her adaptability to them; she was low-spirited, and perplexed as to her course. At moments she felt that she would have been less uncomfortable at Axmouth. The gibes of the village girls would have been less intolerable than the patronage of Mrs Tomkin-Jones. The envy of the rustics was a recognition of superiority, and consequently flattering to her pride, whereas the condescension of the doctor's widow impressed on her a sense of inferiority, and that an inferiority on an uncertain stage. At Axmouth she at all events felt the ground under her feet. Here, at Bath, she did not touch ground at all. She was like one of those glass imps in a water bottle that goes to the bottom at a touch on the elastic cover of the vessel, and the thumb

199

of Mrs T–J was much employed in depressing her.

If Winefred could have said, I am a poor girl, I went about on the seashore collecting pebbles and grinding them, and glad to get a shilling for a good specimen, and my mother peddled tapes and buttons, I have had no more education than could be acquired in a Dame's school – then she would have experienced a sense of relief.

But this she could not do. Her father was a gentleman. She was being polished at his desire, and in fulfilment of her mother's ardent wishes. She was no longer poor, but her mother must ever remain illiterate and excluded from the class into which she, Winefred, was to be introduced. Nor was this all that troubled her. She was in uncertainty as to the actual position of that mother whom she idolised; consequently she was in doubt as to her own.

If her mother had been really married, then Winefred had a perfect right to the name she bore, but it was a mistake for her mother not to carry the same. But if the marriage had been invalid, then she herself was guilty of imposition in assuming a name to which she had no title. In many ways she was sailing under false pretences. Her situation was full of difficulties and productive of embarrassment. To shield her mother, she could not speak of her as her mother; she was constrained to accept the fable that she was her nurse. She was impelled into a course of equivocation and half–truths against which her conscience rebelled.

Were it to leak out that Mrs Marley actually was her mother, what looks would be exchanged, and how precipitate would be her expul- sion from the house! For herself she would not care. But she was aware that her mother's ambition was to see her a lady, and this was a necessary step towards that goal. Were she by her conduct or admissions to forfeit her place there, it would make her mother's heart bitter with disappointment. Moreover, she had been led to believe that she was put with Mrs Tomkin–Jones at her father's desire, and deep in her heart lay the longing desire that she might be the means at some future time of bringing him and her mother together once more. If that consummation were to be obtained, it could only be through fidelity in carrying out their common desire.

She had tact, and yet was in fear of betraying her ignorance, transferred suddenly as she was from one social element into another. When she did make a blunder it involved an elaborate apology and explanation on the part of Mrs Tomkin–Jones to such as had witnessed the error, and this wounded her to the quick.

Had she been a cowardly girl she would have written to her mother to say that her position was unendurable and that she must return to her. But she was brave and strong. She knew her mother's heart, and to satisfy the ambition of that heart she was content to remain and suffer.

But it must be added that, although she was subjected to humiliations and to discomforts, there were compensations. She was quick-witted and perceptive enough to see that an opportunity was given her of making her future. Nor was she so unfeminine as not to feel a relish in being measured, fitted, and brought up to the fashionable pitch. Nor again so inhuman as not to derive pleasure from being complimented by Mr Wardroper, the value of whose flatteries she was too inexperienced to estimate. As Winefred sat thus, her mind a prey to many thoughts and her heart to conflicting emotions, she noticed a man sauntering along the side of the square, by the rail, which he tapped with his umbrella handle and rattled as he came along.

Something in his manner attracted her attention, and diverted it from her own affairs. Owing to the intervention of the rails she could not see his face distinctly till he came near, and then only when having inadvertently missed striking one bar, he stepped back to tap it. At once she leaped to her feel – she had recognised her father – and she ran to the gate, opened it and awaited him. Mrs Tomkin–Jones had studied the *Bath Gazette*, but had not found in it among the fashionable arrivals that of the Governor of Tierra del Fuego, and she had thought that Winefred must have been mistaken when she caught a passing glimpse of a gentleman and took him to be her father. Now there could be no doubt as to the identity.

The same indecision was in the man in the square as had been in him on the beach; but he looked feebler. His action in tapping the bars was like that of a child. She observed that his lips moved, he was counting them, without purpose as a child. His going back to strike a bar that had been omitted was the action of a child.

He was by no means an uncomely man. On the contrary, his features were finely cut, and had the lower jaw been firmer, and the chin less retreating, he would have been pronounced a handsome man. His brow was high and white, his eyebrows well arched, and the eyes fine, soft and full. Winefred's heart beat fast in uncertainty whether he would recognise her or not. He came slowly on, with his eyes looking dreamily before him, and his lips moving as he counted, till he was close upon her. She blocked the way to his advance. Then he drew back, raised his hat and said politely, "A thousand pardons – sixty–eight, sixty–nine – I did not observe you." He looked at Winefred. A trouble came into his eyes. He was not sure. Did he know the young lady? The face was familiar, yet – "I must apologise," said he hesitatingly, "if I – if I –"

"If you do not recollect your own child," said Winefred, "it is not her fault. You are, indeed, my father, who met me on the shore, and here is the watch you then gave me. I am Winefred Holwood."

He recoiled and groped in his pocket for his latchkey, but being unable to find it, put the handle of his umbrella to his lips and blew upon that, then stood, undecided, looking at her with the umbrella held up between them, and the handle at his mouth.

"Father," said Winefred, "will you come through the gate into the garden? I should like to have some talk with you."

"Oh, yes! indeed, indeed, this is surprising. I trust no one overheard you. Unexpected felicity, astounding encounter."

"I saw you some days ago, as I was driving down Pulteney Street."

"You were driving! How come you here? No, do not answer till I see that we are not overheard. Is there anyone else in the garden? Were you in company? I should not like – I mean I should prefer–" Winefred drew him within and shut the gate.

"I do not see why, father, you should be surprised to see me. It was your wish that I should be brought up as a lady, and if you did not choose Mrs Tomkin–Jones's house for me–"

"I do not understand."

"You provided the money; otherwise, of course, my darling mother could not have afforded this."

"I – I provided the money! Oh, yes, certainly, certainly, and with

202

the utmost regularity, and I shall continue to do so. But I did not anticipate–"

"It was all arranged by dear Mrs Jose."

"Mrs Jose! Oh, indeed."

"She knew some people here of distinction, and they agreed to receive me and polish me, so as to make a lady of me; you understand, deal with me as Mr Thomas Gasset does with the pebbles, rub and smooth and bring to a surface. It was your own desire."

"I – well. Oh, certainly. Nothing could be better; but do they know? – excuse me, is it a matter of knowledge?"

"What do you mean, sir?" She fixed her eye on him.

"I mean – I hardly can find words to adequately express my meaning. I would say – What name do you carry here?"

"I have told you, father. Winefred Holwood. Holwood is your name."

"To be sure. Exactly. I wish I had my key, but they have deprived me of it. Yes, of course, inevitable. And your – I mean your –"

"Mother?"

"Precisely. Is she here also?"

"No."

He breathed freer. "And do they know?"

"By they, I suppose you mean Mrs Tomkin–Jones and her daughters?"

"It is with them you are staying?"

"Yes – and they know nothing."

"She – did she – I mean your mother – did she bring you to Bath?"

"No. Mrs Josc did that."

"Mrs Jose, certainly. Charming. But who *is* Mrs Jose?"

"She is the farmer's wife at Bindon."

"Bindon" Oh? I am again at fault. Bindon, very nice; but where *is* Bindon?"

"Bindon is near where mother and I lived. Mrs Jose has been very kind to us, that is, mother and me, when all the folk in Seaton and Axmouth turned against us. She alone held to us and believed in mother. And mother said that it was your intention that I should be brought up a lady, and she and Mrs Jose put their heads together, and I have been sent here to Mrs Tomkin–Jones."

"Mrs Tomkin–Jones! Delicious! Who is this lady?"

"I believe her husband was the maker of Bath. A most eminent physician. There is a story about him and a pill, but I do not know it."

I never heard of him, or of her, or of the pill."

"But Mrs Tomkin–Jones knows about you."

"Merciful powers! Knows *what*!" The man quaked.

"That you are a relative of Lord Finnborough."

"Finnborough! Finnborough has never done anything for me, although I believe there is some sort of connection."

"Then that at least is true. Here I do not know what is lies and what is truth. Will you sit down on this bench, sir? Mrs Tomkin–Jones lives in the corner house yonder, with an eye looking this way and another that."

"Do you think that her eye is on us now?"

"No; the sun shines in at it, so the blind is down."

"How long do you remain with her?" Mr Holwood's chin was too retreating for him to be able to lodge it on the handle of his umbrella, but he attempted to do so repeatedly, and as often failed.

"Till the rubbing and polishing are done. That will be long. I am harder than a chalcedony."

"This is a dreadful shock to me."

"A shock to meet your child?"

"I mean, I mean a surprise. I am taking the waters. Strong emotions I have been instructed to avoid. I am not well. A dreadful menace hangs over me, a sword of Damocles. I have been ordered here by my medical attendant, I feel unhinged at the news." Then, changing his tone, and disengaging his hand from the umbrella, he took Winefred's fingers in his nerveless grasp and said, "My child – yes, my child – it is soothing to the feeling – to the heart of a desolate, a sick, maybe a death–stricken man, to know that he has a child."

"And a wife." He winced and let go her hand.

"There are sundry considerations that have interfered," said he, with a faltering voice and a veil let down over his eyes. "You cannot understand. In the higher circles, you know; but she is your mother, and I would rather say no more."

"Father," said Winefred, "I will tell you right out how matters stand here – here, not at Axmouth, only here in Bath. Here I am your child, but my mother is thought to be dead."

"Dead!" His cheek flushed.

"Only in Bath. She is in Axmouth and alive there."

"I do not understand."

"Mrs Jose had given out that she was my nurse – my nurse only, not my mother. She did this because my dear mother insisted on it."

"Oh! true. I am glad."

"I do not like it. I am unhappy. It is a lie. I hate lies. But I cannot help myself. Here, in Bath, she is known as my nurse."

"Quite so, your nurse."

"Yes, In Bath. Elsewhere she is my mother."

"Ah, your mother. You have her force – her vehemence."

"And she is your wife."

"I am – ah! so agitated. I will see you again. I must go and have some of the waters. I will call on Mrs –"

"Tomkin–Jones. And on me, your child?"

"Yes – I shall see you again – my child." He stood hesitating before her. Then he stooped, looked about him timidly, and, seeing no one, kissed her brow.

Chapter Thirty–Four

Mischief–Making

A rap at the front door, followed by a ring, and then a card was brought up by the servant and presented to Mrs Tomkin–Jones on a blistered Japan tray.

"Oh, certainly – charmed," said the lady. Then to Winefred, "My dear – your father." Next moment Mr Holwood was ushered into the drawing–room, in which, happily, a fire was burning, but the covers had not been removed from the furniture.

He was well dressed, in a plum–coloured coat with high rolling collar, brass buttons, a tall cravat, and two waistcoats, one of which was of figured silk. His trousers were tight–fitting and buttoned at the ankles. At first glance Mrs Jones saw that he was a gentleman and a gentleman of style. He bowed to each lady as he entered and advanced, and his gold–framed eyeglass dangled and swung as a pendulum under these evolutions. As he approached the lady of the house he offered profuse apologies for his intrusion, and then turned and touched Winefred's cheek with his lips.

"So glad to make your acquaintance, Mr Holwood," said Mrs Jones. "It is a real honour to Bath to receive a visit from you."

"I have come," said the gentleman, "positively to throw myself at your feet, madam, in the attitude of a suppliant. I am so much alone in Bath–"

"Yes, the Finnboroughs have left."

"The – oh yes!"

"How is your sister, the Viscountess?"

"My sister! Oh! you mean my cousin, Lady Finnborough. 'Pon my word of honour, I don't know. It is Finnborough himself who is dyspeptic. She is all right, I believe. I never heard anything to the contrary; but 'pon my soul, I know little of them, and they less of me." Mrs Tomkin–Jones sighed.

"It has occured to me," said Mr Holwood, "that my daughter, coming from the country, might like to walk and look at the shops – and possibly – some trifle in the windows – and so far as my limited means reach – ahem! So I came, with all due deference, to ask if she might be spared from the studies and all that kind of thing to come a light stroll with me."

"She is entirely at your service," said the lady. "I only regret that her new set of gowns and her hats are not come home from mantua–maker and milliner – in which she would be more suitably dressed, and do you more justice."

"I thank you – she will pass."

"By the way, sir," said the widow, "have you any objection to Winefred attending the next ball at the Assembly?"

"Not in the least – only – but –"

"There is some difficulty about a chaperon. Since my bereavement I cannot go – by the merest accident I know no one of title at the present moment in Bath who could introduce her. There is Lady Wardroper, but she is in constant attendance on her husband."

"Wardroper!" said Mr Holwood. "Not Sir Barnaby?"

"The same."

"I have met him at my office."

"The son is very intimate here. He takes a lively interest in what relates to dress."

"Sir Barnaby was a bit of a buck."

"Alas! he is now a cripple from rheumatism."

"I was unaware that he was here. I will call and see him certainly. I have not been in Bath many days."

"You are not surely going?" said Mrs Tomkin–Jones, as her visitor rose. "Run, Winefred, and get on your things. You desire her to be with you now, I take it."

"If you please."

When Winefred had left the room, the doctor's widow said, "You will excuse the liberty I take, but the interest I feel in your engaging daughter, and the responsibility laid upon me, induce me to speak with a plainness from which I should otherwise shrink. I think, Mr Holwood, that you have made a mistake. Gentlemen, widowers especially, are liable to fall into errors of judgment that produce results that are deplorable. You have – pardon the remark and my freedom in making it – you have committed a serious error in allowing your daughter to grow up under the influence of that woman."

"That woman!" repeated Mr Holwood timidly, and not having a latchkey to trifle with, put the brim of his hat to his lips.

"The nurse, I mean, whose name is Mrs Marley. It must be confessed that she is a vulgar woman."

"You know her?" His hand shook. He set down his hat and took up his gold–edged glasses.

"Not at all. I judge by results. The girl has fallen so completely under her thraldom that she has come to regard her almost in the light of a mother. It speaks well for her heart, but ill for your judgment. I can quite understand the power over her gained by a woman who attended her in her childish ailments, who dressed her dolls, and put her hair in curlpapers. But although we must admire the quality of Winefred's heart in clinging to this individual, one can do no other than lament that the attachment has been so close between persons so different in rank. Contact, and that so intimate, with one of an inferior quality has had a deteriorating effect. It has imparted a rustical flavour to the speech, mind and manner of your child. Young characters are given shape and bias at an early age, and from their associates. Pardon my asking such a question, but have you married again?"

"No." Mr Holwood put his eyeglass to his lips, breathed on it, then produced a silk kerchief and wiped it. He did not notice in his nervous distress, how steadily and searchingly the eye of Sylvana was fixed upon him.

"I can give you an illustration of the manner in which that female has gained power over the girl. Winefred will not allow the most trifling remark to be made in disparagement of her. She has even taken me to task, and has threatened to leave should I let slip a word to her disadvantage."

"Ah! yes."

"When she refers to that individual, she has spoken of her on more than one occasion as her mother. This is reprehensible, and a practice that must be abandoned."

"Oh! yes – yes!"

"This doubtless commends itself to you in the same light as to me."

"Oh! certainly." Drops stood on his brow and lip. He employed the kerchief to wipe his face. Then, with a quiver in his voice, "Perhaps you would not mind speaking to her on the matter."

"I have spoken; it is, excuse my plain speech, your duty to back me up. I see clearly that if she be allowed to fall under the influence of this female, it will undo all the advantage she has derived from a residence in my house. If you will pardon the liberty I take, I would advise you to dismiss this personage, to send her to her friends – with a pension perhaps."

"She has a liberal allowance."

"Quite so, but let her live on this allowance at a distance, and on the understanding that it will be withdrawn should she attempt to renew her relations with Winefred."

"I – think – I am sure, I cannot do this."

"Then suffer me to take the negotiations out of your hands; it will doubtless come better from me. Empower me to write and place the matter before her in a clear light, inform her that she must never see Winefred again. It will be solely by dissociating your child from vulgar persons that the little peculiarities in her dialect and the provincial mannerism, I note, can be effaced. You agree with me?"

"I – I –"

"You see the necessity."

"Yes, oh, assuredly."

"Hist! Here she comes. I accept the responsibility. Not a word before her."

When Mr Holwood was gone with his daughter, Sylvana fixed her pebbly eyes on her mother, and said, "There is something wrong about that woman."

"About what woman?"

"The Marley."

"My dear, I know there is; she is vulgar."

"I do not mean that. There is a mystery attached to her. Have you not observed how uneasy Winefred becomes when you speak of her?"

"She will not suffer me to speak of her at all."

"And with Mr Holwood it is the more conspicuous. When you were making inquiries about her, or passing remarks upon her, he turned hot and cold, and his lips and brow positively cried. He was thrown into a condition of abject embarrassment. I am really surprised, mother, that you did not see it. But then you see nothing which is not to your advantage, or to the glory of the Tomkin-Joneses. I saw through the man at once."

"My dear, there is nothing to be seen in him save the perfect gentleman. Naturally he was distressed. I should take to my bed and never raise my head again if I knew that one of my daughters mispronounced her vowels or misplaced her prepositions."

"It was not that that troubled and alarmed him."

"What else can you mean?"

"There is some mystery concerning his relation with the Marley."

"Sylvana, I will not listen to a word that savours of impropriety. Besides, I receive five guineas a week for Winefred."

"Quite so, and for the sake of five guineas you shut your eyes."

"Sylvana – you forget the respect due to me."

"You forget the respect due to yourself and to us, and to the name of Tomkin–Jones, of which you think more than you do of Jesse and me. I say you forget that when you harbour in your house a person whose antecedents are equivocal."

"Equivocal! Goodness preserve me! I am known in Bath to be the very Pink of Propriety."

"You run the chance of becoming only the Picotee of Propriety – that I take to be a dappled pink – if you take under your patronage a girl of whom you know nothing, and who may turn out to be –"

"My dear, not a word. All will be right if we can cut off this woman. I do not allow what you suspect; but I can quite see that there is mischief in that woman, and that we must draw a line between her and Winefred that shall absolutely sever them for ever, in the interests of Morality."

Chapter Thirty–Five

The Young Man From Beer

To Mr Holwood it afforded pleasure to be able to walk in Pulteney Street with a fresh, pretty daughter on his arm. For the first time for many years the old buck held up his head and strutted proudly. He had the handle of his rattan to his mouth. His white beaver hat sat jauntily on his head, a little on one side, and his gold–framed glass was in his eye.

He thoroughly enjoyed the looks of admiration wherewith his daughter was greeted. Well dressed she now was. Her costume was no longer of country make; but what man gives a thought to the dress when the frame it encloses is graceful and the face within the bonnet is charming?

Mr Holwood saluted with consequence when an acquaintance passed in a carriage, as one who was conferring that favour of recognition in place of receiving it. An occasional walker caught his eye and bowed, then, seeing the young lady on his arm, drew to him and asked, "Introduce me, Mr Holwood." The father chuckled with delight, and his frilled shirt-front seemed to rise like the crest of a turkey-cock.

Winefred and her father had not been gone many minutes from the house before the house-door bell was again rung, this time with no accompanying rap. The maid soon after came to announce that a young man from near Axmouth was below, waiting, and had brought a hamper for Mrs Tomkin-Jones from Mrs Jose of Bindon. "We cannot receive him in the drawing-room," said the widow. "Jane, show him into the dining apartment." Then to her daughter: "I suppose I must give him a shilling. Have you any change, Sylvana?"

"Upstairs, mamma."

"Well, bring it to me below. I must thank him for his trouble and inquire after Mrs Jose, and offer him a glass of ale."

"Do you think a shilling sufficient remuneration, mamma?"

"Humph! half-a-crown is a good deal of money. It makes a sensible hole in a sovereign. We are not supposed to know, my dear, what the basket contains – possibly only watercress, and for that a shilling would be ample." Then to the servant who tarried: "Jane!"

"Yes, ma'am."

"What has the young man brought? Did he intimate to you what was the contents of the hamper?"

"A pair of spring chickens, ma'am."

"Then, Sylvana, eighteenpence is ample – ample. Bring the silver to me in the dining-room. I will hold my hand behind my back – or, stay! No. I have left my pocket-handkerchief above, and whilst giving me that, slip the change into my hand. Do not be long, as with this sort of people one does not know what to say."

211

Mrs Tomkin–Jones descended majestically to the red dining–room in which Jack Rattenbury was awaiting her, looking like a soul in purgatory. He at once handed her the maund, and stated that it was a little remembrance from Mrs Jose. "How good of you! I really am eternally obliged. And so you have come all the way from Axmouth? Not on purpose to bring this, I trust?"

"Oh no, ma'am. I am here on business for my master."

"What, Mr Jose?"

"No, madam, I am in the Beer quarries with Mrs Jose's brother, who works them. I have come to Bath on concerns of the quarry."

"Quite so. It is very good of you. A fine day this with drifting clouds; the sun is hot, but the wind cold. You have, no doubt, found it to be so?"

"Yes, ma'am; but the weather does not trouble me greatly."

"And how is that excellent Mrs Jose?"

"She is well, active, and as good as ever. There is not a woman for miles about more respected than Mrs Jose. I may even say, more beloved."

"Very pleased to hear it, and suitable to one in her situation. Oh! thank you, Sylvana. This is most considerate of you. How can I have been so neglectful as to leave my pocket–kerchief behind. I fear my memory is not what it was." To Jack: "I have had trials that wear a lady." She then accepted the handkerchief from her daughter, and at the same time closed her fingers and thumb over the change, and passed it into the palm of her hand. Then to Jack: "You will be so good as to thank Mrs Jose on my behalf."

"Would it not be more gracious, mamma," said Sylvana, "for you to write? It might, you know, extract further favours."

"My dear!" Mrs Tomkins–Jones frowned, then, "Ah, to be sure. I was intending to do so. The ink and a blotting book are in the room, but the pens are cross–nibbed. However, I trust I shall manage – oh!"

The exclamation was elicited by the fall of the sixpence from her hand upon the floor. But Mrs T–J was equal to the occasion; fixing the eyes of the visitor, she placed her foot on the coin, and executed the *pas* termed by the dancing–master a *chasse*; and so reached the writing–table with the sixpence carried along under her sole. She seated herself and began to write.

"I beg pardon," said Jack Rattenbury, "but may I be permitted to see Miss Holwood? I am the bearer of a message to her."

"From Mrs Marley?" asked Sylvana sharply.

"No, miss, from Mrs Jose."

"I suppose that you are acquainted with Mrs Marley?" enquired Miss Jones.

"I have seen her," answered Rattenbury.

"But you know something about her, I presume?"

"As to her age?"

"No," retorted Sylvana with sharpness. "As to who she was, whence she came, what her circumstances."

"She was certainly at one time younger than she is now; she lives on one side of the Axe," answered the young man, without a muscle in his face changing, "and there exists a ferry between the Axmouth and the Seaton side. I am at Beer, two miles distant from Seaton, and Seaton lies a quarter of a mile from the landing–stage of the ferry."

"Sylvana bit her lip. Was he stupid?

"Is Miss Holwood in?" he asked.

"No, she is not," snapped Miss Jones. "She is out at present with her father."

"Her father!" Jack let the words escape in an accent of surprise.

"I suppose you know Mr Holwood?" queried she.

"No, miss, I have never seen him."

"But you have heard of him?"

"One has, of course, taken it for granted, if there is a Miss Holwood, that there is a Mr Holwood also." Jack was aware that he was being pumped. It was done clumsily. He was conscious that, if pumped, it would be well for Winefred's sake that he should not reveal all that he knew. Sylvana knitted her brows. "You must have heard Mrs Marley talked about?"

"Really, miss," said Jack, "at our works the men talk mostly of politics, and leave scandal for women."

"Sylvana," said Mrs Tomkin–Jones severely, "I cannot possibly compose a letter whilst conversation is going on behind my back. I have made a blotch of the letter and shall have to write it again. Just listen and say if this will do. 'Dear Mrs Jose, Ten thousand thanks for those splendid spring chickens you have been so good as to send me. I think that I have never seen any before so plump, so delicate and toothsome.'"

"But ma'am," insisted Jack, "the hamper has not yet been opened."

"Ah! true. I had best see the fowls. Will you kindly cut the twine, I have no knife. Sylvana, I must write this letter over again. Listen. 'I have never seen before any so plump, so delicate and so toothsome, and we all look forward to enjoy scandal for women.' There, you see what you have made me say. I must take another sheet and rewrite my letter."

In the meantime Winefred was walking with her father in Pulteney Street. Thence they entered Sydney Gardens. "My dear child," said Mr Holwood, "may I inquire who is that young gentleman, so elegantly dressed, whom you seemed to recognise, and who saluted you with such refinement of manner?"

"Oh! that is Mr Frank Wardroper."

"Really! Then the old gentleman in the bath–chair propelled by a black servant is Sir Barnaby? 'Pon my soul, what a wreck! and I remember him so different." With raised hat, and bows as graceful as those of Mr Frank Wardroper, Mr Holwood approached the chair and introduced himself. The baronet held forth a shaky and contracted hand. "Allow me to introduce my daughter," said Holwood.

"Odds life!" exclaimed the baronet. "I congratulate you. A charming face. But, bless me! Holwood, I did not know you had been married."

"I had the misfortune to lose my wife early," answered Winefred's father in some confusion.

"Ah! by gad! glad it was not I. What I should do without Lady Wardroper to dress me and help me feed I do not know. No valet comes quite up to a wife in these matters. The wind is tempered to the shorn lamb. Gad! I'm glad I did not lose my wife. But, there, you are no cripple, so it don't concern you. Have you married again?"

"No, Sir Barnaby."

"Gad! I like that. Frank, my boy, mark that! It might go among 'The Percy Anecdotes' as an example of fidelity."

"Sir," said Frank, "if the mother at all resembled the daughter, he could do no other."

"Very well put. The boy has wit," said the baronet. "Who was she? Anyone I know? – or the family?"

"I fear not, Sir Barnaby. I am truly sorry to see you in this plight. How long has this been coming on you?"

"Gad! it has been slow in progress, and how long it will continue the Lord alone knows. I can enjoy nothing. The world has used me badly, crumpled me up like an old rag – and you?"

"And I?" Holwood became grave and his face livid. "I am afraid that I am threatened with something more serious, more painful than your affliction. It may be that I shall be let off with the scare – it may be –"

"Then, 'pon my soul! I'm sorry you lost your wife. Take my word for it, you can rely on a wife better than on a valet when *hors de combat*. I am sorry for you. Monstrous fine gal that."

"My daughter – the pleasure of having her with me has for the moment taken me out of myself and made me forget my fears."

"Taking the waters, Holwood? So am I, but they do me no good – harm rather. They are lowering. Excuse me, if I move on. Sambo! Sambo! Going to sleep there? I cannot remain still. I am liable to take a chill. Walk beside me, Holwood. Sambo! wheel me out of the gardens. I would ask you to dine, but, Lord! it is no pleasure. Lady Wardroper has the world of trouble to keep me clean. I cannot hold a knife and fork, and I spill the wine from my glass. However, it is her duty, and she likes it. Frank and the Missie can go on together. Walk by me, Holwood, and say something to amuse me. Gad! there is no wit in the world now. Lady Wardroper is all very well as a nurse, but she hasn't the faculty to answer me. Any new anecdotes out – epigrams? Any scandal? Ah! excuse me, I am having my twinges. Sambo! wheel me home. I must have my liniment rubbed in by Lady Wardroper. A good woman and useful, but dull."

Mr Holwood raised his hat. As Sir Barnaby was being rolled away, he said to his son: "Frank! A fine girl. Find out about her, who her mother was, and whether she left her a fortune. I did not know Holwood had been married; but he was a good-looking fellow, and rather a favourite with the ladies. Gad! So was I, and now I am this battered hulk! In the office, Holwood could not make any way. There will be a retiring pension, and his family is not amiss. Don't make more of an ass of yourself, Frank, than you are by nature. Do not commit yourself till she has been weighed and you have found her worth. Who the deuce is she talking with now? He looks like a seaman out for a holiday."

The person whom Winefred met as she left the Sydney Gardens was Jack Rattenbury. At sight of him she flushed to the temples. He came to her with deference in his manner. He could see that already she had stepped out of his sphere.

"So – you here?" said Winefred, in a tone expressive of annoyance.

"Yes – and an unwelcome sight."

"Indifferent rather."

"Who – who may this be?" asked her father.

"A young man from Seaton," answered Winefred, in a tone of indifference; "on that account it pleases him to address me."

"Not on that account," said Jack, "but because I am commissioned to you with a letter from Mrs Jose." He handed her a packet, folded and sealed.

"I thank you," she said in a tone of constraint. "Are you in Bath for long?"

"No; I return home tomorrow."

"Home! I did not know that you possessed one."

"Winefred!" said her father reproachfully.

"It is not my fault, but my misfortune that I am homeless," said Jack, looking the girl full in the face. And before his intense eyes her countenance fell. "I understand you," he said. "The word was said with intention to hurt. But it hurts me only so far as it shows me what your intention was."

"Did I hurt you?" asked Winefred, turning crimson. Then, "I am sorry." But the expression of regret came too late, Jack had already walked away.

Chapter Thirty-Six

To Bath

How Jack Rattenbury came to Bath must now be told.

Jack had found work, or it had been found for him. Whilst Winefred had been settling into new quarters at Bath he had been finding a temporary home and occupation at Beer. It had come about in this way. He had gone to Mrs Jose, at Winefred's suggestion, and told her his difficulties, and that kind-hearted woman had induced her brother, James Ford, or, as he was locally termed, Captain Ford, to give him employment in the Beer quarries.

These are excavations extending for a great distance underground in a fine-grained stone composed of carbonate of lime, that cuts like cheese, but hardens on exposure to the air. The Beer quarries are no scar and disfigurement to the landscape. They produce but little refuse, and that little is rapidly overrun with grass.

In the face of a cliff of white rock gape square openings and these lead to a labyrinthine underground world, where piers of stone support the upper beds, and every block that is extracted serves for building purposes. The quarries have been worked during many centuries. From them houses, cathedrals, have been built, and yet in outward appearance they are insignificant.

Jack was not employed as a common quarryman, but was given a stool in the office. No sooner was it settled between him and Captain Ford that he was engaged, than he started for Bindon, as in duty bound, to thank Mrs Jose for her intervention in his favour.

But as he passed out of the village of Axmouth he saw the farmer's wife in a tax-cart driving down the road with Winefred at her side, and behind was an arched trunk, covered with hair and traced with brass-headed nails, attached to the back of the cart by ropes. As Mrs Jose approached he noticed how her fresh face beamed with yellow soap and good–nature. She saw him at once and drew up.

"Well, Jack, my boy!"

"I have come to thank you," said he, patting the rough cob. "You have done me a real good turn, Mrs Jose, and if your eyes could look down into my heart as they can into sea–water, you would see true gratitude at the bottom."

"Like a sea–anemone open and asking for more," said Winefred.

"Not another word," said the good woman, ignoring the girl's malicious aside. "I am putting both of you out in the world, both you and Winefred. One is as much indebted as the other. Her I am taking to Bath, you I have disposed of at Beer. Well, good luck attend you, my boy; you have my best wishes – and luck will come to you if you are steady. That is my doctrine. Gee–up, Robin!"

But he would not let go the cob. He held the rein whilst he renewed his thanks. Then the jolly woman became impatient and cracked her whip. "Have done," said she. "You cannot thank me better than by remaining where you are and profiting by your position. Now, Jack, say good–bye to Winefred and wish her luck, as she wishes it for you."

Winefred looked at him without a word, and this paralysed his tongue. Mrs Jose waited for a moment, but as neither spoke she drove on with an impatient lifting of the elbows. Jack looked after the trap, but Winefred did not turn her head to give him a parting salute and kindly look.

"She might have been more gracious," he said, "but one cannot gather figs off thistles. She hates me, moreover, for all the contradictions she has had to endure, and the sours she has been forced to swallow because of that nonsense about my father's savings."

He walked away, reached the ferry, and hailed Olver to take him across. Dench was profuse in his expressions of regret at losing the society of the young man. Jack said a word of civility in response. He disliked and mistrusted the man, and was glad to be rid of his company. Nevertheless, the fellow had been a comrade of his father, and Jack had lived with him since the death of his father, and he accordingly did feel some regret at parting with Olver, though it was a regret largely qualified with relief.

"Come, lad!" said the ferryman. "Let us go to the Lion. We will have a glass to your good fortune." Jack could not refuse. He shouldered his bundle and accompanied the elder man into the village of Seaton, and with him entered the public-house kept by Mrs Warne.

But when there he was unable to talk, his heart was troubled, his mind engaged. He was thinking of the girl Winefred and of her ill-humour, rather than of his new start in life. Happily for him there were others in the house at their beer and with them Dench fell into talk. Jack sipped at his glass, looking dreamily before him.

"This is a poor beginning," said Dench, presently noticing how absent the lad was. "It is not what the captain would have liked – ah! there was a man if you will. He'd have said, 'You were not chipped off the old block, but whittled out of the soft wood of your mother.' He would have had you take to a more stirring life and one connected with the salt water."

"A man must take, in these times, whatsoever offers," answered Jack. "I have been sufficiently long out of work to take up any work with relish."

"But you need not have been without a job," said Dench, with a wink to his fellows at his table.

"I could get none that suited me."

"Well! There is no more understanding the fancies of boys than the whimsies of girls. There is Winefred Marley, or as she is pleased to call herself, Holwood, gone off to be a fine lady at Bath. We shall hear next of her marrying some fine gentleman, and when he comes to learn who and what she is, there will be the deuce to pay. However, she has a tongue that can parry as well as lunge."

Jack stood up. "I cannot remain here," he said. "I have no stomach for ale; moreover Captain Ford expects me at Beer."

"Well, go along with you, boy, and may you soon sicken of sawing stone and take to cutting the waves."

Beer village or hamlet was to be reached by one of two ways. There was the road, which was the shortest, that ran along a dip in the land, between green hedges; and there was the way by the White Cliff, that was pleasantest but longest. Jack chose the latter, solely because it was unfrequented, and in his then mood he was indisposed for conversation. What ailed him?

He had at length obtained that for which he had been in search, and for which he had chafed: work, and work eminently suitable, work, moreover, sufficiently well paid to support him. He was entering the service of a master who, if he possessed a tithe of his sister's good qualities, would be to him a friend and a father. He had accordingly every reason to be elated. On the contrary he was depressed. What ailed him?

Undoubtedly he felt his loneliness, yet he was not so lonely as he had been, for Mrs Jose had been a good friend to him, and had enlisted for him the sympathies of her brother. There is such a sensation in a young breast as home–sickness without a home for which to be sick; it is a vague yearning and regret after something unknown, undefined.

The young spirit is like young wheat – it grows weak, watery, yellow, there has been overmuch rain, overmuch cold. All it needs is the sun. That which burrowed in his heart like a mole was the thought of Winefred's treatment of him. He could understand that there was occasion for it. On his account she and her mother had suffered great annoyance, had undergone wounding suspicion. They had been sent to Coventry by the neighbourhood. Winefred was sensitive to the slights she had encountered, and held him to have been prime mover in the combination against her mother and herself. It was natural that she should regard him with resentment, and yet, that she should do so, knowing as he did that he had personally done nothing to stir up the hostile feeling against her and her mother, distressed him greatly.

Now that Winefred had departed he ought to have felt relieved. There was no further chance of an encounter in which he always came off worsted. Yet he was not so. In all likelihood he would see Winefred no more. She had gone to Bath; there she would make new friends, form new associations, and forget Axmouth and its vexations together with those who had occasioned them. This, again, should have relieved his mind; on the contrary, it depressed it further.

Certainly he was unhappy, without being able to account for his unhappiness. What was Winefred to him but one with whom he measured swords whenever they met? What could Winefred be to him in the future? A recollection, an unpleasant one, and nothing other. Why did he think of her? Why did her angry eyes haunt his soul? Why did her stabbing words still make his heart tingle?

He seated himself on the chalk cliff above the harbour of Beer, this latter a snip taken by the sea out of the soft and crumbling rocks. The choughs were flying beneath his feet, building in the crags that overhung the beach. Below was the pebble strand. Boats were drawn up on it. A thread of weed marked the retreat of the tide from the shore, a fringe of foam on the grey water a few yards from the land told also that the sea was in ebb. Gulls chattered and fluttered and dropped to secure some little fish stranded. The evening was closing in, and a pale light hung over the sea, that looked dull as lead, but gave to the chalk cliffs a moonlight whiteness.

At the flagstaff where the Beer streamlet trickled into the shingle and lost itself were fisher lads congregated in idleness. When nothing can be done at sea, none more listless, inert, pictures of *dolce far niente* than those who live by the harvest of the water. They will occupy a bench by the harbour hour after hour, smoking, occasionally talking, but doing absolutely nothing with hand or foot or brain. These fisher lads, several hundred feet below where sat Jack, were chattering, laughing and sometimes singing.

Then a boy's clear voice sounded:

> I would I were a sparrow
> > To light on every tree;
> At even, noon and morning,
> > My love, I'd sing to thee.
> And as the ship is sailing,
> > So lightly I would fly,
> And perch upon the mainmast,
> > My own true love to spy.
>
> I would I were a goldfish
> > All in the sea to swim,
> At even, noon and morning
> > To follow after him,

> And o'er the bulwark leaning,
>> He'd say, "What see I there,
> That shines so gay and golden?
>> A lock of my love's hair."

Then the boys burst out laughing, and there was a chatter as of birds, so that the singer was not suffered to finish his ballad. They all belonged to an age at which the emotions, the pangs of love, were unfelt, and a song that expressed them touched no fibre in the soul. But it was other with Jack. He knew the song, and his lips moved as he completed it, and his mind travelled away, not seaward but overland.

He remained some time on the cliff, but finally shook himself, picked up his bundle and descended into Beer. He had taken lodgings with a widow at the higher end of the village, in a picturesque cottage that leaned against the hill and faced every way except into the rock against which it leaned. This was near his work and away from the harbour, a double advantage, as he was not favourably eyed by the boatmen, who regarded him as a deserter from the cause of free trade, and as weak-spirited in abandoning a life of adventure for an office stool. Not only could he go to his work from the cottage without running the gauntlet of the inhabitants of the village, but he was also able with the same immunity to go to Seaton or ramble on the cliffs. Jack was not timid, but every lad is thin-skinned and sensitive to ridicule and when it was possible to avoid unpleasantness he very judiciously did so.

He had been resident in Beer before; put there by his ambitious father to be educated by the curate, so that he had many acquaintances in the place, but in his then temper of mind he preferred solitude; and in the evenings, when his work was over, in place of looking up friends in their homes, at the harbour, or in the public-house, he preferred to saunter alone on the downs. His friend and teacher, the curate, had recently departed to another cure. When he rambled on the headland he often stood looking south, where sea and sky melted into each other in the evening haze, and his thoughts, his desires were altogether as indefinite as was that horizon.

He was angry with himself for thinking of Winefred. The sense of his folly in caring for her was as a hot coal in his heart that he laboured to eject, but always ineffectually. If he sat on the top of the White Cliff his eyes often turned in the direction of Bindon Under–cliff, though Winefred, as he knew well enough, was not there; yet there were spots there associated with her in his memory.

No single lad of Axmouth or Beer had any suspicion of what pas–sed in his mind. None would have credited it, had they been assured that he who had been robbed by Winefred's mother had set his heart on the girl. Moreover, in the opinion of these lads there was nothing to attract in Miss Winefred, except her money, and that was ill–gotten. The rustic youth has not a discriminating eye for beauty. He is blind to those points and lines and colours which draw the admiration of the man with the artistic faculty. In the country the ugly girl stands as good a chance of securing a lover as does a beauty, if only she possess an attractive character and pleasant ways. The shy mind of the peasant boy starts back from the ready wit and the nimble tongue. That Winefred was good–looking would have been admitted with listless indifference; that she was a spiteful minx was a conclusion to which all would have leaped and to which held. A bumpkin would handle the girl ready at repartee with as great reluctance as a fisherman would handle an electric eel.

On Sunday Jack had an excuse for crossing the water. He must see Mrs Jose and report to her how he got on. But when he was on the farther bank of the Axe, he bent his steps first of all to the undercliff, to the elder–bushes, where he had retained Winefred from falling over the precipice, to the gate where she had kept him at a distance with a twig of thorns, to the slit in the barn wall through which he had watched her at the dance; and only finally did he enter the farmhouse and present himself before Mrs Jose.

She had much to relate about Bath, and its beauties, about the splendours of the Tomkin–Jones mansion, about the cordiality of her reception, and about the prospects that opened before Winefred.

Jack listened in silence. It pleased him to hear about Winefred, yet it was a pleasure fraught with pain, for it riveted in him the convic–tion that he and she were parted not so much by space as by the wider separation of social standing. And yet, what did he want with her? Nothing could come of his fancy, even were Winefred to lay aside her dislike for him. But he knew, too surely, that she hated

223

him. When they had met, they were like two goats on a plank, clashing horns.

A couple of weeks later Captain Ford said to Jack, "My lad, I have an errand for you. I can't go myself. You must do the job for me. Borrow as many eyes as there are in a peacock's tail, and use every one. I want you to go to Bath. They tell me that there they saw the stone. It is harder than ours, but it is done, I believe, by water power. Make pencil notes of all particulars, and if the outlay be not too great, as it need not be if you bring every contrivance away with you in your head or on paper, and we can rig up the concern with our own workmen, we shall save a lot of cost and time."

Jack flushed with delight, but that delight soon gave way to anxiety. He might, indeed, see Winefred, but only to discover how much further she was removed from him at Bath than she had been at Bindon. Then only the Axe had flowed between, and a current prejudice. He might find that a mightier stream was parting them, and one that was to him impossible to cross. "I wish first to go to Bindon," said Jack. "Mrs Jose may have some message to her cousins at Bath."

"Right," said Captain Ford. "I suppose you cannot see Mrs Marley, and learn if she has anything for her child?" Jack shook his head.

"No," said the captain, "I reckon not. You ain't on speaking terms. Communication made must be through Eliza Jose."

Chapter Thirty–Seven

Confidences

Thus it came about that Jack Rattenbury visited Bath, and the spring chickens arrived in the kitchen of the establishment of Mrs Tomkin-Jones.

After the meeting at the exit from Sydney Gardens, and when Jack had departed, Winefred remained standing where he had left her, motionless, looking before her, but seeing nothing. What fiend had possessed her, that she should have struck at him so cruelly?

At the moment she had not intended to hurt, but the words had come to her lips before she had thought what to say, and had been launched unconsidered. She was roused by her father addressing her.

"Really, my dear, you were – were rather rude. You should not be that, least of all to an inferior. It angers an equal, it cuts an inferior."

"Father, he has occasioned mother and me much wretchedness."

"How?"

"By causing cruel, untrue things to be said of us. He has made our lives miserable."

"Not – not about – ahem! Has he insinuated –"

"I need not tell you about what, further than that it concerns money."

"Oh, money! What about that?"

"If you desire to know more, it is that he said, or perhaps it is more true to say he has caused it to be said, that mother is well off and able to send me here, because she stole money from his father; but I know better, for one reason, because she could not do a wrong thing; and next because the money came from you. But first of all because mother *could* not do it. The money was from you, was it not, father?"

"Certainly it was. I sent to her money repeatedly, and of late, liberally."

"There now!" in a tone of triumph. "Oh, if you would speak that out before all Axmouth! How happy you would make my mother!"

"That – that is not possible."

"Why not?"

"There are reasons. They are weighty. I cannot fully explain. For one, I am here taking the waters."

"Then let me call him back. Say the words before Jack. he is not a bad fellow, honest and true, and he will believe you and tell the truth to everyone."

"For Heaven's sake, no!"

"Why not? It is the truth." She paused. "Are you ashamed of me as your daughter?"

"No, a thousand times no; and since you have been new fitted out by Madame Delmarc and Miss – Miss – I forget the name – ten thousand times no."

"Then why? Are you ashamed of my mother?"

He groped in his pocket with twtching fingers, but could find neither latchkey nor pencil to put to his tongue or lips. "I – I – there are matters, my dear, beyond your comprehension. A little later. Have patience, Winefred; when you are a bit older, have more knowledge of the world–"

"You will make it up with my mother?"

"I – I will think about it."

Her face that had kindled with hope, was again clouded. It was a humiliation to her, that she felt poignantly, to be recognised by her father, and at the same time to have her mother ignored or treated as dead. She had caught the words of Sir Barnaby and her father's reply, and they had been as drops of flaming phosphorus falling on her heart. She would have turned, cried out that her mother lived, and was the noblest and purest of women, but that her sound reason assured her such an action would be fatal to her ambition. She must be patient. She must endure a little longer. The moment had not come. She must first weave herself round her father's heart before she could draw him in the direction she proposed.

She now greatly regretted her rudeness to Jack on other grounds than that she had committed an offence. She would have liked to send back a message to her mother, together with a present, to assure her that she was not forgotten. But she could not ask a favour of one whom she had insulted.

Had the lad deserved the treatment meted out to him? What fault of his was it that he was disappointed of his expectations on the death of his father, and that he had been forced to sell the cottage? He had done this so as honourably to pay his father's debts. Was he really responsible for the stories that circulated anent her mother? Had he not assured her that he did not believe in her mother's guilt? Why, then, was the young man to be snarled at? Her thoughts that had started with her mother and father now circled around Jack.

She was turning the parcel he had given to her in her hand without considering it. Now she looked at it and found that it comprised a small box, tied up in paper and sealed. Doubtless it contained a letter.

Winefred walked back beside her father to the square without uttering another word. Neither did Mr Holwood speak. He, likewise, was engrossed in thoughts, and thoughts set with prickles. At the door they parted. "I shall give myself the pleasure of calling for you again tomorrow," said he. "Your new equipment I must tell Mrs Jose is eminently becoming."

She went to her room, and when she had removed her bonnet and mantle, she seated herself at the window, and unknotted the string that bound the parcel. A hundred, even fifty, years ago, no woman ever dreamed of cutting a string; she laboriously unknotted it, then did it up in a tag and laid it aside for further use. A small square cardboard case was disclosed that contained cotton wool, bedded in which were a pair of imitation pearl drop earrings. Folded about the case was a letter. This she proceeded eagerly to read – it was from Mrs Jose:

> My dear Winefred, – Your good mother and I hope you are well, as it leaves me. I send you two pretty eardrops that I had when I was married. I have grown old and fat and ugly, and shall never wear them no more. They suit young and pretty faces, so take them and when you wear them think of your mother's and my hearts that hang on you. I send them

to you by Jack Rattenbury, who has found a place at last and decent wages, so he tells me, enough to keep him in bread and cheese. He is a good lad and upright, and I am pleased to know it. Your mother is tolerably well. My brindled half–Jersey has dropped her calf, and we have had trouble that way before. I am going to look out for a goat to run with the cows. That is a good thing where they take to dropping their calves. Good–bye, I'm terrible short of breath with writing so much – Your affectionate friend and well–wisher,

ELIZA JOSE

M.P. – Your mother is a curious customer. She was all agog for you to go to Bath, and now she is in a sort of raging fever and ague to boot because you are away. 'Tis exactly like a cow when they've took away her calf.

Winefred sat in the window turning over the earrings, but thinking rather of the 'M.P.' than of anything else, when there came a rap at her door, and, without awaiting a response, Jesse entered. "What have you there?" she asked at once, her feminine eye lighting on the bit of cheap jewellery.

"It is a present from dear Mrs Jose."

"Mercy on us! you cannot wear such absurd fandangles."

"I would not offend Mrs Jose for the world, and she says such pretty things about them."

"She is a darling, and our cousin, though mamma is too gorgeous a personage to admit it. But Nebuchadnezzar's image had feet of clay and the awful erection of the Tomkin–Jones family has common soil at the bottom of it. But those ear–pendants are ridiculous."

"I shall wear them when I go back to Axmouth."

"As you will, but mother will never suffer them here. I may as well take this opportunity to speak to you about our family. Shall I sit down, Winnie? Well, mamma's great delight is blowing wind-bags, and we prick them, Sylvana out of malice, I out of mischief. But no sooner have we shrivelled one up than we find her puffing out another. After all, it hurts no one and it amuses her. Nobody is deceived. no one believes in her stories. They are like wax apricots. They look very well, but bite and you find they are emptiness and

228

your mouth is full of beeswax. Mother is concerned because no street or square in Bath is named after papa. But no one cares about him, or remembers him now he is dead. Moreover, in Bath people come and go, some for a season, some for two. He was a doctor, an estimable man, and, as doctors go, no worse than his fellows. He once put the Prince Regent's insides right with a pill, that is all; and out of that pill mamma has blown up a balloon. He did not make a fortune, or we should be better off, living in the square and not hanging on to it. But with all her grand talk mother is a good woman, and such as know her intimately learn how much better she is than all the flummery with which she surrounds herself. Sylvana and I do our utmost to tear down her piles of pretence, but it is lost labour. She is like Jack the chimneysweep on May Day, who dances under an extinguisher of greens and sham flowers. Unhappily, with him it pays, with mamma it fails. Take these eardrops and put them away till you return to Jose–land. I want to talk to you about Frank Wardroper. Do you care for him?"

"I – no! How should I?" Winefred looked genuinely surprised.

"But," said Jesse, "he has been paying you marked attention."

"He has been civil. He chose my hat and gowns."

"That was it. If anything could rivet his attentions it would be that. You are sure you do not feel for him more than ordinary interest."

"He amuses me; that is all."

"Because," said Jesse, colouring, "at one time he was fond of me. But when you came, then mamma began to throw you at his head."

"But why – if she knew that you liked him?"

"My dear, with her, all her geese are swans except her daughters, who are little common ducks. It has never occurred to her that he could fancy me. You see," said Jesse, colouring deeper, "no one could suit Frank better than I, because I really do not know or care anything about dress, so that it would be an eternal joy and interest to him to keep changing my gowns and bonnets and mantillas and all the rest."

"I would not interfere between you, set your mind at rest thereon," said Winefred, laughing.

"Do you care for anyone else?"

"I!" Winefred now gasped. "I – I know no one. I – of course not. How could you ask such a question?" Then, hurriedly, as though to cut short further catechising, "I know what I will do. I will make you a present of an entirely new and fashionable suit of clothes, hat or bonnet, gown, everything, and Mr Wardroper shall select them for you."

"O my dearest!" exclaimed Jesse, and threw herself on the neck of Winefred. "You could not have thought of anything better, or anything more calculated to secure him. One word in return for this kindness: Be on your guard against Sylvana."

Chapter Thirty–Eight

A Letter from Bath

Jane Marley sat before the door in the shade of a bursting elder, in an atmosphere perfumed by its leaves; the sun was on the white rock against which the cottage was built, and sent a reflection in her face so strong that she was unable to raise her eyes from her knitting. Her brows were contracted, partly against the glaring light, partly through the working of her stormy mind.

Dazzled by the sun, occupied by her thoughts, she did not notice the approach of Mrs Jose, and when the latter spoke Jane started, passed her hand across her brow, and recovered herself with an effort.

"Deary me!" said the farmer's wife. "Always busy. If Satan finds some mischief for idle hands, he need not come to the undercliff. He will never find those fingers at leisure for his work. But, bless my life, Jane, what can be the matter with the birds? I have known them swarm here and sing and chortle like a concert of choristers – jackdaws, starlings, choughs, gulls, magpies – and today not one to be seen or heard."

"I have noticed it. They are gone."

"Gone! But what can have driven them away? Have they been chased or shot?"

"No – I have not heard a gun."

"But this is amazing. What does it mean? I have not started a magpie, not heard the pipe of a blackbird. It has never happened before. This has been a paradise of birds." Mrs Marley shrugged her shoulders. She did not concern herself about feathered creatures and their ways.

"You have not come here to tell me that the birds have flitted," she said; and scrutinising Mrs Jose's face she said, "You have something on your mind. What is it?"

"I have had a letter."

"From Winefred?"

"No, from Mrs Tomkin–Jones."

"Does she ask for money?"

"No."

"What does she say about Winefred?"

"Not very much."

"She is well?"

"Very well – and happy."

"And happy," repeated Jane with a tinge of disappointment in her voice. "Come inside; the light here is too strong."

"How the mint smells!" said Mrs Jose.

"Yes."

"And the elder shoots."

"Yes." Jane led the way within, and the change to the shade of the room was grateful. She signed to her visitor to be seated, but did not take a chair herself. She held a stocking three parts knitted in one hand, in the other a pin. She did not seat herself; she was restless and impatient. "What is it?" she asked. "I know there is something that you have to say which is not easy for you to speak. Had it been good news, it would have come forth already."

"Really the letter I have received is to you or about you. But as you cannot read, it is addressed to me."

"Then let me hear it at once."

"That is not so easy done. In truth, my dear, this letter is not pleasant reading. Mrs Tomkin–Jones informs me – and you – that

231

Winefred has met her father."

"I am not sorry for that."

"Her father is vastly taken with her, and walks her out, and shows her the sights, and goes with her to shops and buys sundry pretty things that he gives to her."

"That is as it should be."

"If that were all, I should not be in such a fluster over it," said Mrs Jose, her pleasant face expressing concern.

"What is there more?"

"Her father has taken a pride in his child, and a liking to her, so that he will not part with her any more."

Jane was silent. Shadows passed over her face, like those that darken the sea. She stood meditating, with her knitting-pin to her lips. "He may see her a bit," she said; then, after a pause, "he may see a good deal of her."

"Ay." Mrs Jose looked up with distress into the clouded face of the mother. "But what if he purposed taking her altogether away from you?"

"He cannot do that! He shall not do that!" almost screamed the mother, and then clenched her teeth and stood glaring at her visitor. Presently she said fiercely, "Bring out that letter and read me every word. pass none over. I must hear all." Mrs Jose looked from side to side in embarrassment. "The letter!" said Jane imperiously, and pressed the end of the knitting-pin on the table. The farmer's wife was compelled to draw the epistle from her pocket and unfold it upon the board. She knew that Jane was illiterate, and it was her intention to soften down as much as possible the harsh expressions, but she could not blunt the edge of the cutting facts. "Begin with the first words," said Mrs Jose. "They are from Mrs Tomkin-Jones about my chicken I sent her. She is a sort of cousin, and she begins affable enough, seeing the difference in our station in life, and all these first lines contain nothing further than what I have already told you, that Winefred has met her father, and that he is mightily taken with her."

"How far does that go?" asked Jane, with the pin on the letter.

"To the point – there you have it – 'pretty things'. It is as I told you. He has bought them for her."

232

"Go on from there. What is that word?"

"Then Mrs Tomkin-Jones continues, 'I think he will not be satisfied until he has removed her entirely.'"

"From what place? From your cousin's?"

"No, not exactly so. From –" She hesitated.

"Show me the words. I can count the letters if I cannot read them. What is that little word followed by a long one?"

"'That creature.'"

"What does she mean by 'that creature'?"

"I think she means you. But mind this, Jane. It is Mrs Tomkin-Jones who writes, and not Winefred nor Mr Holwood; and Mrs Tomkin-Jones has never seen you, does not know more of you than what she has heard from Winefred."

"And did Winefred tell her I was a creature?"

"My dear Jane, no; that is merely her way of expressing herself. We are all creatures of God, made in His image, and so in a fashion equal. She means no offence."

"Very well. That creature – that is me. Read on after 'that creature'."

"'Who has–'" Mrs Jose turned mottled, and her voice betrayed her uneasiness.

"'Who has' – Go on, alter not a word."

"'Who has – has – has a very prejudicial effect on the girl.'"

"Prejudicial effect! What does she mean by that?"

"I think she means that Winefred has learned to talk like us folk of humble life and not like to gentlefolk."

"That's like enough. It is true, quite true, and I do not dispute it. Go on." Mrs Jose fidgeted in her seat, and was reluctant to proceed. She was not a woman of readiness to substitute a word, an expression for another; moreover, Jane Marley overawed her.

"Go on," said the mother sternly. "I will hear every word in that letter. I can bear it. God in heaven knows that I have borne much already."

"Then be prepared for what follows, though it may not be to your liking. You must remember that it is the lady who writes, who has neither seen nor known you."

Jane nodded. She was choking. But she said hoarsely, "Go on!"

233

and pointed with her knitting–pin.

Mrs Jose read, "'Mr Holwood is resolved that the connection between his daughter and that woman shall cease entirely.'"

"Shall cease entirely – that connection," muttered Jane. Then she looked up and laughed bitterly. "Can any man make that connection cease entirely – that – the connection between mother and child? She is my daughter; she is more mine than she is his. She has drunk her young life at my bosom. She has lived all that life with me. She has been, she is still, in my heart of hearts. He may tear my limbs away. But he cannot separate Winefred from me. Go on." Mrs Jose, conscious of the pain that she was giving, aware that every word was as the iron tooth of a harrow drawn over the mother's heart, wiped her eyes that were full.

Then she continued. "'He is prepared to give Marley an annuity, a liberal allowance, but –'"

"But what?"

"'But Winefred and she must never meet again.'"

"It shall not be!" cried Jane, as she beat the table with clenched hand and snapped the steel needle. "He has ruined my happiness, wrecked my life – nothing, nothing whatever has been left me, nothing, nothing, save only my child, and her he will tear from me. He shall not do it."

"Pray do not be excited and angry, Jane," said the farmer's wife. "You must remember that you yourself desired to have Winefred brought up as a lady."

"Yes, as a lady. I desire that still."

"And as a lady she must of necessity be much severed from you."

"Yes. I grant it. But not altogether."

"No, perhaps that need not have been; but the father thinks differently. If he takes her to live with him, what can you do? Can you go to him, uninvited? Will he recognise you as his wife? The situation will be most untoward for yourself, for him, for Winefred. You must weigh this well."

"I do weigh it. I will not be parted from her for ever. If she is made a lady, let me look on her. Let me see her from afar off. But see her I must, or it will kill me. She is my child." Jane looked half fiercely, half imploringly into her visitor's face. "You do not understand what it is to be a mother – and a mother of one child. She lives for one thing only – her child. She has but one pride – her child; one hope – her child. She cannot do without her. Look you. There is a woman at Seaton, a widow. She lost her son, her only son. He clambered after gulls' eggs, fell over the cliffs, and was dashed to pieces. Thenceforth she is no more a woman, she is a moving image. She has no soul, no heart, no life more, nothing in the world to hope for, nothing in the world to love, nothing even to fear. All her life died out in her when she lost her son. I have a daughter. She lives. I may not be with her always. I am content for her sake that it should be so. But not to see her, never to hear her speak, not again to feel her arms round me, and to rock her head on my bosom! – I could not bear it. Promise me but this, twenty years hence I shall kiss her, and I will live in that single hope – but never – never –" She cast herself at full length on the ground and burst into a rage of tears.

"I have sinned – I have sold my soul for this! – to this have I been brought by my wickedness!" was what she wailed. Then she gathered herself up in a crouching position. "I have not heard all. There is something more. After where my pin broke."

"There is no need. You have the substance."

"I will have it. Read me the last lines."

"I will not do so," exclaimed Mrs Jose in desperation. Then the unfortunate mother tore at the letter, and ripped away the conclusion. "I have it," she said, "I will go with it to Olver Dench. He will read it to me."

"No – no. Give it me. Rather than that I will read."

"It must be read," said Jane, surrendering the fragment. Then faltering Mrs Jose read, "In this Winefred fully concurs."

"Concurs! – she agrees!" cried Jane Marley, and again flung herself on the floor and writhed like a bruised worm. Mrs Jose knelt by her, stroked her hair, wiped the tears from her eyes, patted her – uttering kind words; but it was long before she could assuage the paroxysms of grief and despair.

When Mrs Marley was slightly more composed, raising herself on her hands that rested on the floor, and glaring like a wild beast at her consoler, she said hoarsely, "Hearken to me! on the night when every door was shut against me, then I would have thrown myself over the cliffs with Winefred in my arms. I would to God I had done as I purposed. Cursed be he who prevented me, cursed whether in heaven above or in hell beneath, for he is dead. But for him we should have been together now, together inseparable, for ever – in one deep sea, in one eternity. But now–"

She cast herself again with her face to the floor, and rocked from side to side in irrepressible grief. "Jane," said Mrs Jose, "you are in no condition to be left alone. Come with me to Bindon."

"I will not."

"Then I shall come here and stay the night with you. Compose yourself. I shall run home and fetch such things as I may require, and be with you in a jiffy."

The wretched mother tossed but made no reply. Mrs Jose seated herself again, talked to her soothingly, till she considered that the first violence of her grief was over. Then she rose and proposed, "Have a cup of tea."

An hour later she had induced Jane to sit by the hearth. Then, convinced that she might quit her temporarily, she departed for Bindon to make such arrangements there as would be necessitated by her absence during the night. She was back again in three–quarters of an hour, but found the house locked and Jane gone, as she satisfied herself by looking through the window.

In alarm she hurried home. "Please ma'am," said the maid, "just after you was gone that Mrs Marley came here, looking wild–like, and she gave me this key and said it was that of the house, and that you was to take charge of it till she came again."

Chapter Thirty-Nine

The Bath Assembly

The maid-servant at the house round the corner opened the door in response to a sharp ring and an imperious rap, though they came at an unprecendented hour at night. She saw before her, by the flicker of the oil lamp overhead, a woman standing on the step. On asking her business, she answered, "I want to see Winefred Holwood."

"*Miss* Holwood," said the maid, with emphasis. "Miss Holwood is not at home. She has gone with our ladies to the Assembly Ball."

"Assembly Ball! Where is that?"

"In the Assembly Rooms, of course."

"But where are they?"

"Near the Circus."

"How am I to find them?"

"You must go along Gay Street till you reach the Circus, then you turn to the right and see a building with pillars, between Bennett Street and Alfred Street."

"I am a stranger in the place."

"Can't you put off seeing Miss Holwood till tomorrow?"

"I cannot. I must see her. It is important."

"What do you want with her?"

"I have come from Axmouth."

"If you positively must," said the maid, "then there's no help for it. You will have to do one of two things, either wait till our ladies come home after midnight. They will not be late as our mistress is gone, and it is the first time for years – or else you can go with me to the Rooms. Did you say you had come from a great distance?"

"Yes, from Axmouth. I have walked all day, and more than one day."

"Are you not tired?"

"I am too anxious to see her to be tired."

"Well, you may step inside and sit down. I shall be going to the Assembly Rooms shortly myself with the shawls and clogs. Our ladies drove there, but are going to walk home."

"How long before you go?"

"In an hour. I have a mind to see what I can of the dancers in their gay dresses and jewellery."

"I would wish to go with you."

"Come in, then, and be seated. Shall I give you a mouthful first? You must be hungry. We are about to have our supper, and you shall join us. That done, we will go."

Jane Marley consented. The girl was good–natured, simple and fresh, but not devoid of curiosity. In the kitchen she observed the stranger woman, how dirt–soiled, weary and dishevelled she was. Her clothes were of good material, in cut above those of the class of the domestic, and there was a distinction in the manner, and nobility in the face, that imposed on the girl.

"You will do up your hair and be shaken down a bit before you go," said she, "and slip off your shoes and I'll give them a brush up. You see – unless tidied, they are not likely to admit you."

The girl endeavoured to extract some particulars from the stranger concerning herself and relative to her purpose in coming to Bath. But Jane was reticent. Her impatience was so manifest to start for the Assembly Rooms. And when she was prepared, she made Mrs Marley assist in carrying the mantles and shawls. "You see there are four of them," she explained; "the old lady I thought never would have gone out into Society again, but with this Miss Holwood she has made an exception. They say she's a regular beauty, and Mr Wardroper comes here a lot, but whether it be after Miss Jesse or she – that's more than I can guess. Miss Holwood has a power of fine dresses – O my! you should see them, and they set her off beautiful. Her father, he's never tired of making her pretty presents, and she has the beautifullest gold watch."

Mrs Marley listened eagerly, as the girl ran on. And it was thus talking they they arrived at the Rooms, where they readily obtained admission as servants of Mrs Tomkin–Jones. Jane was bewildered at the light, the sound of music, the buzz of voices and tramp of feet, and the, to her, unwonted splendour of the surroundings.

The Bath Assembly Rooms are, perhaps, the best constructed in England. There is not a step or staircase throughout. Ballroom, octagon, card and tea rooms, all are on one level; and the suite is so contrived as to have four exits in the event of fire. A central cross with an octagonal vestibule adorned with columns gives access to the ballroom, great octagon, and tea–room. The whole was gilded, and sparkled with wax lights. We have advanced vast strides in illumination, but no amount of glare can compensate for the mellowness and beauty of the light that came from innumerable wax candles.

Into the principal portions of the building, the servants were not admitted; but they hung about the entrance to the vestibule, and were even allowed to encroach somewhat further, to invade the vestibule itself. Jane penetrated to the pillars sustaining the entablature, and stood there, seeing the gleam of dresses as they flashed by the open door of the ballroom, and observing the dancers, who, heated or thirsty, came forth to sit or become cool, or enter the tea–room for refreshment.

There were benches in the octagonal vestibule against the wall, and near where Jane stood were a couple of elderly bucks, commenting on those who swept by, or exchanging opinions on the difference in style in the woman of the present from the past.

"By the way, Gorges," said one of these in a blue coat with brass buttons and white waistcoat, "what is your opinion of the newcomer?"

"I should say that Audrey had slipped into Rosalind's clothes."

"Ah! a case of female Christopher Sly."

"For shame! That is not fair. There is nothing coarse about her – only rustic and piquante."

"Piquante she is, I hear – with her tongue."

"Do you know her father?"

"Holwood," replied Gorges. "Can't say I do – he is or has been in the Foreign Office. Eminently fitted for his post. I should say."

"I hear he has come in for money, through the death of an aunt."

"It is a deuced shame that some men have all the luck in the world and some none. Why should he come in for money and a beautiful daughter? By Gad! Look at my three rose–buds! Old and cankered every one. I can't dispose of them, because I cannot, like the Pope, offer my roses of gold."

"I am like Henry VI of Germany. Thank God I have none to dispose of. I find it difficult enough to dispose of myself in an easy chair."

Jane but partially understood what was said. The allusions escaped her altogether. Turning to the girl who had accompanied her, she whispered: "I shall never know her – never in the dress she will be wearing."

"I will point her out to you," said the maid. "Here come some. The waltz is over. Stand back, they will pass this way."

"Hang it, Gorges," said the man in blue; "we shall have to vacate our seats. I'd go into the cardroom, but, dem it, I dare not touch cards – I never win, never; and to lose eternally is not fun."

The maid touched Jane. "She's coming on her father's arm."

Mrs Marley drew back, a spike as of ice pierced her heart. For a moment she said nothing. Before her rose a blue vapour, like woodsmoke, and the lights died away to mere sparks. She was about to see him, after a lapse of many years, whom she had once loved with her passionate heart, but now abhorred; the man who had desolated her life and now proposed to render it absolutely desert by bereaving her of her child.

It was as though a vast gulf opened before her, and she looked across it at the man who had once been so near to her – the gulf of time that had swallowed up her youth and all her happiness. She could dimly perceive in the haze a middle–aged man, spruce, with hair curled and shining, high white collars, and a spotless neckcloth, a cream silk uncrumpled waistcoat, and a face bland, with a fine complexion. Slowly, as from a swoon, she rallied. It was the pressure on her arm of the maid's hand that recovered her and brought her back from the region of dream.

"There, there!"

She saw before her a beautiful girl, with low dress and bare arms, gloved hands, in white, with no other colour about her than a rose in her hair and a coral and gold necklet – a girl, lovely, far surpassing all that Jane could have imagined. A cry of joy; and in a moment – "Mother! mother!"

She was clasped in the arms of this girl, her burning cheeks were kissed, and she was enveloped in a cloud of white muslin and in an atmosphere of heliotrope. Jane Marley hastily disengaged herself and thrust Winefred aside. She looked about her with flashing eye, and had reared herself proudly.

A circle had formed around them, a second ring was behind, composed of others looking over the shoulders of those in the first row, then again others, packing in from behind – a circle, a mass, a rising wave of faces and forms, beaux with eyeglasses lifted, ladies in ball dresses, fans fluttering. The orchestra had ceased. The drift was through the vestibule to the tea-room. There were curiosity, malice, surprise in every face. Jane looked from one to another.

"It is not true," she said slowly, distinctly, deliberately. "I am *not* her mother. I am her old nurse. I am nothing but the nurse. But she has a good heart, a heart of gold, and she loves me. Look at me, then look at her. It is her condescension to stoop to such as me. I thank you, miss. I am obleeged for the flattering recognition."

"For mercy's sake, not a scene!" exclaimed Jesse Jones, thrusting herself through the ring. "Here, quick. Into this little room; it is empty. You obstruct the promenaders." And with tact and energy the girl pressed Winefred, her father and Mrs Marley into a small apartment, shut the door, and planted herself without as a guard.

Then with a laugh Jesse said to those who looked and whispered and wondered, "The old goodie is delighted to see the child she nursed. Give them leave a while. It will be a dream of delight for the woman's afterlife. Pray move on."

The room into which the three had been thrust so unceremoniously was poorly illumined by two wax candles on the table. It had been intended as a place to which cronies might retreat to gossip or talk politics, and perhaps also to which couples might retire for the making and answering the eventful proposal. There was stillness within after the noise without. Jane looked hastily around, and seeing that there was no one else present, said to Winefred with vehemence, "My child! my child! They shall not take you from me that I never see you more."

"Mother, no. They shall not."

"And you did not write that it was with your consent?"

"With my consent!"

"That I should be pensioned off and moved away, so that we might never, never, never meet again, that I might never, never, never see your face more."

"Mother, I could not write that, you know it. Nothing would make me do such a thing."

"I felt that," said the woman, surging up, as she pressed her hands to her heart, "I felt here that it could not be. But yet I was uneasy. I could not say – among grand folk, what had been spoken and done to wean you away. I thought that you might feel that I lowered you."

"Never," exclaimed Winefred, and turned sharply about to face her father. "Who wrote that?"

"It was he, then," said Mrs Marley, "he who has been my woe from the moment I came to know him."

"I – I wrote nothing," faltered Mr Holwood; "I am quite innocent in this matter. I believe it was Mrs Tomkin–Jones who wrote."

"You did not write with your hand, but with hers," said Jane wrathfully. "You admit, you know that she wrote. It was you. Cursed be the tongue that proved my undoing, cursed be the heart that devised this new cruelty."

"Mother!" entreated Winefred, and she put her hand on Jane Marley's mouth.

"Look, look!" cried the outraged woman, thrusting her aside, "see him sidle towards the door, instead of facing what is unpleasing. That has ever been his way. He has thrust himself into situations that were uncomfortable, into associations that proved irksome, has contracted ties that galled him, and he has never had the courage to accept the consequences of his own acts. As soon as all is not easy and troubles begin, he sneaks away like a coward – a coward that he is. He will never do that which is right, if right weighs over a couple of ounces. Coward! you who took from me my young hopes will take from me now my child. He contrived it; he is too mean to admit it. No!" She threw herself between the man and the door. "He now seeks only how he may slip away. Coward, listen to what I have to say. Hide behind the window curtains, will you! I rejoice there is so much shame left in you. Listen. I ask of you one thing

alone, and with that alone will I be content. I do not say acknowledge me! Whether I be your wife or no,. God, and the law alone
can tell. Not that. That I do not desire. Nothing on earth would bring
me to acknowledge *you*. That is what it has arrived at now. I scorn,
hate you, so that no power could make me hold out this right hand
and say 'husband'!" to so despicable a wretch. See. I have on the
wedding–ring that you once gave me in the ruined church, blessed
by the unfrocked parson. I pluck it off and cast it from me."

With trembling fingers she suited the action to ther word, and the
little gold hoop rolled to his feet.

"I should despise myself to think that I were linked for the
remainder of my life to such as you. No, no, no! I desire nothing of
you, not your name, not your money, not your protection. I can
elbow my way along without aid from such a grasshopper as you.
But there is one thing I will not endure, that you should tear my
child from me. I know that she is a lady, and a lady let her remain.
I will never do a thing to lower her before the world. And it is
because I will not be parted from her that I humble myself to make
one request of you. I do not ask you to let her acknowledge me as
her mother. I am undeserving of that. But I do ask, let me see her,
let me hear her talk, let me be near her, and for that I will be a
scullery–maid in your house."

"Mother!"

"Let me speak. My heart is bursting. I shall die if you interrupt.
You say that I am a violent woman, unfit to be with other servants,
impossible in a house. Try me. Let me be near her, and you shall
see. You will find me docile and meek. I will give no offence. I will
do nothing, nothing to render myself unendurable. You say I am a
raging fire. I have been, I am now but a heap of grey ash with one
spark in it – my love for Winefred. Let me smoulder away where
she can breathe on the spark; it will only flame into more love for
her. I ask no more. I will be speechless in your house if you will –
but see her I must. I must look on her, as she moves, like a lady that
she is – but I will not approach her to soil her with my touch. Only
now and then, when there be none to see, let me kiss the tip of her
fingers. I will go down on my knees to ask for this – but I will take

243

nothing less." Her voice was hoarse with emotion. "Part from her I will not."

"Mother," interposed Winefred, "I have a word to say. My father had not the purpose that you attribute to him. He spoke no word about it. He never hinted at any such thing. There has been a mistake somewhere. You are hard upon him, too hard. He has been indulgent to me, he could not have been more kind. Whenever he has spoken of you, it has been with a tremble in his voice, and I know that his heart has been full. I do not believe that he has ever forgotten you, ever ceased to love you. Now, dear mother, set your mind at rest. Parted we shall not be, and in token of that I will go home with you tomorrow."

Mr Holwood came hesitatingly forward and raised his hand in deprecation.

"There is no occasion," said Mrs Marley. "I have seen you. That suffices. Stay on. You are learning much here."

"Mother, I also have a longing to be with you – if for a few weeks only. I have spent some little time with my father. It is right that now I should be with you. If he loves me, and he finds that he also cannot do without me, then he will come to Bindon Undercliff and fetch me thence, to take me back to Bath."

Then Winefred put her arms round her mother and kissed her. "How you love me!" she said. She disengaged herself, and putting her arms round the neck of her father she said, "And you, father, have come to love me."

"Yes."

"Surely, father, if you love me; and you, mother, if you also love me, you cannot hate each other."

Chapter Forty

Wanted – Choughs

Winefred had returned to the cottage on the undercliff along with her mother. Her departure had been hurried. She had spoken a few words to Mrs Tomkin–Jones in explanation of her departure, and had promised to return in a fortnight. Mrs Tomkin–Jones was troubled in mind. She had entered into negotiations with a butler to be maintained at Winefred's expense. She was vastly alarmed lest the sudden whim to go to Bindon should be a prelude to entire withdrawal, in which event the lady would be obliged to pay the butler a month's wage for having engaged him prematurely. Moreover, the loss of Winefred would mean stinting in other ways.

As she departed, Winefred said, "I shall not forget my promise about the choughs."

At the undercliff the cottage looked small, the fittings poor after the house at Bath; and the girl was at once aware that her mother's mode of speech differed from that of the society into which she had been introduced. And yet there was a grandeur and force, and even an approximation to culture in her mother's speech, due – she knew not to what – perhaps to the Bible, to the books it had been Winefred's wont to read aloud to her mother every evening.

She was glad to be back. Her mother's happiness at having her there had something pathetic in it, and Winefred was touched to the quick. It was a pleasure to her to scramble about the cliffs, walk on the pebbles, revisit old haunts.

Little did she suspect that her arrival had filled Olver Dench with alarm. He had heard sufficient to cause him considerable uneasiness. Winefred had met her father in Bath. What had passed between them? What had been divulged? When she came to the ferry to be put across to Seaton, he seized the opportunity to question her.

"So – you have been with your father?"

"Yes."

"And what does he think of you?"

"That is a question to be put to him, not to me."

"I suppose he wonders that your mother should go to such expense about you."

"I do not see how he can wonder, when he finds the money."

"Oh! he finds the money, does he?"

"Certainly." Winefred coloured with anger. "You do not dare to insinuate that she got the money in any other way?"

"Dear me, no. Very natural that he should provide the blunt. It will be a lot. Have you talked with him about the matter? Said that it did not suffice? Your expenses are piling up."

"He knows what they are, and provides. I have not spoken with him about them. But really, Mr Dench, this does not concern you."

"Certainly not. But we are old friends and neighbours. So I like to know that you are in deep water."

After a pause, Winefred said, "I want to obtain a couple of young choughs. Can you help me?"

"No," he replied. "All the birds have abandoned the cliffs on the Bindon side. But there are some in the White Cliff; yet I will not adventure my life there."

"I will pay," said Winefred.

"A hundred pounds would be no good to me if I lay at the foot with every bone in my body broken." Then she stepped out of the boat. Olver, so far, was satisfied. No suspicion had crossed the minds of Mr Holwood or of Winefred, as far as he could judge, that the remittances had been embezzled.

But was it likely that his proceedings should remain undiscovered? The presence of Winefred in Bath with her father was a menace to him. He did not anticipate a reconciliation between Jane Marley and Mr Holwood, but he did fear lest the father should cease to pay the annuity through his hands, and especially lest his fraudulent conduct during many years should come to light and entail his transportation. He had laid by the accumulations with the object of taking an inn. His highest ambition was to end his days as a publican. His future was secure, should he not be found out, and he had already his eye on a suitable tavern, and had opened negotiations with the owner. Now discovery of his malpractices threatened from the side of Bath.

He had not slept soundly since he had heard through Mrs Jose that Mr Holwood had recognised his daughter and was much in her society. He sought to stifle his anxieties by having recourse to spirits; but when he drank himself to sleep he found that his dreams were more terrifying than his waking fears.

All would be well, he thought, could Holwood and his daughter be kept apart. That nothing as yet had transpired did not content him. Holwood was almost certain now to take it into his head to rearrange his expenditure, and in so doing to take account of what had already been paid to Jane, and then the exposure would ensue.

Hitherto he had not entertained any fear of Winefred, but now he not only mistrusted her, but regarded her with animosity. If she could be kept away from Bath, and retained at Axmouth, all might be well. Her father was affectionately disposed towards her, but not very likely to desire to renew relations with her mother. Then he considered that he had seen Winefred on the edge of the cliff, walking unconcernedly where a false step would precipitate her to the shore. Why had not her foot slipped? Why had not the crumbling chalk yielded beneath her weight? He recalled tales of persons who had turned giddy when on an edge, and cursed his folly in telling her that the birds had deserted the chalk cliffs on the Bindon side of the estuary, for otherwise she would have leaned over the edge and pried after their nests, and might have overbalanced; she might even have ventured to climb to their places of breeding and in doing this have fallen.

A fog came on, enveloping everything as in cotton wool, obscuring all sights, deadening all sounds. Presently Winefred would be on her way back from Seaton, to be put across, and then she would ascend the steep hill opposite and strike across the down to the cottage of her mother. In such a mist, what more likely than that she should lose her way, stumble over some obstruction, go over the cliff? And yet – no – likely it was not, seeing how familiar the girl was with every inch of the way.

There was a jetty from which a passenger stepped into the ferry-boat. It consisted of planks sustained on poles driven into the mud.

The planks were slippery with the distilling vapour. The stage was not particularly secure, as Olver had noticed that morning. In another half hour the tide would be racing out, swirling about the piles on which the footway rested. It was precisely the swirl that had loosened one of them and made the planks incline and become infirm.

When a passenger arrived and asked to be ferried across, it was Olver's wont to extend a hand and help him into the boat. But what if the step were missed and there ensued a fall into the water? In the fog, at the rate at which the tide would be sweeping out, that person who was submerged would be carried away, and the veil of vapour would make it difficult, if not impossible, to recover him.

Olver sat in his boat musing and motionless, with the oar poised in his hand. The mist condensed on his glazed cap, and formed a chain of drops about the rim. His brows, his beard, were beaded. His jersey became sodden. The seat in the boat ran over with water. But all these discomforts he regarded not. The fog became thicker as the day declined. It lost its white opacity and became brown as coal-smoke, it deepened from that into darkness that was black-grey.

In the meantime Winefred had been in Seaton. She had gone there to inquire about choughs, and knowing where to learn something about what she desired, make her way at once to the Red Lion, where she was certain to find the young boatmen congregated. She was not disappointed in her expectation, but to her vexation she saw that Jack Rattenbury was there, one whom she particularly desired to avoid. On her appearing, he started up, and would have addressed her, but she turned her head aside and would not notice him.

"I have come, lads," said she, "to know if any of you will procure me a pair of young choughs. I will pay a guinea for them."

"They are not easily got," answered one of those addressed. "It is a bit late in the spring, and, besides, choughs are becoming yearly more scarce."

"I know that they are scarce, that is why I offer for them twenty-one shillings."

"There are none to be found except in the face of the White Cliff," said another.

"Well, then, get them from the White Cliff."

"Easier said than done," was the retort. "The brow overhangs."

"Sailor lads should not shirk a climb," said Winefred impatiently.

"That is not rigging," said a boy; "you want a land–lubber for that cliff."

"Here, take Jack Rattenbury," shouted one. "He has cut the sea and taken to the land." The sally was greeted with a laugh.

"I do not care who procures the birds; so long as I have what I want, I am content," said Winefred.

"If the choughs are to be had, I will get them for you," said Jack quietly.

"And you shall receive a guinea."

"I will not take the money."

"And I refuse them as a present."

"Settle the terms later," called a young sailor. "I would bargain for a kiss."

"I will get them," said Jack.

"And I shall hold you to your promise," returned Winefred, and left the room and the tavern. A moment later Jack went out, and, walking quickly, overtook her.

"I will see you to the ferry," he said quietly.

"I can find the way by myself," was her reply. They paced side by side in silence. presently she said, "Remember, I hold you to your undertaking, unless what you offered were mere idle brag. Have you come after me to beg off?"

"I have not. You shall have the choughs."

"And you shall have the guinea."

"I will not touch it. All I ask, if I bring you the pair, is that you will think of me with less bitterness." Again a pause ensued. The chill of the evening, the heavy vapour clogged their tongues.

Presently, feeling the irksomeness, she said, "When will you go after them – unless your heart fails?"

"My heart will not fail. I will try tomorrow at sunrise." Again she was silent. Their steps in the wet mud was like the sound of children eating.

After a while she said hesitatingly, "I do not yet believe that you will venture. If you do, I am not responsible for your safety."

"I risk it of my own free choice."

In the dense mist and gathering darkness sat Olver. With his oar and a boathook he had been working for some time at the loose pile that sustained the landing–stage, and he had succeeded in making it doubly insecure. The planks were greasy. He put the blade of his oar against the footway and with the pressure it declined. Then he sat motioness. Suddenly he lifted his head and listened. He thought that he heard steps. He was not mistaken. The pebbles sounded under the tread of feet. He stood up, and balanced himself in the boat on his oar, and drew his brows together and set his teeth. He peered into the fog but saw no one.

But – was that the sound of one pair of feet that approached? Then he uttered an angry, disappointed growl. He had distinguished voices. Next moment from out the envelope of vapour emerged Winefred and Jack Rattenbury. "Take my hand," said the latter. "The wood is slippery."

"I can steady myself unassisted," answered the girl; and she went forward on the plank. Then it yielded; she uttered an exclamation and caught Jack's hand.

"But for this," said he, "you would have been soused in the tide."

"Then Dench would have drawn me out. I have been in no real danger," was her ungracious reply; and, without a parting salutation, she stepped into the boat. Jack remained on the insecure stage.

"Will you not say 'Good night'?" he asked. She was silent.

Presently relenting, she said, "I will call 'Good night' from the further side, when safe over the water." He waited. Presently, muffled by the fog, from the further shore, "Good night!"

Then only did Jack turn and retire.

Chapter Forty-One

The White Cliff

In the dead of night, Jane Marley came to the side of her daughter's bed, and asked: "Why are you tossing so unceasingly?"

"I cannot sleep."

"What disturbs you?"

"O mother! I have done wrong. I was desirous of procuring a pair of choughs. No one would trouble himself, and risk his neck to get them for me but Jack Rattenbury, and he will go over the White Cliff in search for them. If anything were to happen to him −" she choked.

"Nothing will happen to him," said her mother. "Compose yourself. *He* would not risk himself for either of us. He hates us too heartily. He probably knows where are some birds easily reached, or he is fooling you with a promise to do that which he has no intention of performing. He will run into no danger on *our* account, be certain of that."

Somewhat relieved in mind, Winefred lay quieter. There was reason in her mother's words. She herself would adventure nothing for Jack, and why should he run into danger on her account? Nevertheless she was not wholly reassured, and rising before daybreak unperceived by her mother, she went down to the ferry, crossed with a couple of women bound for Seaton with eggs, and made her way to the White Cliff along the beach; then, turning up a cleft at the junction of the chalk and the red sandstone, she ascended to the summit, which rises four hundred and twenty-five feet above the sea, not perpendicularly, but so as to overhang. A haze covered the water, and the bald white crag, stood up as a horn of the moon issuing from the clouds.

Winefred was out of breath from the ascent, which was steep, and a catch came in her throat when she saw three figures, of which one was Jack, by an old thornbush that grew close to the edge. As she had walked along the shore she had used the opportunity to observe the face of the crag more attentively than she had ever done before, and she had seen how that it had been gnawed into by the sea–winds till it resembled a piece of old Stilton cheese of which little save the rind is firm, and how difficult and perilous it would be for anyone to attempt to reach the recesses and ledges where the birds harboured. To ascend from the beach would be a sheer impossibility; moreover, the places employed by the sea–birds for breeding were all near the summit, and were protected by the beetling brows of that summit.

With quivering lip, Winefred went to the three young men she saw before her, and singling out Jack, said roughly, "It is nonsense – I do not want the choughs."

"You offered a guinea for them," he replied.

"Take the guinea. I do not choose to endanger anyone's life. I had not noticed before how the brow overhangs. I will not have the choughs."

"I am satisfied that they are possible to be got," said he; "I can but try."

"I will not have you try."

"You held me to my promise."

"I hold you no more. I withdraw everything I said. But you shall have the guinea."

"I do not want your guinea. I shall go after the birds all the same."

"I beg you will not go."

He smiled. "I," said he, "am obstinate, as was my father. It is in our blood. When I have undertaken to do a thing, I do it."

"You will not, when I beseech you to desist."

"Yes. I shall get the choughs if they are to be had." She was silent. She saw that it was in vain to use further entreaty, and yet her alarm was great. Her bosom heaved.

"We are not friends," she said at last. "We have been enemies. Perhaps for that very reason I do not relish that your death should be due to any fancies of mine."

"I am not dead yet, nor have I got the choughs."

She stooped; there was at her feet moss that was studded with dewdrops, and with it she wiped her hands. "I am clear of it. I have entreated you not to venture on this mad expedition. If you go on now it is due to your own wilfulness. I am guiltless."

"You will not be held responsible," said Jack. Then turning to his companions, "Now, mates, slew the cable about the thorn, and mind that it runs over the roller." He indicated a piece of beechwood on the cliff-edge. The rope by which he was to be suspended was to cross this, so as not to fret on the edge of the cliff. This also would allow him, when climbing up or descending, to get his fingers under the cord. Without this contrivance they would be torn to the bone. Winefred stood aside panting. She had been heated by climbing, but now she turned cold; all her nerves tingled as though she had been whipped by nettles.

"You must have a rope round your waist, Jack," said one of the lads.

"No, thank you, it would encumber me. I must be free. It is not so bad. I shall not swing but cling to the rocks and work myself down and along with my hands. I shall sit astride on the pole and have a crook to help me along." Words of renewed entreaty to desist rose to Winefred's lips, but she could not speak them, and she knew that further remonstrance was profitless. Jack threw a bag across his shoulder, and bound it about his waist. He stepped to the edge, cast himself flat on the turf and looked over. The end of the rope, attached to the middle of a short pole, swung in space.

"All right, lads," said he, and slipped over the verge. Winefred's heart rose, and her head swam, as she saw him disappear. As he went, he looked at her and smiled.

Should the rope give way, should he lose his balance on the crosspole, there was for him a sheer fall of over four hundred feet. Below were broken masses of rock, fallen from above, about which the sea chafed and frothed, and among which it burrowed. The cable was strong; it was passed twice round the trunk of the thorn, and was held fast by two lusty youths, who paid out gradually, as required. One of them, turning his head over his shoulder, said to the girl, "Go below, missie, and see how he manages."

She made no reply, but turned to obey. Her knees trembled under her, and she was sick at heart. As she descended, tears came coursing down her cheeks. Tears of vexation and of alarm. How would she feel ever after should an accident occur? The wiping of her hands with dew could not brush away responsibility. Jack would not have ventured his life had she not urged him to it.

When she had reached the shore she looked up. The White Cliff is composed of a cap of chalk, a hundred feet thick, striated with beds of flint, and this rests on a series of shelving cherty sandstone beds of a tawny hue. The inclination of these gives to the whole headland an appearance of lurching to its fall. Water sinking through the chalk oozes through the sand and dissolves it, undermining the white bed above till masses of chalk that have lost all support hurtle down. But the chalk itself is full of cavosities caused by the soft rock being eaten into by the sea-winds. Consequently the entire mass is in incessant decompostiion and is crumbling down.

The mist had blown away, and Winefred was able, on looking up, to see the whole cliff towering above her, the white summit caught by the light of the rising sun. Jackdaws, gulls, choughs, alarmed at the sight of a man descending towards their haunts, were wheeling, plunging, screaming. The cord by which Jack was descending appeared to Winefred but as a thread of black horsehair.

He had grappled the protuberances of chalk and progressed, creeping downwards and inwards, about the humps and into corrosions wrought by the sea blasts. The surface was not only scooped out, but was also pockmarked, where nodules of flint had dropped away exposing the sockets in which they had lain. So friable was the rock that there was ever present the danger of the flints detaching themselves and raining down on the head of the climber. There were projections on which the foot might rest and to which the fingers might cling, but each projection had to be tested before being used, so deficient in tenacity was the chalk.

Winefred could not distinguish the little steel crook employed by Jack, but it served him in good stead; he could dig it into the rock, and by its aid draw himself along.

For a moment he disappeared behind a protruding mass, then he re-emerged, creeping like a fly. Now he stood balancing himself on a ledge so narrow as to be imperceptible from below, and seemed to be studying what looked like a smooth wall along which he purposed to advance by clinging. A profile of rock stood out that bore a resemblance to George III. This the climber had to circumvent, but he was slow in accomplishing his work. He penetrated into every recess, searching among the nests of the sea-birds – so it seemed to Winefred, and so only could she account for the delay and his occasional disappearance. Then, if too much cord had been let out, he was constrained to gather it up as he crawled farther till it was again taut.

He was on the chin of King George, groping in the jaw for some hollow into which he could insert a foot, some nodule sufficiently firm to which he could hold. Now he was plastered against His Majesty's cheek, sliding towards the ear. Then down came a hail of dislodged flints and a snow shower of chalk, as Jack slipped. Next moment a scud of vapour swept past and blotted out the summit of the cliff. Winefred had her knuckles pressed into her mouth to check the cry that she could not otherwise restrain, or the gasp that accompanied every venturesome movement of the climber.

When the fog passed away she saw him again. He had reached a green ledge where grew samphire. She wondered what he was about. She could see that he was shaking the cord. This was passed over projecting ribs of rock overhead. Clearly at last she made out that he needed more of the rope to be let out. He was on a terrace that ran in under arches of rock, and there doubtless nests abounded. But the line was entangled by the rock over which it passed, and so strained that no amount of shaking would communicate a signal to those above.

Winefred could see Jack, his feet at the edge, looking up, shaking the cord, then desisting, then striving to disengage it, so that the vibration might be continuous, but all his efforts were ineffectual. Should she ascend to those aloft, by the torn tree? It would take her twenty minutes to reach them, and by that time Jack's object in signalling would be gained or abandoned. She saw him stand motionless, considering what his course should be. Then she saw him release himself from the rope and fix the crosspole upon which he had been seated and fasten it between two horns of chalk. At that moment down rushed something that turned and whirled through the air. It was the roller over which the rope had passed. With the relaxation of the strain, it had shot over the brink. With the fall of the roller the cord had become loosned, and, to her horror, Winefred saw the end with the crosspole dangling free at a distance of several feet from the shelf on which stood the climber.

The fall of the roller had disengaged the crosspole. She knew at once that he was a prisoner fast in the face of the terrible precipice, with fifty feet of impending crag above, and nearly four hundred feet of sheer drop below. With a cry of dismay she cast herself on the pebbles.

Then a hand was laid on her shoulder, and she was shaken, and she heard her mother's voice, agitated with feeling: "Winefred, this is too much! After that I robbed him, are you about to kill him?"

"Mother!" She started to her knees. "Mother!"

"On me only is the guilt of the robbery, on you – that of his death."

"Mother!" In a tempest of conflicting feelings – fear for Jack, horror at what had been revealed, she gasped: "You say that, mother!" Jane Marley shrank back. But Winefred could not even now withdraw eyes and mind, save for one staggering moment, from the swaying rope and the green shelf. She saw Jack issue from the depths of the cave, come to the verge and look at the pole. It was beyond his reach. Then he tried the side of the rock to which he had adhered as he worked his way forward to the cave. Apparently that way could not be retraced. He attempted it, but retreated, foiled. Then again he stood on the turf, measuring his distance. There was but one way of escape possible, and that was to reach the rope and pendent pole.

He drew back. A piercing shriek burst from the lips of Winefred, as, next moment, she saw him leap – leap towards the suspended crosspole. And in that shriek her consciousness went. She fell forward as a log upon the pebbles, and passed out of knowledge whether his young arms and accurate eye had saved him, or whether he had missed and had fallen headlong, or whether, again, he had succeeded in catching, slinging for a moment, but had been unable to maintain himself swaying as a pendulum in mid–air.

Chapter Forty-Two

A Revelation

The lapse into unconsciousness was but momentary – it was like the shock produced by a crash of thunder attended with a blinding blaze of the electric fluid – that stuns for an instant. Winefred recovered rapidly, and staggered to her feet.

"He is safe," said Jane Marley. The girl waved her mother back, and started for the path that conducted her to the summit. But she had not mounted halfway before her powers failed her. The strain on her nerves had been too great, the horror of being responsible for the life or death of the young man had so shaken her that limbs and breath failed, and she sank on a bank of red earth near where a spring oozed forth and trickled to the beach. Then she covered her face with her hands and panted. The drops ran off her brow, the tears from her eyes. What if he had missed the swaying pole and had fallen, and been now lying at the bottom, a mass of broken bone! Would not the guilt of having driven him to his death lie on her? The coroner's jury might not find her guilty, but her own conscience would condemn her. She had asked him to go after the choughs, had taunted him till he could do no other than keep his promise; when he had provided companions and rope, he could not retreat, even when she begged him at the last moment to desist. And now, like a dash of poisonous exhalation, rose the thought that he had been robbed by her mother. In the supreme moment of alarm, the mother had let slip the truth.

She could not think out all that suggested itself to her mind, could not resolve what to do. Only one desire filled her mind: "That I were dead. Oh, that I were dead!" Then she thrilled through every nerve, as she heard a voice say: "Here they are."

Before her stood Jack with a little wickerwork cage in his hand,

and in it two choughs. She saw them not, nor the cage, only Jack. She sprang to her feet with a cry, in a moment was in his arms, and the cage and birds had fallen. Not a word was spoken. Jack held the girl to his heart and felt how she shivered as with an ague, that she could not utter a word, only sob as though her heart were broken.

In a German tale a monk who doubted about immortality listened to the song of a bird, entranced, and when roused found that a hundred years had passed as a watch in the night. It was the reverse with Winefred. As her heart broke forth into song – the new strange song of love – it was as though that one moment were expanded into a hundred days.

With a flash that filled her at once with ecstasy and with awe came the revelation that she loved Jack. All her roughness and rudeness trowards him had been due to a misconception of the state of her own feelings. Throughout she had loved him, but had not known it, and had resisted; misunderstanding the movements of her heart had given to them a perverse bias.

"So," said he, "we have found each other at last."

"Oh, God forgive me! God in his pity pardon me!" she sobbed. "Oh, the anguish that I have endured! Jack, if you had perished, been dashed to pieces, I would have cast myself over as well."

His breast swelled. He looked around. The vapours of morning had drifted away. Whither they were gone he knew not – only that gone they were. The sun shone upon Winefred and himself from out of a blue morning sky full of promise. And she was happy resting in his arms, too humbled to lift up her head, quivering in every limb, fluttering in every nerve. The conflict of emotions was almost unendurable. After a while she drew herself back, and with hands extended, and with tear-stained cheeks, she said: "Jack, can you ever forgive me?"

He caught her to him again. When one has endured a spasm of exquisite pain but a single thing is possible, to rest, breathe, and recover force – though that may be merely to undergo another throe. So she rested in his arms, panting, rallying, and yet with the prospect before her of renewed pain. "Jack," she sobbed, "I have spoken cruel words to you." He kissed her. "And I might have caused your death."

"I forget everything now. I would do more. I would do anything for you."

"I could die now you have forgiven me," said she, disengaging herself and sinking on a bank of turf.

"No, Winefred," he said, "this is not a moment in which to speak of death, but rather of life – ay, and of two lives flowing into one."

She shook her head. "I can never forgive myself."

"See, Winefred, I have had bitter thoughts of you, but they have all passed away like the morning mist. We were both entangled in a fog of misunderstandings. Now the sun is out and shines on both our heads and down into both our hearts, and all within as without is light." But again she expressed dissent. It was not light in her heart. In its depths lay the hateful thought of her mother's wrong-doing. "Do not concern yourself about the matter of the choughs," said he, misunderstanding her, "I went over the cliff of my own accord. I was glad of the excuse. Ever since I have broken with the smugglers I have had trouble with the young fellows of Beer. They have sneered at me as wanting in pluck. They could not account otherwise for my withdrawal. So I was glad to catch at a chance of showing that I still had a cool head and a stout heart. It was nothing in itself but it served my purpose. Winefred, it was you who advised me to have done with smuggling. I have kept my word to you, but it has involved me in unpleasantness, and I am thankful to you for having given me the occasion for doing something which may possibly help to set me right in public opinion at Beer."

She shuddered. "Oh, God have mercy on me!" she said, with a new outburst of compunction. "I did it in malice, because I thought that I hated you."

"Winefred, but for this we should not have met as we meet now. I should have gone on thinking that you hated me."

"And I – I quite believed that I did hate you."

"Now you know better. But for those choughs you would have been believing the same now and evermore." Then after a long pause he said, "We have each something to forgive and much to unlearn. I, at one time, really did suppose that your mother had stolen my inheritance." She uttered a cry and shrank from him.

"But only for a short while," he continued. "After that meeting

259

with you I was convinced that neither she nor you had injured me in that way. Your looks, your words, assured me of your entire innocence. Some folks have gone so far as to assert that your mother had employed my father's savings to send you to Bath, but I have spoken strongly against that." He was started by the expression of her face, by the mute agony and despair that were in it.

She looked at him with blank eyes, and every particle of colour had deserted her face, even her lips. As he put out his hand to take hers, she drew back with a shiver. "Winefred! what is the matter? I tell you that I believe this no more. Why are you frightened? Why do you look at me thus?"

"Do not ask me," she answered. "I cannot explain." She laid her face in her hands.

"I will ask no questions at all, " he said. "I am content now that I have your love. I forget all the past, with its misunderstandings. But be yourself again. I love you with all my heart – let that be our one thought now." She wrung her hands despairingly, looking at his with a deathlike face. Her lips moved, but no words came over them.

"I love you – I love you," she said, after a long and painful pause. "But that is all. In the bright day comes darkness. We are two wretched creatures. We must not love each other, for we can never, never belong to each other."

"But why not?" he asked. He looked steadily into her face, and a suspicion stole serpentlike into his mind. His breath came slow and laboured. A veil formed before his eyes. Was that it – that which he feared? Then, in a subdued voice, he said, "Winefred, we cannot remain longer here and I must know the meaning of this."

"We cannot remain, and you will not ask."

"I hear steps. Someone is coming. We must meet again."

"Better for both if we part here, and for ever."

260

Chapter Forty-Three

A Refusal

Winefred descended the path to meet her mother, who was slowly mounting the path. "You have been long," said Jane.

"Yes, but I have got the choughs. Mother, I have been endeavouring to make amends for a cruel wrong that has been done. I have been guilty of risking a life for a fancy."

"Amends! What amends? A guinea is what you offered. Have you made it thirty shillings? That is ample and overflowing."

"No, mother. Let us turn and go home. When we are on the beach we will talk; here we must walk in file, and the red marl is greasy."

Jane Marley turned about and led the way; but she looked over her shoulder to observe her daughter. She was not easy in her mind about her. She was frightened at what the consequences might be of what she had uttered in sudden alarm at seeing Jack Rattenbury on the brink of a terrible death. At length they reached the bottom of the declivity. Here lay the shingle beach before them, backed by Indian-red cliffs in which lay the strips of curious verdigris shale, and all crowned with intense green and rich vegetation. At intervals oozed a liquid like blood, the drainage of the sandstone. No one was in sight; but owing to the noise made by walking on the flint and chert pebbles, mother and daughter could not converse in a low tone and be heard by one another. It was necessary for them to speak aloud and in high-pitched voices.

"Well," said Mrs Marley, "what amends, but money? I have offered him help, and he threw my offer back in my face. As to the choughs – any lad would risk his neck for guinea – you owe him nothing, now he is paid."

"No other lad would take my offer, mother."

"If he had fallen, it would have been his own doing. There is nothing to be won without risk. My father risked his life and liberty – my brother did the same, and lost his life."

"I urged – I drove him to it, mother. If any catastrophe had happened, I should have felt that I could not live longer. If Jack had been killed, I would have thrown myself down."

Her mother laughed scornfully. "Once – and that for me, you would not face a fall over the cliffs, but fought like a wildcat with teeth and nails. Now, for this clodpole you are prepared to do it! I cannot understand you. What is this bumpkin to you, that you should be in such a way about him?"

"That is what I desire to speak with you about, mother," said Winefred, and there was a ripple in her voice. "I have tried to repair some of the wrong done him by myself. Now I ask you – will you not do the like?"

Mrs Marley looked sharply at her sideways. "What do you mean?" she inquired in a low tone, so low that Winefred could not hear the words, lost in the clicker of the pebbles displaced by their feet; but she knew what her mother said, for she was observing her face, and she read it in the movement of her lips.

"Mother," she replied, "you know what I mean. Recollect what the words were that you uttered, when he had let slip the rope, and was preparing to leap. Then you cried out –"

"Do not repeat them. Bah! It was nonsense. I spoke any foolish words that came at random into my head."

"I do not believe you when you say this," said Winefred. "Then, when off your guard the truth came out." Jane Marley looked down. Her veins swelled, her face became dark. "Mother," continued the girl very gravely, "I believe what you then cried out. I believe that you found and kept the money that should have belonged to Jack Rattenbury. I shall have no peace of mind till every penny has been restored."

"I have nothing of his."

"Mother – you shall know something more. I cannot tell how it is, it came over me like the bursting of a wave over my head. I and Jack – that is – I – I mean that I love him." Her red cheeks had become suffused, and she turned her face to the red rocks.

"What?" Jane Marley stood still, and became rigid, with both arms extended at her side, stiff and her hands clinched. Every muscle in her face was knotted. "What! You – you and that fellow, Captain Rattenbury's son! Love *him*? Him of all people! Are you mad? You can never take him."

"No, mother, that is true. I cannot take him, so long as this wicked injustice stands between us. I know that well enough. No, I cannot be his. You have parted us."

"It is well. I would have broken his neck."

"Then I would have died also. Of what profit would it be to you to have and keep that which you have got, if through retaining it you were crushed with the knowledge that you had wronged him, and that I, for love of him whose death I had caused, had also perished?"

"I do not say that I have anything of his. But suppose it were as you fancy. Do you think anything would have brought me to do it – but care for you?"

"If for me you did what is wrong – for my sake now undo it."

"I cannot."

"Till that be done, he and I remain apart."

"If for that alone, I will not do it."

Then Winefred caught her mother's arm, and drawing her round so that they faced each other, she said, in muffled, quivering tones, "Mother, I have held up my head and scorned and flouted the people at Axmouth, because I believed that what they said was a lie. I did not, I would not, suppose that you could commit such a wickedness. I was proud of you. I believed in you. I held it to be a false accusation. I thought you too good, too noble, too upright to be – to be –" She hesitated.

"Say the word, to be a thief."

"You gave way to temptation out of love for me. Out of love for me restore what you took." She panted for breath. She was white with the deadly earnestness with which she pleaded.

"And you – to be brought up as a lady," muttered Jane, scowling, "and to throw yourself away on a village lout – one, too, who had not the manhood in him to take to the sea and be what his fathers have been."

"I do not desire to be a lady."

"I do – it is my one thought, my only ambition."

"And at Bath," pursued Winefred, "everything about me is false. I am expected to pass as one who has lost her mother. You are supposed to be only a nurse! I hate it, I will not bear it any longer. No – not although my father – no, not although you join with him to force me to this deception. I will have the truth. I will not be false and deceitful. Let all be honest and clear as sea–water, and nothing be held back and muffled up in lies. I have hated it throughout. I have felt like a fly tangled in a cobweb, like a fish in a drawnet. I will not go back unless it be as your daughter. I was so proud of my dear mother, she was poor but honest, and now –" She burst into tears. Jane continued looking down with knitted brows; she stirred the shingle with one foot, playing with the pebbles, yet regarding them not.

"I do not admit anything," she said sullenly. "You are troubled with a bad fancy. But even –"

"It is no fancy. I could not mistake your words."

"Suppose it has been as you think. I do not allow it, but let us say that old Captain Job did leave a trifle of money, and that I found and kept it. I had a right to it. It was money taken from my father, squeezed out of his veins. It was the price of my brother's blood."

"O mother, you do not know this."

"I do know that my father worked for years under the captain, and died penniless. I do know that my brother was shot when he set up himself apart from the captain."

"But you do not know that Captain Rattenbury was responsible in either case."

"They were in the same business. The money stuck in some hands, and none in those of my father."

"Mother, dear, you owe all this to what Olver Dench has been saying to you. What is his word worth?"

"Of all men none is so likely to know the truth as Olver."

"But is he a man who speaks the truth?"

"I care not. You shall be a lady, and you shall marry a gentleman – a real gentleman – such as was your father."

"But were you happy with him?"

"We were ill–assorted. You shall be a lady."

"Do not, for ever, dear mother, turn back like a wheel to the same point. I have no wish to be a lady. I was happy as a poor girl, picking up pebbles and grinding them. Mother, my heart is full of Jack. I cannot endure that this wrong should have been done him."

"What!" asked Mrs Marley, looking up with a dark shadow in her eyes, "you will tell him all?"

"No – that, never."

"A girl in love is a fool; she blabs everything."

"I can be silent. I shall not utter a word. What would it profit me to say to him, Jack, you might be rich, but are poor, because we have got your money. I am dressed out with coin that should be yours. I am pushed with your money into a position in life above that to which I was born. What would he think of me and of you if I were to say this? I cannot possibly tell him my shame and yours. For your sake I will not. No never!"

Jane, with curling lip, said, "What would folk exclaim suppose I were to do as you desire?"

"It does not concern us what they would exclaim. Do what is right. Then only is the barrier down between Jack and me."

Mrs Marley ground her heel among the rolled stones. Presently she looked up, and said roughly, "Come along."

"Mother, what will you do?"

"I will not. You shall be a lady. It is my fixed purpose. I am not such a fool as to cast away what I hold. Would you – if you found a rare chalcedony, throw it into the sea?"

"If it belonged to another, I would put it into his hand. Mother, why is it that dear Mrs Jose has been so good to us? Why has she stood up so stoutly for you against the whole neighbourhood, but because in her honest heart she thought you could not have done such a thing."

"Need she know it now? Will you set her against me?"

"I shall not breathe a word of it to her."

"That fellow, Jack – he shall not have you."

"Mother, I am sure if Jack knew how he had been defrauded by us, he could not love me. He does love me, because he cannot believe this to be possible."

"And yet you would tell him!"

"No, you and you alone must tell him the truth. Let him have what is his own, and I am content to lose him."

"Come on, enough of this."

"You will not, mother?"

"No." Winefred heaved a despairing sigh. She knew the resolute character of her mother. Suddenly she flung her arms about her, kissed her passionately, and said, "O mother, if you love me, if you love me at all, do it."

"No, because I love you; you shall be a lady. No, I will not."

Chapter Forty-Four

The Gate of Thorns

Jack had worked diligently in the office all day. He had been late in arriving, but he apologised, told the truth about his adventure, and promised to work overtime so as to make up for his default. His heart was light. Whilst engaged over his books the figures danced before his eyes, and the lines in the ledger became music staves from which his heart read a joyous melody. He had loved Winefred for so long a time, and had done so in anticipation of nothing but rebuff; and now, all at once, he found his love returned.

Verily he was the happiest of boys. In the evening he walked through Seaton. The night was still and starlit. There was frost in the air, but he did not feel it; the sea grumbled as it chewed the flints on the Chesil Bank, but he regarded it not. His pulses leaped and his heart sang.

He arrived at the ferry and was put across. Olver marvelled to find him in such buoyant humour, and asked the reason.

"I have had a good day," said Jack, but entered into no explanation.

"Had a rise in your salary?" observed Dench.

Then Jack ascended the combe, and took his way over the common to the cottage on the undercliff. A light was burning in the kitchen. No other window was illumined. He could look in, and he saw Mrs Marley only, engaged in some domestic employment. Then Jack turned in the direction of Bindon. If Winefred were not at home, she could be nowhere else. Nor was he out in his reckoning.

The relations between mother and daughter had been strained. Throughout the day each had felt uneasy, and conscious of the barrier that divided them, and shy of being in each other's presence and society. The situation had become unendurable, and for their mutual relief Winefred had gone in the afternoon to Bindon, to see Mrs Jose and have tea with her. She did not herself feel in a humour for a visit. She would have preferred to remain alone in her chamber with her thoughts, but as matters stood she considered that it would be best for her to be away from the cottage, and as she owed Mrs Jose a visit and a talk, she went to her. She could at all events freely speak with her of Jack's daring feat in getting the choughs, and she carried with her the cage to show the birds to the farmer's wife. She further harboured the hope that, when by herself, her mother might reconsider her determination.

Night had fallen when Winefred left Bindon to return to the undercliff, and she went up the lane to the gate that opened on to the down. And there, in the starlight, she saw someone. She knew who it must be thus awaiting her, standing there where she had formerly menaced him with a bush.

"Winefred," said he, and threw open the gate, "see, I have plucked away briars and thorns. Pass through to me on the down."

"O Jack, why have you come?"

"Because I could not stay away. I felt that I must once more see you, hear you – kiss you."

"Jack, I am returning home, and am late. I have stayed too long at Bindon."

"You shall not go home yet. Your time belongs now to me."

"No; have you forgotten what I said to you?"

"I have no memory but for bright and pleasant things. I can recall but one thing distinctly – that you love me." She heaved a sigh and laid her brow on his shoulder.

"My dear one," said he, "why are you so downhearted? I love no

267

one in the world but you, never have loved another, not even with a boy's fancy, and never can love anyone else."

"It is sweet to me to hear this, Jack; it is like the singing of larks in early spring, and yet it troubles my heart. A thick fog is about me. I can see no way."

"But I have your hand and can lead you."

"We can never go hand in hand together."

"Why not? I want no other companion. I will have no other; and if you can put up with such an one as I –"

"I! – oh, how I would it could be so! But it cannot be. Indeed, indeed, believe me, it cannot be."

"Why not?"

She was unable to answer him, at least openly. She could not tell him her reason. As for Jack, if, in the morning a suspicion had traversed his mind that he really had been robbed by Mrs Marley, and that Winefred was aware of it, in his overwhelming happiness at knowing that he was beloved, he had forgotten this wholly.

"I am hanged if I see any just cause or impediment, dear Winnie. I am not rich; indeed that is my disadvantage. Otherwise I venture to think I am not an undesirable party." He laughed good-naturedly. "I have robust health, strong arms, as you saw this morning; commonplace wits, and a very firm, dogged resolution that I will have you and no one else. I am earning something already; I get on famously with Captain Ford, Mrs Jose's brother, and see no reason why I should not in a little while be sufficiently comfortably off to keep two – with moderate requirements."

"Consider my mother, Jack."

"She wishes to make a lady of you, and will not give consent. But, Winnie, what if you plant your feet, put up your lip and say that you are disinclined to be made into manufactured goods? Any man can take a horse to water, but ten cannot make him drink."

He was in jubilant spirits. "Winnie," said he, "a caravan came to Colyton last summer with wild beasts. They went in procession through the town; there was a zebra, striped like a tiger. But a thunder shower came on just as the procession moved, and after it all the stripes had been washed from the beast, and out of the rain stepped a plain Neddy. I object to painted donkeys."

Winefred laughed – she could not help it. She said, "You are very uncivil, Jack."

"I don't care whether it be a donkey or a gazelle, let us have the real thing –"

"Jack, I am altogether with you. Let us have the real thing."

"That is a kiss," said he. "No sham there." Jack was in excellent spirits. He could see no cloud in the sky. Winefred's love for him had broken like dawn upon his soul, and within him all was light, and twitter, and bloom.

"I must go back to Bath," she said.

"What – to have the stripes painted on?"

"There are the choughs."

"I will take them."

"No – my father is there."

Jack became grave. "You fear that he will not give consent?"

"I know that he will not, any more than will my mother."

"Winnie, my dear. Parents have had to undergo this sort of thing before, but children can bring them to reason. The inevitable is the most convincing of arguments. You do not suppose that cattle in pastures eat only buttercups? They nip up sorrel leaves as well. But presently they lie down and chew the cud – and it all gets chewed up together and turns into sweet milk. This little opposition to dad and mam is but sorrel leaves."

"No, Jack, it is in vain. I cannot go against both. You do not know what my mother has been to me. But that is not all. O Jack, I do indeed love you, love you with every scrap of my heart. I would do anything for you that was possible. But do you not see that there are other impossibilities than those which can be beat down by brute force? I do not want to be a lady, to have stripes painted on me." She laughed and cried at once. "Heaven be my witness, I would go down on my knees and scrub the floor, and whiten the doorstep of our house, and be happy, and warble for joy of heart, and keep, as I worked, an eye on the lookout to see you coming home from the office to me – to my heart." He clasped her to him.

"But it cannot be," she said, disengaging herself.

"Why not – I ask again?"

"I am not able to tell you. I am not, indeed. It concerns others

269

besides me."

"You are full of secrets," said he, somewhat peevishly. "Look here. I have torn down all the thorns that stood in your way, and now you are wilfully setting them up again. Winnie, it is just the old stupid story over again. You whisk thorns in my face, and will not let me draw near to you. If you really love me, tell me everything."

She burst into tears. "I cannot do so. There are things I dare not say. I have had my tongue tied."

He became graver, for he recalled now for the first time that ugly suspicion, which had occurred to him in the morning. "Winefred," said he leisurely, "perhaps your father or mother may say that I cannot have you, because I have inherited nothing from my father, who was supposed to have laid by a good deal of money. Believe me when I tell you this. Look up at those glittering stars overhead. I assure you solemnly, before those eyes of heaven, that if my father had accumulated a fortune, and had left it to me, I would not touch one penny of it, no, not one penny, for I know how it was got, by ways that I do not think straightforward, and perhaps even dishonest by smuggling. I do not know whether there is any right or wrong in the matter – it was an underhand business, and that is enough. I will earn my livelihood honestly and openly, with my hands and head, and on that alone will I live, so help me God. If my father ever did lay by a store – I do not say that he did – and if by some accident it had gone astray so that I have not had the fingering of it – then, Winefred, mark my words – to that person into whose hands it has fallen I freely, cheerfully surrender it all. From this moment I give up all claim to it. I look upon it as though I have not, and never had, any right to it. I will bear no grudge against any such person as may have got hold of it by accident, and have hesitated about surrendering it. Winnie, if at any time you should chance to hear that it had been found and retained, then tell whomsoever it concerns to throw it into the sea, or give it to a hospital, or do what he likes with it. I will ask no questions, and not trouble my head about it – here is my real treasure, and I ask for none more."

He would have clasped Winefred, but she forestalled him by catching his hand, and kissing it, and as she did so, a tear fell upon it. "You are good," she said, "nevertheless, it remains the same – it cannot be."

"But then – what is to become of us?"

"I do not know." They walked side by side on the open down for a while. The stars glinted overhead. Below, the flints that had been fractured reflected the glint. The sea murmured unintelligible things below, and their minds were as that sea, fretting, chafing, uttering unintelligible murmurs. At last Jack burst forth with:

"Is there no way out of this hobble?"

"There is none," said she in a low voice.

"Bah!" exclaimed Jack. "There is no tangle that cannot be unravelled with patience. We are both young. We must not set our noses against a wall and say that is the world's end." Thus they parted.

And thenceforth every evening he was at the gate, and every evening she was there also. In vain did she torture her mind to find a way out of the difficulties that obstructed her. Sometimes she was tempted to confess everything – she knew that he suspected the worst. He was so generous that he would forgive her mother, and the story would never become public. Everything would be arranged between them. But the secret was not her own. She had promised her mother to be silent, and she could not endure to admit the fault of a mother who had loved her so dearly, and who had sinned only out of love for her. It was at the same time intolerable to her to know that Jack suspected the truth, and to be unable to speak in extenuation of her mother's conduct.

Moreover, she felt that some of her mother's guilt adhered to her. She was so far a participator in the wrong done that she profited by it. To what extent her expenses at Bath were defrayed by her father, and to what extent they were paid for out of Captain Rattenbury's savings, she did not know, but she could not free herself from the consciousness that some of this stolen money had been expended on herself. The hopelessness of their love weighed on both their hearts. Love was sweet, and yet was bitter, like the little book which the prophet ate.

Of the two Winefred was the more unhappy, for she did not possess the sanguine temperament of Jack. She felt an unutterable joy at having his love, and yet it was a joy that turned to despair. How was this to end? This was what they asked each other and themselves, and never received an answer.

"It shall end for a while, now," said Winefred, "for tomorrow I return to Bath."

"How is this? I thought you would not go back till your father came to fetch you away."

"That was my first intention. But I have been obliged to give way. Things are not ripe for that yet. I take the choughs with me. I shall see my father again."

"And how long will you be away?"

"That I cannot tell."

"Winefred," said Jack, "we are at the gate of thorns. If you will set your hands along with me to unweave them and pluck them out, we shall make an opening in time. Never mind your fingers. We shall get the gap large enough in time for both of us to pass through to freedom."

Chapter Forty-Five

Holwood or Marley?

"My dear Sylvana, I wish you particularly to look at this tureen. Very handsome, is it not?"

"Beautiful, but surely very costly."

"It is costly, my dear, as it is plated, but not so costly as it would be if it were silver. Happily, at a dinner party the guests cannot examine it for the plate mark, as they can forks and spoons. In our position we must possess a handsome soup-tureen."

"We have done without one of metal hitherto. Why buy one now?"

"Sylvana," said Mrs Tomkin-Jones, "I have engaged a butler. With him we must have a suitable tureen."

"Why, mother?"

"Because, my dear, we shall be constrained to give dinner-parties."

"We have given nothing above high teas hitherto."

"But with a butler, dear."

"Well, with that adjunct?"

"We must give dinner-parties, and giving dinner-parties must have what looks like a silver soup-tureen on the table."

"What an explosion of gentility!" exclaimed Sylvana.

"My dear, hitherto we have not been in a position to buy a tureen. Now it is somewhat different."

"Oh! because we have a paying pupil whom you can trot out. How long is she to be with us? Perhaps a month, perhaps may not come back to us at all, and then away flies this butler with the soup-tureen under his arm, and the last state of the Tomkin-Joneses is worse than the first."

"My dear, don't be profane."

"I am stating a fact. But how do you know that the girl Winefred is a fit person for you to patronise?" asked Miss Jones, with a malicious intonation in her voice.

"She is related to the Finnborough family."

"Have the Finnboroughs acknowledged her?"

"They are not in Bath at present. When they learn how greatly admired she is and how much she is talked about –"

"Because of her dialect."

"No, Sylvana, because of her beauty. How can you be so disagreeable?"

"Mother, send back the tureen as not suited, and cancel your engagement to the butler."

"Sylvana! how offensively you put things! I am not engaged to any butler. It is the butler who is engaged by me."

"Well, rid yourself of both."

"I cannot; I have bought the plated tureen."

"And the butler bought also?"

"Engaged, as I said."

"Then you are throwing away money that we can ill afford. When young Maskell came of age his father had a blaze of fireworks, and afterwards informed the youth he had nothing to give him and nothing to leave him; his inheritance was debts."

273

"There is no analogy in the cases."

"You want to blaze out, mother, before you know that with any self-respect you can keep Winefred in the house."

"Indeed!"

"Indeed, yes. I have received some information. I have an old school friend at Axminster, and I have inquired of her about the Holwoods."

"Axminster is not Axmouth."

"It is on the same river."

"So are Pangbourne and Tilbury. You do not inquire at one place relative to persons at the other. Besides, I will trouble you to mind your own business and not be so officious as to inquire into things that in no way concern you."

"They do concern me, mamma. We have – or rather have not – this girl in the house, and she is involving you in soup tureens and butlers."

"I want to know nothing of what you have been inquiring after."

"Of course you do not. After having spent something like ten or a dozen pounds on a tureen. But I will tell you, nevertheless. My friend says that there are no persons of the name of Holwood, that anyone knows, in the county, and the name is not in the *Court Directory*. As to their country seat, it resolves itself into a castle in Spain."

"Mrs Jose told me that they lived at The Undercliff."

"There is no gentleman's seat so called. I further inquired of my friend – "

"I want to hear no more."

"I further inquired," pursued the relentless Sylvana, "about a person of the name of Marley."

"How ridiculous!" exclaimed Mrs Tomkin–Jones; "how should anyone know about Mrs Marley? She was a common menial, a nurse, nothing more."

"There is no knowing what one may learn by mentioning names."

"Of course you heard nothing of her?"

"I did not expect to hear from my friend at Axminster, but she has a friend married at Seaton, and she will write to her."

"I insist on you desisting from this sort of thing," said the doctor's widow. "We were dropping out of consideration in Bath because we did not entertain."

"And, mamma, you are leaping – "

"Leaping, Sylvana, be decent; I never leap."

"Leaping into notoriety, mother, if you choose to patronise a young woman of equivocal origin."

"My dear, you entirely forget who I am."

"Not at all. It is because you are a Tomkin–Jones that I am constrained to look after you. There was a peacock in Bedfont that got into the lodge and spread its tail before the kitchen fire, and it blazed like a Catherine–wheel. The funny thing is that all that summer the peacock continued to bristle up and spread the bare and charred stumps, wholly unconscious that it was making itself ridiculous. Take care, mother, that you have feathers before you make a spread."

"You forget what is due to you," said the widow angrily.

"I am solicitous for you. Have you ever asked Winefred, or her father, what was her mother's maiden name?"

"No."

"But I have."

"My dear!"

"I asked Winefred, and she flared up and refused an answer. I next asked Mr Holwood, and he became so nervous and bewildered as to be speechless. That tells its own tale – it does not look nice."

"How can you, Sylvana? What an improper mind you possess! Besides – such questions – most reprehensible."

"This must be searched to the bottom."

"But – but!" gasped Mrs Tomkin–Jones, "consider the tureen!"

"You cannot afford to know the truth," pursued Sylvana, "because you have bought a soup–tureen and hired a butler! So, to preserve both, you thrust your head into a bush."

Then Jesse, who had been seated in the window engaged in domestic needlework, darning a kitchen tablecloth that a stupid maid had cut through when slicing bread – and had been unnoticed by her mother and sister, as taking no part in the conversation – now started from her chair, threw down the tablecloth, and coming forward, laid her thimble-shod finger on the round rosewood table, and said: "What does it matter to any of us who was Winefred's mother and whence she came, and what was her maiden name? Winefred is sent to us, not that we may pick holes in her pedigree, but patch up gaps in her education. What does society care about her mother? Not a rush. It is solely those who are disappointed and soured who go about with the muck-rake scraping in the gutters for dirty, inconsidered, and castaway trifles, and rejoice in the foulest find the fork brings up. Society does not ask these questions, does not care about the mothers of those whom it admires. Society does recognise in Winefred a wholesome mind, a fresh nature, and a sound heart. These are things not brought ot the surface by the muck-rake. Society recognises her good qualities and respects her, regardless of father or mother, for her own sake."

"Oh yes," sneered Sylvana, "you fight her battles because she has promised you a new gown and bonnet."

"I fight the battles of anyone who is an object of envy and spite to the gutter-scrapers." At that moment the front door bell was rung, and a knock followed.

"Quick – quick, Jesse!" exclaimed the mother. "Put the dreadful tablecloth under the sofa. It ought never to have been brought in here. Sylvana, hide the tureen, and for mercy's sake, Jesse, take off your thimble, slip it into your pocket, and pretend you were reading *Rogers on the Imagination.*"

In another minute the door was opened and Mr Holwood entered, accompanied by his daughter. After the first salutations, always made with the most laboured politeness by him, and responded to with formal courtesy by Mrs Tomkin-Jones, as though they were practising a figure under the supervision of a dancing master, Winefred said: "I went first to my father's lodgings to see him, and have brought him on here."

"You have certainly tumbled upon us quite unexpectedly," said Sylvana. "I must confess that in Bath we are accustomed to send a letter beforehand to notify our coming. But customs differ in different latitudes. That may not be usual at Axmouth which is *de rigueur* at Bath."

"Sylvana, be silent," ordered Mrs Tomkin–Jones, frowning at her elder daughter; then with a face wreathed in smiles she said to Winefred, "My dear, delighted to see you. At all times you are welcome."

"I am sorry if I have acted wrongly," said the girl. "When I left, I said that I would return in a fortnight. I have not exceeded my time. I have brought the choughs; they are in the passage."

"In the hall," was Mrs Tomkin–Jones's correction. "How good of you, and how gratified the Square will be at our contribution to the garden! It will be noticed in the *Bath Gazette*."

"I hope the ancestral mansion is looking its best," said Sylvana, who stood by the fireplace playing with the spills on the mantel-piece.

"I do not understand your meaning," answered Winefred, looking fixedly at her face. Jesse drew to her side. She saw a crisis approached.

"And the venerable fossil – in good repair, I trust?" asked Sylvana.

"What or whom do you mean by that term, venerable fossil?" asked Winefred quietly but firmly. Sylvana, trifling with the spills, threw out some from the vase that had contained them. These she leisurely collected to return them to the same receptacle. A provoking smile was on her face, but she made no answer.

"I asked you a question, Miss Jones. Whom did you mean when you spoke of a venerable fossil?"

"Oh, you and Mr Holwood know best," sneered Sylvana, turning her head about to contemplate the "Flight into Egypt."

"If you refer to my mother, she is well."

Mr Holwood gasped and fell back.

"Oh, your mother – I thought her name was Marley. I beg pardon for my mistake." A long silence ensued. Mrs Tomkin–Jones endeavoured by looks and signals to silence her daughter. Jesse took Winefred's arm. Sylvana continued playing with the spills with the same exasperating smile on her lips.

Winefred was composed. She answered, "My father can give you the best reply as to her name." Mr Holwood shook like an aspen

277

leaf, and turned about as though he sought the door by which to run away. "My name is the same as hers," said Winefred. "I will bear that of Holwood only if I have a right to do so."

She waited. No word came from her father. "I am glad of this opportunity having arisen at once," said the girl. "I returned to Bath with full intent to have everything cleared up. On descending from the coach, I went direct to my father. I have brought him here that misunderstandings might at once be got rid of. I wish everything to be open and plain before those who have so kindly received me."

Jesse pressed her arm. "I hate everything that is not true and aboveboard. I have been unhappy here hitherto, through no lack of kindness or consideration on the part of Mrs Tomkin–Jones and of you, Jesse, but because I was in a false position. I myself did not know, I do not know now, how I stand. Am I Winefred Holwood or am I Winefred Marley? Father, answer me that."

He was turned half round and was blowing at his fingertips as though playing on pan–pipes. She waited, and then repeated her question in a peremptory tone. "Really, my dear, you take me aback. I was unprepared. This is wholly, entirely unexpected."

"It is but a plain answer that I ask for as to facts," said Winefred. "I will accept whichever name you say, but remember this, father, I will no longer – no, not for a day – suffer my poor mother to be thrust out of all consideration and called my nurse. Anyhow, after what has occurred, I shall return to her again, be she Marley or Holwood. My mother she is, and dear past words to say, she has always been, is, and ever will be to me. Father, if you desire to have me here at any time with you, and if you value a daughter's love, you may seek and find me in my mother's arms; whether that mother be Marley or Holwood by name, she is mother to me. Which is it?"

He was groping in his waistcoat pocket, then in the tails of his bottle–green coat. He turned round and round again, like a parrot on a perch, but with none of the coolness, the audacity of a parrot.

"Very well – I go back to Axmouth at once," said the girl.

"O Winefred!" – he returned stationary for a moment – "do not leave me! You do not know all. I cannot explain everything at once. There are many things to be considered."

"Father, I must know what is my real name. Is it Marley, or is it

278

Holwood?"

"Oh, do not worry and distract me. I am very ill. The doctors say that they cannot sure me – it may be long – it may be short –"

"I am indeed sorry to leave you, dear father. But you know where at all times I may be found – with my mother." Again the feeble man began twisting about.

"Come," said Jesse. She let go her hold of Winefred, and caught the father, gripping both his arms and holding him fast so that he could no more revolve. "Come, Mr Holwood, I will shake you. Positively I will shake you to bits unless you answer Winefred. Now –" She had him by the shoulders.

"Oh! don't, I cannot bear it."

"Which is it?" with an initial premonitory shake. "I will shake your wig off."

"Oh! don't, I am in poor health."

"Which is it, Marley or Holwood?"

"My teeth, my teeth!"

"I will shake them out of your head. Which is it?"

"She is my – my daughter."

"And the mother – speak plainly – what is she?" She shook him again. He gasped, he put his hand to his cravat. "

My – my wife – really, really – my lawful wife."

"Then," said Jesse, letting go her clutch, "Winefred is rightly named. She is Miss Holwood."

"Sir," said Mrs Tomkin–Jones, with great stateliness, rising, rustling and curtseying, "under the painful circumstances, as your daughter says that she intends to leave at once, bear in mind that I have not received a notice of any sort – I am quite ashamed to seem mercenary – and positively I know nothing about money and business and all that sort of thing – but I have been drawn into numerous expenses to make all ready to accommodate your daughter. And I regret to say that I expect – "

"The soup–tureen to be paid for," threw in Sylvana.

"Certainly! certainly!" said the trembling man, "anything, only do not retain me longer. I am very unwell, and my cravat is – is – is all on one side. I confess everything. Jane is my wife, and Winefred is my daughter. So they both have a right to my name."

279

Chapter Forty-Six

Over a Tea-Table

Winefred accompanied her father to his lodgings. These were comfortable and well-situated, spacious and elegantly furnished; clearly not chosen with a view to economy. He bowed and made her enter, with old-fashioned courtesy, and then ordered tea.

A certain amount of constraint existed between them, and yet he had lost much of his timidity of manner since he had been forced to avow the nature of his relation to Jane. The Rubicon was passed. He had dismissed his ships. It may, however, be questioned whether even when shaken to the undoing of his cravat and the loosening of his teeth he would have made the admission but for two considerations.

In the first place, he had become warmly attached to his daughter, of whom, moreover, he was vastly proud, so that he had felt the deprivation when she had gone back to Axmouth; and secondly, he was aware that he was afflicted with an incurable complaint, and the thought of dying in solitude without a loving hand to smooth his pillow filled him with dismay.

During the absence of Winefred he had thought much of this. "Miss Jesse was wrong," he said, "in her allusion to my head of hair. I do not wear a wig. I have my hair dressed by a French barber before I leave the house, but it is my own hair. You may pull a lock if you doubt my word. I am positively not so old as some persons are disposed to make me. I may look a little aged – of late. I have had a trying life; and recent troubles of mind – relative to what the doctors have told me – have had their effect on me. May I ask you to favour me by pouring out the tea?"

Presently he said, "I like crumpets. They crunch like hard biscuits, but have no deleterious effect on the teeth."

"Are you fond of hard biscuits, father?"

"Of Abernethy's I have always been fond. I even enjoyed a ship–biscuit once, when the world was young, and when – when I first knew your mother." He sighed deeply.

"Were you thinking of her, papa?"

"To be honest, of Abernethy biscuits. I did relish them. I shall never eat one again."

"Why not?"

"Because my teeth are gone. I have at least some that are not my own. Miss Jesse would have shaken them into my mouth on to my tongue – had I not spoken. That, you see, would have been humiliating."

"Father, you said something of being ill."

"Yes, I am ill, but not very. That is to say I am threatened, but do not suffer seriously at present. I do not like to think about it, still less to speak of it – but to you it is another matter. You must know about it. When I came here I had some hopes. But the doctors afford me none. Let the subject drop. I have enough of that when alone, and at night. Then it haunts me and will not let me rest. During the day, and with company, I shake it off. I like crumpets. When I hear the crumpets crackle it carries me back to the time when I ate Abernethies and had no false teeth."

"Tell me about your marriage with my mother," said Winefred, desirous of drawing him from crumpets, and Abernethies to matters of more enduring interest. "Father, how was it that she did not take your name?"

"Well, well, my dear, the story is painful, but it must come out now. The facts were these. We were married privately by a rogue of a parson at St. Pancras Church at Rousden. It is ruinous, but it had a rector, who lived in Lyme, and did no duty, as there were no parisioners. I do not think he was unfrocked. It would have been hardly worth the bishop's while to do that, you see, as he did no duty, and there was no roof on the church. For my sake, and at my request, the marriage was kept secret. When young, your mother was a beautiful woman; you remind me of her greatly. In fact you get your good looks from her."

"But, father, why were you – "

281

"I know what you would say. Why were we separated? You see the marriage was not known, and I was given a place in the Foreign Office, and as everyone supposed that I was calculated by character and capacities to get advancement in it I began to see that my marriage presented serious difficulties." He began to fumble with the teaspoon at his tongue, and spoke accordingly indistinctly. "I mean this – that I feared it might prevent my preferment, and then again it would alienate all my family from me. I had an aunt who was wealthy, and she doted on me; but she was ambitious, and would not have forgiven me. So I got your mother to keep our marriage dark, and then – then –"

"Then you were appointed Governor–General of Terra del Fuego."

"No – come – no. That was not really the case. I believe poor Jane – I mean your mother – was led to think I had gone abroad, lest she should come to town after me and make scenes. She had a violent temper."

"So you parted from my mother for the sake of your prospects with an aunt and for preferment in the Foreign Office?"

"I would not put it quite that way. Of course they could not turn me out because I had married your mother, but they would have seen that she was not wholly qualified to shine in a Foreign Embassy. You see she could speak neither French nor Chinese. You comprehend – it would have caused difficulties, embarrassments."

"But did you get an Embassy?"

"No, no; I remained in the office."

"Then you threw her over for nothing!"

"No; not quite that. My aunt died a year ago at an advanced age, and has left me very comfortably provided for. I have applied for a pension, and am really in easy circumstances at present – now, just at the time when –" He shivered, and his weak mouth fell. "It is too tragic to contemplate. I did hope that the Bath waters might have expelled the poison from my veins, but my disorder remains unarrested. It may be rapid in its course, and my dissolution may be near, or it may be slow. I cannot tell. The doctors give me very little hope, in fact, to be candid, none at all. O Winefred, you will nurse me through it?"

"Yes, father, and so will mother."

"But she hates me. She can never forgive me – and then she is a violent woman. She frightened me years ago. I dislike rough ways and strong tempers. I always did at the time when I was young and strong. Now I cannot endure the least roughness."

"She is not rough, she is vastly tender. But her strong heart has had its beatings stayed, and her ideas have become twisted about."

"Ah, yes – she is a passionate woman."

"She loves passionately, but has had her heart wounded and bruised."

"Yes, I suppose she has suffered – so have I."

"She has suffered, therefore she can have compassion."

He remained silent, and shook his head dubiously. "Tell me about yourself," he said at last. No doubt he had undergone stormy scenes with Jane that had frightened him, and left on him an impression that could not be eradicated.

"What shall I tell you?" asked Winefred.

"About your youth, and where you lived, and how."

"We got along, mother and I, as best we could, she hawking tapes and needles, and I – collecting pebbles."

"There was really no necessity for that."

"We must live. We had a cottage on the cliffs, but it went to pieces as the cliff cracked and made a chasm. So we were obliged to leave it, and then we had a very bad time, for no one would take us in."

"You should have gone into lodgings. Your mother had means."

"Hardly any. One may earn a few pence by the sale of combs and laces, thread and needles, but not much. And I was indeed proud if I got ninepence for a cornelian."

"I do not understand. Why did you go to that man – that captain – I do not recall his name?"

"Oh, you mean Captain Rattenbury. He took us in one night when we were in despair, wet to the bone, and had no shelter for our heads, and every door was shut against us."

"But if you had asked Olver Dench, he would have provided for you."

"He! he is our worst enemy."

"That cannot be."

"He is. Mother cannot endure him. He does not love us."

"I see no reason for this. He has been my paymaster."

"What do you mean, father?"

"I have sent him money every quarter for your mother. I have done so for eighteen or nineteen years."

"You have sent him money!" exclaimed Winefred in amazement. "I am certain that my mother has received nothing."

"Impossible that he can have withheld it!" said Mr Holwood, really aghast. "Did your mother not tell you that she had an allowance from me?"

"My mother hid nothing from me. At times, when we had sold nothing, we really had not enough to eat. I am positive that she never had anything from Olver Dench."

Mr Holwood beat his brow. "I am innocent in this matter," he said. "Write to your mother and explain. I am innocent indeed. I have wronged her in many ways, but not in this. I sent her money when I could ill afford to part with it, but I never failed to send regularly. Whenever my salary came in, I transmitted a share to her before I spent anything on myself. But Olver said – " He hesitated and looked down.

"What did Olver Dench say?"

"He – he did not speak well of your mother. he led me to – to think; but I will enter into no particulars."

"Olver is our mortal enemy. I do not know wherefore, unless it be that he has been filching the money all these years. He hates mother, and he dislikes me. If he has dared to speak against *her*, he shall be called to account. There is one whom I can trust" – she held up her head – "one who will take him by the throat and make him unsay every word."

Mr Holwood knew that she did not refer to himself, and he was humbled at the thought that his child should look to another to vindicate her mother's good name.

"No," said Winefred, with heightened nolour and sparkling eyes, and speaking with vehemence, "my dear mother has done nothing to forfeit your esteem, nothing to dishonour your name. She has been poor, and has huxtered tapes and packets of pins, and has trudged through rain and mire, and there is none in all the country round who can say an ill word against her that has in it a spice even of truth."

"And she is now in poverty?"

Then, and not till this moment, did the recollection of the one great and terrible fault committed by her mother recur to Winefred. She suddenly dropped her head and covered her face with her hands.

Chapter Forty-Seven

The Curtain Drawn

Jane Marley was unaccountably restless. She sat at her needlework, but could not remain at it. A disquiet that was inexplicable kept her on the move throughout the day.

Her daughter had left her precipitately, had gone back to Bath, without a word of explanation as to her purpose, whether to remain there or to return.

Jane could not sound Winefred's heart. She was in doubt whether the girl intended to abandon her and adhere to her father, or whether she proposed to pay her occasional visits. The girl had been reticent towards her regarding Jack Rattenbury. From what she had said, and this was not much, Jane judged that Winefred acknowledged that union with him was not possible, and yet adhered to her resolution not to banish him from her heart. Jane was well aware that the two had met on the downs almost every evening.

The girl was altered in her demeanour towards her mother since the discovery of the appropriation of Captain Rattenbury's hoard. Jane could have bitten out her tongue with mortification at having blurted forth the truth. But in the moment of excessive agitation, under the pang of remorse, of fear lest Jack's life should be sacrificed, she has lost control over her words. Her conscience had cried out in audible tones, and though the words had been few, the accent had sufficed to convey to Winefred the revelation of the fraud committed. And yet, as Jane reasoned with herself, Winefred must have arrived at the truth shortly by another road.

If she got into conversation with her father about the past he was certain to mention to her, in self-exculpation, how that her mother had haughtily, resentfully refused assistance from him; how that from the day that he left her she had not accepted a stiver from him.

When Winefred learned this she would at once ask, whence then came the money that had enabled her mother to purchase the under-cliff, and to send her to be educated in a private family of some pretensions? And Winefred was not one to leave such a question unanswered. She would work at it till she had arrived at a satis-factory explanation. When the girl discovered that no money had been transmitted to her mother from Mr Holwood, her mind would at once fasten on the rumours that circulated relative to what her mother had done. She could come to no other possible conclusion save that there was some good ground for the suspicion so generally entertained.

That Winefred did resent such an appropriation of the savings of a dead man Jane could understand, but not why she did not accept those excuses for it with which Jane salved her own conscience. The fable about the murder of her brother at the instigation of Job Rattenbury, and that of her father having been defrauded of his legitimate gains by the same man, she had accepted as certain truths, and clung to them as such with tenacity.

She had not that sharpness of vision in the matter of right and wrong, nor that fineness of texture of conscience that had Winefred. Like a vast number of other people, any pretext served as an excuse for the commission of a wrong; a colourable pretext was the cocaine with which moral sensation was benumbed. Various causes had combined to make Winefred high principled as she was. Un-questionably there was natural downrightness in her character from the outstart; this had been accentuated by her work in selecting and polishing stones for the lapidary. Too often she had been deceived by a pebble that promised well, and which only after laborious grinding and smoothing had revealed itself to be worthless. This had contributed to foster in her resentment against an exterior that did not correspond with what was within. She had been obliged to deal with shifty personages, and had seen through their evasions. Further, she had enjoyed that supreme advantage of having been taught in a dame's school where the two duties were made the basis of all instruction, and the mind was educated instead of being taught.

But it was not trouble of mind concerning Winefred that alone allowed Jane Marley no rest. There was a something indescribable, sensible but inexplicable, that set all her nerves in a tingle, that impressed her with a feeling of insecurity. Once and again, haunted by an unreasonable dread, she went to the wardrobe to examine the range of crooks and pendent garments and assure herself that they had not been touched. Once and again she started as though the ground beneath her feet had given way suddenly, and when she recovered herself it was to be seized with fear lest her brain was reeling. Then there came over her a qualm, and she sank on a seat with sickness at her heart and a spinning in her head.

As she shut the wardrobe door after one of these looks at her secret drawer, she saw the shadow of a man pass the window, and this was followed by a sharp rap at the door. Without awaiting an answer, a preventive man entered unceremoniously.

"Missus," said he, "I advise you to budge. Something is going to take place; we don't know what, and I've had orders to give you warning."

"I do not understand you."

"Come and see for yourself." Jane followed the officer, and he led her from the house, through the bushes, to a point on the edge of the cliff that commanded the beach and the sea some three hundred feet beneath. She was silent. No wind was stirring. The moment was that of the turn of the tide. At a distance of half a mile from the shore the surface of the water heaved like the bosom of a sleeper in rhythmic throb. There were no rollers, no white horses.

But nearer land the sea was boiling. Volumes of muddy water surged up in bells as from a great depth, and spread in glistening sheets, that threw out wavelets which clashed with the undulations of the tide. Moreover, there appeared something like a mighty monster of the deep, ruddy brown, heaving his back above the water.

"That which is coming in is sweet water," said the man. "One of our chaps has ventured down and tasted it. It is not the fountains of the deep that are broken up, but the land springs are feeding the ocean. Did you ever witness the like?"

"Yes," said Jane, "there was something of the kind took place, but only in a small way, before the crack formed when my old cottage was ruined."

"Exactly, missus. And there is going to happen something of the same sort here, but on a mighty scale, to which that was but as nothing. Where it will begin, how far it will extend, all that is what no mortal can guess. Now you know why I have been sent to tell you to clear out as fast as you can. If you want my help, you are welcome to it."

"My house! – I have but just bought it."

"The sea and the freshwater springs were not parties to the agreement, I reckon," said the preventive officer.

"But this new house of mine is some way from the edge."

"For all that you must shift. It is unsafe to remain in it another hour."

"Whither shall I go?"

"Mrs Jose, I reckon, will gladly receive you." He was in the right. Some appalling convulsion was threatening. To what extent the coast would be affected, and for how far inland it would extend, none could predict. The sky overhead was grey, the air tranquil. A filmy mist lay over everything so fine as hardly to obscure the sight of any object, certainly not the upheaving volumes of turbid water and the bulging shoals of mud.

Jane turned, terrified at the prospect, aghast – not knowing what to do. How was she to remove her store of money in broad daylight, before all eyes? and already she saw that spectators were gathering on the common in expectation of witnessing a great convulsion of nature. She declined the assistance of the man so civilly proffered, and, locking her door, ran towards Bindon. On reaching the farm she threw herself breathless on a form by the kitchen table, panting, and entreated to be afforded shelter.

"My dear Jane," said the kind farmer's wife, "what do you want? Take what is ours and welcome. There was a cow once –"

"Oh, never mind about the cow now. What am I to do about all the things in my house?"

"About your furniture and clock and bedding?"

"I must remove first of all the things of greatest value that are in the smallest compass. Give me some box that I can lock them in, or a strong drawer."

Mrs Jose showed Jane a stout cypress chest in a room over the porch. "You may have that and welcome," she said. "But I reckon you will require something in which to carry your traps. Here is an old–fashioned carpet–bag that I will lend you. Shall I go with you and assist you? Shall I summon the men?"

"No – no. I must go first. Later, I shall be glad of assistance."

"You know best, Jane; but look here. There was the most curious sight imaginable this morning. The rabbits have come off the common on to our lands in flocks as of sheep; they are all over our fields now."

"And the birds have deserted the cliffs. Something is certainly going to happen."

"We, thank God, are well inland at Bindon, and on the safe side of the hill."

"There is no time to be lost," said Jane in feverish unrest and impatience. "I must go." Then she hurried from the house.

The number of persons assembled on the down had increased. Most stood at a considerable distance from the cliffs, but a few audacious boys dashed forward to the brink, and were screamed at by their mothers, and sworn at by the coastguardmen, who bellowed to them to return.

"Has there been any change?" asked Jane as she came among the spectators.

"Nothing so far, but something will happen before very long. Hush! Did you hear that?" No – there was no sound, either from sea or land.

"You are surely not going back to your house?" said one of those looking on, as Jane passed him.

"I must go. I have all my little possessions there."

"However got," threw in one hard by. Jane Marley accelerated her pace to be away from the crowd and to reach her home.

None seemed to know whence the menace came, and where

danger would be found. Some individuals more timid than others lurked behind hedges, putting a bank and quickset between themselves and danger. Others held to gates and rails. Others again looked out for a clear space, in rear, over which to beat a precipitate retreat, if necessary. After Jane had pushed through the line of onlookers, she descended to the undercliff, reached her door, looked about her, listened and entered.

When she had gone forth with the preventive man, half an hour previously, she had not observed a face watching her from behind a rock. When she traversed the bushes, she had not seen how a man stole forth from his place of concealment. She had not suspected, whilst she stood on the cliff observing the tumescent waters, that this man had slipped in at her door left unlocked, and had secreted himself within the house.

When Jane now entered her habitation, she carefully locked the door on the inside. By so doing she had, unconsciously, locked herself in with this man.

On finding herself within, she looked around her. Everything was as she had left it. Nothing had been in the smallest degree deranged. No one was to be seen. Not a sound was to be heard. She looked up. The clock had ceased to tick. There was nothing to lead her to suppose that she was not alone.

So little did she conceive this as possible, that she at once went to the window, pulled down the blind, and then drew the curtain, lest that by any chance, anyone might see what she purposed doing behind the locked door and the shrouded window.

Chapter Forty-Eight

The Beginning of the End

The carpet-bag was light, portable and capacious. It was a contrivance for the convenience of travellers upon which we have not improved, and yet it has been relegated to the limbo of antiquated articles, is no more in commerce, and is replaced by portmanteaus and Gladstone bags, metal armed, and with vulnerable sides, that are scarred by the impact of other baggage equally furnished with iron or brass scutcheons and corner pieces that curl, add no strength, but serve vixenishly to scratch and tear whatever baggage is brought in contact with them. Our children will hardly know what the old, worthy, serviceable carpet-bag was like – a bag simply constructed, as its name implies, out of bits of carpet.

Furnished with this article, that was of inconsiderable weight, Jane Marley drew a long breath. The bag was supplied with lock and key, but this was a matter of no consideration, as, when filled, she would not let it pass from her hand till its contents were secured in the cypress chest at Bindon, that had been put at her service by Mrs Jose.

She drew apart the jaws of the bag, disclosing its striped canvas lining, and she set it beside her near the wardrobe. Her next proceeding was to open the doors of this article of furniture. She started, thinking that she heard a step. She looked about her, but nobody was visible. She held her breath. Nothing was to be heard save the shouts, very distant, of those gathered on the downs.

No one would be surprised, she considered, to see her pass with the bag. Nothing more reasonable than that she should be concerned to remove her portable goods to a place of security. When the valves of the wardrobe had been thrown wide apart, and the range of dependent dresses revealed in the twilight caused by the darkened window, then she placed the stool in position. This she mounted and pulled at the crooks. At once the drawer slid forward smoothly and noiselessly, bringing with it the series of garments.

Jane put her hand in and pulled out as many bundles and purses of gold as she could compass in her hand, and dropped them into the yawning carpet bag. They fell with a muffled thud. She was too much occupied, and in too great haste now to look about her. Time was precious. There was no knowing when the catastrophe would take place. It was by no means sure than some officious coast-guardsman would not come to her door with offers of assistance or insistence on her immediately vacating the place.

She laid hold of a small metal case that contained jewels. She had formerly looked at and admired the contents, and had fondly dreamed of the time when they would be worn by her Winefred. She was removing this case to drop it where the gold had fallen, when her arms were grasped from behind. She uttered a cry and strove to turn about.

"Ay! scream with all your lungs! None will help you now. At last I have found out what I long wanted to know!" The voice was fam-iliar. It was that of Olver Dench – a conviction by no means reassuring. Jane's first impulse was to shut the drawer, but her hands were fast. She thrust at it with her head.

Olver contemptuously laughed, and threw her from the stool, and still gripping her arms above the elbows, with hands like vices, hard and sinuous with working the oars, till their strength was irresistible, he looked into the receptacle. "Ha, ha!" said he, chuckling; "a clever trick, i' faith. I have hunted twice through this house, and never thought of this."

Unable to resist the attraction of the gold, he let go one arm, that he might thrust the freed hand among the packages of coin. Jane seized her opportunity to wrench herself loose; she caught up the carpet bag and sprang towards the door.

"Not so!" said Dench with an oath. With a stride he caught her before she had attained her object, and twisted the handle of the bag out of her hand. "Ah! scream away! No one can hear you."

Then, frantic with despair and rage, she threw herself upon him, like a wild beast, and he found her more difficult to master than he had anticipated. She writhed, bent, caught him by the arm, by the throat, she tore, she bit at his hand, and made her teeth meet in his flesh. The frenzy and the force of a demoniac were in her. Roused to desperation at the prospect of losing that which was to make the fortunes of her child, she forgot herself in the fury of onslaught. If he was strong, she was wiry and nimble. She bowed herself, she beat at him, she strove to drive her bony fingers into his eyes, to rip his skin with her nails. At one moment she all but tripped him up.

He dared not mount the stool. He could not explore the receptacle of so much gold. His every faculty was engaged in self-defence. As he held the carpet-bag, she cast all her weight on his arm, and as she could not break the bones in it, she snapped at his fingers like a dog.

Time was flying. An end must be put to this conflict. In her rage she lost breath. The cataclysm might come upon them at any moment, and to be beneath a roof then might prove fatal. With a curse, Olver gathered up his masculine strength, and having drawn from his pocket some whipcord, he twisted her arms behind her back; plunge, toss, sway herself as she might, he held her wrists together, threw her down on her face, planted his knee on her back, and deliberately bound her arms behind her so securely that it was impossible for her to disengage them.

She did her utmost to be free. She plucked one arm this way, the other that, but, although the cord tore the skin and blood came, she was unable to release her wrists. Then he rent away a piece of one of the dresses and rammed the rag between her teeth into her mouth, after which he bound his spotted red-and-white kerchief over her mouth. This accomplished he stood up and laughed, and, mounting the stool, proceeded to empty the drawer. Some of the parcels of gold he put into his pockets, others he threw down to be carried in the carpet-bag.

Jane, now hopeless of securing the spoil for herself and child, was filled with a raging desire to prevent Olver from enjoying it. She sought to prolong the struggle till one of two things should happen, either the earth should reel and bring down the house over their heads, or else till some of the preventive men should come, and intervene, when she would declare all, so that neither might possess the treasure.

Lifting herself with difficulty to her knees, having no power with her hands, and unable to tear with her teeth, glaring at Olver with inextinguishable, insatiable hate in her eyes, she struggled forward on her knees till she was able to fling her weight against the man as he was engaged, standing on the stool, with the drawer. With a curse he roared, "Jane! Leave me alone, or, by heaven, I will knock you over the head with the stool!"

She did not heed his threats. With tigerish eyes she followed his every motion. He aimed at her with his fist weighted with a purse of gold, but she ducked. He missed his aim, and as he staggered, she struck the stool from under him, and he came reeling over and nearly lost his feet. She at once kicked the stool into the fire.

But he had not fallen. He was brought up by the clock which at the impact went over with a crash. He sprang to the hearth, took the stool and swung it over his head in menace. Possibly he was afraid to completely silence her lest in the event of discovery he might be called to account. He replaced the stool where he required it, and said, "I dare you to touch me again! If you do, you shall be reduced to quiet so as to trouble me no more! Beware, Jane, you she–devil!"

When he had mounted the stool, she rose to her feet and made her way to the door. He continued to clear the drawer of the money that was in it, but he observed her out of the corner of his eye, and he soon discerned her purpose.

She had retreated backwards till she had reached the door and now facing him, with her bound hands she was endeavouring to turn the key.

"No!" he shouted. "I see your game." He dashed at her, spun her about, and dealt her such a blow with his fist that she fell on the floor. "You will remain still now," said he; and he resumed his work.

Jane was partially stunned. For a moment only she was unable to rally her senses, but she was incapable of offering further resistance. She saw what was going on, lying with gagged mouth and labouring lungs. She could not breathe fast enough, and the air screamed through her nostrils. The blood mounted and purpled her face, and swelled her veins to bursting.

At last everything had been removed, and the carpet–bag was

filled with the contents of the drawer. Dench thrust back the row of crooks and swaying garments to the place normally occupied by them and again chuckled at the ingenuity of the contrivance that had twice baffled him. Then he leisurely descended from the stool, and halted on his way to the door to look at Jane Marley as she lay bound at his feet. The laugh was still on his lips.

Her head in falling had struck the overturned clock, or been cut by the broken glass of the face, and it was bleeding. Her profuse black hair, tinged with grey, was dishevelled, and lay in a tangle about and under her head; the face was turned on one side, and the eyes flared at him like coals in a blast furnace. He set his teeth. A malignant expression came over his face.

"Eh, Jane! Better to have gone shares as I once proposed, than lose all and come to this!"

He prepared with lifted foot to kick her in the face with his boatman's shod boot, when a shiver ran through the house – a shiver like that which passes over a man when, so it is asserted, an enemy treads on his predestined grave. "Time to be off, by –," said he, and darted to the door. "Jane – I leave you to your fate."

He unlocked the door, passed through; he had removed the key. He locked it from without, and threw the key away among the bushes. For a few moments he stood irresolute what to do, in which direction to turn.

He was unwilling, carrying the carpet–bag, to pass through the crowd of spectators, and he stayed to consider whether by any means he could reach the ferry unobserved. There was an open patch before the cottage, screened by bushes so as not to be overlooked from the down. he took a few steps in one direction on it, then halted – and took another. He had the carpet–bag in his hand.

Meanwhile, within, Jane had heaved herself to her knees, and then to her feet. She staggered to the window. The table was before it. By an effort she succeeded in mounting the table, and then, with her bound hands she plucked at the curtain and drew it, next by a pull tore down the little blind. And now she could look out.

Looking out she saw Dench standing irresolute – as one dazed. She saw something more. At that moment the house swayed like a ship. The surface of the land broke up, and seemed transmuted into fluid, for in one place it heaved like a mounting billow, and in another sank like the trough of a wave.

It was to Jane, peering through the little window as though she were looking at a tumbling sea through the porthole of a cabin.

Again the house lurched, and so suddenly and to such an acute angle, that Jane fell from the table.

Chapter Forty-Nine

Rent Asunder

Winefred and her father were on their way to the down, passing up from Axmouth through Bindon, when Mrs Jose appeared in the archway that gives access to the court, and saluted them. She was in a condition of considerable perturbation, as was perceptible in her face, which mirrored the state of her mind.

Winefred, catching her hand, inquired breathlessly, "What is the meaning of this? It is as though everyone were on the cliffs. Surely not an invasion from France?"

"It is rabbits. They are running from the downs and the people are going on to it."

"What is the matter?"

"I cannot tell. No one knows. Something is going to happen, and your mother has not returned."

"My mother!"

"She went to the cottage with a carpet-bag to remove her knick-knacks, and has not come back. But perhaps she has got together men to carry the furniture and all the whole bag of tricks out of the house."

"But why?"

"And all my men and maids have gone too. And Jose has toddled after them, he as don't care for phenomena, as the parson calls it, but only his pipe and ale."

"But what is the matter?"

"The Lord only knows. The sea is boiling and throwing up mud, and they think that the rocks are about to fall. But I can't say. Lord preserve us all! It may be the Last Day coming on us in Axmouth and going on next to Seaton, and destroy it by instalments. If so, I wish it had begun t'other end of England."

"Where is my mother – at the cottage?"

"That is just what I do not know, but want to find out."

Winefred waited no longer. She ran up the lane leaving her father to follow at a pace more suited to his age and tight–lacing. She came to the gate – once set with thorns – with a number of people running also up the lane, and could see that there were a great many on the common, forming as it were a wavering black ribbon on the short turf. Some impelled by curiosity advanced considerably, but next moment alarmed at their own temerity, scared by some trifle, recoiled. One cried out that he heard a grinding sound under his bootsoles, and at once there was a rush inland. There broke out an argument as to where the fall would be. Some said along the line of the old undercliff, there would be the cleavage. This was disputed on the ground that the undercliff represented an earlier and exhausted subsidence.

One point there was on the down higher than the rest, that commanded a general view, and this was a point to which the curious trended partly because it gave such an extensive prospect, but also because it was esteemed secure. Winefred enquired of the groups she encountered whether they had seen her mother, and received contradictory replies.

She was taking the path that led to the cottage, when she was arrested by a loud and general cry that ran from west to east; and immediately she heard a strange rending sound as of thick cloth ripped asunder; this produced a rush backwards of the people, and shouts of command rang from some of the preventive men. At once was seen a jagged fissure running like a lightning–flash through the turf, followed by a gape, an upheaval, a lurch, then a sinkage, and a starring and splitting of the surface. In another moment a chasm yawned before their eyes, three–quarters of a mile long, torn across the path, athwart hedges, separating a vast tract of down and undercliff from the mainland, and descending into the bowels of the earth.

Winefred was caught by the shoulder and hurled back. It was not safe to stand near the lip of this hideous rent, for that lip broke up and fell in masses into the abyss. Cracks started from it, or behind it, and widened, and whole blocks of rock and tracts of turf disappeared. The surface beyond the chasm presented the most appalling appearance. It was in wild movement, breaking up like an ice-pack in a thaw. It swayed, danced, fell apart into isolated blocks, some stood up as pillars, some bent as horns, others balanced themselves, then leaned forward, and finally toppled over and disappeared.

In an agony of alarm for her mother, Winefred ran to the bit of isolated land whence the whole scene was visible, even the cottage, and she was followed by Mrs Jose and Mr Holwood, who had come up with her. From this spot of vantage could be discerned how that a wide tract of land, many acres in length, had separated from the main body and was sliding seaward in a tilted position. At the same moment from out of the sea rose a black ridge, like the back of a whale, but this drew out and stretched itself parallel to the fissure.

An awed silence had fallen on the spectators as they held their breath to watch the progress of the convulsion that was changing the outline of the coast and transforming its appearance. But suddenly a cry was heard, and next moment someone was seen running on the sloping andf still sliding mass.

It was not Jane Marley. It was a man carrying a carpet-bag. For some time none could make out who he was; but the Captain of the Excise, who had a glass, exclaimed that he was Dench, the ferryman. Olver appeared to be panic-stricken to such an extent as to have almost lost his senses. Seeing the crowd he ran towards it, along the path from the cottage till he came upon the gap that was rapidly widening and dividing him at every moment farther from the mainland. He seemed as though on board a vessel that was being swept out to sea, and frantically strove to escape from her to those who stood on the wharf observing him. Down into the separating chasm eyes looked, but could not make out the bottom; the depth contained a tossing mass of crumbled chalk and erupted pebble, with occasional squirts of water, some two or three hundred feet below the surface on the land side. It was like a mighty polypus mouth that had opened and was chewing and digesting its food in its throat and belly.

Seeing this, mad with fear, shrieking like a woman, Olver turned and fled, to be again arrested by a mound that lifted before his eyes as though thrown up by a monstrous burrowing mole. Almost immediately this ridge changed its character, it split with a sharp snap, became a rent, and Dench's way was again cut off. Once more he turned, and this time ran in a seaward direction down the inclination, but when he caught sight of the churning water throwing up volumes of mud, and at the uprising slimy reef lifting itself out of the sea, he turned again, never letting go his hold of the bag, shrieking still, for in the unparalleled horror of the situation his brain had lost its balance.

Those who looked on at the frantic man knew that it was not within human power to aid him. It was a mighty arena, and the spectators contemplated the solitary flying wretch pursued to his death by the relentless, invisible forces of Nature. Now he sought the cottage. It seemed to him in his dazed condition that he might find shelter there. But the door had been locked by himself and the key cast away.

He stood and wiped from his brow the sweat that rained down and blinded him. And then a gleam of thought lighted his troubled mind. He considered that if he ran eastward and could outstrip the rent as it formed, he might yet attain solid and stationary land.

But those who looked on with bated breath and trembling pulses saw that the attempt must end in failure. Such as stood on the height in security roared out advice to him. He halted, looked in their direction, endeavoured vainly to catch what was said. Men yelled louder, waved their arms, but as none agreed in the advice tendered, the wretch was confused and not assisted.

He continued his run eastward, ran – ran with his full strength, and came abruptly on the edge of a mural precipice, with another world far below his feet covered with brushwood, from which he was cut off by a perpendicular escarpment like one of the walls of a crater in the moon. To that lower world he could not descend. Then again he turned to run in an opposite direction. To such as saw him he was like a fox throwing the hounds off his scent, doubling, retrieving, dodging, but always headed.

And now as he ran he was brought down by his foot suddenly sinking into a crack that was in process of formation, and which he had not seen in his precipitate haste. By the time he had extracted his leg, this crack had become a gash that descended into darkness.

Clinging to a bush, kneeling, as he withdrew his foot, he saw the crumbling chalk dribble into this depth below, and the thought quivered through him that he was going down alive into the bottomless pit.

Rendered crazy with fear he mounted a fragment of rock and saw about him the wreckage as of a world – prostrate trees, leaning pillars of rock, disrupted masses of soil, bushes draggling over to drop into the throats open to swallow them.

There was but one possibility of salvation open to him, to leap the chasm that divided him from the mainland at one point where as yet the width was not extreme, and the feat was not impossible. But to do this he must act with promptitude. To fail was to fall down that throat to be mumbled and chumped with the grinding rocks. The leap would be considerable, but feasible by any man of moderate activity.

Dench retreated to run. Those who saw his purpose shouted to him. He looked up at them bewildered. They called to him to lay aside the carpet-bag. His hand was passed through the loops, and it hung from his wrist.

He did not understand what was shouted. Possibly in his then condition of mind he was unconscious that he was still weighted with the bag. He ran, leaped, was flying in space over the chasm, touched the rock on the farther side, caught at the grass; but was overbalanced, dragged backward from the crest by the weight of the bag, and went down with a tuft of wiry grass and hawkweed in his right hand, and disappeared in the midst of the rock and earth that was in process of being chewed. Now the carpet-bag, then a leg, next a hand appeared, and went under again. Then up came the head, only next moment to be drawn beneath and disappear in the mighty mill.

Chapter Fifty

Joined Together

Not till evening was setting in was it possible for any to cross the gulf and reach the subsided portion. The chasm itself was some three hundred and sixty feet across, and into this all the tract between the lips had gone down at various inclinations. Beyond that to the sea something like four hundred and forty yards had slipped away in an incline, much dislocated, but with an abrupt face forming one side of the great chasm.

It was of imperious necessity to get to the cottage that could be seen, not ruined, still standing, but leaning to one side, that search might be made for Jane Marley.

It was only made possible by the efforts of Jack Rattenbury, assisted by some of the Bindon labourers placed at his disposal by Mrs Jose. By his direction a pathway was cut down the face of the chalk precipice on the land side at a point where the ravine was choked with accumulations that had fallen in, and by means of planks and ropes the chasm was passed and the farther side ascended and then Winefred, followed by her father and Mrs Jose, was enabled, with the assistance of Jack, and walking with wariness, to arrive at the cottage. It was locked, but when Winefred called, she heard a muffled voice reply from within.

The front door was too stout to be easily broken open, but that at the back yielded and the rescue party entered. They found Mrs Marley on the floor. She was in a sitting posture, her hands still bound, her hair dishevelled, but the blood from the wound in her head was staunched. She had succeeded, by some means, in freeing her mouth from the gags. Her eyes were dull. The colour had died from her face, the fire from her heart. She breathed, looked dazedly before her, and seemed listless when her daughter, Mr Holwood and the rest entered.

Winefred pulled back what of the curtain remained obscuring the chamber. Through the back door that faced west a stronger light entered and penetrated to the room where Jane crouched. Jack Rattenbury had at once cut the bands that confined her hands, and although the woman was able to bring her arms forward, they were stiff, and her hands frightfully swollen.

Mrs Jose had run for water, but the spring that had supplied the cottage was dried up. There remained, however, a little in a vessel in the back kitchen, and with this Jane's face was bathed as Winefred rested her mother's head on her bosom. The cuts in her head were not serious. The girl hasted to tie up the draggled hair.

The men who had assisted to make a path had been relegated to the outside. It was probable, if Jane Marley were unable to walk, they they would be required to carry her. Mr Holwood remained looking at her intently, his weak lower lip fallen. She did not notice him. Her eyes were for her daughter only, who bowed over her, kissed her repeatedly, and whose tears dripped upon her face.

"Are you better now, mother darling? Do you think you could rise?"

Winefred supporting her on one side, Jack on the other, the woman staggered to her feet, and at once recovered self-possession. She raised her head, looked at the wrists and swollen fingers and passed her hands over her eyes.

"It has been a dream, a nightmare," she said. And then asked, "Where is Olver Dench?"

"O mother, do not ask."

"But I desire to know. He has robbed me."

"He is gone to his account."

Jane was silent for a while. Presently she said, "He carried off everything in a carpet-bag."

"That," said Winefred, "will never be recovered. It has gone down along with him."

"Gone down!" repeated Mrs Marley, with trouble in her eyes.

"Yes, mother, ask no further. It shall be explained later. If Olver Dench has wronged you – and that he did so I know – God has judged him. Whatsoever of yours he had in that bag is lost, never to be recovered."

Jane turned her eyes slowly to Jack and said, "It was your father's savings, hundreds of pounds of gold. I had kept it. I did wrong. I am punished."

"Mother, are you better?" asked Winefred. "Can you see who is before you?"

"Yes, you are here."

"Not I alone. Here is father."

Jane looked at Mr Holwood. Perhaps she was too shaken, too exhausted to manifest the resentment that had possessed her. She looked at him steadily, without hate, but also without affection in her eyes.

"Jane, my wife," said he in a faltering voice. "I also have done wrong, and like you I acknowledge it openly. But not all the wrong you suppose. I have sent every quarter a liberal share of money to you through Dench, which he retained for himself, and I – I have often had an ache of heart and yearning after you, but have been prevented from coming to see you by the reports of what you were and what you did – slanderous and wicked reports – sent me by that infamous man. I believed him."

"Then you never knew me," said Jane slowly, "or you would not, you could not have believed him."

"I never knew your worth, Jane," said he, "because I had not that worth in me which could appreciate how noble and how good you were. Can you forgive me?"

"I do not know," she said slowly – dreamily. "It is a long story. Nineteen years of desolation and heartbreak; nineteen years is a long time, and in that chain, each day is a link, and each link is full of pain."

"Jane," said Mr Holwood, "here is your ring, that you threw on the floor at the Assembly Rooms at Bath. Will you not take it on again?"

"I do not know." She looked at her hand. "My fingers are so swelled."

"Jane," he went on – and Winefred, holding her mother, looked earnestly into her face, so changed from what it had been.

"Jane," pursued Mr Holwood, "I have come here as a suppliant. I am smitten with an incurable disease – perhaps the most terrible and painful that can afflict man. How rapidly it will act I cannot say – but in a year at the outside all will be over. In a little while I shall not be able to speak, for it will begin from my tongue – the tongue you cursed. Jane, Jane! May I not die in your arms?"

Then a shudder ran through the woman; she shook herself free from Winefred, stretched her purple hands towards him, and in thrilling tones said: "O Jos! my own Jos! Come to my heart once more."

Thereat Mrs Jose took Winefred by the arm and drew her into the back kitchen; thither Jack had already withdrawn, and then the good woman wiped her eyes and kissed Winefred – thrust her towards Jack, and said: "You, boy – kiss her too."

Next moment Jane called them. "I want you here," she said. Once more her voice had acquired some of its firmness and imperiousness. And they saw her – she was herself again, nay other – younger, with a tender look in her face and love in her eyes.

"I want you here," she said. "I desire you to hear me ask for pardon of Jack Rattenbury. I have done you a great wrong, Jack, for which I can make no amends. Can you forgive me?"

"No, no," answered the young man. "You have done me no wrong. Whatever it was my father saved could not have been better expended that in the purcase of this house, and in the education of Winefred. Give her to me as the balance."

"You must ask him," said Jane, indicating Mr Holwood.

"If Winefred has her mother's strong will, as I do not doubt she has, Jane, you and I can but accept her selection."

"In a year," said Jack, "I shall be in a position to support a wife."

"About that do not concern yourself," said Mr Holwood. "I am well off, and all I have shall be hers."

"Nevertheless, I will work," said Jack. "If at some future time I get something with her, I daresay Captain Ford will take me into partnership, and we can set up machinery and make of the Beer quarries something great."

"I had a cow, once on a time–" began Mrs Jose.

"Never mind about the cow now, you dear thing," interrupted Winefred. "We positively must get back to the mainland whilst there is light, and at Bindon we will hear the cow story from beginning to end and will not interrupt."

"But the cow had a calf–"

"And we will listen also to the history of the calf."

"Well, well," said Mrs Jose. "You and Winefred go on, and Mr Holwood and I will follow with your mother. What a day this has been for rending asunder – and for joining together."

THE END

THE NEW BARING-GOULD COLLECTION

A BOOK OF FOLKLORE. First published 1913. A treasure trove of stories, legends, myths, written by a most enthusiastic collector of this kind of material. Regarded as a classic source book in its time. Paperback. 176 pages. ISBN 0-9518729-4-X. £5.00.

RED SPIDER. First published 1887, this has always been one of Baring-Gould's most popular novels. Set in the real Devon village of Bratton Clovelly, it is a Gothic romance, full of action, social history and local colour. Many of the beliefs and legends in the *Book of Folklore* reappear here in fictional form. Paperback 256 pages. ISBN 0-9518729-1-5. £5.00.

THE MANA OF LEW by Cicely Briggs. The author is Baring-Gould's grand-daughter, and the book covers the whole history of Lew House, which Sabine rebuilt throughout much of his life. Richly illustrated, and packed with information concerning the man, the house, the family and the local area. Paperback. 64 pages, with 33 illustrations and family tree. ISBN 0-9518729-3-1. £5.00

Order direct from Praxis Books, "Sheridan", Broomers Hill Lane, Pulborough, West Sussex. RH20 2DU.